Sarah Stryker
The Outcast

Hanif Muhammad

Table of Contents

Chapter 1: Hunted

Inside an old musty apartment lived a young woman capable of crushing a man with a single thought. Her name was Amy Stryker. She was a seemingly average specimen; a girl with an athletic build and pale blonde hair wrapped in a long-braided ponytail, petite and fair in complexion but her circumstances made her more cautious than most. She knew what was out there, which is why she generally preferred to be on her own. She scurried through her kitchen with a fly swatter in hand after spotting an intrusive bug, determined to prevent an infestation.

"There you are," she said in a conniving tone. The cock roach quickly scurried underneath her refrigerator and with ease Amy lifted it off the ground with one hand, watching as the roach fled and climbed onto the countertop near the sink. She set the Fridge back down with a steady hand before standing up straight and raising her hand. One good swat was all that was needed to end the conflict.

"That's it. Easy does it," Amy muttered before bringing her arm down in an authoritative attack.

The swatter broke in half the moment that it hit the countertop. She had managed to kill the bug but at the cost of her tool. She sighed in disappointment as she examined the broken stick that used to be her favorite weapon of choice against a girl's worst nightmare.

Amy jumped up from where she stood at the sound of an unsuspecting knock on the door. Who had come to visit her? She hadn't been expecting anyone and as a security measure informed very few people of her whereabouts, so whoever was knocking must have had an important reason for doing so. With that thought sawing its way into her conscious mind Amy leaned against her front door and squinted her eye through the peephole.

A young man stood with the front door less than an inch away from his grasp. Sweat darkened his ginger hair to brown, his freckles thrown to an even starker relief than usual on his pale skin. He was tall though compared to a girl of Amy's small stature almost everyone seemed tall. He gritted his teeth before taking a few deep breaths in and out and knocking on the door once again. Amy opened the door and his eyes widened.

"Leland?"

"H-hey Amy. Long time no see," Leland mumbled in reply.

"Oh my god," Amy exclaimed. "What are you doing here?"

"Well, to see you obviously. What do you think?"

"Seriously?"

"Yeah. So, can I get a 'hey, how are you? Or it's nice to see you?"

"Oh, I'm sorry." Amy chuckled before reaching up and wrapping her arms around Leland's thin frame in a brief but affectionate hug. "I was just so thrown. It's been like years since we've seen each other. And you just show up? Out of the blue?"

"Well, I told you that I was coming, didn't I? That I would visit?"

"Yeah, but I didn't think that you meant today."

"Well, I-I mean if you're available I thought that we'd catch up, y'know maybe spend some time in the park?"

"Really?" Amy beamed.

"If you're hungry we can grab a bite to eat too. You like hotdogs?" Leland asked. Amy smiled; her face shone with soft tenderness. She leaned against the doorway as her soft blue eyes fixated on him.

"Yeah. Yeah, I like hotdogs," she said.

Leland treated Amy at a local hotdog stand and drove her through downtown Seattle until arriving at the woods in a secluded part of the city.

The two sat in the vehicle for hours after that, reminiscing about their days in high school and coming to terms with how far apart they've grown.

"So, Amy? How's life been treating you?"

"Pretty good. Pretty good," she replied, feigning a casual tone of voice as she sat up in the passenger seat of the vehicle. "I've just been a little busy lately."

"Oh yeah? Busy with what?" Leland leaned back and draped his arm over the front seat.

Amy bit her bottom lip. "Things."

"Things?" Leland repeated, raising his eyebrows at her. Amy fought a cracked smile but then Leland poked her in the ribs eliciting a burst of contagious laughter.

"Yeah, I know you. I know you're hiding something. Word is that you've been up to a lot for the past few years."

"Maybe I have," Amy admitted. "But it's no big deal. Nothing that you need to worry about."

"Maybe I'm not worried, just curious."

"Well, what about you? You're so curious about me, what have you been up to?" Amy asked.

Leland's face melted in response. "What do you mean?"

"I mean why are you here visiting me all of a sudden. Aren't you supposed to be in Bellingham? Why are you in Seattle?"

"Oh well, I moved. I've changed a lot over the past few years. I'm not the same man that I was back then."

"Yeah? And what kind of man was that?"

"I don't know if you remember but I fell in with the wrong crowd back in high school. Most of my old crew fell in with the law. But not me. There's no way I'm being put behind bars. Especially not now during our current climate."

"That's smart," Amy agreed before taking a bite of some leftover food.

The two spoke for a few hours as the darkness of the night consumed the once blue skies. Just being near this man did much to put Amy's mind at ease. So much so in fact that she hadn't noticed the conversation venture into shark-infested waters, not until it was too late to turn back.

"Amy, I gotta tell you something. Something that may make me sound like a total creep if I admit it out loud, but I feel I should say it anyway. Just so things are clear between you and me," Leland whispered. Amy squinted at him with a skeptical eye.

"What?"

"I missed you. When you went away. Like really missed you. Things just weren't the same after you left."

"I missed you too," Amy lied.

He hadn't been on her mind prior to that day. However, sitting alone with him produced emotions within Amy Stryker that she never knew that she had; the sort of thoughts that she was generally too shy of expressing. She was a girl who until very recently seldom interacted with the opposite sex and hadn't pursued a relationship. Now she was alone with a man she knew from high school. In just a few moments everything in her life was about to change.

"I heard stories you know. Lots. Things that I didn't want to believe but the more rumors spread the less I was able to ignore them."

"Yeah," Amy muttered. She had a feeling that she knew where the conversation was going.

"How's your sister doing?" Leland asked, his eyes squinting at her with a mixture of bemused curiosity and stiffening fear.

"She's good. Very busy at the moment but overall, she's fine."

"There are a lot of rumors going around in Bellingham. About what she has been up to for the past two years." "They're probably all true," Amy admitted.

"All of them?" He asked. Amy nodded.

"So, did she really go to Africa? During the Invasion, I mean?" Leland asked, his face shone with disbelief.

"I was there with her," she said. "I got out before she did, but I was there through most of it."

"That must have been terrifying."

"It was but we made it out okay." Amy turned towards the floor. "Thanks to her we made it out okay."

"Being related to someone like that must be a badge of honor. You should be proud."

Amy bit her bottom lip. Who was he to tell her how to feel? Her expression grew cold the longer she kept her eyes averted away from him. It took him a moment to pick up on it.

"Oh god I-I'm sorry. I overstepped my bounds, didn't I?"

"No. No, it's not that. I-it's nothing." Amy retreated into her dismissive tone.

"No, I did. I didn't mean to pry. It's just something that I've been curious about ever since the two of you left and the stories began to circulate around town. I guess I just wanted an insider's perspective. You know without risking any direct confrontation."

Amy turned towards Leland. With his honest reply, she saw an opportunity; the chance to be herself without judgment or reprisal.

"Well, then ask me."

"What?"

"You heard me. Ask away. What do you want to know about my sister?"

Amy's insistence made Leland shift his sitting posture. "Are you sure? You won't get upset if-"

"No, I won't get upset," Amy interrupted. "What is it that you want to know? About her past? About what it was like growing up with her? Or where she is now?"

"Well since you're in share mode, how about all of it?"

Amy returned his reply with a stern glare. "Dude, you're killing me."

Leland raised his eyebrows. "You said I could ask?"

Amy sighed, shifting her gaze away from his once again. She knew what he was doing but Leland's constant pushing made the increasing temperature of the car more apparent.

"Just tell me this. All those years growing up with her. Did you have any idea? Any idea that she would grow up to be what she is? What was it like?"

Leland spoke in a whisper that somehow gave his words even more volume. Amy curled her lips, examining her feet and the floor of the car once again.

"My sister.... well, she's always been this really quiet calm sort of crazy. For years I thought that I was the odd one. And maybe in some ways I am but," Amy squinted in deep thought as she looked up and gazed through the car door mirror. "I've never met anyone quite like my sister. Which should be a good thing. I mean who wants to be like everyone else right? But then you also want something normal. Something to keep everything at an equilibrium."

"But because of her, you'll never be normal right?" Leland prompted. He was too perceptive for his own good. Amy gave him a knowing look before speaking.

"I shouldn't be thinking this," she confessed. "God knows that I wouldn't be able to tie my own shoes without her. But she's completely secluded. She usually only goes out when she's on a mission. And when she does nothing else matters. Like she'd just as easily stab you as she would say hello. Honestly, she scares me sometimes."

At that moment, the gravity around Amy seemed to have lessened. Part of her couldn't believe what she was saying but another part was surprised it took her this long to say it. What was it about this man that allowed her to open up so easily?

"Wow... that's quite a mouthful." It was all that Leland could say at first. He was still reeling from Amy's sudden confession.

"Yeah, and it's something that I don't know if I'll ever bring myself to tell her face to face. I don't know if I'm more scared of her or for her. She's caught in a storm, and I have no idea what to do about it."

"So, you're afraid then?"

Amy affirmed Leland's estimation with a reluctant nod. "That's pretty much the long and short of it."

"Well allow me to let you in on a little secret." He leaned in close before carrying on, this time speaking in a more intimate tone than before. "Everyone's afraid, Amy. We all experience it. I bet even she is afraid."

Amy shook her head. "Oh no. She isn't. Trust me my sister is anything but scared."

"Yes, she is. I guarantee it. She just doesn't let you see it. That's all."

"What makes you so sure?" Amy said, squinting at him.

"It's obvious. Anyway, I just wanted you to know that despite everything that you're going through you can trust me. I'm not someone that you need to be afraid of."

Leland seemed sincere, but Amy couldn't help but question him. "And what makes you think that I'm afraid of you? Maybe I'm the one that you should be scared of."

She raised her eyebrows as she leaned towards him, lowering her voice to a hushed and calculating whisper. Leland felt a sudden spike in his body heat. His skin tingled in anticipation as Amy drew closer to him. In all his life he had never been weakened by a person so seemingly petite.

"Really, you think so?"

"Oh, I know so." Amy placed both of her hands against Leland's chest. The hardness of his muscles made all her hairs stand up at once. "Believe me I've tussled with the best." She could tell that he had been working out, perhaps in preparation for this very day and the thought spurred her on.

"Well, I think I would like to see you in action," Leland muttered. Amy let out a silent chuckle, revealing her beautiful shiny white teeth.

Her breath smelled like peppermint and a slight tingle surged through Leland's skin. For a moment, time itself was at a standstill. His heart rate dropped, and the world around the two dissolved. Leland could feel himself almost hovering in midair as Amy's lips inched closer to his own. Closer and closer. One more second was all that he needed but a bit of rustling in the bushes and the sudden *crunch* of a tree trunk a few yards from them made Amy jump in her seat.

"What was that?" She exclaimed.

"What?"

"Didn't you hear that? It was like something was moving out there."

"There's no one out here, Amy."

"You sure?" Amy said. She scanned the bushes ahead of them with a wide-eyed expression. She could see a pair of white lights nestled in them.

"Of course. It's just like I said. There's nothing to be afraid of," Leland assured her.

"I don't know. It's getting late. I think that maybe we should leave."

"Or maybe we should continue where we left off," he said, his voice oozing with seduction as he leaned in for another attempt at a kiss. But his moment was gone. Amy wrinkled her nose in disgust and turned away. Something had disrupted her train of thought, creating a sense of unease that was hard to decipher and even harder to ignore.

"N-no. No," she said before giving him a slight push backward.

"What? Whaaaat?" Leland whined before slouching in his seat. "Come on. Don't tell me you're getting cold feet now. I thought we were opening up here."

"We were. But now-I- I just-" Amy paused. She didn't owe this man an explanation.

"What? Come on. I'll take you somewhere nice. Buy you some more food."

"NO. I said no okay. Let's just go." Amy curled her lips and averted her gaze toward the ground.

"Ah, I know what it is. There's someone else, isn't there?" Amy said nothing.

"Yeah, that's it. You have feelings for someone else. More than one. Several someone else's if my hunch is correct."

"Excuse me?" Amy snapped her head towards him, her face contorted in confusion. "Just who do you think that you're talking to?"

"What? Did I touch a nerve?" Leland teased.

"Yeah, you did. But it doesn't matter. Let's just get out of here okay. We can hang out somewhere else."

"What's the matter? Is poor whittle Amy scared of the dark?" Leland said, mimicking a child's voice.

"Stop it. It's not funny."

"Ah, poor Amy. It's okay." He reached over and tickled her, hoping to change her mood. It wasn't working.

"Leland stop. I'm serious," She barked, growing more annoyed and anxious by the second.

"Don't worry I'll make it all better."

"STOP."

It was only a second afterward that the man in front of her did exactly that. He stopped and so did everything around her. Something smashed into the windshield, creating a web-like pattern on the glass. "Start the car!" Amy cried.

Leland fumbled with the key fob. Before he could press the ignition button, his door was yanked open. Leland gasped as someone stabbed his left shoulder with a knife. It stayed there as blood spurted. Then, he was pulled from the car.

Amy opened her door and ran around the car. Leland was on the ground with several dark figures gathered around him. She rammed her fist into the closest one's back, sending the apparition sprawling. A well-placed kick propelled a second figure to the right and into a bush. Several others pulled back as she glowered at them. She stomped the ground. The resulting shockwave sent them reeling back into the bushes. Amy knelt by Leland. A knife whizzed by her and buried itself in the car seat behind her.

Frantically, Amy tugged at Leland's right arm. He groggily got slowly to his knees. She pulled him toward the car. Opening the back door, she shoved him inside. Blood oozed down his nice shirt and created a crazy pattern on his bare arm. He managed to pull out the knife and was staring at it with a bewildered look on his face.

She slammed his door shut and tried to get into the front seat. To get there, she had to kick and punch as hard as she could. Several apparitions still had knives. She dodged glancing blows, picking up several small cuts on her forearm. Still, she drove back the creatures and got into the car. The fob was on the floor. She pushed the ignition; the car started. The door wouldn't close. She didn't care. She began to back up, gritting her teeth as the car hit a few bumps and came to a crashing halt, ramming backward into a tree. The impact sent Leland to the floor and shoved Amy into the steering wheel.

"Leland. LELAND! Are you okay?" She pleaded, shaking him with fervor. Leland groaned. Amy's eyes widened. The two of them couldn't stay there. She barged out of the car and dragged the boy out with her.

"Leland? Leland! Can you stand? We have to get out of here!" She brought the boy to his feet and draped his arm over her shoulders.

Amy's jaw dropped. Small Lights appeared in the bushes all around them. They shifted and began to rustle the leaves as they emerged. With horror, Amy backed away, realizing that what she saw wasn't artificial light but pairs of eyes that belonged to nocturnal beings.

"We have to get out of here. Come on!" She ushered him forward, putting every bit of strength into her legs. Amy ran, sensing the stammering feet following behind her. *Why are these people after me?* She thought. *Why now? I've kept to myself for weeks. It doesn't make sense.*

Amy scanned her environment as she ran through the darkened forest. The sound of metal slicing the air sounded in her ear as she dragged the injured man beside her. The knives twirled around them, cutting strands of her hair as galloped frantically. There were a few safe houses nearby. Amy zigzagged, hoping to confuse her pursuers before barging into a warehouse and locking the door behind them after entering one of the rooms.

"Just hold still. We'll get you out of this, okay?" Amy sat Leland against the bench, and he winced as he attempted to fight the pain of his stab wound.

"Just relax okay. We'll get through this. We need to get you to a hospital," Amy said.

"Jesus. What the hell just happened? Who were those guys?" Leland asked, struggling to catch his breath.

"Those weren't guys."

Amy Stryker was alone; surrounded from all sides by a powerful enemy that wanted to subdue her. She helped Leland to his feet and escorted him to another room in the warehouse. With any luck, the two of them could find another shelter before any of their attackers spotted them. She turned her eyes to the boy beside her and noticed that he was beginning to lose color in his cheeks.

"Amy I-I don't think I feel so," He broke off and chuckled before finishing his remark. "I think I need to lie down."

"It's alright. Just relax. I'll get you out of here," She promised. "Just try not to move too much or talk. You'll only waste your energy."

"I should've listened to you. We should have left. I just- I really liked you and wanted to stay. I wanted you to want me as badly as I want you."

"Shh, don't say anything else okay. We'll talk later."

"I just want you to know. Seeing you today after all these years it-"

The floor trembled beneath the two before Leland was able to finish. Amy was thrown against the wall by an unseen force. A pair of hands burst out of the ground, clutching Leland by the ankle, and pulling him underground. The hands were distinctly feminine, and their nails were covered in dirt. Leland let out a hoarse breath as the hands tightened their grip. His skin began to turn shockingly pale as his lower torso was pulled underground.

"Leland!"

Amy dove after him, wrapping her hands around his wrist and pulling with as much force as her unseen attacker. Her friend was halfway underground, and for a while, it seemed that they were at a stalemate but then two unsuspecting hands seized Amy and pulled her from behind. One opponent wrapped its hands around her waist and the other in a painful hold around her throat. Amy felt her grip slipping.

With a forceful tug, Amy was yanked into the room behind her. She crashed into the wall, and everything went spinning. She placed a hand on the ground and as her vision returned looked up at the two women who had attacked her. Their long hair covered their faces, its blackness resembling the atmosphere of the room in totality. Their skin appeared to have been peeled off and as they moved with slow and methodical steps their bones crunched and contorted in unnatural ways.

Amy gritted her teeth as each pulled a knife from behind their backs. *Just stay calm. Remember what my sister taught me.* she thought. She planted her feet against the wooden floor and tightened her fists until her veins popped.

The two female creatures lunged toward Amy in unison, and she decided to meet them halfway. She stomped her feet as she attacked, unleashing a shockwave that split the ground asunder. Amy swung at her opponents with the full force of her upper body, dodging the reactive swipe of their knives by a narrow margin. Amy punched one in the shin, breaking the woman's leg bones with a sickening crack before raising her hand to grab ahold of the wrist of the second attacker who attempted to stab her. She struck the girl across the jaw with a head-spinning right hook before grabbing her from behind and hurling her into the other opponent, against the wall.

Amy took deep breaths in and out as her opponents stood up. The two females revealed their misshapen faces; the skin on their cheekbones appeared to be either peeled off or burnt. Amy winced, a mixture of disgust and horror enveloped her senses. The two women, if they could be called that, turned their faces toward Amy. Their pupils were invisible, and their white eyeballs were blank, yet Amy could tell that they were fixated on her.

The two creatures twisted and contorted their bodies. Their bones cracked and their heads spun back into place, Amy's jaw dropped. One of her attackers reached into its spine, pulling out something white and hardened. It took Amy a moment to realize that it was one of the creature's bones. She braced herself for a second assault only to be frozen in place in an instant.

A third creature wrapped its scaly decrepit hands around Amy's waist and, with a sudden burst of strength smashed her into the ground. Amy roared and with tense shaking hands launched herself into the air, smashing her attacker against the ceiling. She regained her footing just in time to pluck the disassembled bone from its grasp and send the creature flying with a thundering uppercut. Amy took the offensive and utilized the hardened bone as a weapon, smacking the creature in front of and behind her in rapid succession. She swung at every inch of her opponents that she could reach, smashing their feet with her new weapon before either could land a blow. Amy then wedged her weapon between the two at just the right moment; with one end rammed into the neck of the creature behind her and the other in the mouth of the creature in front.

Amy floored the enemy behind her with a kick to the shin and another to the face that sent it flying backward. She chose to focus all her resentment on the creature in front of her. She snapped off half of the weapon made of bone, with the other still lodged into the creature's throat. She stabbed it in the ribs and the abdomen, hitting it more than twenty times before it keeled over. She shoved the other end of the bone deep into her opponent's throat before the creature landed. It was left lying on the pavement, subdued, and twitching involuntarily.

Amy barged back into the room that she had been yanked from, hoping to find her lost friend but all she saw were the remnants of the scuffle that had taken place. The walls and floor had been smashed to pieces and the benches had been chucked across the room.

"Leland? LELAND!"

Amy lifted her fist into the air and in one swift motion she pounded the ground, sending a current through the earth that turned the wooden floor upside down and sent debris flying in every direction.

Amy burst out of the warehouse. Her eyes darted in a frantic motion as she breathed heavily. Then something grabbed onto Amy's ankle from underground.

An entire swarm of hands popped out of the ground in unison. Two of them held Amy in place as they emerged, each revealing themselves to be creatures like the ones that had attacked her before. Two of them sank their nails into the raw flesh of her arms. Amy cried out as several more followed suit, biting on her face and piling themselves on top of her. There were too many. They were much stronger than the previous opponents as well, and with the darkness engulfing her vision, making it out of the meadow in one piece seemed to be less likely with each passing second.

An abrupt whistle alerted Amy to the presence of another unwelcome guest. She heard a knife fly by. It struck one of the creatures. Another knife followed. Amy could feel the creatures moving away from her. The hands on her legs released their grip.

She saw a powdery mist oozing across the ground. She backed away on her hands and feet as the odd cloud began dragging the creatures with it. It seemed to attach to each one. One tried to hold onto the ground, leaving fingernail scratches in the soil as it was pulled away. Another froze. Then a large hole appeared in its chest as the mist flowed through its body.

In a moment, the creature collapsed into a dark heap. Others were simply whisked away.

Chapter 2: Emergence

"Haven't I told you? Always remain on your guard; no matter what."

Amy's jaw dropped. At first, all she could see was a silhouette of the long-haired figure who had rescued her. But she knew that voice anywhere. It was the voice of the one person who mattered most to her.

The figure leaned closer toward Amy. The darkness of the surrounding environment was replaced by a chilling glow. The person in question was a girl with identical pale blonde hair. The girl's clear blue eyes glistened with a grace that provided stark contrast to her long hair, a gesture that oozed with the sort of authority and power that only an older sister could provide.

"Sarah!"

Amy jumped off the ground and pulled her older sibling into a warm embrace. At that moment despite the dire circumstances, there was nowhere else that she would rather be.

Sarah Stryker stood a little over two inches taller than her sister. The look in her eyes was severe and her expression poised. She had a lean athletic build that complemented her stature and served as but a glimpse of the true power that dwelled within her. Amy punched her in the shoulder.

"Why did you take so long to get here? I was almost done for."

Sarah shrugged, her expression nonchalant despite the circumstances. "Just wanted to gauge your skills."

"Yeah? Well, how did I do?"

"You could use some practice."

Amy rolled her eyes and chuckled. "Yeah? Well, you're lucky that we're being ambushed, otherwise, I'd pop you in the face for that one."

Sarah smiled. "It's good to see you, Amy."

"Yeah, you too. It's been weeks. I almost thought that you'd forgotten about me or something," Amy said feigning meekness with bashful eyes.

"Never."

"It's a good thing that you came when you did too. The Pride was about to do us in; me and Leland both."

"Who?" Sarah's face contorted in confusion.

"Leland Sheffield from school, remember? He had a few classes with us."

Sarah shook her head. "Amy, about the only thing I remember from school was soccer."

"Well, we've got to find him! He had come to take me out today and well we were having a good time but then they attacked. Oh god. They stabbed him and dragged him through the warehouse and then underground. I tried to help but then they attacked me and-"

"Don't worry. We'll find him."

Sarah placed a comforting hand around her sister's shoulders. Her voice was an ocean without waves, full of such reassuring confidence that the world had become less dark in Amy's eyes.

"I'm not worried."

"We just need to remain calm. Remember panicking won't help."

"Panicking won't help," Amy repeated, though the voice was less than certain.

"Yes. Don't worry. We fought The Pride before and survived. Just consider this practice," Sarah said with a sly smile as she led the way forward.

The Pride was a global organization; considered by many to be the most formidable on earth. All its members were female, and most could kill with their bare hands thanks to their gargantuan strength and martial arts prowess. They had little competition and even the few organizations that could measure up would have to rely on special abilities to counteract the overwhelming physicality of the merciless felines that dwelled within The Pride. Sarah Stryker couldn't have encountered a more deadly adversary, still she was unfazed. The Pride was but a spitting image of the monster that she saw every night that she looked inward.

Sarah and Amy ventured through the meadow with their ears perked and their eyes widened. Both were in peak physical condition but there was only so much that two lone women could do against an entire army. Pretty soon their numbers would be overwhelming. Sarah made sure to stay a few steps ahead of her younger sibling.

After a few moments, the sisters stopped in their tracks. A group of women stood in a line a few yards ahead, blocking the path. They were slim built, black-haired, and each stood upright with perfect posture.

"Stay behind me. I'll be your pair of eyes from now on. Just follow my lead," Sarah instructed.

"O-okay," Amy muttered.

Sarah shut her eyes and the world went silent. She inhaled, taking in all the purified oxygen around her. Sarah then exhaled and a white mist blew out of her mouth. The mist engulfed both girls in its presence.

Sarah opened her eyes, revealing pupils that shone in the night the same as the women from The Pride. All that was left to do was to hunt and protect what mattered to her along the way. Amy's hands shook as she took slow and purposeful steps toward her opposition.

Sarah spread her arms out, revealing two small throwing knives in each hand. Her long, elegant hair flapped in the wind as she twirled the weapons in her grasp, getting a good feel for each. She had the enemy's ignorance to her advantage. The darkness of the night as well as the cold mist would provide all the cover that she needed. All that was left to do was to act.

Sarah threw one of her knives in a swift motion. It soared through the air before penetrating a girl in her back. She spread her arms out and gasped. Specs of frost appeared on the girl's face and her protruding jaw was locked in a perpetual scream that was dulled out by the loss of motor control. The girl fell to the floor in disgrace, her body frozen from the inside out.

Sarah and Amy continued at a snail's pace toward the next warehouse. Sarah made it a point to go around the opposing team that was searching for them, walking behind trees and beneath various bushes along the path. There were two more guards on watch ahead of them and Sarah took the opportunity to floor them with more of her makeshift weapons before entering a small building, the mist dissipated after they walked inside.

Amy gasped the moment that she walked in. There, sprawled out in the middle of the floor was the man she had known since high school. A thick line of blood extended from the forehead to his right cheek and his neck had been cut open. Amy cupped her hand over her mouth as the reality of what had happened to him hit her like a freight train.

"No, no, no."

Sarah's eyes widened as she took in the look of the man whose eyes remained fixed in place while his jaw hung open. She examined his body but there was no need. Based on what her sister had told her it was obvious what had transpired. She could only hope that they hadn't

forced him to endure much pain before the end.

"NO, no, no. Oh god Leland, no."

Amy knelt beside him as her cheeks reddened and her eyes watered. She placed a gentle hand on his chest and another on his forehead. She ran her smooth hand along his wounded face, taking in every detail. The cuts on his face were fresh as were the ones on his neck. How long had he been like this?

Sarah shot her head backward, hearing something outside the warehouse. The enemy was still out there. The world didn't stop, even for a girl who had just lost a friend. Sarah wrapped a firm grip around Amy's forearm.

"Amy, we have to go. Come on. There's nothing that we can do here," She lifted her off the ground.

"No! No, I can't! I can't just leave him! I can't!" Amy's mind tumbled through the abyss. She couldn't believe that what was supposed to be a simple evening had turned into such a disaster.

"We have to. It's over. He's gone." Sarah tugged at her arm, but Amy retaliated once again.

"NO. No I- I can't leave him. He's not gone. He's right there. He's-"

"Amy. AMY." Sarah placed her against the wall and shook her, speaking in a stern tone. "Amy! He's gone. There's nothing that you or I can do."

Amy tore her face away from her sister's gaze and toward the body on the ground. It was an expression that Sarah had seen on her many times before. This man, this strange man whose name Sarah hadn't even remembered must have meant more to her sister than what she was letting on. And with that simple look, Sarah began to realize why the two of them had been targeted by the Pride, but she would need further confirmation to be sure.

"But he- we were on a date. At least that's what he called it. He was good to me, took me out. He-he said that he liked me."

"Amy, we need to get out of here. My car is right outside. But we have to hurry. There's no telling how far The Pride will tail us. I'm going to need you to hold it together long enough for us to get out of here.
Can you do that? For me?"

Amy nodded.

"Alright. Let's go."

Sarah led her sister outside, noticing a silver car parked a few yards away. But she also noticed several women blocking the path to her vehicle.

"Remember when I give the signal we attack," Sarah said.

Sarah fixated her stern gaze on the women in front of her. She twirled a small dagger made of ice in her hand. Her movements had to be swift. Just a second of hesitation would be time wasted.

Amy balled her hands into an angry fist as she harnessed her energy and burning tears poured down her cheeks.

"Now."

The sisters bolted through the meadow at top speed. Sarah lunged toward one of the girls and slugged her across the face, putting her entire body weight into the blow. The girl tumbled across the pavement, submerging herself in the dirt, grass, and broken tree branches just before her body went limp.

The ground exploded and Amy knocked several of her attackers through the sheer force of the energy surrounding her. She lifted one woman in the air and threw her with gargantuan strength, causing her back to collide with a tree trunk with a sudden *crack.*

Sarah took out her female opponents in quick succession, one after another. She overwhelmed two opponents with a barrage of punches to the gut before catapulting one in the air with a jaw- clenching uppercut to the chin and the second with a swift spin kick.

Adrenaline bubbled up in Amy like boiling water. She bent one of her attackers over and knead them in the chest before lifting them up by the collar and swinging them in a full three-hundred-and-sixty-degree motion. The girl was thrown into a group of her peers and the gang contorted into a pretzel as they tumbled across the pavement in unison.

Amy took deep hoarse breaths in and out. It had been weeks since she had been in a fight. Sarah could tell. She wasn't holding back but she was usually much faster than this. During her time away Sarah had been in several battles while her sister had clearly been living the quiet life. This wasn't her world. It was Sarah's and yet somehow her old enemies had managed to drag her sister into her problems as well.

Sarah scanned her surroundings. She took notice of the athletic, predatory women walking toward the two of them. Their eyes glowed white from a distance same as Sarah's. Not only was the converging enemy great in number but the creatures that had grabbed Amy from underground dug themselves from the surface, revealing their long disheveled hair and skeleton faces. Amy's jaw dropped. There were dozens of them.

"Sarah Stryker."

Sarah's cold merciless blue eyes met the cocky expression of the squad leader. She was someone that Sarah was certain she had never met before.

"I have a message for you. On behalf of The Pride."

"Well, I'm here, aren't I?"

The girl smiled, her eyes wide with hunger and intrigue. "Knock this bitch down a few pegs. Then if she is still breathing, maybe we'll talk."

The ten guards huddled together beside the squad leader; some were preparing to fight Sarah bare-handed though there were a few armed with daggers that needed to be considered.

"Now."

The other ten warriors lunged toward Sarah and Amy in unison, believing them to be nothing more than the sort of opposition they would face on any given day. Sarah blocked and countered the advances of her enemies with stunning speed. She struck two in the face with debilitating fists and before one girl could catch her off guard from behind Sarah clutched onto her throat with nothing more than the bare tips of her fingers. The girl gasped as white smoke blew out of her mouth and the world seemed to dissolve around her. Sarah yanked the girl's arm; a sudden *pop* alerted the others to the fact that she had pulled it out of socket before lifting her up and throwing her over her shoulder.

The squad leader jumped into the fray, realizing that her teammates were not faring as well as she hoped. She was a black-haired girl with a peculiar Arcane symbol tattooed on her left cheek. She pulled a dagger out of her sleeve and lunged toward her opponent, but Sarah was ready for her. She dodged the squad leader's advances before seizing the girl's wrist and squeezing it, forcibly opening her hand, and dropping the knife. Sarah stuck her fingernails into the girl's wrist forcing her mind to tunnel into an avalanche. Her breath became hoarse as a feeling of numbness entered her bloodstream. Sarah narrowed her expression.

"If my intuition serves me right, you must be the one in charge of this little expedition. That's good. With you here, I just might be able to make an impression."

Sarah perked her ears. There were two more enemies behind her, and she could feel the panic in their movements. She caught one with her elbow. Her timing was precise. The blow made the wind crack and the girl's vision blurred from it. The second girl to attack Sarah from behind fared even worse. Sarah stomped on her foot before winding her arm backward and striking the attacker between the eyes with the full force of her fist. The attacker flew several yards away and was buried beneath the bushes.

"Now where was I?" Sarah said.

She turned her attention back to the squad leader and examined as she pulled out a knife using her free hand. Without so much as a thought, Sarah halted her advance with a swift punch to the gut and a light headbutt that knocked her to the ground.

"Oh yes, before we were rudely interrupted."

Sarah placed an authoritative foot on the squad leader's chest.

"Who are you?"

"The name's Greta," The squad leader replied.

"Why did you come here?'

Sarah spoke in a low tone voice with just a tinge of malice hidden beneath it that made Greta's bones rattle inside of her skin. She hesitated and Sarah applied pressure with her foot. Greta winced as the suffocating cold of Sarah's touch entered her bloodstream.

"If you like your bones where they are you'll answer me when I ask you a question. Why did you come here? Why did you attack-"

"Isn't it obvious?" Greta managed to squeeze a chuckle out of her tightened lungs. "We came here for you. To send a message. Targeting your next of kin seemed like the way to do it."

Sarah cocked her head to the side, a swell of smug fearlessness seeped into her pores. "By all means, if you have something to say now's the time."

"Oh, the message is not from me. It's from your dear friend Anastasia."

Sarah raised her eyebrows, startled by Greta's revelation. "Anastasia?"

"Half the Pride is loyal to her now. She's been hiding, building up her strength and why do you think that is?" Greta prompted. "That's right. The most powerful woman in the world has set you in her sights. She's coming for you Sarah and there's not a thing that you can do about it. There's nowhere to run and nowhere to hide."

"Well since I wasn't planning on doing either I don't think that'll be much of a problem."

Amy turned towards her older sister, gazing at her with a bemused expression. There was also a much larger group of women approaching them in the distance that needed to be accounted for.

"There's no escape. The Pride will never stop. We'll hunt you across continents if need be."

Greta spread her lips into a wide conniving smile after she spoke. Sarah took note of her smug expression. It would make what was to come next even more enjoyable.

"That's fine. It's just another thing that we both have in common. I'll deal with Anastasia soon enough but you're going to help me send a message in the meantime."

Sarah's words prickled at Greta's skin, triggering an alarm that she knew she wouldn't be able to turn off. Her heart was racing so much that it burned. She had heard about this girl's reputation and ending up in her clutches was the last thing that Greta wanted.

"Sarah! Come on. We have to get out of here." Amy approached the passenger seat of Sarah's car.

"Amy hold on a second. Stay right there."

Amy stopped in her tracks and stared at her sister with a wide-eyed gaze. The tone in her voice was alarming and one that Amy had heard in her sister before. Both sisters knew exactly what Sarah was capable of when her words were uttered in that tone. The only person who didn't was the soon-to-be victim of her wrath.

"You attacked my sister and murdered a close friend of hers. It put her in a lot of distress and that- that is going to cost you."

Greta's eyes sunk deep into the pit of her sockets. "Cost me what?" Sarah lifted her leg off the ground.

"No. Wait."

"You obviously don't know me very well," Sarah said. "If you had you would know that I don't respond well to begging."

Sarah turned the girl over on her back and in a single motion smashed the area between her calf and upper thigh, breaking her kneecap in the process. Greta bellowed, utilizing the full force of her lungs, and shattering her vocal cords. The maneuver put the rest of the squad on alert. Amy saw them running several yards away.

"Come on Sarah. We have to go."

Sarah took one last look at her opponent as she backed away. Her heart swelled up in her chest. This girl had gotten a taste of it, but this was nothing compared to the retribution that her enemies would face once she was done with them. Sarah promised herself that as she climbed into the driver's seat.

"GET HER!! BRING THOSE BITCHES TO THEIR KNEES!!! BOTH OF THEM!" Greta yelled in a blood-curdling shriek. "I want them mauled. Bring them to Anastasia on a platter. Do you understand me?"

Greta wriggled in agony as and rolled over on her back. The pain she felt was greater than any she had experienced in her life. It would be a permanent staple in her mind. Even as she shut her eyes, using all her willpower to block reality out of her mind she could still see those same penetrating pupils staring down at her like a hawk. It was those eyes that would haunt the squad leader in her sleep, long after the encounter. Because the number one target of The Pride's scorn was once one of their own and though Sarah had endured unspeakable torment at the hands of others it was only by their hands that she became known as The Outcast.

Chapter 3: A Day in the life of

Sarah Stryker was jolted awake. She was pulled from slumber by a sharp morning breeze. Her glacier-like pupils glistened in the sunlight as the world came into focus. Her gaze shifted, taking in as much of her surroundings as she could without moving a muscle. She laid on her right shoulder. Her days of tossing and turning in the middle of the night were over but it seemed as if the nightmares would never cease. For as long as she lived, the memories of her chastisement would continue to haunt her.

Oh Sarah

The voice was like an echo. It was what had awoken Sarah from her slumber in the first place. That and a few frozen images that had been stamped on her heart since they occurred. She saw men with forked snake-like tongues and women with glowing white eyes, both of whom had set their fiendish sights on her. She saw images of a dungeon, one in which women were violated beyond recognition. But the sight that suffocated Sarah was an image of her mother placing a trusting hand on her cheek on a hospital bed. She couldn't believe that it had been so long since that was at the forefront of her mind.

Most people take life for granted. They have no idea how hard it can be for some to get out of bed in the morning, but Sarah knew all too well and it was that knowledge that made every day a trying ordeal. After a few minutes, Sarah sat up on her bed. The air was cool and tranquil. The sun beamed on her from the windowsill, highlighting her smooth fair skin and shining hair. She stood up and the weight of the world became less than unbearable.

Sarah stared into the bathroom mirror, taking in the sight that served as a vessel for her wounded spirit. She was a twenty-year-old woman with the physique of an Olympian thanks to her rigorous training regimen. She wore a thin sleeveless shirt that exposed her bulky muscular biceps. She had the Sun-drenched blonde hair of a Viking warrior and stood at five feet eight inches. Her icy clear eyes radiated with unquantifiable strength. What was most peculiar of all was a Chinese tattoo written along her left shoulder that read nǚ hái hái zhàn zhe. Even after two years as a solidified warrior it fascinated Sarah to no end. That was when she got the call.

"Hello?"

Sarah placed the phone against her ear, the air thickening with dread as she waited for a reply. She didn't prefer to be called so early in the morning. Despite her disposition, Sarah felt her defenses weaken after the person on the other end spoke.

"Hello, Sarah. I've been looking forward to speaking to you for a long time. I hear that you're planning on entering Georgetown and those of us on the outside want to know what your intentions are."

Sarah squinted her eyes. "Who is this?"

"Oh, I'm sorry. I was told that you would be expecting me. My name is Stephanie White. I work with the national media. I'll be your liaison to much of the world at large for the time being."

"Oh yes, yes." Sarah shut her eyes, embarrassed that she had forgotten. "I didn't think that you would be calling so soon. But yes, I remember."

Sarah never met the girl in person though she had seen her photograph online and had spent a lot of time learning about her, visiting her social media, and even exchanging a few emails in preparation for her call. From what she could recall Stephanie White was a diplomat for many of the most powerful organizations in the world. She was a black woman with straightened hair and a face that shone with innocence and youthful optimism. But there was something else about this woman. Something that inspired trust and intrigue that she hadn't felt it years. It was for that reason about all others that Sarah agreed to the interview in the first place.

"Sorry for the sudden drop in but I like to get a jump on things."

"Great," Sarah said, with less enthusiasm and more sarcasm than what she intended.

"I'm getting that you don't feel the same way. "

Sarah shrugged, giving herself permission to be blunt. "Well, if you're looking for someone to bail you out of a fight, possibly break a few kneecaps I'm your girl. But this, talking about my issues with a stranger? Well, that's something I'm less than proficient in."

Sarah could hear Stephanie sigh from the other end of the receiver. A slight pause alerted Sarah to the fact that her interviewer was just now coming to grips with the awkwardness of the situation.

"Sarah look, I understand that you never signed up for this. But what you have here is a golden opportunity. A chance to set the record straight. To explain what it is that you do and why. Try not to think of it as a burden."

Sarah didn't see how she could see this exercise as anything besides a burden, yet the woman's words were full of reassurance. "What is it that you want to know? Why do I fight? Or why have I specifically chosen to go after The Pride?"

"We'll get to The Pride in just a second but first I want to know about you. What is it that drives you? I've read through your file. So, I have the cliff notes, but I need more. Why choose the path of a warrior? Willingly? Your life could have gone in another direction entirely. What is it about this life that entices you?"

Sarah leaned against the side of the bed as she sat down. The questions had just begun and already the girl was sure not to make things easy on her. Sarah rested her free hand on top of the bed.

"Why fight? Because I need to. Because every day I feel anger and resentment swelling in my chest. I feel it in my throat, in my gut, and prickling at my skin and I want it to stop. So, I fight every day that I can in the hopes that it will."

Stephanie took a moment to take in Sarah's words. "I see. So, it's therapeutic. It's your coping mechanism."

"One of many," Sarah answered. "That's the thing that most people don't understand. It's not until you've experienced real trauma that you come to realize how much of a hold it can have on a person's life. Every day is a trial. My mind is desperate to remember. Always. So, I've trained my body to fight it. Every second that I can."

"And how is this battle between mind and body fought? How is it won?"

"A daily routine helps," Sarah added. "I wake up, train, meditate and get dressed before going on an afternoon drive. If I have plans for the day that's usually when I take care of them. I come back and meditate some more before nightfall. Then I hunt."

"Hunt?" Stephanie was startled by the sharp change in Sarah's tone.

"For a third of the night. I go out. It's when they are most active."

"You mean The Pride?"

"Yes. I can sense them. Their bloodlust and oftentimes their location. It's only a matter of staying one step ahead and keeping track of their swelling numbers."

Stephanie bit her lip. "Maybe it's not my place to say but one might think you're looking for trouble. You could choose to wait until it comes to you."

Sarah shook her head. "I'm done waiting."

"I see. So, you said that you engage in combat or hunt, if you will, for a third of the night. That's quite a busy schedule. Are you able to get some quality rest?"

"Yeah, I've developed a schedule for that."

"How's your sleep?"

"I get about three hours a day. If I'm lucky."

"Three hours? Only three hours."

Sarah shrugged. "I'm used to it."

"Goodness. How are you able to cope with all the stress?" "One day at a time," Sarah replied.

Sarah spent the better part of the afternoon driving through downtown Seattle with Amy sitting in the passenger seat next to her. She decided to use this time to answer a few of her sister's questions regarding The Pride and the hit that one of their deadliest warriors had placed on her. It helped keep her mind from tunneling too deep into darkness.

"Sarah, who's Anastasia?"

"Someone that you don't want to meet."

"That bad huh?" Amy added.

"The worst."

"And The Pride answer to her now?"

"Not all; just a fraction of them. There are a few loyal rebels out there that recognize her for what she is."

"And what is she exactly?" Amy asked, her face contorted with a mixture of intrigue and confusion. "What is it that makes her any different from the rest?"

Sarah kept her firm gaze on the highway, her eyes hidden by a pair of thin protective sunglasses that she occasionally wore while driving. Her expression remained placid, giving away little except the slight curling of her lips and a momentary pause before she spoke.

"Well to keep it short; it's how unhinged she is. Most of The Pride are killers. That's nothing special but Anastasia? She lives for it. Pretty sure all the power, money, and status are just a bonus for her. She's a sadist of the most perverse breed. She rules over her subordinates through fear and intimidation. Honestly out of all the people I've met I can't think of a more frightening person."

Amy scoffed. "Frightening? Please. I bet I could take her."

"I'm sure you could. If you put your mind to it," Sarah replied. She gestured with her forefinger, pointing at her in a fervent warning. "But don't think for a second that you're going anywhere near her without my say-so."

"Yeah, yeah. I hear yah. All I'm saying though is that if we were locked together alone in a room I wouldn't complain. It would give her plenty of time to be well acquainted with my fists. I've been training just like you have. Every day. It's amazing. How much stronger I feel. I hardly ever get tired either."

"That's good. Just keep in mind that there's a lot more to a fight than brute strength Amy. You could have all the power in the world within your grasp but if you lack the necessary skill and discipline in harnessing it said power will only cripple you," Sarah warned. "It's a lesson that I've learned, time and time again."

Sarah drove to a nearby gas station. She stepped out to fuel her car and to speak to the clerk in the convenience store while Amy sat still on the curb in silence, allowing her inner thoughts to take form and clutter her surroundings. It was only now that Amy was beginning to realize how utterly unfair this entire situation had been for her. Ten minutes later the steady voice of her older sibling brought her back to reality.

"I got us both a drink, but I didn't know if you were hungry. If you want, I could go back in and get you something."

Sarah stood outside the store as she examined her sister. She had already finished fueling her tank, but Amy hadn't noticed. Her gaze remained fixated on the ground. Sarah could feel her heart skip a beat. "I-I can't eat," Amy said. "I just- I've been thinking about things. About how screwed up everything is. It just isn't right."

Sarah took note of her sister's mannerisms and her mumbling voice. Amy could hardly bring herself to meet her sister's gaze, and that was enough to trigger an alarm.

"Is this about what happened last night? About what's his name?"

"Leland. He's dead Sarah. They killed him and here we are just going on with our lives as if nothing happened. It just isn't right."

"I know," Sarah said, her voice softening up at the sheer magnitude of Amy's words. She edged towards her with quiet steps before sitting down beside her. "You said he was from school, right?"

Amy nodded.

"Did you like him?"

Amy's face contorted in confusion. "That's what I've been trying to figure out. I don't know. I mean I think I did. He was cute but also kind of annoying. You know the way most guys are?"

Amy had found the strength to look her sister in the eye, her eyes searching for acknowledgment and Sarah replied with a gentle nod, illustrating that she was on the same page.

"But I-I mean. He liked me, really liked me. He moved all the way from Bellingham just to see me. I mean, that means something right?" Amy averted her gaze to the ground once again. She fidgeted with her cuticles, hoping to keep herself from crumbling under the weight of her words. "Maybe we could have been something. Maybe there was a chance. But now we'll never know."

"I'm sorry," Sarah said. She rubbed her sister's back with gentle hands, hoping the gesture would soothe her in a way that her words couldn't. The two sisters sat in silence for the next ten minutes. It was the least Sarah could do to honor a man that had impacted her sister's life, if only marginally so.

Sarah's mind remained fixed on the road ahead as she drove Amy back home. She couldn't shake the feeling that she was headed for disaster, but an open challenge was something that Sarah never backed down from and Anastasia knew it. This was a part of The Pride's plan and if she proceeded half-cocked, she could very well be walking into their trap. Still, there was no other option that made sense to her. The coming battle would be an act of faith; like the one that had inspired her to begin her life as a warrior in the first place.

"So, what are you going to do? About Anastasia I mean? What are you going to do to keep her from hunting you down?"

Sarah had just parked near the curb of Amy's current apartment. It was small, one of the few that Amy could afford on her salary. She was the one who had insisted on the move, despite Sarah's insistence on close contact and keeping a watchful eye.

"The only thing I can do," Sarah said. "I'm going to hunt her first. Preferably sooner rather than later."

"Are you sure? I mean you said it yourself; she's a lot more frightening than the rest and most of The Pride answers to her now. How are you going to beat her?"

"I'll find a way."

"What if you're not ready?"

"I'll make myself ready."

Amy curled her lips and averted her gaze. The time had come for her to make her move.

"Anyway, I should probably go. I told Kyle to meet me at five and if my hunch is correct, he'll be pretty upset about now. I'll make it up to him. How are you on rent by the way? I have a bit to spare if you needed-"

"I'm coming with you. On the hunt for Anastasia. I'm coming with you."

Sarah's heart sank under the weight of Amy's interruption. She wanted to ask her to repeat it but there was no doubt about what she had just heard. This was a fear that Sarah didn't realize that she had before that very moment.

"I-I don't think that's such a good idea. You still have a lot to learn Amy," she said, her eyebrows raised.

"And this is the perfect opportunity. This will be good practice."

"This isn't practice. This is the real thing. It's not something to take lightly."

"I'm not asking. I'm telling."

Amy's words were precise and full of thunder. Sarah's forehead curled as she turned to meet her fierce gaze. What had come over Amy was something that she hadn't sensed in months.

"Now I'm coming with you whether you like it or not. Just thought that I'd warn you first," Amy said.

"Amy, who do you think that you're talking to?" Sarah squinted as she examined her sister. "I think you're forgetting which of us is the older sibling."

"Sarah, you can't expect me to sit back and wait. After what just happened. After what they did to Leland? I can't. I'm part of this just as much as you are. They'll hunt me just like they hunted you. So why not have me lend a hand? I mean two are better than one, right? You're up against an entire army."

Sarah's squinting eyes morphed into a slight glare as Amy dug a bit deeper into her plea for approval, bringing some of her older sister's insecurities up to the forefront. She knew how to pull on her heartstrings better than anyone that Sarah had ever known.

"I know you don't like to ask for help but sometimes you need it, and you need it now more than ever Sarah. If this girl is as dangerous as you say then all the more reason for me to be there by your side. You say she isn't to be taken lightly? Then act like it and stop being so stubborn. This isn't a game where you have to play by the rules to win. This is life and death."

"That's quite a way of twisting my words," Sarah said, with a tinge of irritability oozing out of her voice though to her dismay Amy shrugged off her retort with a fierce reprimand of her own.

"Yeah. So? Doesn't make me wrong now does it?"

"No. You're not wrong. I'll give you that," Sarah said with a defeated sigh before turning her gaze to the road ahead. She was miles away from her goal just like Amy but maybe together that road would be just a bit more bearable. She turned her observant glare back towards her sister, squinting at her for almost a minute before uttering her one-word response.

"Alright."

"Thank you, Sarah. You don't know what this means to me. I've always wanted to fight beside you. I know I can keep up. I just need a-"

But Sarah raised a finger to silence Amy before she could finish her celebratory rant.

"Do what I say at all times. You'll be there for support, but Anastasia is mine. Don't risk a direct confrontation with her. You only attack if and when I say so. No back talk. I mean it. You give me a reason to think that you'll jeopardize the mission in any way you're out. No exceptions."

"Don't worry Sarah. I'll be fine. You don't need-"

"Ah, ah, ah don't interrupt me," Sarah said, raising her finger in protest once again. "I wasn't finished. Remember you follow my lead.
Which means when I speak you don't. Are we clear?"

Amy placed a fake zipper over her lips in a playful gesture, her face shone with amusement. Despite her previous stern demeanor Sarah couldn't help but soften her expression as a result. It was a game that the two sisters had engaged in since they were children and one that Amy possessed a mastery over.

"Just be careful okay," Sarah's voice had lost its edge. She was no longer the commander that she had been a second ago. Amy crossed her heart with her forefinger in reply.

"You can speak now Amy," Sarah said, allowing a slight smile to escape her expression.

"No, I was finished. I said all I needed to say. Just make sure you don't leave me behind. If you do, I'll hunt you across town myself."

"Good to know," Sarah said, as she turned her focus back to her steering wheel.

"You're the best, you know that?"

"Yeah, yeah I know," Sarah said with a defeated sigh. Amy wrapped her arms around her and rested her cranium on her shoulder.

"I love you, Sarah."

"Same."

Sarah returned her affection with a subtle pat on the cheek. Amy exited the vehicle and Sarah was alone; alone with inner turmoil and her decision; a decision that she may soon regret.

"She drives me crazy," Sarah remarked before putting on her sunglasses and driving off.

Sarah arrived at a local diner fifteen minutes later. Her stomach growled in anticipation as the warm smell of buttery toast and waffles entered her nostrils. She walked inside and found her friend sitting at the far end table of the restaurant, disappointment, and annoyance plastered over his face. Sarah decided in advance that she wasn't going to let his negativity get to her. She would make the most out of their meeting, no matter what.

"You're late," The man said the moment Sarah approached his table.

"Hey Kyle. Good to see you. How are things?" She reprimanded, determined to match his words every step of the way.

"Oh please. Let's just skip the pleasantries. You're here because you want something from me like always. Let's just get to it."

Kyle Harper was one of the most unusual people that Sarah had ever met and that was due to both his appearance as well as demeanor. He had a full head of jet-black hair that he only partially chose to keep in a tidy fashion, small strands of it extended over his forehead and eyes, which were the most striking shade of bright green. He had a scrawny build; one that allowed most people to overlook him though Sarah knew better.

This man was a pivotal player. He held all the keys; including one to what may very well be Sarah's salvation. Doing business with this man was essential, even if she would have to deal with his most cumbersome idiosyncrasies along the way. It was that simple truth that gave Sarah the courage to sit down in front of him.

"What's with the attitude?" Sarah asked, her voice gentler than what she had expected.

"What?" Kyle murmured, as he picked at his cuticles. "There's no attitude. I just prefer not to waste our time, you least of all. Since you obviously have other places that you would rather be."

Kyle hadn't looked her in the eye upon uttering that statement. He didn't want to meet her fierce gaze so soon, though he could feel it beaming and examining him like an X-ray. He could see Sarah's glare even before he looked up though when he did Kyle was surprised to find a bit more amusement in her expression than what he had expected.

"Kyle, we're all adults here, aren't we? If you're upset because I was late, then just say so."

"Hmm? I never said that I was upset." Kyle then changed his tone; his eyes lit up and his voice raised as if he were on stage. "Although if I was, could one really blame me? I mean here I am; sticking my neck out when I could be halfway around the world if I wanted to. I mean the fact that I'm considered to be the smartest man in the world by anyone at all must mean that there's plenty in other continents that know who I am. I'm sure I could get their support, make a solid living for myself. But I don't. I'm here. Because I want to be."

"So am I. I'm here, aren't I?" Sarah challenged.

Kyle scoffed. "Barely."

"Kyle," Sarah muttered, leaning forward, and speaking in a more intimate tone. "It's nothing personal. I've just had a lot on my plate these past couple of days."

"Yeah, and maybe that's the problem. Maybe I want things to be more personal between us. Instead of you just contacting me whenever you feel like you need something."

"What do you mean?" Sarah asked, squinting at him.

"I mean that I want you to let me in. About your life; how you're coping with the day-to-day stress of living. It's what I'm passionate about and I feel like I can really help you."

"Kyle, don't take this the wrong way because I'm pretty sure I'm in the same boat but your bedside manner leaves a lot to be desired."

"What? What are you talking about? I can talk to you about your problems, insecurities; all that. I mean I'll just tell you that you're being an idiot, which you are. Which everyone is; except me. Because I'm a certified genius but uh-"

Kyle stopped in his tracks. Sarah's gaze was razor-sharp. He couldn't continue his tirade in good conscience. "Oh uh. I guess I'm not really helping my case much huh?"

Sarah shook her head. A waitress approached the two of them just as he was about to give a counter argument.

"Hi what can I get for you today? Your usual?" She said, addressing Kyle first.

"Yeah. I'll take the pancake platter with sausage. With a side of bacon. And scrambled eggs. And a piece of toast on the side."

"And what can I do for the ma'am?" The waitress asked.

"Buttery croissant, egg muffin. And a vine of grapes if you have them."

"Alright. And what would you two like to drink?" She asked.

"Orange juice." Sarah and Kyle spoke in unison. The waitress jotted down the order of her two guests with lightning speed before departing.

"Alright, I'll get that out to you Asap."

"Anyway," He carried on, turning back towards Sarah. "Look I can't do the things that you can do. I can't pummel people with my fists and freeze their internal organs. But I can help you if you'll let me. And I feel that I should. To repay you."

A slight frown appeared on Sarah's face at the sound of Kyle's plea. The conversation had just taken a sharp detour.

"For saving my life two years ago. When we were both at our lowest. I've never been the same since that day. Don't tell me that you've forgotten."

"I haven't forgotten," Sarah admitted. "How could I?"

"There's no way that I'll ever be able to repay you for what you did. To make it up to you."

"Kyle, we've been through this. You don't owe me anything. And besides, I'm pretty sure you did make it up to me when you helped save my life remember?"

"Yeah, I guess. But it just doesn't feel the same."

"Well, I have just the thing to lift your spirits," Sarah revealed. "A job that I entrust only to you. One that involves hacking, uncovering a buried secret, and most likely saving the little shred of sanity that I have left."

Kyle's entire being flared up, optimism shined through his widening eyes. "What? You mean it?"

"Mmm-hmm. And this secret has been hidden for a long time. It'll be a challenge, but I know you're up for it."

"Seriously?"

"In addition to our current mission, I'm going to need you to work on this special assignment for me okay. And let's keep it confidential. No one else needs to know."

Kyle's mouth hung open for a moment. "Uh, sure. Who else would want to know?"

"I'm going to need you to look for someone for me. A man," Sarah revealed.

Kyle shrugged. "Okay. A man. Sure. That narrows it down to about half the population of the entire planet. Want to be more specific?"

Sarah bit her lip. "I don't know his name. I only remember his face and what he did to me. But that'll have to be enough.

"What do you mean?"

Sarah gave him a look. "Kyle, you're smart. You should know. I'm not ashamed or anything but I'd rather not say it out loud," she said, her eyes shifting to examine the diner and the people around her. "Take a peek inside." Sarah raised a finger in a stern warning. "Take a peek but don't wander."

Kyle squinted as his gaze locked onto the crystal glaciers inside of her pupils. A few images popped into his head and at that moment Kyle's eyes widened greater than Sarah had seen in years.

"Oh Sarah, Sarah wait a minute. Sarah. Now, wait just a minute." He raised his hands in protest after just barely being able to decipher what she was referring to. She shook her head, a gesture that was slow and methodical.

"I'm done waiting."

Her voice oozed with maturity. Kyle saw the small details in her facial expression that alerted him to the seriousness of their conversation. He couldn't risk saying the wrong things especially not in this delicate time. Kyle sighed, summoning up all his courage to respond to her sudden request.

"Sarah, I know you're upset. God knows you have every right to be. Those men- the dozen or so that did this to you,"

"Fifty," Sarah corrected, her voice as thin as the hiss of a snake.

"Sorry. Fifty. The gang that did this to you. They are pure evil, every single one that had a hand in your suffering. The worst of human filth and they deserve whatever calamity befalls them."

"But-" Sarah prompted. Kyle swallowed a bit before responding to her challenge.

"But you might want to consider going about this from another angle. Maybe-"

"Letting go. Live and let live? Find a place in my heart for forgiveness? Is that really what you wanna tell me?"

Kyle lowered his head in shame. He had always felt that sarcasm was his specialty. "You make it sound so crass."

"I wonder why."

"I don't mean to be."

"I know," Sarah said. "Which is why I give you respite. But make no mistake. One way or another I will find this man. Now you can either help me or get out of the way. It's your call."

"Damn girl. Take it easy. We're just having a conversation here."

Sarah shrugged. "I'm just being transparent. Isn't that what you feel most people are lacking?"

"Yeah, but your aura is practically screaming right now." Kyle sighed. "Alright, I'll do it. But it'll be quite a wide search. I can't promise anything overnight."

"Take as much time as you need. I'm a patient woman."

"Well now that that's out of the way let's say we get down to business, shall we?"

Sarah nodded. "We shall." The waitress brought out several plates of food, only one of which belonged to Sarah. She set them in front of the two just as Kyle prepared to get into the meat of their conversation.

"Okay as you already know Anastasia has placed a hit on you. My guess is that given your elusive nature she saw your sister as an easy target. Now just like with the other mission I would urge you not to let your personal dislike of the girl get to your head. She was given a position of authority for a reason. She's as deadly and as cunning as they come; possibly more than any you've faced."

"I'll keep that in mind," Sarah assured him, between small nibbles of food.

"Based on all the research I've done since yesterday The Pride is split about fifty-fifty on her. Many think she's the real deal but there are still a few rebels who want to take her down as badly as you do. One such warrior being Maryam Bahira. A resident of Georgetown."

"Georgetown?"

"Yeah, and with any organization as influential as The Pride many of them have decided to spread their power throughout every town and city in America. Maryam Bahira is an up-and-coming prizefighter with several impressive victories under her belt. So much so that she was put in charge of her local district. Georgetown is the most dangerous part of Seattle, and it just so happens to be where Anastasia was last rumored to have been. As far as I can tell Maryam is not a friend to Anastasia so you shouldn't have any problems dealing with her."

"We'll see."

"Just be careful okay. I know fighting is an inevitable part of this whole gig but try to avoid the unnecessary ones."

"If I didn't know any better, I'd say that you were worried about me," Sarah said before taking a bite out of her muffin.

"Of course. Contrary to what you might think I care about you a great deal. Which is why I get a little ticked when that feeling isn't always mutual."

Sarah took a swig of her orange juice as she studied the man in front of her. Just what was his deal? She had known him only for a short while and already he believed that she owed him something. Still, she was humored by his interest and took it as an opportunity to play her hand.

"Well, I have trust issues. You know how I am."

"Yeah, yeah, yeah. I have heard all the excuses. They don't impress."

"But between you and me," Sarah said, lowering her voice and leaning closer towards Kyle. "You're the one that I'm going to depend on the most during this little adventure. Your expertise and knowledge will be vital in the coming years. Most of the important work that I have will need to be regulated by you. Which might also mean that I will have to reveal all the little secrets inside of my head that you are desperate to get your hands on."

Kyle's eyes widened. "Really? You mean it?"

Sarah nodded. "Mmm-hmm."

"Sarah, are you just telling me what I want to hear so that I'm more likely to cooperate?" Kyle asked, being too perceptive for his own good.

Sarah squinted in reply, the fierceness of it pierced through Kyle like a laser. "Are you calling me a liar?"

"No, uh no I'm not," Kyle said, his voice rising just a bit.

'Good. I meant every word. You might feel like I'm holding out on you now but that's only because I got a wealth of jobs lined up for you in the future. Some of which I know can only be done by you."

"Really? Only by me? Well, when you put it that way-"

Sarah shrugged. “People call you the smartest man in the world, right? Well, now you’ll have the opportunity to prove it.”

“Sounds promising,” Kyle said.

“But just remember that I’m less likely to be as generous if you give me lip.” Sarah tapped on the tip of his nose with her forefinger. “Okay?” Kyle lit up; a half-smile appeared on his face.

“Yeah okay. I got this. I’ll search for the identity of this man while you’re tracking Anastasia. With any luck, I should be able to report back within the next few days.”

“That’s what I like to hear,” Sarah said.

“Would you like me to split the bill?” The waitress had appeared before the two again, noticing that they were almost finished. Sarah looked up at her.

“No. It’s all on me.”

“No! What? I was supposed to pay. I invited you,” Kyle said, his voice raised in protest. Sarah clicked her tongue and wagged her finger at him.

“Nope. I’m not letting you spend a dime. You should know better.”

“But Sarah you hardly even ate anything. I’d just hate to put you out.”

“Trust me, Kyle, you couldn’t put me out if you tried.” Sarah stood up and placed her green bag over her neck, pulling out a wad of cash that she would hand to the cashier before she left. She placed a comforting hand on Kyle’s shoulder. “Besides just think of it as my way of repaying you for being late.”

“Alright. But I’m going to need to see you again before you leave. There’re a few areas of Georgetown that may be of particular interest.”

“I’m free tomorrow. What do you say that we meet at your place? I’ll bring Amy. She could use a friendly face right now.”

“Oh goodness. Amy.” Kyle said, his expression melting a bit. “How’s she holding up?”

“She could be better. Hopefully, this trip will do us both some good. But let’s keep this business with our current mystery man between us. She’s already involved enough. We don’t need to burden her with this.”

"Sure, though last time I tried to hide something from her it didn't go so well. I doubt this will be any different."

"Guess you'll just have to trust me."

Kyle scoffed. "Gee I wonder what could go wrong there."

Sarah allowed a sly smile to escape her lips before walking away. She brushed her hair backward and bit off a grape from the vine in her grasp. She approached the cashier, leaving Kyle alone to finish the rest of his food in silence. He sighed in defeat, realizing that despite his convictions the conversation had gone exactly as Sarah had planned it.

"She drives me crazy."

Chapter 4: The Fighter

"Welcome ladies and gentlemen. Thank you all for coming. It is my pleasure to announce this week's state championship match. And from what I've heard it'll be the bout to shake the heavens."

The sound of the announcer's thunderous voice rang in the ears of the crowd within the stadium. They raised their hands and bellowed at the height of their lungs. This was a fight they were eager to watch. The announcer scanned the stadium as the bald referee and the two contestants stepped into the ring.

"In the challenger's corner, we have a lieutenant from The Serpent army. One of the organization's most powerful fighters.'

A bulky man with short ginger hair stepped into the ring. He was a man not only of massive stature but a unique pair of eyes that resembled the slit pupils of a snake and made him distinct from most of the competition.

"Our champion is a resident of Seattle. Having several titles under her belt, taking on opponents from around the world. A woman said to have the strongest fists in Seattle. MARYAM BAHIRA!!!"

The moment she entered the ring the crowd went wild though Maryam paid them no attention. Her long braids hung in pigtails and her dark brown eyes gleamed with a ruthless tint. She had beautiful dark skin that highlighted the lean muscular body that she sharpened day after day.

Maryam's forehead furrowed as she examined the warrior in front of her. Her blood began to sizzle as the weight of the world welled up in her hands. She knew what he was, even before examining his pupils his entire aura screamed predator. He was a member of The Serpents, a ruthless all-male army. And not just any member but a lieutenant who often dominated this side of the underground fighting scene. She had entered The Lion's den and there was no way out, especially if she won. All eyes were on her.

One of Maryam's trainers placed a protective guard in her mouth before she was allowed to step forward. She knew that she didn't need it but figured it was best to cooperate, give the fools surrounding her a sense of normalcy before the slaughter.

"Now I want a good clean fight. That means no biting, eye-gouging, and no hitting below the belt." The referee turned towards The Serpent man. "And no innuendo either. I know about your kind, and I know how messy you can get. What'd you say we leave the personal vendettas for the streets?"

Maryam stared deep into the thin slit pupils of her muscular opponent. The referee's words went in one ear and out the other. "Fine with me. Long as this punk plays by the rules so will I."

The Serpent hissed, enchanted by Maryam's words. "Cooperative. Good. I like that in a woman. What do you say you and I hook up later on?" The man stuck out his thin snake-like tongue at her.

"I know you're one of them," she said ignoring his remark.

"The name is Henry. I think I speak for most of us when I say we've had our eye on you for some time now. Your power is impressive though troubling. We feel that there's much that can be done to tame it."

"Now if you're both ready will you please step into your corners?"

Maryam Bahira and Henry each backed away a few paces at the sound of the announcer's request. Maryam's blood boiled as she pounded her fists against each other and bounced up and down to find her footing.

The bell sounded and both warriors circled the arena, making sure to watch each other's footing and their own before springing into fisticuffs. Maryam began by jabbing at her opponent's jaw and darting back and forth before finally swinging at him with just a sizable portion of her strength to test his skills. He blocked several of her attacks before unleashing a fierce combination of his own. The crunch of fists colliding with the forearm and solid bone of the two fighters vibrated through Maryam so hard that she was sure that the first two rows of the crowd must have heard it too.

Maryam struck her opponent in the stomach causing him to heave under the weight of such a precise blow. The moment of superiority was all that was needed to begin her stride. She ducked and felt the whoosh of wind blow her hair backward as Henry's fist grazed over her head. He then staggered backward after being socked across the jaw with a severe left hook. It took him a second to regain control over his body and vision and by then Maryam was already in attack mode once again.

Henry's neck snapped backward the minute Maryam's hardened fist connected with his face. The swiftness of her thrust turned rubber into steel and set The Serpent's world ablaze. Blood splattered on the ground. Maryam gritted her teeth before swinging again, this time with twice as much fervor.

Henry clutched his opponent's fist, halting her movement in the process. Maryam tugged at her wrist, but she couldn't budge. Then something happened that caused her eyes to widen in dismay. A snake suddenly appeared in front of her, extending its scaly body, encircling Henry's arm, and wrapping itself around hers. It seemed in her excitement she had managed to underestimate this man.

Maryam winced as the creature squeezed her arm. The snake widened its jaws and latched onto the skin near her shoulder. She dropped to her knees as a sense of numbness overcame her.

"That's it. Give in. Submit."

Henry's voice rang in her ear like an alarm. She couldn't believe that she had given this man an upper hand even for a moment. The thought entered her bloodstream as the snake stuck its fangs deeper into her flesh. She couldn't give in. No matter what.

"FOUL!"

"That's a FOUL. He can't do that. It's against the rules."

Several members of the audience bellowed in protest. Their shouting drowned in Maryam's ear. She placed her fist on the ground as she summoned her strength.

"Poor girl. There's nowhere you can go where we won't follow. You're on our radar now. We'll track you just like the rest. It would be wise of you to give in while you had the chance. You'll save yourself a lot of pain that way."

Maryam ignored Henry's chastisement and with a sudden burst of power yanked at the snake wrapped around her arm. The man tripped as he was pulled forward and was caught with a punch to the gut. Maryam popped off the ground and turned his gaze towards the ceiling with a ruthless uppercut. She cut him in the chin with another ferocious punch. Henry's face reddened and his forehead curled. He lunged towards his target with the full force of his power, using both his fists and the pet snake he summoned.

The strength inside of Maryam was as unstable as boiling acid. She bobbed and weaved, dodging the snake's hungry jaws at the last possible second. She swung at her prey with a ferocity that eclipsed her previous attacks by a country mile. She hit her opponent, in the chest, abdomen, in-between the eyes and his jawline; anywhere that she could reach. She blocked and parried all attacks by the man with finesse before connecting with a second uppercut that launched him off his feet.

The Serpent landed on the ropes and had to wrap his arms around them to keep from toppling over the ring. Henry's mind spiraled out of its orbit. He was unaware of the world around him and felt as though his head was detached from his body, but Maryam wasn't finished with him yet. She continued to pound on his limp body for a solid minute; the crunching of her steel fists against flesh vibrated through the stadium, causing the audience to cringe in their seats. She knocked Henry into the corner of the ring with a brutal right hook before unleashing a severe barrage of punches that were sure to cause lasting damage. Several of Henry's teeth were knocked out of his mouth in the frenzy and the crushing pain of her blows crept into every inch of him.

Maryam ended her barrage just as Henry lost all sensation in his body. She stopped in her tracks and froze in place for a few seconds, seconds that seemed to echo in his mind for eternity. She took a step backward, realizing that her work was done.

Henry felt his legs give out on him first, despite that being one of the few areas that Maryam hadn't touched. His fall was involuntary and as such was the most painful part of the experience. He tipped over like a teapot, unable to brace himself for the sudden collision when his body hit the ground. Henry landed sprawled on his stomach with his face glued to the ground.

Maryam used her foot to flip the man over on his back. He was unconscious, his eyes shut, and his mouth gaped open. She took notice of the cuts and blood splattered over his face. Despite her enraged breathlessness, Maryam raised her chin and allowed a look of approval to escape her lips as her heart welled up inside of her.

"Still strong after thirty-seven consecutive victories. The winner is MARYAM BAHIRA!"

The referee lifted Maryam's hand in a triumphant gesture and the crowd erupted. She smiled; her perfect whitened teeth shone even in the distance. She was sure that there was nothing else in the world that could make her feel more elevated. Everything in her life was exactly as it should be.

Maryam retreated to the locker room after the fight was over. She washed up and retrieved a pair of navy-blue jeans, a t-shirt, and an unbuttoned jean jacket amongst her belongings. Despite her opponent's best efforts, he hadn't managed to make any lasting marks on her and that was impressive considering who he was.

Maryam sat on the bench in the locker room. During the fight, adrenaline surged through her. The confusion and the constant heartache that her life had become dwindled into nothingness. She and her opponent were the only ones present and it was only after Maryam left the arena that the world came into focus.

"That was incredible! Absolutely incredible!"

Maryam twisted her neck, her face contorted into a frown as she gazed up at one of her biggest fans. He had somehow managed to follow her from the arena without anyone noticing.

"Boy, what are you doing here?"

"Well, I was in the neighborhood, and I thought I'd come and watch your latest fight. And by golly wow was that a fight."

"It waddit nothing," Maryam said, slipping her arms through the sleeves of her jean jacket as she spoke. "Punk ass bitch can't even fight anyway. He uses dirty tricks to throw people off their game. And I meant what are you doing here in the locker room? Can't you wait outside?"

The man lowered his gaze as he picked at his cuticles. He was slender. Maryam doubted he had ever been in a fight a single day of his life yet there was something about his naivete that made her study every inch of him, his widened smile, wavy hair; even the fact that he was Caucasian. All pointed to opportunity; one of the few she would get to have something normal.

"I could have waited but I wanted to see you," The man took a moment to pause. His next words were laced with meaning. "You know, after the fight?"

"Why?"

"Well, I thought that maybe we could go out sometime. You know maybe do something fun?"

"Fun like what?" Maryam asked, her eyes squinting with skepticism.

"I don't know. Whatever you want. Come on work with me here. I'm taking some initiative. The least you could do is give me some leeway."

"Whatchu say?" Maryam's body flared up. The man felt a massive weight drop onto his chest and yet despite it chose to carry on with his plea, in the hopes that it would provide him with just the slightest inch that he needed.

"All I'm asking is that you give me a chance, that's all. The world is full of people, and I think you'll find amongst them are a lot of pretty decent guys. Unlike the animal that you decimated in the ring just now.

We just might surprise you."

"Yeah? Well, maybe I don't want no more surprises. Maybe I just want to be all by my lonesome. That's how I've always gotten by." Maryam turned her gaze away from the man in front of her and bent down to buckle her shoelaces.

"I think you want to do more than get by," The man said. Maryam looked up.

"You don't know me," she said.

"Yeah well. Maybe I'd like to."

"Then get in line," Maryam's voice rose in a declarative tone. I've got dozens of men in my contacts that want to get to know me. What makes you think that you're any different?"

"Well, I'm sure not many of them have watched all of your matches. Not like I have."

Maryam approached the man until she stood at less than an inch away from him, her protruding chest nearly touching his. "And you what, think that that makes you special? That because you watched my matches, I owe you my time? Or worse yet, my body?"

The man's eyes widened protruding from their sockets. "No. No, that's not what I meant at all. Just that maybe you could give it some thought, maybe some consideration. That's all."

"The only thing that I'm considering is whether or not to call the guard outside or throw yo ass out of here myself."

"For what?"

"For barging in here uninvited. That's not something that I take lightly," Maryam said, her voice oozing with menace.

"Well, I- I'm sorry. I didn't mean to um- well I won't do it again," The man swallowed down hard as he used willpower to form simple words. "So, it's a no on the date then huh?"

A warm smile appeared on Maryam's face, one that alarmed the man even more than her threats had. "I'm playin." She gave the man the slightest tap on the chest, causing him to stagger backward. "Just don't sneak up on me like that again. Give me a warning or something. I was about to knock you out."

"I'll keep that in mind," The man said, masking his fear with nervous laughter.

"Now about that date," She prompted. The man braced himself for something big. He would either win the day or come crashing down hard in the next second. Though to his surprise, neither happened, which made Maryam's answer even more disappointing.

"I'll get back witcha." She tapped his cheek with her open hand before walking past him towards the door. The man twisted his head back to address her.

"What? That's it? You're not going to at least give me your number?"

"Why? That would spoil the fun of the chase," she said, turning towards him after opening the door. "Besides you said you were a fan, right? Then I'll see you at my next fight. I'll let you know how I feel then." She pointed a finger at him. "Don't be late."

The man rubbed his cheek where Maryam had touched him. The warmth of it sunk into his pores, making him twitch and melt at the same time. Her fragrant scent echoed in his mind as his hands grazed over his skin. For several minutes after she left it was all that he could think about.

"Well, at least she didn't say no."

Maryam kept her gym bag wrapped fervently around her neck as she walked through the streets of Georgetown. The night was quick to settle in and it wasn't long before the darkness engulfed much of Maryam's surroundings. The eeriness of the situation was not lost on her, but she welcomed it all the same. These were her streets, and she knew them better than anyone.

"Maryam. MARYAM BAHIRA."

She shot her head backward. The man who called her name had a demonic look in his eye; the most hideous and unnerving she had ever seen. She had noticed him following her before. His tongue hissed with predator instincts as he approached her.

"You never should have evaded us. You never should have beaten Henry. He was a lieutenant. He may end up being our leader someday."

Maryam stood upright, a gesture that was sure to trigger The Serpent even further. "Really? Well, he shouldn't have stepped into the ring with me. Anyone who does that is sure for a beatdown."

"Mind your tongue. If we possessed even half the strength, we once did you wouldn't be so cocky. Hell, you probably wouldn't even be standing in front of us now."

Maryam shrugged; smugness shone through her unflinching brown eyes. "And yet here I am. Why don't you step up and do what your so-called leader couldn't? Or are you scared?"

"You're the one who should be scared," he said. Maryam shifted her eyes, noticing a few more men stepping out of the shadows on her left and a few on her right. There were five men in total and each had a hissing pet snake wrapped around their wrists. The obstacle that Maryam had anticipated since her match in the ring had finally arrived. "You're going to regret what you did," The man threatened.

"Then stop talking and put yo hands up. I ain't got time to be here all night," she said before throwing her bag up in the air. It landed around the top of a caged fence near a basketball court. The Serpent's lips curled in disgust as they summoned up their nerves and fortitude. Despite their numbers, they all knew that they had entered The Lion's den and there was no way out.

"I'll tell you what. I'll let one of y'all make the first move." She scanned the faces of the men surrounding her; their eyes shone with contempt though the one who had addressed her first seemed to be the most unhinged of them all. She pointed an authoritative finger in his direction. "How about you?"

The Serpent lunged toward Maryam and threw the fiercest punch that he could throw. She clutched his hand, halting his advance with nothing more than her open palm. The man pulled and tugged but he couldn't remove himself from her grasp. He watched as she squeezed his trapped fist.

A sudden *pop* caused the other four men to jump from where they stood. The attacker felt himself sinking into an unseen abyss. His hand and wrist bones had been snapped in two. He fell to his knees and cried out as the pain circulated through his body, preventing him from removing his hand from Maryam's death grip. She took the opportunity to punch him square in the jaw, knocking him several feet before he landed on his back.

There was an explosion of rage and violent outbursts as the men attempted to overwhelm their target along with the carnivorous pets wrapped around their wrists. Maryam hit one with a stunning left hook that caused him to bounce on the concrete. Another attempted to tackle her, and she kneed him in the stomach before throwing him into the wired fence.

The men each gritted their teeth as their attacks grew more chaotic and uncontrolled. One lunged towards her with a live snake to which Maryam responded by pulling it and trapping the man's arm between hers. She pulled it out of socket before bending him backward and slamming him into the concrete with her elbow. A Serpent then pulled out a knife and slit at her clothes, just barely grazing the surface. She ducked out of the way just as The Serpent attempted to cut her face with the knife before connecting dead in the center of his jaw with an angry right hook that caused his head to spin.

Two Serpents lunged toward her with live snakes and Maryam was forced to fortify her defenses. She clutched onto both creatures and yanked the men forward, lifting them both off the ground and knocking them backward with a precise punch with both hands just in time for a third to lunge into the offensive. He threw attack after attack, but outboxing Maryam would prove to be a most futile endeavor. It was like punching concrete and eventually, his arms gave up on him and Maryam wasted no time in picking him to pieces with her smooth debilitating strikes.

The Serpents were being tossed around the courtyard like rag dolls. Their opponent used them for mere sport despite their desperation and intent to kill. She stomped on a Serpent's foot, an attack which sent a jolt of pain surging through his system. He curled his knee up to his chest, realizing that all the feeling of mobility in his lower body had been removed in the process. Maryam then seized the wrist of a Serpent just before he attempted to hit her over the head with a battering ram. She dropped to the floor and placed her foot on his midsection, flipping him into the wired fence behind her.

She tightened her fists before proceeding into her final onslaught, connecting her attacks with such precision that opponents were rendered numb. She caught one man behind her with a crushing elbow before pinning another to the wired fence, unloading explosive rapid-fire attacks that rendered the man groggy. The twenty-punch combination had done its job and Maryam was given just enough time to intercept the attacks from the last two fighters. She held her elbow out in front of her, parrying a single right hook from one before striking him in the stomach with fists as hard as concrete. She pulled her arm backward before connecting with a punch so severe that it threw his entire upper body and mind out of orbit. If there was an instance in which time itself could be frozen this, was it. The Serpent's jaw clenched, and his bones crunched as blood and pieces of teeth splattered around him. The harsh maneuver was bound to leave him bruised and in aching pain for weeks to come.

Maryam dropped her hand to her sides, noticing the protruding eyes and hesitant pitter-patter of the last man's footsteps. After a few seconds, he found the nerve to lunge toward her. He threw a swift kick, but his opponent caught his leg with minimal effort. She then swept him off his feet before mounting herself on top of him. The Serpent man had one last trick up his sleeve. A literal one. But Maryam caught the snake in her grasp at the last second, squeezing its throat before it could bite her.

"You bitch!! You miserable bitch! The Serpents will kill you for this, worthless black ape!!!"

The sound of his surroundings was muted within seconds. He had been struck with a blow so severe that not only had it rattled his brain but crushed his eardrums as well. The faint sound of the earthshattering and the shaking of a metal pole that held the wired fence together rang in his ear. He thrashed in a desperate attempt to gain control. He wanted to leap out of his own skin. He was willing to flee with nothing but his endoskeleton intact. He was at Maryam's mercy, and she intended on showing him none.

Maryam gritted her teeth as she pounded her opponent into submission. Her foreleg rested on top of his arm, smashing it into the dirt. The adrenaline that flowed through her was like a drug. She threw the strangled snake behind her and rotated between both hands, striking not only across the jaw but punching his nose in as well. Her knuckles stung as the blood from her fallen victim splattered onto her.

Maryam stopped beating on her fallen victim after a few dozen hits, even though she didn't want to. Her fists remained outstretched towards the spot his face had been, realizing that it had been submerged underneath the ground. She fell on her rear end, resting her shaking hands behind her.

"This is just practice. That's all it is. Just practice."

It was what Maryam often told herself after a match. She took a few deep breaths in and out and loosened her jaw. There were cuts along her cheek that began prickling at her skin. It took her a moment to realize that several of the pets of the demonic men had bitten her during the scuffle. She noticed a thin line of blood dripping down the corner of her mouth and felt a small cut near her eyebrow. It was the most she had been hurt in the past month.

Maryam arrived at her home to find it conspicuous. Everything was silent and all the lights were turned off. After locking the door behind her, the first place she went was the kitchen. There were still a few plates of unfinished food on the counter and a few bottles and glasses of wine; some of which had spilled all over the sink. She shuddered and ventured to one of the rooms where she found an old man, sitting alone, and rocking back and forth as slumber overtook him.

Maryam bent down to where the man was sitting before lifting him by his arm, hoisting him over her shoulder, and carrying him to another room. The man sat on the bed and Maryam aided him in sprawling out his legs and laying his head against the pillow with a feather-like touch that would have felt unrecognizable to anyone who met her in the ring.

"Maryam."

His whisper was faint yet distinct from any voice she had spoken to all day. She knelt beside him and leaned in close.

"Hey, grandpa."

Her voice was low as well, masking the fatigue engulfing her insides. Her lips twitched as the man placed a gentle hand on her cheek. His touch was cold and sent a tremor through her body.

"Did you fight today?"

"Yeah, yeah I fought today."

"Did you win?"

Maryam replied with a gentle nod. "I took care of business."

"That's my girl," The man said, his voice shone with pride. Maryam lowered her gaze, breaking free of his touch. "Always a fighter, just like your father."

The man trailed off. Maryam sat still beside his bed, staring at his sleeping body for several minutes as his mind ventured off into the far reaches of the unknown.

The world had become a dark foggy haze. Sarah could feel her insides churning, desperate to cling to life as she tumbled down the steps. Her hair was a disheveled mess, many strands of it had been removed from her once neat ponytail. She coughed and gagged as streams of blood poured down her nose and mouth. She was certain that her attackers had cut and slapped every inch of her. Her once smooth skin sizzled with a crippling reminder of what they had done. They had only struck her with a closed fist on occasion. This was nothing more than a game to them. To the men that had abducted her she wasn't a person. She was nothing more than a toy that they could break at their leisure.

Sarah's dark blue eyes darted frantically around the cell. Running was no longer an option, and neither was fighting. She had been rendered useless to the will of the forked-tongued men that were infamous throughout the world. They walked towards Sarah, cackling to their heart's content and her chest heaved. The daily beatings were humiliating and demoralizing but it was the laughter of the snake-possessed men that wounded her most of all. It violated her eardrums as they drew near.

"Oh Sarah."

"Ssssaaraaaah."

Their shadow engulfed the light on top of the stairs. It was dim but it was that small light that had kept her spirit alive. Now all that was left was the suffocating darkness of the dungeon. Eighteen-year-old Sarah closed her eyes as the men took their final steps and proceeded to press their diseased bodies against hers.

Sarah Stryker opened her eyes as reality returned to her. She sat still in her car, exhibiting perfect posture. The world seemed distant, seen through the dark lighting of her brown shades. The calm stillness would do much to ease the trembling in her heart, but she would only be able to stand it for so long. Like a thirst that needed to be quenched Sarah knew that her time for battle would come.

Sarah was jolted by a sudden knock on the window. She lifted her sunglasses above her forehead and unlocked the door, letting Amy inside.

"Hey."

"Hey," Sarah replied. "You ready?"

"I was born ready."

"Amy." Sarah's voice was laced with a stern warning. She gave her sister a stern look. "Seriously. Are you sure? There's no going back from here."

Amy met Sarah's gaze, determined to match the look in her eyes. "Yeah, I'm sure. This is where I'm supposed to be. By your side. No matter what."

"Alright then," Sarah said before backing out of the driveway.

Sarah drove to an old warehouse downtown. An entire team of welders and designers were present, all busy working to their heart's content. Just a few feet to their right there was a building that was near halfway complete. The two sisters approached the warehouse, spotting Kyle Harper amongst the crowd before he saw them.

"Well, you certainly took your time. Been waiting hours for you."

"Yeah well, I got a little held up. Had to wait for her," Sarah said, pointing at her sister.

"Kyle!" Amy lunged towards the scrawny man, wrapped her arms around his waist, and locked his arms together. She lifted him into the air with ease and cracked his back. Kyle yelped and tightened his mouth shut. Amy's affections always came with a price thanks to her superhuman strength.

"Yeah, yeah. Good to see you too Amy," he said, pulling away from her grip as fast as he could.

"Oh sorry," she said, realizing her strength as Kyle massaged his back.

"Yeah. It's alright. I'm used to it by now." He stretched his back. "So, are you two leaving today?"

"Yep. Might need to make a few stops on the way but barring that we should be there before nightfall," Sarah replied.

"Yeah, as long as you don't hold us up," Amy teased.

"It'll just take a minute. I promise. Sarah, let me see your phone."

Sarah gave Kyle a suspicious look. "Why?"

"Just trust me. What, do you think I'd steal from you?"

Sarah reached into her pocket and took out her cell phone. She placed it in Kyle's hand.

"You break it, you buy it," She warned.

Amy sat on one of the benches against the wall of the warehouse. She rested her chin in a bald hand, letting her mind wander. The loud thundering sounds of the welders and the drilling of various objects were drowned out by her inner thoughts. Amy was so deep in thought that she was startled when Kyle sat down to join her.

"Hey."

"Hey." Amy popped her head up and her eyes widened. She scanned her surroundings and wrinkled her nose. "Shouldn't you be fixing or downloading something on Sarah's phone?"

"I got one of my guys doing it. What's eating you?" He prompted.

Amy shook her head and sighed. "Nothing."

"I'm sorry about what happened, about Leland."

Amy turned towards him; a slight glare appeared on her face. "Did you read that, just now?"

"No, I-" Kyle paused. "I mean I did just now to get his name. But I already knew what happened. Want to talk about it?"

"Not right now. Maybe later okay."

"Are you sure?"

"Want to get punched?"

Kyle shrugged. "Not at the moment but I'll let you know when I'm feeling masochistic."

Amy thrust her shoulder into his and Kyle returned the gesture. The two exchanged a warm smile. At that moment the weight of the world had become less than unbearable in their eyes.

Kyle Harper finished all preparations that he had made for Sarah ten minutes later. He walked outside of the warehouse, letting the men resume their work as he exchanged final words with the sisters. They stood outside of Sarah's car as they spoke.

"Alright, inside here is a full GPS of Georgetown, not only general directions but I even managed to hack into a few secret files and provide intel on specific locations. There's one showing where Maryam Bahira works and the arena in which her fights are held. She's the first person that you should talk to; given that you're entering her district."

Kyle handed Sarah her cell phone and she quickly skimmed through it. "I'll keep that in mind."

Kyle shifted his eyes. He could sense something strange within the minds of the sisters and he didn't like it. "You know if you needed an extra pair of hands I could come with, you know lend a helping hand?"

"No!" Sarah shut him down in an instant. She opened the door of the driver's seat and threw her bag inside. She pointed a finger at him in a firm gesture. "I need you right here."

"I know. You want me here to help you find-"

Sarah raised an eyebrow in sharp warning. An alarm sounded in Kyle's ear as he gave a glance toward Amy. "To help you catch Anastasia. I got it. But I can do two things at once. I'm a man of many talents you know?"

"Sorry, Kyle. It's girls only this time," Amy said, giving him a sympathetic look before joining her sister by the car. "It's really dangerous over there and we don't want you getting hurt."

"Still three heads are better than one and I think I know just the girl to help us," Sarah said with a knowing look towards her sister. "She'll want in on the action. Besides, that little pinch of street-savvy might be just what we need."

Amy beamed at Kyle, rubbing her hands together in uncontrollable excitement though for some reason he was slow to catch onto what Sarah had revealed to him.

"What are you...no!" His eyes widened in disbelief. "No, no, no. Sarah no."

"Yes," Sarah declared.

"Sarah no, not that bitch."

"That bitch," Amy confirmed, still reeling in anticipation.

"Oh Jesus Christ," Kyle exclaimed.

Chapter 5:

Three's Company

Carmen Rivera stood upright; her knees buckled as she clenched her fists. There were at least seven women surrounding her, each black-haired and at seemingly peak physical condition. They knew her reputation and their feet twitched at the mere sight of her. The girls were in a confined room inside one of her old warehouses that the gang often used; a few stood in a fierce combat stance while some sat on a small couch in front of Carmen.

She was a Hispanic girl whose tiny stature stood in direct contrast to her scorned expression. Her hair was pitch black, wrapped in a disheveled ponytail. Her long fingernails scratched the skin of her palm and her brown eyes shifted left and right, sizing up her opponents. The rage oozing out of her pours did much to make her forget the thin line of blood along the corner of her lip.

"Come on Carmen. This is pointless."

"No, it isn't, dumb bitch. Now, are the rest of you just going to stand there or are we going to fight?"

The squad leader squirmed in her seat. Her heartbeat rose as Carmen's laser eyes homed in on her. Out of all the rebels whose wrath The Pride had incurred why did it have to be her?

"Carmen, please? It was just a game sister."

"I'm not your sister. I'm done. I stopped working for you bitches weeks ago."

"I know. Which you have every right but-" The squad leader shifted her eyes. "We still would like to think of you as one of our own. Once a Feline always a feline."

"Aw, that's sweet," Carmen said, sporting a half-smile- half glare. She lowered her voice, mimicking the squad leader's soothing tone. "Really, you're breaking my heart. And as a fellow sister, I feel obliged to return the favor."

For a moment the squad leader believed that she had reached her but then Carmen leaned in close and spoke in a voice that made her muscles churn.

"By breaking your bones," Carmen declared. By the time this fight was over she would have the leader down on her knees, submitting to the true Queen of Seattle. That much was certain in her mind. "Now get the hell up."

"You're not breaking anyone sis-"

But Carmen elbowed a girl behind her before she had the opportunity to finish her retort. The girl's jaw dropped, and her hands gripped Carmen's shoulders. The blow zapped all the air out of her lungs. Carmen's elbow penetrated the girl's stomach like a knife. She punched the girl in the ribs, causing her to hunch over, providing the opportunity for Carmen to floor her with a knee to the face.

"That's what you can expect in your immediate future. Assuming of course that you have one. I've been known to get a little carried away in confrontations like this."

"Carmen, please," The squad leader begged. "We don't have to fight. She had no idea that you're related. Things got out of hand, and we got a little carried away."

"HE'S SEVEN!" The sound of Carmen's voice hit the girls' ears like a bomb. The fact that these bitches thought that they could attack a member of her family and get away with triggered the angry siren within. "Do you know that! Did you even think about that? I don't care about your lame-ass explanations. All I care about is this Queen-sized ass-kicking with your name on it. And yours, and yours, yours, yours, and yours." She pointed to each of the girls, their eyes widened the moment Carmen addressed them. "So, how are we going to do this? One-on-one? Or all together? I really don't care."

"Look, we'll give you back the money alright. Just calm down."

"This ain't about the money. And I was going to be cordial. You know, just send you a message by beating up on your cronies. I once had a gang of my own and I almost felt just the tiniest bit of solidarity. But then you had to go and open your mouth, revealing that you're just another dumb bitch that The Pride should have thrown out years ago. And just for that comment, I think I'm going to beat you a little bloodier than usual. Now, who's first?"

Carmen's words sounded an alarm inside the minds of every woman in the room. The squad leader opened her mouth, hoping to find some clever retort to steer Carmen away from her current course of action; but no words came.

"Well?"

The air grew thick with anxiety. Some of the girls stood on the tips of their toes in a half attempt at an authoritative step forward. But no decision was made.

"No? Alright."

Carmen had enough. She approached one of the girls sitting on the couch and yanked her by the collar. The girl tugged and struck her fingernails into Carmen's forearm. She was rewarded for her efforts with a knee to the gut and a slug to the face. When The punch connected Carmen could feel the girl's jaw snap.

The girl's vision was engulfed in darkness. Her teeth churned and her body lost its equilibrium. Despair glistened in her eyes as Carmen's knuckles grazed against her cheekbone. She had never felt a punch like it. The attack echoed in her mind as she tumbled over, rolling for a few seconds before smacking into the wall. She lay in a state of limbo, only half-conscious.

The squad sprung into attack mode, the sight of one of their own humiliated spurring them on. They lunged toward her in an all-out assault, swinging left and right with their bare fists. Carmen parried their attacks before unleashing a severe combination that rattled the girl's skulls. She had seen the fight in her head and was now a mere observer in the clash of raging knuckles. She utilized the strength of her arms as well as the thrust of her hips to send her enemies out of orbit with excruciating strikes to the head and body.

Like most of The Pride, fighting was Carmen's life. It had been since she was a small girl. She timed her attacks with the rhythm of a beating drum, every movement in perfect sync with her opponents. Blood and dust appeared on the faces of the women as Carmen plowed through them with her speedy strikes.

Carmen bent to the ground just in time to watch a battering ram brush over her hair. She then latched onto the bat with her two hands before shoving her foot between the girl's legs. Carmen swung the bat in a smooth motion, knocking heads in quick succession. She twirled the bat in her grip, making sure to get a feel for it before unleashing her next round of attacks. The sound of the bat bashing against raw flesh was invigorating. Carmen utilized both ends of the bat, the front end for bashing, and the back for penetrating. Hatred and venom gleamed in her eyes as she struck her opponents; hitting them at least five times with a bat before sweeping a few off their feet.

A girl lunged towards her with a knife and was poked with the back end of the bat before she had even fully extended her thrust. She hunched over as the suffocating pain overcame her. Carmen smashed the girl over the head, knocking her out cold before launching another girl into the air with a massive swing that shattered the weapon into pieces.

There were three fighters left and from the swaying of their bodies as well as the blood spattered over their cheeks and forehead they could keel over at any minute. It wasn't enough for these women to be subdued. Carmen wanted them humiliated. She placed a thumb and forefinger on her chin before tilting her head to the right and then to the left. The rest of the squad swallowed the saliva and blood in their mouths as Carmen cracked her neck; the sound of it violating their eardrums, creating nightmares that each of them would have long after the fight was over.

One of the girls found the courage to spring into attack once again and was rewarded with a swift kick to her midsection that caused her to crash through a wall. She was submerged in debris and concrete as the world dissolved around her. The remaining two fighters lunged at Carmen in unison. She used her forearm to parry their advances with an embarrassing amount of ease. The girl's vision blurred as Carmen struck them in the ribs and on top of their breasts. She knocked one into a wall before flooring the second with a brutal backhand, the sound of it echoed across the room and made the squad leader grimace from where she sat. Carmen then turned her attention to the girl she had pinned to the wall; her gaze laced with malice as she prepared for her deadliest combination yet.

The girl felt as though she had fallen into a vortex; a well of pain and punishment exclusively for her. She wanted to cry out; to beg for mercy but her attacker moved at such tremendous speed that it seemed impossible to reach or to do much of anything. Her body rattled and her head rocked back and forth as Carmen's tightened rock fists rammed against her. It was all a blur. Flashes of Carmen's movements and disgruntled face penetrated her mind moments later. She couldn't even see the punches as they came but she felt every ounce of it just as Carmen intended.

"Oh no. We're not done yet."

She had hit the girl over twenty times and her body had gone limp, but it wasn't enough. It could never be enough for how far these girls had crossed the line. She lifted the girl up by her hair before she had fallen, pulling it to where it stood an inch over her face. Her eyes were shut, and a thin line of blood dripped down her mouth and nose. She wasn't even conscious, but she would wake up in as painful of a state as possible after Carmen's beating. She allowed her to fall to her knees, stretching her arm backward before delivering a right hook that left her sprawled out on her stomach.

Amid her barrage of attacks, Carmen hadn't noticed one of the fighters approach her from behind. She turned around just in time for the girl to wrap a firm grip intrusively around her throat. The girl was taller and thick and should have been able to overpower her with ease, but she didn't know Carmen Rivera. She jabbed a fingernail into the girl's eye before smashing her cranium into the girl's head. Carmen wrapped her hand around the girl's neck after she staggered backward and lifted her in the air. Her feet dangled and her reddened eye sizzled in pain but that was nothing compared to what was in store for her next.

Carmen slammed the girl to the ground before mounting herself on top of her. She smashed her aching fist against the girl's temple. The girl moaned as she wriggled her body with fervor and desperation, but it wasn't enough. Carmen seized the girl's wrist before placing them under her thighs, locking her arms into place. She then proceeded to pound the girl into submission. For Carmen, the feat required minimal effort but for her victim time stretched for eons. Her brain turned into jelly and her nerves lost all sense of equilibrium. Every punch seemed to possess more weight behind it than the last. By the time Carmen was finished the girl's bones vibrated like a musical instrument. When unconsciousness finally reached her, she welcomed it as a luxury.

Carmen stood up and shot her head to the right. The squad leader sat in the middle of the couch with a woman sitting to her left. She could tell that they were attempting to keep their composure and mask their fear. She wanted nothing more than to change that; to cause them as much discomfort as possible.

"Are you happy now, sister?' The Squad leader asked.

"Happy? Oh no. When the begging starts, that's when I get happy," Carmen snarled, a demon rising in her throat. She wrapped her grip around the squad leader's collar and stood upright.

"Please sister. There's no need for this."

"Oh, trust me. I see plenty of need."

"No! Don't hurt her. You've already made your point." The girl to the right of the squad leader stood up in her defense.

"Don't worry. You'll get your turn next," Carmen said, contempt glistening in her eyes.

"It wasn't her. It was me. I was the one that took his money. I brought him to the others, and we roughed him up a bit before she split us up. I promise."

"Really?" Carmen sized the girl up and down, her expression growing narrow as she considered her words. If what she said was true, this would be a major turning point in the conflict. Her fury couldn't be contained but it needed to be properly channeled.

"It's true. I stopped it before it got out of hand," The squad leader said. Within seconds Carmen swung like a battering ram and knocked her on the couch with a two-fisted hammer across the face. The squad leader sunk into her seat as she lost consciousness, giving Carmen the opportunity to turn her attention to the woman who had just confessed to the very thing that had spurred her on in the first place.

"Look I-I'm sorry okay. Like she said it was a game. A stupid game that went too far. Honestly, I didn't mean anything by it. I didn't know that he was your-"

Carmen interrupted the girl's excuses with a swift backhand that echoed in the silence of the building. The girl's cheeks reddened, and her eyes moistened as she was yanked by the collar, the same as her leader had been earlier.

"Let her go." The last combatant still conscious attempted to intervene and was shut down before she had even had the chance to initiate an attack. Carmen struck her in the stomach with pinpoint accuracy without even turning to face her. She grabbed her by the back of her collar before hurling her into the air. The girl ran smack into the wall face first and flipped backward before landing unconscious.

"That was very rude," Carmen said, her eyes zoning in on her soon to-be victim. Hot tears rolled down the assailant's cheeks, realizing what she was in store for.

“I’m s-o-sorry.”

“You’re sorry? Oh no.” Carmen stomped on the girl’s legs, crippling her in an instant as she fell. “But don’t worry. By the time I’m finished with you lord knows that you will be. Now come on!”

“No, no. NO please.” Carmen dragged the girl by her ankle as she thrashed her body around and screamed at the top of her lungs. Her tears had become soggy wet and everything in her perimeter became cloudy. She dug her fingernails into the ground but the stunt only agitated Carmen, who yanked her skitting body across the concrete in response.

“Come on bitch! This was just a game remember? Isn’t that what you said? Well, now it’s my turn to play.”

The girl was brought to a meadow near the warehouse. The maneuver had left multiple scraps and scratches on the girl’s skin. The grass of the meadow beneath her was almost a welcome change of pace and scenery but what wasn’t was the presence of a small boy in the middle of the open field. His name was Ricardo and he stood in a solemn position, his left cheek red and swollen shut by the strength of the girls’ attacks. She could tell from the boy’s expression that he had been crying though by now his eyes were locked in a stern gaze. Carmen grabbed the girl by the back of her head and sat her up in front of the boy.

“You see this? You see what your little game did? Do you think it’s worth it? Did you have fun?”

The girl gritted her teeth to mask her discomfort, but Carmen saw right through it. She yanked on the girl’s hair, sending a surge of agonizing pain through her, and jolting her into immediate compliance.Good.

“Answer me when I’m talking to you!” her voice blasted through the girl’s ear like a dysfunctional microphone.

“I’m sorry. I’m sorry. I swear. I’ll never do it again.”

"You'll never do it again?" Carmen contorted her face into a frown. "No, you'll never set foot within a hundred yards of him again. If I even so much as see you look at him, whether it be on the street or anywhere else I'll kill you. You got it?"

"Please. Please stop."

"You better answer me before I end you right here. I'm not playin with you." Carmen tilted the girl's head back further, applying pressure on her that was sure to do some lasting damage if she didn't act soon. Carmen's fierce death stare met hers as she spoke in an intimate tone that sent a winter's chill through her veins. "You will not go near my nephew again! Do you understand-"

"YES." The girl bellowed. "Yes, I swear. I won't touch him. I won't go near him. Just please P-please."

The girl began to sob, it was relentless, and as far as Carmen could tell it was a clear sign of defeat. There was no point in harming her any further though Carmen had half a mind to continue.

"Alright good. Now take a nap." She said before kicking the girl square in the face. She collapsed in an instant and Carmen took a deep breath in and out. She turned to face Ricardo and took notice of his bulging eyes and the protruding mark on his cheek that had turned purple and red over time. Carmen loosened her muscles as well as her expression.

"Sorry, you had to see that. But I needed to teach those bitches a lesson."

Ricardo said nothing in reply. His gaping mouth and fixated glare were enough to bring out the mother in Carmen.

"What? Why are you staring at me like that?" She said with a chuckle.

"A-are you okay?" Ricardo shook as he spoke. Carmen's eyes locked onto him, noticing that his vulnerability had stretched even greater than what she had thought.

"Yeah, I'm okay but what about you dum dum?" She knelt on the ground and prompted him with a poke in the ribs. "Remember what we talked about? I told you to stay clear of those girls. No matter what they try to offer you."

"Yeah but-"

"No buts." Ricardo averted his gaze to the ground.

"But I-I was hungry. And the girls, they said that-"

"Ah, ah, ah no back talk." Carmen wagged her finger at him. "All I want to hear you say is yes Carmen."

Ricardo sighed. "Yes, Carmen."

"Or yes Queen C but I'll let that one be optional." The two exchanged a warm smile, their mood changing in an instant. Carmen lifted her hand and ran her thumb along the boy's swollen cheek.

"They messed you up pretty good, didn't they? Weak ass bitches. Don't worry. We'll get you fixed."

"You." Ricardo pointed at her face; his expression contorted in confusion. "Your face."

"What?"

"You're hurt," he said, noticing the thin line of blood along the corner of her mouth. Amid all the hysteria and fighting, Carmen had almost forgotten about it. She stuck out her left cheek until it grazed Ricardo's thumb. With delicate fingers, he rubbed the blood. It smeared her chin at first but after a bit of friction, he removed the stain from his line of sight. Carmen returned the gesture by rubbing his head in a fervent motion. She stood up.

"Come on. I'll buy you an icy." Carmen extended her hand and cupped his gentle fingers into her own. "Just make sure that you eat something wholesome when you go back to your parents okay?"

Carmen Rivera was a girl who grew up in the streets yet generally preferred a life of glamor and tranquility. She was twenty-three years old and lived on her own, a choice made after the sudden disappearance of her former lover. Now she had little else to live for besides the thrill of the hunt; a lifestyle that would on occasion allow her to spend time with her two newest friends; Sarah and Amy Stryker.

"Well look at you. Finally back in the states huh?"

"Hey, Carmen."

Carmen greeted Sarah first upon opening the door of her house, beaming as she brought her into an affectionate embrace. She stood with a moist towel wrapped around her body and another over her hair. Sarah could feel the soggy wetness still on the girl.

"Sorry for the sudden drop in but we're on a tight schedule."

"Oh please. Don't apologize. How are my girls doing?" Carmen then turned to Amy, pulling her into a longer and more attentive hug. The two stood at around the same height, giving Carmen the opportunity to be more intimate. Carmen released her hold on her, noticing Amy's solemn expression. "And how about you? How are you holding up?"

"I'm okay, been better," Amy said. Carmen gave her a look of deep sympathy before cupping her fragile hands into her own.

"Yeah, still hurts huh?" Carmen said, her voice soft and caring. Sarah had informed her of what happened to Leland and the hit placed on them by The Pride.

"It comes and goes." The attempt at flippancy was solid but Carmen saw right through it. She tugged a strand of Amy's hair behind her ear and spoke in a conniving whisper.

"We'll get those bitches."

Amy allowed the slightest smile to escape her pouting face. It was subtle but would do much to alleviate her mood in the coming hours.

"And if you need anything else just holler alright? I mean it. Anything you need. You know I'm here." Carmen shook Amy's hands with fervor, locking onto her with widened eyes.

"Yeah, I know."

"Now, are you going to stand there all day or are you going to come in? Come on, come on," She ushered the two girls inside, noticing her agitated German Shepherd begin to bark.

"Down girl," Carmen ordered. "So, Anastasia is back in business huh?"

"Yeah. It was only a matter of time." Sarah crossed her arms, speaking in as casual of a tone as possible despite the mere mention of that girl's name twisting her stomach in knots.

"But why now though? Why attack her boy toy? Why put out a hit on you?"

"She probably knows that I came back. Her name was one that I heard rather often while I was away."

Carmen's eyes widened. "Wait. Are you saying that bitch has followers outside the states? As in she's building her own global empire?"

Sarah shrugged. "Pretty much."

"Damn. Well, whatever you're planning I'm your girl. I'm always ready for a good scrap. Speaking of which-"

Carmen ventured towards the dining table and fetched her cell phone. She clicked on it and tapped on the screen.

"Let me know what you think."

A video of one of Carmen's previous street fights appeared on the screen. She handed the phone to Sarah before proceeding to the washroom. Carmen examined her body in the mirror as Sarah and Amy watched the video footage of her fight. She was eager to hear what they had to say but wanted to make sure that she was ready before their trip.

"Oh my god." Amy's eyes popped from their sockets as she peered at the screen along with her older sister.

"Yup. I've been fighting consistently for the past month now, rebuilding my rep from the ground up." Carmen flossed her teeth as she spoke, her gaze locked onto her mirror, examining the full circumference of her mouth. "I guarantee you that there are at least a few people in Georgetown who have heard of me by now."

Sarah's eyes were glued to the screen, not once wanting to turn away from the action. Her eyes shifted left and right as Carmen traversed through the screen like a blur, swerving left and right as the opposing gang swung at her with their fists and various wooden poles. At one point she took out two women at once with a single right hook. Sarah raised her eyebrows in a stern expression, realizing that she couldn't remember when she had done the same thing.

"Damn girl. You got hands." Amy beamed as she watched the footage, her eyes shone in reverence.

"Oh, honey you ain't seen nothing yet. You should see my matches with some of the squad leaders."

"How long did it take you to improve your skills like this?" Sarah asked.

"Honestly? I saw quite a bit of improvement within the first week," Carmen said, flossing after each sentence. "After about a month I would say my newfound strength was solidified. You should see how I punch."

"So, is this just a hobby or what?" Because if so, I think you might need some back up," Amy warned.

"Well, I don't know. At first it was just a rush. A means to vent but after A while it started to become really invigorating. I'm so full of energy. Like all the time. It's unreal. After a fight my hands shake a bit but I'm usually fine after that."

Sarah shrugged. "And here I was thinking that you were all bark and no bite."

"No that would be her," Carmen said, approaching the two girls and pointing at her barking dog. "Hey, hey." She clicked her teeth in an authoritative tone. "Cut that out. You want me to take your chew toy?" The German Shepherd sank to the floor in response, tucking its ears in as it sat down.

"We were both talking before we arrived about whether you'll be okay over there. But after seeing this?" Amy shook her head. "Don't know about Sarah but I'm pretty much convinced."

"I have to admit you're much tougher than you look." Sarah placed her tongue in her cheek as she peered up to meet her friend's gaze.

"Look who's talking," Carmen said, raising her eyebrows and allowing a sly smile to escape her lips. "You know I consider myself to be a person who dances to the beat of my own drum. I mean I used to be but seeing you two. It changed things. Especially you," Carmen said pointing at Amy.

"You were hardly on The Pride's radar and yet still you choose to excel." Amy smiled.

"I lit a fire under my ass. I figured that if you two could do it then so can I. It's just like what you told me once," Carmen said, addressing Sarah again. "There's nothing that a woman isn't capable of when you push her far enough right? Well, this time I'm the one that did the pushing."

"I'm proud of you," Sarah said. Carmen averted her eyes. A bashful smile appeared on her expression, one that she rarely ever used. She was afraid that it would turn her into mush and decided to put on her tough exterior.

"Yeah, well maybe someday soon we'll have that match that we spoke about before." Carmen locked onto the woman in front of her as she spoke, a look of menace shone through her glazing eyes. She took a sip of her mango tea, feigning casualness as if she was stating the weather.

Sarah cocked her head to the side, the lioness rattled inside of her caged mind and let out a thunderous roar. "Well, I wouldn't say no."

"Oh, honey believe me. You wouldn't have the chance."

Sarah's eyes widened. Carmen Rivera was one of the few people in her immediate circle who dared challenge her. She was also one of the few people in Sarah's life that she couldn't predict. Her gaze matched her own in both its ferocity and potency.

"Still think that you can take me, girlfriend?"

Sarah nodded in reply, locking onto Carmen with pinpoint accuracy. The two women's eyes never wavered and never lost sight of each other. Both knew that the other could sense their weakness and would take full advantage of it should they have the opportunity.

"Well guess we'll just have to put our skills to the test one of these days huh?"

"Guess so."

Sarah glared and sized up the woman in front of her. Carmen mirrored the expression. Their fierce staring contest was interrupted by Amy, who seized both girls with a fervent grip around the neck and pulled them into a tight embrace.

"Come on. You guys know that you're not going to fight."

"Wait, wait. There's more. Go back to the footage," Carmen ordered, shaking Amy's grip off her. Sarah picked up the phone, noticing a point in the video in which Carmen interrogated a girl that she had beaten in a fist fight.

"Answer me when I'm talking to you!"

Carmen shouted at the girl in the video, holding her with both hands around her neck. She pinned the girl to a wall afterward before punching her repeatedly in the stomach.

"That's my line," Sarah said, noticing her words.

"Yeah, we're going to have to sue you for copyright," Amy added. Carmen smiled, but before she could provide her own commentary two little boys barged down the room of her house, running and giggling at the highest pitch of their lungs. Carmen whistled in their direction, and they came to a screeching halt.

"Ricardo. What do you think that you're doing?" One of the boys turned around while the other stood still, fidgeting with his hands as he waited.

"W-we were just playing." Carmen raised her eyebrows and the boy's eyes sunk into the back of his head.

"In the middle of the house? Can't you see that we have guests here?"

"Yeah b-but we-"

"But nothing. What did I tell you? Either go outside or play with your friend quietly?"

"But-"

"Ricardo!" Carmen shut down his protests in an instant. She pointed two fingers at her squinting eyelids before pointing them in his direction. The boy sighed in defeat.

"Yes Carmen," he said before walking towards the stairs.

"Thank you." Her expression returned to its usual calm demeanor.

"You're welcome, Queen C," The boy replied, sporting a phony grin. Carmen glared but couldn't help but smile, appreciating the callback. She shook her head and turned back toward the sisters. "I swear

one of these days that boy is going to drive me nuts."

"I know the feeling," Sarah agreed.

"I'm going to start using the belt. He's old enough. It'll do him some good. His parents spoil him. "

Sarah shrugged. "Whatever works."

"I mean don't get me wrong. I'd kill for him, but that boy's got a mouth. I'm older and I've been around and yet whenever I tell him to do something he has to say something smart. It's like he wants to undermine me on purpose."

"Children can be a lot to deal with."

"He probably thinks that he can get away with it because I'm not his parent." Carmen shook her head. "Honey, you may not be my kid but keep giving me lip and I'll sure as hell beat you like you are."

"Pretty much sums up my thoughts on this girl right here."

Amy jabbed Sarah in the shoulder, catching onto her teasing. In response, Sarah pinched her sister in the arm.

The three girls left the house an hour later. Carmen dressed mostly in casual attire, with her most distinct features being gold hoop earrings and purple nail polish. Sarah entered the driver's seat of her car and took a subtle breath through her nose. There was still a part of her that dreaded this trip, but she was more than grateful that she would be able to spend the better part of it with two people that she was most fond of.

"Want to sit in the front?" Amy asked Carmen.

"Sure."

Amy squeezed inside of the car and took her place in the back, leaving Carmen to take the passenger seat. "You know I'm surprised that you two decided to invite me along."

"Why? Why wouldn't we invite you?" Amy asked as the two of them put on their seatbelts.

"Well, I was just thinking that you'd rather have your little freak with you. Isn't he supposed to be the brains of the whole operation?"

"Getting through Georgetown with our heads still attached requires a lot more than brains," Sarah said with a quick look at the blind spot behind her before backing out of the driveway.

"So, homeboy didn't make the cut huh?" Carmen asked.

"Yeah, and homeboy was pretty pissed off about it too. We tried to explain that we were doing it to protect him, but he wasn't having it," Amy chimed.

"He'll be fine," Sarah said as they drove off. "There's important work for him to do here. Plus, with The Pride in full force and making an example of the male populace it's best that he keeps his distance. We can't afford to risk it."

Carmen's eyes widened just the slightest bit. She spoke in a low voice that she hoped would mask her concern. "So, it's true. The Pride is going to war against the menaces of women? On a global scale?"

"Every man that they set their sights on."

"Good. Who needs them anyway?"

"Carmen," Sarah scolded her.

"Relax, I was just kidding," she said, softening her tone.

"The Pride is dangerous and considering how bad things got last time there's no way we're letting Kyle anywhere near them." Amy's tone became solemn and heavy. She could feel herself tunneling through her memories, reliving an earlier trauma that she had only recently recovered from. "After the battle, he was sent to the hospital with a broken leg and a few broken rips. He was almost killed. We both were."

Carmen couldn't resist sinking her teeth into who she saw as a lesser man. "It's a good thing that you didn't invite him then. His scrawny bod would only slow us down."

"Yeah, but you should have seen him when we told him we were bringing you along." A humorous grin spread across Amy's face and her voice rose. "He was like what? Not that bitch."

Carmen's protruding eyes locked onto the road ahead as her lips curled. "Is that what he said?"

Amy chuckled. "Oh yeah. He was pissed. But it was in the heat of the moment. I wouldn't stress it."

"Oh no. No one's stressing. He's right. I am a bitch. I see no shame in it. But the next time that boy decides to call me out of my name you tell him to say it to my face, okay?"

Amy's heart sunk into her chest. "Ookay."

"You got me?"

"Yeah, yeah I got it. Whatever you say."

Carmen allowed the faintest grin to escape her lips. "Good girl."

"So, when's our first stop?" Amy couldn't change the subject fast enough.

"We're staying at the Georgetown inn tonight. We'll speak to Maryam Bahira tomorrow," Sarah answered, keeping the stern passionate gaze of her crystal blue eyes on the road ahead of her. The team was still in Downtown Seattle. It would be about half an hour before they made it to their destination.

"Who is this chick anyway?" Carmen asked. "What's her deal?"

Sarah shrugged. "Don't know much. Just that she was put in charge of keeping the peace in Georgetown. But apparently, that hasn't turned out well for her so far. There's an increasing epidemic of missing boys within the district. Kyle wasn't able to find a causal link but judging from the pattern laid out for us one could only assume the worst."

"So, Anastasia's already attacking people? In Georgetown?" Amy asked, her eyes glazing with fear.

"Looks that way," Sarah replied.

"Well, whatever it is I'm ready. The bitches that I tore up earlier today were made of glass. It's been a minute since I had a real grueling scrap." Carmen's blood boiled and her fist clenched.

"Don't let your newfound confidence get the better of you, sister." Sarah pointed her forefinger at the girl to her right as she spoke, her expression stern. "Since I've met you, you've been the most abrasive person that I've ever known. Like me, you have a grudge. Your heart is swelling with anger."

Carmen's eyes widened with intense fervor. Finally, someone who understood and could articulate her feelings in such succinct language. "Oh, you better believe it."

"That anger is a vice. It's important. Utilize it. Harness it. But don't let it consume your entire being." Sarah pressed harder on the gas pedal and her knuckles turned white on the steering wheel. "You're a lot more than that Carmen. Despite what many in The Pride may have you believe."

Carmen lowered her voice, speaking in a hushed whisper, masking her tone. "It wasn't The Pride who made me this way."

"Me neither." Sarah shook her head. "We each have our own path to take. And it's difficult for all of us. Just know that there are a select few of us that you can count on."

"Yeah, you can count on us," Amy said, her face shining with tenderness. Carmen turned around, studying her demeanor. Amy smiled; her white teeth glistened in the near-setting sun. Carmen returned the smile before averting her gaze back to the road ahead of them.

"It's not that I don't believe you. At least I want to. It's just that women like me, like us, we can't afford to take any chances. The world is going to find a way to screw us over. No matter what we do."

"It doesn't have to be that way," Sarah said. A beeping noise interrupted the flow of thought, and she was forced to divert her attention. "Hold on a second. Let me take this."

Sarah turned on the monitor below her radio and the screen lit up.

After a few seconds of static, the fascinating yet freakish face of Kyle Harper appeared on the radio. He sat at a dining room table; his full attention focused on the three women in front of him.

"Kyle, can you hear me?" There were a few seconds of static before the response was given.

"Sarah? Yeah, I can hear you."

"What's up?"

"Well, I just want to make sure that everything went okay picking up your," Kyle paused for a moment and hardened his voice. "Guest."

"Yeah. Carmen is with us. we've been on the road for about ten minutes"

"Oh okay. Right on schedule then."

"Any luck finding that info I asked for?"

"Well, you see that's sort of a tricky question," Kyle said, mumbling the words through his teeth.

"Tricky how?"

"Well by luck do you mean the good kind or the bad kind?"

"Kyle." Sarah raised her eyebrows, sporting a stern expression.
"I'm counting on you to do this for me."

"I know. I know. and I'll get it done alright. Just-" Kyle raised his hands in surrender. "This is a lot that you're asking for. You gotta give me time. A few days at least."

Sarah curled her lips. She hated not being able to exercise her authority. "Alright."

"Good. Well, I guess I'll leave you ladies to it then. Sarah, Amy. Good luck."

"What about me?" Carmen asked. Kyle shifted his freakish gaze in her direction. "Aren't I one of the ladies?"

"Technically," Kyle said, squinting in her direction, his voice distant and robotic.

"Well? You got something that you want to say to me?" She prompted, matching his look with a sinister glare.

"Not particularly."

"Come on. Aren't you the one always going on about sharing your feelings? Opening up? Well, here's your golden opportunity."

"I think I'll pass," Kyle said, not at all amused by her advances.

"What's the matter? Scared?"

Kyle turned his gaze toward Sarah. "You hearing this?"

"Hey, hey, hey." Carmen snapped her fingers. "I'm the one who's talking to you. Your girlfriend can wait."

"Come on. He didn't mean anything by it," Amy said, leaning over the back seat. Carmen wagged her finger.

"Mmm-hmm. That's not going to fly girlfriend. I want to hear it from the horse's mouth."

Kyle shrugged. "What do you want to hear? You know how I feel about you and I was bummed out that I didn't get to tag along. I could use some action right about now."

"Call me what you called me earlier. We'll see what we can do," Carmen said, her voice low and fused with malice.

"And the typical Carmen comes out once again," Kyle muttered. "Okay, so what? I call you a name then you threaten me and what, violence ensues? What are we, back in high school again?"

"Oh honey, honey, you don't know me. I don't do threats. But-" She then pointed with her forefinger. "Let's see what we can do about that last part."

"That was another threat."

Carmen shook her head. "No."

"I can read the threat in your words. Remember I can read people? My supernatural ability? Like, how dense can you be?"

"If you really could read people, I highly doubt you would be talking that way right now."

Kyle shifted his protruding gaze up and to the right. "Well, apparently you don't know me either because I talk this way to people all the time."

"Well, then I guess it's no wonder you got your ass kicked in the last time The Pride attacked."

Kyle threw his arms into the air. He had had enough. "Sarah, can you believe this woman? How can you stand to be around this?"

"Kyle relax. She's just trying to scare you that's all." Sarah had finally decided to chime in. Kyle's eyes widened in dismay.

"Those were legitimate threats. Pretty sure that I can tell the difference."

Sarah shrugged. "Doesn't matter regardless. She's not going to hurt you, Kyle. I won't let her."

Carmen let out a slight chuckle. "Bitch please."

"Well, when you put it that way," Kyle said, his voice settling a bit. Carmen lowered her gaze, realizing that she had said more than enough despite her disposition. "You've guys got a long road ahead and I've got more than my fair share of work to do so I guess I'll let you guys go."

"Sure. I'll call you later. See what you've gathered and let you know how things are going in Georgetown."

"Alright. Be safe. All of you. Georgetown is no joke. Chances are you'll get jumped within hours of entering. You'll be recognized as outsiders and an immediate threat. No matter how diplomatic you attempt to be. Which is why I insisted on not bringing on someone who's just going to knock down the hornet's nest with a tree branch."

"We can handle ourselves. But the concern is appreciated."

"Alright. Be safe Amy."

"Bye Kyle!" Amy waved; her face shone with tenderness.

"Talk to you later Sarah." He then shot a scathing look in Carmen's direction and she waved with the tips of her fingers in reply.

"Tootles."

Kyle glared before shielding the computer screen with his hands and shutting the monitor off.

The team arrived in Georgetown twenty minutes later. Despite that, Sarah decided to extend the trip and locate the best hotel in the area. The time would come for conflict and by then she would be ready. Though for the time being, spending time with the two young women that she was most comfortable with would do much to rejuvenate her.

"Who's hungry?"

"ME!" Amy was the first to respond in the affirmative just as Sarah predicted.

"Yeah, I could eat. Why? You paying?" Carmen asked.

"Sure. But we're just going to get something fast. I don't want to stop until we've reached the hotel."

Sarah entered the drive-through of a nearby fast-food chain, allowing her teammates to order first. Both girls ordered big hearty burgers, fries, and large drinks. Whereas Sarah only got a grilled chicken sandwich and a smoothie for herself, and even that was much more than what she was used to eating.

"That'll be $36.95, ma'am."

A cashier addressed Sarah after she pulled up at the first window. She reached into her back pocket but found it empty.

"Amy, have you seen my wallet?" She peered beneath the seat with squinting eyes, scanning it just to make sure she hadn't gone crazy. She looked up at the cashier. "Mind giving me a minute?"

"I got it," Amy said. Sarah glared over her shoulder. "I ran out of lip gloss, and I needed to buy some."

"And you didn't think to tell me?"

"Well, it was on your desk. I didn't think you would mind."

Sarah locked onto the girl behind her with stern eyes. "Just be glad that we're related. Or that would've cost you. Literally."

Amy spread her lips into a wide phony grin. Sarah held out her palm.

"How much did you spend?" She asked after Amy placed the wallet in her grasp.

"Not much. Just shy around $500."

Sarah's neck stiffened in response, her eyes were wide and as sharp as a needle. It was a look that she gave when gazing on would-be prey. Amy burst into laughter.

"I'm kidding. I'm kidding. Like I would spend that much all willie nillie. I mean I would if I was behind on rent or food, and there was that one time when I forgot-"

"Amy if you don't answer me-"

"It was like twenty bucks, that's it. It was a joke."

Sarah shook her head and averted her gaze towards her wallet, scanning through it to make sure that everything was intact and as she left it. "Next time just ask me."

"Yeah okay. I hear yah. You mad at me or what?"

"No Amy. I'm not mad."

"Better not be," Amy said with a playful punch to her sister's arm. Sarah allowed a smile to escape her expression.

Before Sarah could pull out her wallet, a wad of cash appeared right in front of her. "Carmen? What are you?"

"Down girl. I got this one." The Hispanic Queen had already planned this from the moment that they entered the drive-through and took her flustered state as the moment to play her hand. "You paid for what? Like the past ten times we've gone out? Well, now it's my turn."

"Uh, no." Sarah struggled to speak through her gaped expression. "No, it's okay."

"No, it's not," Carmen revealed. "I know you girl. I know you're too proud to admit it but you're going through the wringer right now. And what you really need is a break. Consider this it."

"I-I can't take that."

"Bitch yes you can. You give and you give, and you give. I know. I was once a giver too but at some point, you're not going to have anything left for yourself. And so, from time to time, you take. There's no shame in it. It's a normal healthy part of being a woman. And so as long as you're one of mine when I offer you take. No questions asked."

"One of yours?"

"Yeah, one of mine. My posse. Told you I had my own gang once upon a time remember? Well, this is part of how I maintained order. I offered as much as I took. You're halfway there but you could use a bit of a push in the right direction. Fortunately, you have me."

"It's just food," Sarah said feigning casualness with a shrug.

"No girl, it's a lot more than that and you know it. Now, are you going to take it or am I going to have to get ugly? I don't care. I'll claw that wallet right out of your hands if I have to."

"You'll fight me? Over who gets to pay?" Sarah raised her eyebrows.

"I'm helping you. Whether you see it or not. So, are you going to take it or are you going to make things difficult?" Sarah sighed and sank back into her chair.

"If you don't take it, I'll call your boy toy. The Psychologist. I'll tell him that I think you have a self-destructive personality and to start those weekly counseling sessions up again."

Sarah couldn't believe it. Carmen had hit below the belt, mentioning a man who had meant more to her than any other, even Kyle. Sarah rolled her eyes before snatching the money out of Carmen's hand.

A sly grin spread across Carmen's face. "That's what I thought."

Amy tucked her head beneath Carmen's seat and spoke in a low whisper as Sarah addressed the cashier. "How did you do that? I've never gotten Sarah to let me pay."

"The trick is to get inside of her head," Carmen whispered back. "To prod at the things she's sensitive about."

"Oh yeah, I've done that." Amy lowered her voice, even more, shielding the corner of her mouth with her hand. "Literally, all I have to do is pout and I can get her to do anything for me. Like anything."

"Amy, you say something?" Sarah turned around after she finished paying the cashier.

"No, no, no. I didn't say anything." Amy's eyes widened as she sank back in her seat.

"You sure? Whatever it is I would love to hear it."

Amy zipped her lips shut and threw away the key in a playful motion. Sarah glared at her, doing her best to hide her amusement.

"Keep it that way, okay?" Sarah then turned her gaze toward the woman sitting beside her. "Don't expect this to be a frequent occurrence."

Carmen shook her head. "Oh no, no one ever said all the time." Sarah pulled up to the next window of the drive-through. "Just whenever I feel like it."

Sarah returned her remark with a sinister side glare before addressing the male fast-food employee at the window. He was a tall adolescent with a lean build, chiseled jaw, and short curly hair. Carmen slouched back in her seat as she examined him.

"Damn. Would you look at that?" Carmen's lustful gaze locked onto the young man as He handed the bag of food to Sarah. Amy rested her forearm on the top of the passenger seat and peered up at the boy, her eyes glistening with curiosity.

"He's cute, isn't he?" Carmen said. Amy nodded in agreement, smirking a bit as she placed her chin on her forearm. Carmen leaned closer. "You know it sucks, what happened to your boy and all but think of the upside. All of the able-bodied men of the world are ripe for the picking."

Amy corked her head with a slow methodical turn towards the girl in front of her.

"What?" Carmen gestured with her hands as Amy glared at her. "What?"

Sarah handed Carmen a bag of food and a carriage with two large drinks inside.

"Hey. Which one's mine?" Amy peered over her seat as Carmen shifted through the contents of the bag.

"Relax. No one's taking your food," she said.

"Okay, the first thing that we need to do is find a hotel."

"Anxious to get in touch with that freaky friend of yours?' Carmen asked, handing Amy her soda.

"Kyle? Sort of. There's no rush. He said to give him a couple of days to gather info. No there's someone else I need to talk to before we go." "Who?"

"None of your business Carmen," Sarah said, amused by her friend's curiosity.

"Oh, getting a tad defensive, are we? What do you have a secret admirer? Someone that I need to check up on to make sure that they're clean?"

"It's private."

"Uh uh, we don't do private. I'm going to need something. At least a name."

"You're not getting one," Sarah said, turning her attention to the road ahead of her as she drove off.

"Mmm-hmm, we'll see. You should know me by now. There's nothing that you can hide from me if I don't want you to."

"So tonight we rest," Sarah said, ignoring Carmen's challenge. "Tomorrow The hunt for Anastasia begins."

Chapter 6: Settling Inn

Maryam Bahira stood in front of the wired fence in silence. She stood in front of a basketball court at a local park in her hometown. Everyone around her was consumed with their daily activities, oblivious to the danger that much of the town posed to them.

The group of young women in front of her were in the middle of an intense game of basketball. One of the players raced down the court and leaped into the air past the defender and scored the winning layup. She was a light-skinned girl with a red cap and braided locks. Her name was Desiree. She noticed Maryam standing behind the fence, staring at the girls through her dark sunglasses. She threw the ball to her teammates and approached the veteran boxer with slow cautious steps.

"I thought you stopped playing years ago?" Maryam asked.

"Nah. Not as active as I used to be but I'm always looking to show these youngsters a thing or two."

Desiree noticed two muscular women standing behind Maryam. They were so still in posture that Desiree had to second guess if they were alive. "What's up with the muscle?"

Maryam gave a quick glance behind her. "Oh, them? They insisted on tagging along because what happened after my last match."

"You mean when those snake men tried to jump you?" Desiree asked.

Maryam nodded. "I told them I was fine, but they mentioned things tend to escalate where gangs are concerned. There will be a lot more coming in their place."

"Did they manage to hurt you?"

Maryam glared in response. "What you think?"

She examined Maryam from head to toe before replying with a confused shrug. " The hell I know, I ain't seent yah in weeks. How you been, girl?"

"I've been busy." Maryam's voice had lowered to a hushed whisper. Something that both girls took immediate notice of. She approached the girl from the other side of the fence. "I need your help."

Desiree lowered her eyes. "Let me guess. You have another lead on them boys?"

Maryam took a deep breath. "I found this girl. She was last seen near an attack."

"Maryam." Desiree rolled her eyes.

"She was there! I know it. If we can make her talk, we may just be able to find a few of them while they're still alive."

"The Pride are sworn to secrecy ain't they? What if she doesn't talk?"

"She'll talk to me." Maryam's eyes lit up as her heart stomped in her chest.

"Look what happened with those boys was wrong. I know it. All of us know it. And we'll do what we can to keep something like that from happening again but at some point, you have to let go. You have to accept that,"

"NO!" Maryam shut down her friend's plea in an instant. "I won't. I can't. If there's even a slight chance that they are still alive, then I have to keep looking. If I knew that they were dead, then I could move on but what if they out there? Starvin. Beaten. helpless. parentless."

"I understand. But if you let this run your life-"

"Desiree," Maryam snapped. "I'm doing this regardless. But I have a much better chance of getting out of this alive with you. Are you in?"

Desiree threw her hands up in mocking surrender. "I'm your girl. What do you want me to do?"

Maryam arrived at a local precinct an hour later. The girl in question sat in front of them at a small desk in an isolated decrypt room. She fidgeted and picked at her cuticles with protruding eyes. The police had found the girl at the scene of The Pride's most recent attack. Maryam's eyes locked onto her as she waited. Her blood sizzled the longer that she stared and at some point, the festering madness would have to be unleashed.

"Tell us what you know."

"I-I don't know anything. I already told you. When I woke up The Pride was already gone. They didn't tell me hardly anything. Please, you gotta believe me on this. I never joined to hurt anybody. I swear."

"Desiree. The Files." Maryam's gaze never left her suspect, even when she addressed her friend. Desiree took out a large envelope and emptied its contents in haste. Among the disheveled paperwork five photos, each of a black boy below the age of thirteen.

"Have you seen this? Do you know their names? Rashad, Theo, Ahmad, Chris, Devin." Maryam pointed to each of the pictures. "These boys have been missing for over a month. For two of them, their parents were murdered during their abduction. So, I'm going to need a little more from you than I don't know, or they didn't tell me hardly anything. Why don't we start with what you do know?"

The girl swallowed her saliva before speaking. "Look, they didn't tell me anything. They didn't show me anything. Just- sometimes they gossip. And when they gossip, they get nasty. They let a few details slip. I heard a few of them say that they keep some of the boys to do jobs for them."

Maryam squinted at the girl; a tinge of inquisitiveness shone through her angered expression. "What jobs?"

"I don't know." The girl pleaded. "I didn't ask. I didn't want to know. I just wanted to get out of there. Those girls. They give me the creeps. They are not normal. I'm not even sure that most of them are human. if I, were you, I would stay as far away from them as possible."

"What else do you know? Where can I find these girls? Are some of them here in Georgetown?"

"I-I can't say." The girls' voice shook as she spoke. Maryam could feel herself approaching shark-infested waters and with that, she knew that she was on the verge of something big.

"If you don't want your head stomped in you will."

"Look. I only just became part of the squad a few weeks ago. I didn't spend enough time to gain any real intel. And I intend on keeping it that way. You have every right to be upset but those girls scare me a hell of a lot more than you do." the girl stood up, believing the conversation to be over. "I'm sorry about those boys. I really am. But there's no way I'm getting myself any deeper into-"

"Sit yo ass down!" Maryam popped out of the seat in a split second, her expression laced with venom and contempt.

The girl sank into her chair.

"Now you're going to tell me what I want to know and you're going to tell me now or so help me. I will break all the bones in yo body until I get it. Ya heard?"

The girl's mouth twitched before she spoke in reply. "Why are you so hostile? I'm not the bad guy."

"You in my way. Which makes y'all one and the same as far as I know."

"Mary Chillax. I don't think she knows anything else." Desiree was becoming as uncomfortable as the girl beside her.

"Naw. She knows. She's just too scared to do anything about it. Same as the rest of this punk ass town."

The girl's eyes watered in confusion. "Look I already told you. I'm not with them anymore okay. I left when things got dangerous. I never saw those boys or any of the men they kidnapped. I swear."

Maryam's eyes lit up. Her tone became dangerous. "They kidnapping grown-ass men too?"

The girl lowered her gaze. Her fear had become a demon that stared her down with intent.

"Girl, you better answer me when I'm talking to you."

Maryam noticed that the girl's teeth rattled just the slightest bit. Good. If she put the fear of God in her the chances were high that she would squeeze every bit of information out.

"You may not have the location but what about where you were? What about the women who did this?" There was no response. "Alright."

Maryam had had enough. Desiree and the suspect in question went into full panic mode the moment she stood up. "Mary! Girl, wait! She ain't worth it."

"The hell she ain't."

"No, no, please. Please don't." But Maryam grabbed the girl by the collar and shoved her into the wall before her plea could carry any weight in her mind.

"You got thirty seconds to tell me something useful." Desiree had heard that voice in her friend many times before and knew that it spelled disaster.

"Please! I never had any problem with you, sister. Why are you-"

"Shut up! I ain't yo sista. These boys are lost. This whole town is crumbling. I ain't got no time for games. So, the way I see it you got two options. You can either tell me something, a name or location. Or you can take this ass whoopin. And I promise you it'll hurt. Now I'm going to count to ten."

"ANASTASIA!" The girl bellowed.

"Anas who?"

"Anastasia. You said you wanted a name, right? Well, that's the name; the name seemed to mean the most whenever it was mentioned.
The name of their leader."

Maryam squinted her eyes. "The leader is gone."

"She's the new one! I swear." The girl stretched out her lungs as she spoke. "From what I heard it was just recently, but she wasted no time. Already has half The Pride under her thumb."

"If you lyin-" Maryam's voice was laced in a harsh warning.

"I'm not. Check for yourself if you don't believe me. She's the one who kidnapped those boys; her and her crew."

"Where are they at? Where's this girl?"

"Apparently she's already here. You can check the place you found me in but I'm sure most of them moved on from there. Look I already told you everything I know okay? In fact, I told you too much. They might find out that I talked."

"Yeah, and by then you'll be a dead woman walking." Maryam pressed the girl against the wall before letting her go, realizing that she had gotten everything that she could from her.

"So?" The girl shrugged, realizing that she had finally been shown mercy. "You gonna protect me? I feel like I kinda earned it since I just helped you."

"Yeah, yeah I gotchu," Maryam said, still glaring at the girl. She pointed a finger at her. "But I see you taking any more handouts from them evil females again that's yo ass."

"Yes, yes, yes. I promise. I'll never deal with them again. I'm done." Maryam turned around, her gaze not leaving the girl until she had given her back. "Thank you, Maryam. Thank you. Thank you. Thank you."

"Get her out of my sight," Maryam said, waving her hand behind her. She opened the door and shut it behind her before taking a deep breath in and out. She hated it; being angry all the time. It took far more out of her than she would like to admit. She lowered her gaze to find the two female guards who had located the suspect in front of her and based on their hesitant footing and protruding eyes she knew that the news couldn't be good.

"What is it?" She asked.

"Haven't you heard? One of those girls just entered Georgetown."

"Which girls? The Pride?"

"Yeah, who else?" One of the guards flipped through the contents of her clipboard.

"Are you talking about Anesthesia or whatever her name is?" Maryam asked.

"Hmm? uh uh," The girl replied without looking up from the pages on the clipboard. "But she also had a funny-sounding name."

Before she was able to respond Desiree burst out of the door of the interrogation room, along with the suspect. "I'm about to take this bitch home." She turned towards Maryam as she ruffled with her keys. "Don't go after this girl. Anastasia."

"Why? Why should I worry about her?"

Desiree pointed to the girl behind her. "Tell her."

"Well, She's disturbed. I mean really, really disturbed. More than the rest of them. She likes pain. I mean really does. That's like her mission statement or something. She lives for it. Not to mention the fact that if the rumors are right, she has control over most of em."

"How does she control em?" Maryam's eyes widened in curiosity.

The girl shrugged.

"I didn't ask. Just hearing about her freaks me out."

"We'll talk about it later when I get back. But don't do anything crazy yah heard?" Desiree pointed a finger at Maryam. "If these bitches really are that dangerous then we need to go after them together."

"I need to bring them boys' home," Maryam said, her mind as narrow as an open road.

"I know but we need to be smart otherwise we'll-"

"Here it is!" The girl with the clipboard interrupted the two women in front of her. "The girl that just arrived. her name is. Sarah Streaker-
No Sarah Stryker."

Maryam and Desiree addressed the girl in unison; their faces contorted in bemusement.

"Who?"

"Good afternoon ma'am. Welcome to the Georgetown Inn. How may I help you?"

The team arrived at the hotel on schedule. Sarah exited the car and entered the building first, instructing Carmen and Amy to wait until she checked in. Upon entering Sarah found that the building was much smaller than she had expected.

"Yes, I have a reservation here. Under the name Stryker."

"One moment," The man at the front desk said as she scanned his computer. "Ah, here we are. You said that you wanted a two-room suite, correct?"

Sarah nodded, making a slight humming sound with her lips.

"Alright, so we got you in for three nights. That'll be $389, ma'am."

Sarah handed the clerk her credit card and he scanned it before handing her a receipt.

"Thank you for choosing the Georgetown inn. Hope you enjoy your stay."

"Thanks," Sarah said with a gentle smile before exiting the building.

Carmen and Amy sat in the car, their eyes staring into space as they waited and chomped on the rest of their food.

"Want the rest of my fries girlfriend?" Carmen extended her arm.

"Yes please." Amy plucked the carton of french fries from the girl's grasp without a second of hesitation.

"So, I got a two-bedroom," Sarah said, approaching the car and resting her elbows against the windowsill.

"How much did you spend?"

"I-it doesn't mat-"

"How much." Carmen's tone was precise.

"389," Sarah said, almost as if she was admitting to a crime. Carmen reached into her wallet and pulled out $190 in cash.

"There. That's almost half."

"It's no big deal," Sarah said. "Not even a third of what I make in a week. So, let's just leave it-"

"Sarah, sweetie remember what we talked about?"

Sarah bit the corner of her lip.

"Now are you going to take the money or am I going to have to get ugly?"

Sarah sighed. She placed her thumb and forefinger on each end of the wad of cash. With a swift motion, she snatched the money, indicating her reluctance.

"Good girl," Carmen said. "Don't worry. I'll train you right. Within a month of my tutelage, you'll fall in line just like the rest."

Sarah shook her head. "That's not how it works Carmen. I'm in charge and for the duration of this trip, you'll follow my lead. We clear?"

Carmen shrugged. "Sure. Got no problem following orders; at least not the ones I'm going to anyway."

The two girls glared at one another, a slight smirk protruding from both of their expressions. Amy exchanged bemused looks from one to the other. After almost a full minute Sarah broke the awkward silence, turning toward her sister.

"Want to go for a ride? There's a gym and boxing ring a few miles from here. If we're lucky we might just run into the woman we're looking for."

"Yeah, I'd love to." Amy spread her lips into a wide smile, her eyes and teeth shone with excitement. Sarah turned toward the girl in front of her.

"Carmen?"

"Sure." Carmen shrugged. "Whatever you say. You're the one in charge."

Sarah gave one last glaring look at the girl before entering the driver's seat and backing out of the parking lot.

Sarah, Amy, and Carmen decided to spend much of the trip catching up on the conversation they had back in Downtown Seattle. The beaming sun, hot air, and the movement of the speedy vehicle did much to keep the girls relaxed. They all knew this was only the calm before the storm but were determined to milk it for what it was worth.

"I still can't get over those videos. I mean the way you punch. The way you're able to take on three girls single-handedly. It's incredible."

Amy's flattery had an immediate effect on Carmen's mood. She allowed a subtle smile to escape her lips as she spoke.

"Yeah girl, there's nothing to it. Once you put your mind to something you just go for it. You never know what you can accomplish after that."

"I bet Sarah's given you a lot of really good advice that has helped improve your skills. Just like she did me.

"Excuse me?" Carmen's eyes flared up in protest. "Sarah's given me what?"

"Advice. You know pointers and whatnot. Didn't you train with her?"

"You know for the record I've fended for myself since I was eight years old. Before either of you two took off your training wheels. Believe it or not, some of us knew how to fight long before your big brave sister entered the picture. So, I'd appreciate it if you put a bit more respect to my name."

Carmen's tone was razor-sharp. Though to her surprise, Amy was unflustered by the reprimand.

"Okay."

"You got it, girlfriend?" Carmen said, her tone rising.

"Yeah, I gotcha. No need for the attitude though."

"Excuse me?"

Amy narrowed her expression. "You heard me. Watch the attitude. It's going to get you hurt one of these days."

Carmen's expression flared in protest. She turned her full body towards the girl behind her, addressing her in a more intimate tone. "Oh no, no honey somebody should have warned you. Nobody talks to me like that."

"I just did."

"You looking to start something Biatch!"

"Maybe I am. What are you going to do about it?" Amy raised her eyebrows, locking her gaze on the girl in front of her.

"I'm going to shut that smart-ass mouth of yours. That's what I'm going to do."

"Then do it. Talk is cheap."

Carmen gestured towards her knuckles. "You've seen these hands in action?"

Amy shrugged. "I got hands too. And they ball into fists."

Carmen raised her eyebrows in return. "You think yours can compare with mine?"

Amy nodded. "Yeah. I think I could take you."

"Well, you better know it. Because once you decide to step up there's no escape."

"You'll want to escape once I'm done with you."

Carmen burst into laughter. She turned to address the woman in the driver's seat. "Do you hear this girl?"

Most of Sarah's focus was on the road ahead of her, though her sister and friend's teasing were the soothing background noise that prevented her from getting lost in the darkened tunnel of her mind. " You shouldn't underestimate her. She's quite headstrong and a lot braver than what she might appear to be."

Amy beamed. The sound of her older sister's words fueled her entire being.

"Oh, I know." Carmen averted her eyes back towards Amy. "Trust me I know. I've had my eyes on this girl since we met. Probably one of the strongest out there. Which is why she needs to fall in line." She pointed her forefinger at her. "Keep that strength of hers under control. And her mouth too."

"You're not the boss of me."

"Oh okay, just for that me and you are going to throw down."

"Where? In the ring?"

"Why wait? As soon as we get out of the car."

"Fine by me. As long as you know what you're getting into. Just don't start crying if you get hurt, okay?" Carmen chuckled, taken by surprise at Amy's snarky comment. She turned to address Sarah.

"What do you think? In a fight between us who do you think will win?"

"Sarah already knows," Amy said. "We took karate when we were little. She knows I can fight."

Sarah's eyes widened behind her horned-rimmed sunglasses. "Honestly I'm not sure."

Amy's jaw dropped. Her head made a sharp turn towards the driver's seat. "Sarah."

Carmen replied with a gentle nod. "Uh-huh. It's not so easy, is it?"

"Amy, you've made tremendous progress in more ways than one. Your natural talents give you an edge but there's something to be said for Carmen's ferocity. It's been a while since I've seen one of The Pride fight the way she does."

"What? But I have ferocity too," Amy whined.

"You're strong Amy. It's just that you have a gentle heart. Hurting people isn't something you desire," Sarah said, choosing her words carefully.

"In other words, you're soft." Carmen threw all manner of tact out the window. "You're too nice. You're the kind of girl that most men will eat alive."

Amy's heart sank. So much so that she could feel herself sucking the air out of the vehicle. "Sarah, you think I'm too nice?"

"I never said that," Sarah corrected her. "Just that when it comes to battle instincts Carmen's got the edge. She's less likely to hold back."

"Thank you," Carmen replied. "Good to know that I can count on you to be objective; even where she is concerned."

"I feel so betrayed right now," Amy said, lowering her gaze in disbelief.

"You'll get over it," Sarah said, with no change in tone or demeanor whatsoever.

"Relax girlfriend, it's not that we're putting you down." Carmen softened her voice. "It's just that between the three of us you're still innocent. You haven't been pushed over the edge yet. You haven't been through what we've been through."

Amy raised her palms, her face contorting in confusion as she spoke. "Haven't been pushed over the edge? My date was just murdered," She exclaimed. "I'm pretty sure that constitutes a bit of a nudge."

"It's a start," Carmen replied, though her sympathetic tone hadn't changed. Amy's demeanor grew into genuine annoyance.

"What? So, I'm not ferocious enough because I only watched him die?" Amy leaned in close before raising her voice. "At least I didn't try to murder my boyfriend like you did."

'Hey," Carmen said, her voice becoming stern. "Now that is a place. You best believe it. Once you enter that realm there's no turning back. Sarah knows. She's been there and back again, haven't you?"

Sarah said nothing; even as Carmen's mischievous eyes gazed at her. There were no words to describe what she had done or what she had gone through and to make matters worse Carmen knew it. This was merely a ploy to play her hand.

"Yep. I thought so. She has the look. The look of a thousand cuts and bruises."

"Hey!" Amy exclaimed. "Hey, don't look at her. Your girlfriend can wait. I'm the one who's talking to you."

"Are you mimicking me?" Carmen squinted her glaring eyes as she sized up her soon-to-be opponent.

"That's what you said to Kyle right?" Well, maybe it's bout time you got a taste of your own medicine."

Carmen's jaw dropped. She turned around and leaned forward in her chair, still reeling from Amy's challenge. "Oh, so that's how you want to play this?"

"Yeah, that's right."

"If what I said offended you then maybe you should have spoken up for your boy earlier."

"It didn't offend me," Amy clarified. "But if you're going to play games with me then I'll return the same courtesy. That's how I roll."

"Alright," Carmen said, sporting an amused expression. "Just wait till we get out of the car. I'm going to get you back for that."

"Yeah right."

"You two might want to conserve your energy," Sarah interjected. The sun had set, and she removed her shades, deciding to speak more intimately with the two women. "Because if we find Maryam Bahira then there's a good chance that we're going hunting. First thing tomorrow."

"Oh yeah, I was going to ask you about that. Who is this girl anyway?" Amy asked. "This Maryam girl. Why she's so important?"

"She's a professional boxer; both a state and national champion. And she just so happens to be a former member of The Pride. She was put in charge of Georgetown years ago. If Anastasia really is here, then Maryam Bahira is our best chance at locating her."

"Huh, this chick must have hands if she's a champion. Taking her down in the ring would be a good test of my skills, wouldn't it?

Sarah gave a side glance to the girl beside her. "Maybe but remember we're here on business, not pleasure. Anastasia is the one that we need to take down. We don't have time for distractions."

The team parked in front of the gym and Sarah entered the building, leaving the other two women accompanying her to mind the car.

Amy stepped outside of the vehicle to stretch her legs, but Carmen stepped in front of her before she was able to move an inch. Her facial expression was placid, and her eyes remained locked in place staring at the girl with intent. Amy extended her arms and let out an exaggerated yawn.

"Yes? Can I help you?" Amy asked after she was finished. Carmen stood still for a few seconds before responding with a sudden jab to her midsection. Amy involuntarily wrapped her forearm around the girl's neck and pulled her into a headlock. Carmen mimicked her attack, and the battle was nearly underway but a slight bump on the ground caused them to stumble out of place.

The two girls burst into laughter; their teeth shone in the setting light. Amy tightened her affectionate grip around her friend's neck and Carmen returned the same courtesy. The two stood at eye level, ignoring much of the world around them and giggling their sorrows away.

Sarah entered the gym to find it full of both men and women training to their heart's content. Some were using a punching bag, others jumping rope, while some chose to spar in the arena. She saw no one familiar so Sarah decided to approach the man at the front desk.

"Evening ma'am."

"Hello."

"You a new member or an old one from way back?"

"Neither actually. I'm here on business," Sarah greeted.

The man's face contorted in confusion. "What sort of business?"

Sarah leaned her forearms against the countertop, speaking in the most welcoming voice that she could muster. "I'm looking for a woman. Maryam Bahira."

The man's eyes widened. "I-I see. And how is it that you've come to do business with a warrior of that caliber?"

Sarah cocked her head to the side. "We have a common enemy, she and I."

"Oh well, this common enemy you speak of. This by any chance doesn't happen to be the same group of women that have been attacking and abducting for the past few weeks, does it?"

"It might," Sarah said, lowering her voice to little more than a whisper.

"Then you must be her." The man's eyes widened even further. "The one girl who survived all odds. Who was trained personally by-"

"I am." Sarah finished his train of thought before he did. The man swallowed hard in response to the sudden revelation.

"W-well I'm sorry- sorry to waste your time ma'am but Maryam Bahira isn't here right now."

"Really?" Sarah squinted her eyes. "I thought she usually trained here."

"She does but recent issues have surfaced, and she decided to take most of their work concerning our little invasion on herself you see. It's left little time for anything else."

"Alright," Sarah said. Her voice softened. "Do you know where I could find her?"

"Last I heard she was in the innermost part of town. I can't give you her exact address out of fear that she might kill me," The man said with a humored expression.

"No worries. I'll find her." Sarah took a step backward towards the door.

"Hey," The man called out to her. "Since you're here could I perhaps spark an interest in a membership? The first month is free." The clerk spread his lips into a warm smile. Sarah turned her attention towards the arena, noticing two men engaged in a fierce competitive boxing match, their gloves tightened, and headgear firmly fixed on top of them.

Sarah curled her lip. "Maybe later."

"You sure? From what I heard it sounds like you could give these guys a run for their money? Perhaps you could grace us with a little demonstration of your unique abilities that I heard so much about?" Sarah's intent glacier-like pupils shifted towards the man in front of her. "I'll be around."

Sarah exited the facility, placing her horned rim shades over her eyes, to find Carmen nestled in Amy's fierce headlock.

"Still think you can beat me?"

"You better get off." Carmen tugged at her arm in between giggles. Sarah walked past the two of them, not taking much notice besides a brief smile that escaped her lips. She opened the car door and whistled behind her, a gesture that ended the wrestling match between the two girls indefinitely. By then Carmen was the one who had Amy in her headlock.

"Lucky that your girl was here to stop us."

"Lucky for you, you mean," Amy replied as she raced Carmen to the car.

"What was that?"

"You heard me."

"Alright. Next time I'm not holding back."

"Oh, please don't," Amy challenged.

The team decided to change the topic of discussion on the ride back. With only the three of them present they would be free to discuss the one thing they would be uncomfortable talking about otherwise. The opposite sex.

"I hope we're not just going off looks here. Because unlike you two I tend to see the full package. But in case either of you two were wondering, from all of the men we've encountered Drake Hawkins would be the most adequate partner in my opinion."

Sarah spoke first and just like the rest; her statement left a few eyebrows raised to say the least.

"No way! Team Jenson all the way. Now that's a man," Amy replied.

"Okay, so you two will have to remind me. These days when it comes to men, I pick the tightest able-bodied piece of ass and just roll with it." Carmen gestured at Sarah, hoping for clarity. "So, which one is Drake again?"

"He's a psychologist." Amy addressed her first. "He was assigned to talk to Sarah when she first joined The Pride.

"Okay and the man we spoke to earlier who called me a B?"

"That's Kyle," Sarah said.

"Also a psychologist," Amy added. "Bit more of an advanced one. The point is they're two different people."

"Much different." Sarah annunciated her words, giving clarity to Amy's comment.

"And I'm guessing that guy wouldn't be at the top of your list, would he?" Carmen asked, knowing the answer beforehand.

Sarah shook her head and mouthed an inaudible "no," in response.

"Wait. So, I noticed Kyle is rather unkempt. Drake is the clean tidy one, isn't he?"

"Yeah."

"Oh, Sarah, that's your type?" Carmen grimaced.

"What's wrong with Drake?"

"He's fake. I can see right through that joker."

"Drake's not fake. "He's a sweetie," Amy protested. "Kyle I can understand, he takes time to get used to but Drake? Really, girlfriend?" She mimicked her voice, something that Carmen ignored as she carried on.

"He's fake sweet. He's putting on a show. The dude's obviously hiding something. Can't y'all see it?"

"If he's a phony then the oscar goes to-" Sarah said.

"Nah he's nothing special girl. I've known many a man like him. You're just a little slow in picking up on it."

"Excuse me?" Sarah's tone was sharp. Carmen knew that she needed to clarify her words.

"No offense. You're just not as perceptive as me. Now I know that man touched your heart but once upon a time a man touched mine too. I know what it's like. He'll give you a big epic rousing speech and you'll think bam he's yours; that you're the most important person in his world. But sooner or later you'll learn that that isn't the case; to him, you're just another bag of bones. So might as well return the same courtesy; use and discard him first."

"Damn girl; that's bleak," Amy said, examining her with a gaped expression.

"That's life," Carmen said, confidence shone through her tone of voice.

"You're projecting," Sarah said, squinting through her glasses at the road ahead of her.

"Am I?"

"Yeah. You really should see somebody Carmen. Like a professional," Amy said.

"Did I ask you for your opinion?" Carmen barked.

"No. But I'm giving it to you anyway. Consider it a gift, free of charge."

Carmen smiled. "Do you hear this girl? So, what guy tickles your fancy anyway? What's his name?"

"I told you. His name is Jenson. Always was. Always will be."

"So, your recently deceased was just your boy toy after all huh?"

"Leland," Amy said with a stern expression. "May he rest in peace. He tickled my fancy too. But he was no Jenson."

"And what was Jenson like? Have I ever seen him?"

"He's strong, commanding but also sensitive and respectful," Amy beamed. She leaned in close to Carmen. "And no, you haven't met him. If you did you would know what the perfect man looks like."

Carmen chuckled in reply. "Girl please."

"I will admit Jenson has earned my respect," Sarah chimed in. Amy's eyes lit up like a beacon.

"Really?"

"Yep." Sarah pointed her finger, addressing Carmen. "You wouldn't like him though."

"Oh, you already know, don't you?" Carmen raised her eyebrows in curiosity. "What's wrong with him?"

"The man has some mouth on him," Sarah said.

Amy chuckled. "Yeah, he kinda does. But hey he just tries to stand up for himself. He doesn't mean anything by it."

"So, he's like the guy we were just talking to before we got here?" Carmen said, a threatening expression washing over her.

Sarah tipped her hand like a seesaw, confirming the girl's suspicions. "He's a bit different but on a similar level."

"Look all I need to know is if a woman gives him a signal or warning will he listen? Is he pig-headed? Even in the slightest tiniest bit?" Carmen prompted, gesturing with her fingertips.

Sarah shrugged. "You would have to deal with quite a bit of backtalk."

"Oh no, I couldn't deal with that. If he's not trained, keep him far away."

"Yeah, I thought so."

"Trained? He's a man, not a dog," Amy shouted.

Carmen raised her palms. "What's the difference?" Amy's jaw dropped.

"Hey, I'm just keeping it real girlfriend. Better you learn now than later."

"If you met Jenson, you'd change your tune real quick."

"I doubt it."

"I mean it. Just seeing him gives you hope, hope in humanity. That there is someone out there just for you; that will treat you right; always hear what you have to say; cherish you no matter-"

"Yeah, yeah, yeah we got the cliff notes," Carmen cut Amy off in an instant before going on a tirade. "All I'm saying is if you're going to drive stick you got to take the proper precautions. Now maybe this Jenson is your honey but if at any point he decides to let his down under do the thinking for him instead of you, you know what you have to do right?"

"Carmen," Sarah warned her.

"She already knows what's coming." Sarah shut her eyes in embarrassment.

Amy frowned. "What do I have to do?"

"You need just two objects." Carmen gestured with her hands. "A collar with a leash and a whip. Safeguards any future interaction you'll have with a man; guaranteed."

"A leash?" Amy squinted her eyes at the girl. It took a few seconds for the implications of Carmen's words to reach her but when they did it hit like a lightning bolt. Her eyes widened.

"Oh my god. That's terrible." Amy shot her gaping expression towards the front seat. "Sarah, did you hear what she just said?"

"Unfortunately," Sarah replied, with an annoyed sigh.

"Hey what I'm offering is priceless. It just might save your neck one day."

Amy cupped her hands over her mouth. "Carmen, I can't believe you just said that."

"Yeah well, you better remember it. Collar, bullwhip."

"I'm not whipping a grown man. Are you crazy?"

"Hey, it's either you or him. What, you think I'm joking?"

Amy tightened her grip over her mouth to fight back the incessant giggles but to no avail. "You're terrible." She turned towards Sarah.

"This girl's terrible. Why are we hanging out with her?"

Sarah shook her head, though her expression shone with the faintest bit of amusement.

"This girl knows," Carmen peered over the front seat, taking in Sarah's

demeanor. "She's dealt with far too many a man-beast not to."

'I've got nothing to say to you, Carmen," Sarah replied.

"You don't have to. You're my girl. I already know."

"Know what? I know my sister better than you ever could," Amy said. "She would never do that-"

"Oh no, the bullwhip idea was for you. This girl doesn't need that. She's way ahead of either of us. She has a method of bringing every man that she meets under her thumb. Including the one you recently left behind; that's why she didn't want me going anywhere near him."

"What are you talking about?"

"I'm talking about the sister that you claim to know so well?" Carmen exclaimed; her eyes widened with fervor. "You think I'm a bitch? I'm a schoolgirl all tied up in a feather boa compared to this Queen. Despite how much it pains me to admit, and it even hurts a little mentioning it now, her reach extends quite a bit further than mine."

"Sarah, what is she talking about?" Amy asked, turning towards her.

Sarah squinted her eyes before giving a reply.

"It's just Carmen and another one of her games. Pay her no mind Amy."

"Tell me I'm wrong?" Carmen exclaimed, leaning closer to Sarah than what felt comfortable. "Tell her I'm lying. Go on. Say it?" Carmen raised her chin. "Well? Say it." Sarah sat still, curling her lips, and wriggling her tongue in her closed mouth. There was no response. "Yeah, that's what I thought."

"I have plans," Sarah admitted. "But they involve mutually beneficial arrangements, not collars or chains."

"Uh, when one of your loser boyfriends decides to cross you, it will." Carmen shot a scathing look at the blonde-haired feline. Sarah returned the remark with a critical glare out of the corner of her eye.

"You really think you know me, don't you? After only a few months you honestly think that you have me all figured out?"

Carmen sat back in her chair, as expected Sarah had fallen right into her clutches. "Girl, I had you figured out since the moment I met you, don't even trip."

The two girls remained quiet after the exchange. Too much had been said for Sarah's comfort and yet there was a strange emptiness that was beginning to build up within the pit of her stomach. She couldn't get home fast enough. Amy shook her head in disbelief before sinking back into her seat.

"You guys are both crazy."

After checking into the hotel room Sarah was able to spend so much needed time alone, which she began by taking a cold shower. The hotel was separated into two sections by a door stationed in the middle of the room: baring one bed from the other. Sarah would have quite a bit of time to herself before she went to bed, a fact that she chose not to take for granted. After showering She fastened a moist towel over her bosom before taking a seat on the bed. There was someone that she needed to call. She decided to use the hotel phone stationed on the dresser, giving her cell time to recharge.

"Hello, Stephanie."

"Hello, Sarah. How was your day?"

"Pretty good so far. Just now settling in."

"Have you spoken to Maryam Bahira?" Stephanie asked.

"No. We're going to see her tomorrow. I thought it a good idea that we get a bit of rest before going to work. The others seem a bit tired."

"Rest is good," Stephanie said. Sarah squinted as she took in the girl's awkward tone. There was something that she wanted to get off her chest, but she needed to search for the words.

"Stephanie. Why do you want to talk to me?"

"I'm sorry?" Sarah could tell from the sound of her voice that she was flustered.

"It's just- as far as I can tell we've never met in person."

"Well, it's like I said before. Your story captured my attention. And as you already know a lot of it is public knowledge."

Sarah bit her lip and mulled over Stephanie's words. "True. I'm an open book. Doesn't mean that I let just anyone take a peek."

There was a brief pause before Stephanie spoke again. "Look if this makes you uncomfortable in any way I understand. We don't have to continue-"

"No, no I didn't mean it like that. It's just that a woman in my position can't afford to take any unnecessary risks. I've got a lot of enemies out there."

"Yes, I'm aware of that. You have every right to feel the way you do. Just know that those enemies that you're worried about- I'm not one of them. I promise."

"I believe you," Sarah said, her voice steady once again. "I'm not sure why though. Maybe there's just the dimmest ray of optimism in my blackened heart after all."

"You don't have a black heart, Sarah. You're just wounded the same as anyone else in your position."

"You don't know me," Sarah said, amused by the girl's attempt to read her.

"Yeah well, maybe I'd like to."

"Well stick around long enough and-" But before Sarah could finish her reply Carmen opened the door to her room.

"Hey girl, want to get some grub?"

"Hang on a sec," Sarah lowered the phone before looking up. "What's up?"

"There's some food in the lounge. Amy's down there now. Wanna come?"

"Nah I'm good; not really hungry. You should go though. Amy could probably use the company."

"Who are you talking to?" Carmen asked, noticing the phone in her hand. "Let me guess. One of your boys?"

"No. It's a woman actually."

Carmen's face contorted in confusion. "You're talking to another woman?"

Sarah shrugged.

"Sarah is there something that you wanna tell me?"

Sarah squinted her eyes in bemusement.

"Have you gone and switched lanes on me? It's okay. I don't judge. You're still my girl regardless. We just need to make sure to set boundaries between us. I don't want you sticking your hands underneath the covers when I'm asleep okay?"

Sarah glared before giving her the finger. Carmen chuckled; her teeth shone with delight. She was just about to close the door before Sarah addressed her.

"You sure you're okay with the two of you sharing a room?"

"Sure. Give us a chance to get to know each other a little better. But just so we're clear between the two of us I'm in charge, right?" Carmen asked, referring to Amy.

Sarah nodded in affirmation.

"Thought so. So tomorrow we bust some heads, right?"

"Most likely."

"Alright. Well, I'll leave you ladies to it then." Carmen turned and proceeded to shut the door behind her.

"Night," Sarah called out after her. The brief conversation did much to ease the tension and clean her pores, even more than the shower. Sarah would hang up the phone shortly after Carmen left, promising to speak with Stephanie White more in the morning. She knew that she would need all the rest that she could get. This would be the last night for it. The hunt was nearly upon her.

Chapter 7: Intrusion

Sarah Stryker awoke to find her surroundings and her mind intact. Everything was as it should be, that was until someone barged into the room uninvited.

"Sarah, I need your help. Could you come out here? Please?"

Sarah wiped her eyes with her fingertips. "What is it?"

"I'm about to slap a bitch."

Sarah could feel her sister's blood boiling from where she lay on the bed. It was easy for her to decipher what was going on based on that simple statement. Things could get out of hand if she didn't step in.

"Alright. I'll be right there."

The minute Amy left the shouting began. Despite how tired she was Sarah wouldn't be able to go back to sleep even if she wanted to.

"I'm not letting you back in this bed till you apologize to me. Are you going to apologize to me? Yes, or no?"

"Bitch, I've got nothing to apologize to you for. You pushed me."

"Take that tone with me again and we're going to have problems."

Sarah entered Carmen's section of the hotel room to find her comfortable in bed while Amy stood with her hands balled into enraged fists.

'What's going on?" Sarah exchanged bemused looks from one girl to the other.

"What's going on is this girl pushed me off the bed," Amy revealed.

Sarah raised her eyebrows at Carmen. She shrugged in protest.

"I get a little irritable at night. I forgot she was even there."

"So why don't you let me in?" Amy asked, leaning towards her.

"Simple. I don't want to. I don't like the way she spoke to me. She was like bitch you pushed me like it was some capital offense." Carmen mimicked Amy's tone of voice, something that only triggered her even more.

"What's the big deal? You call people bitch all the time."

"Yeah, but I say it in a different tone. When I call you a bitch it's a term of endearment. You said it as if you wanted to step up."

"Yeah, because you pushed me," Amy spat. "It was just a reaction. I didn't mean anything by it."

Carmen shrugged. "Me pushing you off the bed was a reaction. I didn't mean anything by it either."

Amy squinted her eyes. "Oh, whatever. You knew exactly what you were doing. Sarah, tell her."

"Are you two seriously fighting over a bed?" Sarah said. "What, are we back in high school?"

"She's more than welcome to come back in. She just has to mind her tone, that's all."

Amy scoffed. "As if you've never gotten mad and cursed someone out before. You were the one who said I was being too nice right? What? Can't handle getting some of your own medicine?"

"What you are is spoiled. Like I said before you're not on our level. You've yet to mature."

"You don't know me," Amy rebutted.

Carmen scoffed. "Yeah, I do. I know you just as well as I know her," she said pointing at Sarah. "We're women. You're not. You've got quite a way to go before you're ready to take off the training wheels. So don't go acting like you are, okay?"

"So that's why you're mad? Because I'm acting too much like you?" Amy said, in a failed attempt to read her.

"Oh no. You haven't seen me mad. Trust me. I have been nice to you, this entire trip. But you disrespect me and we're going to have problems. The only reason I haven't done anything is that your sister is here, and she's got a lot on her plate right now." Carmen pointed a finger at Amy, her words laced in a warning. "But FYI back in the day if you were a part of my crew and you spoke to me like that you would have gotten slapped. So, watch yourself, little girl."

"Bitch, I'm not scared of you," Amy barked. Carmen sprung off the bed in an instant and approached her. The maneuver awakened the referee in Sarah, and she stepped in the middle of the two girls. The tips of Carmen's toes touched Amy's as they stood at eye level, sizing each other up; both of their eyes contorted in annoyance and frustration.

"Okay, both of you need to settle down," Sarah said, raising her eyebrows in a fierce warning.

"You think that you're some kind of woman, don't you?" Carmen said, ignoring Sarah's words. "Well? Do you think that you're a real woman?"

"I know I am."

"Do you know that I've been in about a hundred fights in my life? It comes naturally. I can turn it on just like that," Carmen said as she snapped her fingers. Amy shrugged before delivering a sharp rebuttal.

"So? It's not all about quantity but quality."

"Oh, you wanna see quality?" Carmen took an authoritative step forward, but her advance was halted by Sarah who positioned her hand like a stone wall between them.

"That's enough. There's only one woman that you need to concern yourselves with fighting. It's the middle of the night and you two are tired and cranky. I get it. I am too. But the quicker that we finish this, the quicker that we can go home." Sarah folded her arms before carrying on. "Now Carmen, you still tired?"

"Yeah, yeah I could use some more shut-eye."

"Then go back to bed." Carmen exchanged looks between Sarah and Amy before sitting back down in her original position.

"Yeah, that's what I thought. Go back to bed." Amy exclaimed.

"Amy." Sarah shot a stern look at her sister before shaking her head in disapproval.

"But she-"

"Amy," Sarah repeated, raising her voice just the slightest bit. "Now Carmen has done us a favor by agreeing to come along. She's helped pay for a lot of the expenses and as such she gets more of a say in this room than you do. It would be courteous of you to come up with some sort of compromise."

"But why do I have to-"

"Amy. Remember what we talked about?"

Amy sighed, "Yeah, yeah I remember."

"Then do what I ask." Sarah turned towards the door to her room. "And Carmen, I'd appreciate it if you didn't push my sister, okay?"

Carmen rolled her eyes.

"But Sarah- where- what about the bed?" Amy protested. Sarah waved her hand in a dismissive gesture before departing.

"I'm done. You two can work it out amongst yourselves. You're grown women, remember?"

"See? Now you've gone and made her mad," Amy said, shooting a fierce gaze towards Carmen.

"Bitch please, you're the one she cares about. Meaning you're the one who disappoints her. I'm just the third wheel along for the ride."

Amy placed her tongue on her cheek. Carmen had pinched a nerve; a sensation akin to hot boiling water being poured down her esophagus.

"You're really starting to test my patience," she said, in a hushed whisper, unlike her normal tone.

A sly smile escaped Carmen's lips. "Maybe I am. What are you going to do about it?"

Sarah only managed to get thirty additional minutes after breaking up the argument between Amy and Carmen. There was too much on her mind and she couldn't afford to waste any more time. She woke up at four-thirty and began her daily routine, meditating for twenty minutes before washing her face and straitening her hair. At around five Sarah picked up the phone and dialed the number of her newest contact,

Stephanie White. She would need the normalcy of a casual conversation before the approaching conflict.

"You and your sister are going to see Maryam today, right?"

"Yep. We should be leaving in about two hours. Which gives us a bit of time."

Sarah sat on her bed, more relaxed than she had been in ages as she tended to the nail polish that she brought with her on the trip. She had just finished painting her fingernails ice blue and proceeded to apply the same nail polish to her toes. She stroked them with slow delicate movements while keeping the phone pressed against her shoulder for stability. Despite her stiff neck, this was an activity that she would choose to do for hours on end if she had the time.

"So, what's the plan? When you meet her, I mean? From what I hear Maryam Bahira is a proud woman. She won't just accept help from anyone. Her trust is hard to achieve and the few who have did so by proving themselves to her."

Stephanie's warning gave Sarah pause. Since she had learned about the threat against her life her only concern had been Anastasia, the one responsible for her status as a wanted woman. The idea that she may end up clashing fists with other well-known sisters within her former organization was a possibility that she pushed to the back of her mind whenever possible.

"Well, I'm sure you've heard the rumors. I've already proven myself in more ways than one. That's not why I'm here. I have to stop Anastasia before she hurts anyone else. Maryam may be a proud woman but if she has a vested interest in protecting her city then she'll understand that a mutually beneficial partnership is the best option. Though something tells me I might have to explain just how lethal Anastasia is."

"And exactly how lethal is she? I mean I've heard the rumors, but you've had first-hand experience," Stephanie asked.

Sarah shrugged. "Well, most of my knowledge is based on rumors too. And a bit of independent research. We only clashed once, and something tells me that she wasn't putting her best foot forward. She's crafty and slimy; more so than any person you're likely to meet. She likes to play mind games; it's how she's managed to garner so many of The Pride under her thumb."

"Wow. She sounds like someone not to be trifled with."

"Yes, not only that but several of her top enforcers are immensely powerful in their own right. Take Olga for example. The woman's over ten feet tall and sporting over four hundred pounds of pure muscle. This mission has to be handled with the utmost care; just one careless mistake and it'll all be over."

Sarah's mind tunneled through her memories. She had experienced so much in the past two years, including being dragged through the Earth by Olga. The hulking brute of a woman had thrown her around like a rag doll during their encounter; something that would most likely happen the next time they met.

"You're worried about Amy, aren't you? You're worried that if you come up against these women that she'll get in the way or worse she'll get hurt trying to help you?"

Stephanie's question was as precise as an arrow to the heart. Sarah narrowed her eyes in suspicion. "You don't waste time getting to the point do you sister?"

"Like I said I'm here to get to know you better."

"Well with questions like that you're well on your way."

Despite the sensitivity of the subject, Sarah was surprised to find that the question hadn't bothered her. It had been an unspoken fear for so long that being able to get it out in the open was freeing.

"To answer your question, yes Amy's safety does concern me as does Carmen's and even my own. I'm used to putting my life on the line but since The Pride placed a hit on me, I don't know. It's like looking at my own mortality, examining it from the outside. I can't allow Anastasia to gain any more momentum. It's time to face her head-on."

There was a thoughtful pause before Stephanie spoke in reply. Both girls could feel a tremor in their chest. The next question would be of the utmost concern.

"And should it come down to that, a fight between you and her do you think you could win?"

Sarah took a breath and exhaled through her nose. "To be honest I don't know. I'd like to think I would. I've been trained by the best. But Anastasia is another breed entirely. The way she carries herself, I'm not sure she's even human. I can't quite place it, but few people unnerve me the way she does."

Sarah entered Carmen's bedroom to find her fully dressed and Amy still unconscious on the bed. Carmen sat by a desk near the corner of the room, applying her bright purple nail polish to her fingernails.

"Hey," Sarah greeted.

"What's up? You and your girl have a good talk?"

Sarah narrowed her eyes. "She's just someone that I found online. She's working in Seattle and wanted to know more about me. Not much more to it than that."

Carmen kept her gaze locked on her nails. A sly smile spread across her lips in response. "Mmm-hmm."

Amy let out a loud snort and Sarah was grateful to use it as a means of shifting the conversation. "I see that you finally let her back into the bed," Sarah said.

Carmen changed her style, wearing her black hair out long in a similar look to Sarah. She dressed casually, sporting boots, a jean jacket, and leather pants. "Yeah, I wasn't even that tired. I just like to yank my girl's chain every now and then." She looked up at Sarah and shrugged. "You know how I am."

Sarah returned the gesture with a slow understanding nod.

"Probably should have woken her up but she looked so cute wrapped up like that. I was watching a bit of TV earlier and she just snored through the whole thing."

"Once she's out she's out for a while."

"Yeah." Carmen lowered her voice; her expression became like steel as she met Sarah's gaze. "Remember when you used to be able to sleep like that?"

"Yeah, I remember."

"So soundly; no worries. No care in the world. Seems like a lifetime ago." Carmen exchanged looks from the unconscious girl in bed up to Sarah. "You ready to get this bitch?"

"I'm ready."

Sarah placed her forefinger and pinkie in her mouth and Carmen mimicked the same action. The two girls whistled in unison, utilizing the full strength of their vocal cords to do so. Amy popped up from where she lay on the bed. She squinted and scanned the room in a disoriented state. The first person she addressed was her sister.

"Sarah? What- what's going-"

"Time to rise and shine little girl," Carmen said. "You said that you're no longer a child; that you have what it takes to ascend into a fully fledged woman. Well, that's what we're going to find out."

"Remember you volunteered for this. No one asked you to come here," Sarah reminded her. "So, I'll ask you again what I asked you before we left. Are you sure you're ready for this?"

"Yeah, yeah." Amy wiped her eyes and forehead with her palms. "Just give me- give me a minute, okay?"

Sarah folded her arms across her chest. "We leave in half an hour. Don't keep me waiting," she said before turning away.

Sarah, Amy, and Carmen were right on schedule. It would be a ten minute drive to their destination, and each was sure to take nothing with them. The journey would only be less predictable moving forward. Sarah diverted her attention between the road and the screen beneath her radio. A mission like this one needed a knowing eye to guide them and there wasn't a person on that side of the hemisphere who possessed more intel than Kyle Harper.

"So, I sent you the schematics for Georgetown as well as the neighborhood in which Maryam Bahira lives. It was a bit tricky as the woman moves around a lot, but I managed to narrow it down."

Kyle spoke in his usual matter-of-fact tone, taking his time to remind the girls of his intelligence.

"I expect nothing less from you, Kyle," Sarah said. Kyle smiled, his mystifying green eyes shone with pride.

"Thanks, Kyle! You're the best," Amy exclaimed.

"I already know I'm the best," Kyle said, playing it cool. "But it helps hearing it from fine ladies such as yourselves."

"Whatever," Carmen interjected. "It's not like it requires any real effort on your part anyway. What? Haven't you had that information swimming in your head for like weeks now?"

"Two months," Kyle replied, glaring at her. He shrugged, feigning nonchalance. "But who's keeping score anyway?"

"I know I'm not," Carmen bit back. "Hell, a so-called smart man is twice the culprit in my book." She pointed a finger in warning. "Because they know never to cross a scorned woman, yet most do it anyway."

"How have I crossed you?"

"Did I say you?"

"Yes, well no not out loud but I'm almost certain you said it in here," Kyle replied, pointing to his head.

"You know you're pretty cute for a freak. Like my Ex."

"Flattery will get you nowhere with me."

Carmen flared her nostrils. "What did you just say to me? What in the hell makes you think I'm trying to get anywhere with you?"

"Let's not lose our heads," Sarah suggested.

"What, you think you're someone because you know calculus or because you're an inventor or whatever the hell?"

Kyle sighed. "I'm a psychoanalyst, and computer hacker, and I work at a construction company and auto repair shop on the side. Just FYI."

Carmen shrugged. "And what, that makes you better than us or something?"

"No. Just you," Kyle said in a casual tone.

"Well, let me tell you something. I've met dozens of guys exactly like you. Men who think they own the world just because they were born with certain privileges. But in reality,"

"In reality, you're projecting," Kyle reprimanded. Carmen squinted her eyes, focusing on the man in front of her with laser-like vision.

"Maybe so. But I'm pretty good at reading people too. And I'll bet there's a whole colony of female types with dirt on you. I bet that they have some exciting stories to tell."

"And your point is?"

Carmen shrugged. "No point really. I'm just yanking your chain. We're just talking. An exchange between two individuals. That's all."

"Right," Kyle said, his face contorted in skepticism.

"Just know that when I give a compliment, no matter how insignificant it's because I mean it. It's not to flatter you. It's something that I can remember should we end up alone in a room together. You read me?"

"Yeah, I got it," Kyle said.

"You sure? You don't need me to draw a diagram that your megabyte-sized brain of yours can understand?"

"No." Kyle shrugged. "Are we done?"

"Honey, we haven't even started."

Sarah cleared her throat. Carmen shot a stern sideways glance at her before addressing Kyle.

"But I'll let you off the hook for now."

"Lucky me," Kyle spoke through his teeth.

"We'll keep in touch. Don't forget what you promised me," Sarah said with a sharp point of her forefinger.

"Right back at ya," Kyle replied. "Be safe. All of you. Even you," He gave a fierce stare towards Carmen. "We may have our differences but these two care about you and thus I don't want you dead."

Carmen glared in response. "You might want to reconsider that."

Kyle chuckled, realizing that there was no getting through to this girl. "Alright, I'm signing off. I had enough of this." The screen went blank.

"When we meet Maryam allow me to do most of the talking," Sarah said, addressing the girl beside her. "Between the two of us, I think you'll agree I'm the most diplomatic."

"Sure, whatever," Carmen said.

"What about me? I'm diplomatic, aren't I?" Amy's voice shone with tenderness as she spoke.

"I need you to guard the car. If you see anything suspicious, call us or shout if you have to. There's a good chance that The Pride already knows that we're here. We have to be ready for anything."

"But I'm sure we could make a quick getaway if we see them outside."

"No. That won't be good enough."

"But why do I have to man the car? If-"

"Amy," Sarah said, her voice hardening. "Are you talking back to me?"

Amy sighed. "No." She slumped back in her chair. "Sorry Sarah."

"It's okay," Sarah said, her voice becoming as light as a feather in an instant. "Just trust me on this. You're my ace. You'll have an important part to play soon enough."

"Alright."

"So how are we going to deal with her posse?" Carmen asked.

Sarah curled her eyebrows and squinted her vision from behind her sunglasses. "What?"

"This girl that we're going to see. She's in charge, isn't she? Well, odds are her gang will be nearby."

"Yeah, what about them?"

"They're going to be trouble. Gangs tend to be rather overprotective of their leader."

Sarah shrugged. "Well, we'll deal with the situation as it arises."

The team arrived at their destination. The neighborhood was old fashioned and a little run down with graffiti painted over the walls and homes but there were a few well-built apartments in the mix. One of them was bound to be the dwelling place of Maryam Bahira. All Sarah had to do was look.

"Alright. Let's do this."

Sarah's declaration was like a bell, the most authoritative that Carmen and Amy had ever heard. They put on their game face at once, the incoming conflict like a siren in their minds. Sarah opened the door to the driver's seat to her left while Carmen opened the passenger side to her right.

"Guys wait."

Amy halted their movement in an instant. She stretched her arm forward, balling her hand into a hardened fist.

"Bring it in," She commanded. "Come on. Bring it in."

The three girls connected their fists into one binding pact, their knuckles grazing each other, increasing, and unifying their powers at the same time.

"No matter what. We have to promise that we'll do everything that we can to make sure that we make it out of this place in one piece. That we'll have each other's back no matter what."

"She loves doing this part," Sarah said.

"Just do it okay.," Amy exclaimed. "We have no idea what we're getting into. We don't know what Anastasia has planned for us. But no matter what, promise me that we'll have each other's backs. I promise to have yours."

"I promise," Sarah agreed.

"I gotcha girlfriend," Carmen said.

"Let's go kick some ass," Amy said, as she leaped out of the vehicle.

"Uh, Amy." Sarah stepped in front of her sister, stopping her from moving more than an inch away from the vehicle. "Just curious, are you deaf?"

Amy's eyes widened. "Um, no?"

"What did I just tell you?"

Amy's jaw dropped. "Oh, you mean about me manning the car."

"Yes," Sarah said, annunciating her response with precision.

"Well, I just thought I'd come in with you guys for a bit. I can always come in and check the car later. Three of us are better than two."

"Amy." Sarah squinted her eyes. "Are you seriously going to start with me right now?"

"It was just a suggestion," Amy exclaimed. "Geez, you don't have to take my head off. What can an underling not offer suggestions? Am I undermining your authority?"

Sarah rewarded Amy's teasing with an affectionate pinch on the arm.

"Owe." Amy rubbed her arm and pouted.

"You're lucky that we're related." Sarah turned toward Carmen after she exited the vehicle. "You ready?"

"I'm waiting on you."

Sarah placed a hand on Amy's shoulder. "We'll be back in half an hour."

Amy leaned against the car as her two teammates walked off. "Sure. I'll just stand here. And..... wait."

Sarah and Carmen kept their eyes peeled as they ventured around the block. There were several women out during the morning but very few men. Sarah pulled out her cell phone and examined her GPS. From what she could tell the two girls were near the location that Kyle had sent her.

"So? Where is this bitch?" Carmen asked.

Sarah exchanged looks from her phone to the apartment in front of her. "It should be right here."

"This trashy place? The girl sure knows how to pick em doesn't she?" She placed a hand on Sarah's forearm. "I'm going to have a look around okay. I'll be back in a bit."

Sarah ignored her friend and proceeded to walk forward. The air was musty and thick, causing all senses to scream in unison. It wasn't until this very moment that Sarah realized she was venturing into unknown territory, what happened next would be out of her control. The thought slowed her steps and when three dark-skinned girls stepped in front of her, she stopped in her tracks.

"Whatchu want?"

Sarah took a moment to study the women in front of her. One of them, the shortest wore a red cap, with an array of braided locks underneath them. The other two dressed in Cornrows and from their expressions they were ready for a fight. They had stepped in front of the apartment complex as if to guard it.

"Do you live here?"

The one with the red cap, Desiree spoke first. "Girl, you better answer us when we're talking to you."

Sarah didn't appreciate the girl's attitude but knew that it was best to cooperate. There was a much bigger fight on the horizon, and she would need all the help she could get.

"I'm looking for Maryam Bahira. I was told that she lives here."

The group took an authoritative step forward as their expressions lit up. "Whatchu want with Mariam?"

"Like her, I was once a member of The Pride. It's important that I speak with her."

"Oh, so you with them Pride bitches I see."

Sarah shook her head. "Not anymore."

"Well, if she is then she must know something about the missing boys," Another girl chimed in.

"Do you?"

"I might know a thing or two," Sarah said. A voice shouted from the balcony before she was able to elaborate any further."

"Hey, Who Dat?"

"This white girl want to talk to you."

Desiree yelled at the top of her lungs. For a second Sarah thought she had gone deaf. Thankfully she wouldn't have to listen to these two exchange words for very long.

"What girl? Let me see."

Desiree sized Sarah up before speaking again. She leaned in close.

"You lucky. Lately, she's been sending folks away. But you try anything"

"I'm here only to talk. That's all," Sarah promised.

"Well, aight din." Desiree took a step to the side and her posse followed suit. Despite this one of them muttered under her breath as Sarah passed.

"You lucky she said yes."

"You best watch yo back around here little missy."

Sarah ignored their retorts and walked towards the woman on top of the balcony.

"What's yo name?"

"My name is Sarah. Sarah Stryker. I was once a member of the group that is plaguing your town." Sarah stopped in her tracks after reaching the third step from the top of the stairs. She stood less than a foot away from Maryam.

"You must be crazy. Coming here all by yo self." Maryam leaned against the railing in a relaxed position. Sarah could tell from her posture that she wasn't worried in the slightest. Which would have been a good thing had it not been for the current threat.

"Well, I didn't come all by myself exactly. Like you, I have a posse of my own. You're more than welcome to meet them if you have time."

Maryam allowed a sly smile to pass her cool expression. For some reason Sarah's nonchalance humored her. "Girl, Getchyo ass up here."

Sarah smiled and followed Maryam around the balcony. The two women walked until they made it to a room at the far end of the complex. Maryam opened it and Sarah followed with slow suspicious steps.

"Here we are. You want anything? I could fix yah something if you were hungry?"

"No thanks," Sarah said.

"You sure?"

"Yes."

Maryam sat on the sofa in front of the dining room and took a hard look at the girl in front of her.

"So, you're her? The one I heard about. The one they said was so special."

I'm her," Sarah said without changing her tone. "For lack of a better term."

"Say, we met one time, didn't we?" Maryam's eyes popped as she pointed at Sarah. "Yeah, we couldn't talk but a minute, but I remember seeing you. Those Pride girls really went on about you."

"Our reputations precede us."

Maryam squinted, taking in the full scale of the woman that she was dealing with. "It must be nice. To be chosen. To be approved by the head honcho herself."

Sarah shrugged. "It has its perks. But also, quite a few burdens as well."

Maryam pursed her lips and averted her gaze to the floor for a moment. She couldn't remember the last time that she felt bashful enough to do that. "Yeah, well most of us don't have it so lucky."

"I'm aware of that."

"Are you?" There was the attitude that Maryam was used to responding with. It had fluttered away but she knew it would come back sooner or later. She waved her hand dismissively. "It don't matter."

"Look I don't have a lot of time. I came to warn you about-"

"Hang on, hang on, slow your roll." Maryam raised a defiant hand. "We just getting situated here. I got to know who I'm dealing with before we talk shop."

"I'm more than willing to cooperate but what I've come to warn you about is rather urgent."

Maryam's eyes lit up. "Yeah well, who you are and why you've come here is rather urgent to me," she said, jabbing a finger into her own chest. "You see, we've had a sleuth of girls visiting these parts looking for trouble recently. Girls, might I add, that looked like you. So right now, you're in my house, which means that for as long as you're welcome, you'll answer my questions."

"Fine. Sure," Sarah mumbled.

"Ya coo with that?"

Sarah shrugged. "Yeah, I'm cool with that." She folded her arms over her chest and awaited the next round of questions, bracing herself for how personal and intrusive they could be.

"Now if memory serves me right you been to Africa ain't ya?" Maryam shifted her gaze across the room as she took a brief detour down memory lane. "Yeah, that's right. That's what em girls were talking about. About how you went to Africa to help em folks. And against The Serpents of all people."

"It's a long story but that's more or less accurate."

"I had a run-in with em boys myself recently. A handful of em tried to jump me the night after my last match."

"You okay?" Sarah asked, squinting her eyes in alarm.

"I'm coo. They not," Maryam replied.

Sarah nodded in affirmation.

"You know I can usually keep my composure during an encounter but those men?" Maryam shook her head. "Left them a bloody mess on the pavement after I was finished. Word is that you did the same thing when you were in the home country. You got hands?"

Sarah shrugged. "I get by."

"They told me you were the best fighter in The Pride, but I always wondered. I tend not to buy the hype. I only believe it when I see it."

Sarah placed her tongue on her cheek. "Well stick around long enough and maybe you'll find out."

Maryam's eyes widened in response. Her entire being flared up, though not in protest but fervor. The blood that coursed through her veins began to stir with such force as to turn it into molten lava.

"Well, those are some big words right there missy. Be careful. You don't want to end up biting down on too much for you to chew."

"Wouldn't be the first time," Sarah revealed.

Maryam smiled; her expression lightened a bit. "Well in any case I appreciate what you did for our people. But don't think that means we owe you anything. You'll still have to earn trust around here, ya heard?"

"I understand."

Maryam nodded. "So, what is that you wanted to ask me?"

"Well, I'm here for one reason; one name. The name of the person who put a hit on me. The name that helped lead a scourge on the entire population of North America. Anastasia.

Maryam nodded, slowly putting the pieces of the puzzle together. "So that's why you here."

"Yes. A few of her cronies attacked my sister a few days ago. She's here Maryam. In Georgetown and I have no doubt that she's fortifying her army for another all-out assault, possibly on your squad."

Maryam shrugged. "So? If she wants to throw down, she knows where to find me."

"Maryam," Sarah lowered her voice. "Between the two of us, I'm the only one who has met the woman face to face so when I tell you to worry you best listen."

"Why should I be worried? I've been fighting stuck-up bitches like her my entire life. Insofar as I'm concerned, she's just another apple in the barrel."

"And right there with that statement, you've exposed your ignorance and where you're most vulnerable."

Maryam furrowed her eyebrows. "I ain't exposed nothing. And you best mind your tone, little missy. You don't know me like that."

"Anastasia won't hesitate to take advantage of it; not a single solitary second," Sarah continued. "She's not just another fighter, she's another breed entirely. She's taken in dozens, possibly hundreds of women under her wing; young women like yourself and me. By now they've far eclipsed The Serpents in their power and influence."

Maryam raised her palms in the air. "And again, I ask the question you have yet to answer. What is it that you want?"

"Well, I thought that we could track The Pride together. Seeing as how once upon a time we were both members it wouldn't take us long to gain some sort of advantage. She's close Maryam, dangerously close and it's only a matter of time before you and her forces clash. Why not go into battle with a little extra help?"

Maryam took a minute to ponder Sarah's words before giving her a reply. Everything that she had said made sense, but it was what was behind her words that offended Maryam and it was for that reason that she gave her answer.

"Appreciate ya but I don't need no help. I got this."

Sarah's face contorted in confusion. "Excuse me?"

"If you're right and this bitch is here in Georgetown then she'll turn up sooner or later and when she does, I'll beat her bloody."

"It isn't that simple," Sarah said, her eyes widening in alarm.

Maryam allowed a faint smile to escape her lips. "It is to me."

"Did you not hear what I just said? She's far craftier than any warrior that you've ever faced. Most of The Pride answer to her now. We need to play this smart."

"No, what you need to do is worry about your own. I'll handle mine."

Sarah spoke in a hushed whisper. "We have a common interest."

"Do we?" Maryam questioned. "I've lived in Georgetown most of my life. These past few years have been nothing but suffering for us. Half of our people are starving, missing, or worse. In all this time I ain't seen ya, I ain't heard of y'all until about a few months ago. Now all of a sudden you show up and I'm supposed to just go along because what? You were chosen? Well, I certainly didn't choose ya."

"Look I know how strange this must be. Me barging in like this, demanding your cooperation. But I wouldn't do this if I didn't have a good reason. The Pride is dangerous, more so than they have ever been. Those of us who are still sane need to stand together. That's why I was chosen. You have a part to play in this too Maryam."

Maryam squinted and raised her head. She found Sarah's words intriguing but there was still something about them that bugged her.

"You were one of the few whose will wasn't completely taken over by The Pride's influence. That's not something to take lightly," Sarah said. "It's a sign of endurance and character. You're strong Maryam. It's why I came to you. You're exactly the type of person that I want on my team."

Sarah's words stirred something inside of Maryam that she hadn't felt in ages. But all that was interrupted by the sound of fierce shouting outside.

"What was that?" Maryam popped up from the sofa and rolled up the blindfolds on her window. Two women were standing outside yelling in each other's faces, increasing their volume with every second. Sarah recognized one of them as the black girl with the red cap on her head. The other girl was tan with jet black hair. It took Sarah less than a minute to realize who it was. The standout physical feature was the purple polish on her fingernails.

"She with you?" Maryam asked.

Sarah sighed. "Unfortunately."

"Well, you better get her. My girls don't play."

"Are they always standing in watch like that?"

Maryam turned towards Sarah and leaned against the windowsill. "Yeah. When your town is in the position that ours is in you can't afford to take any chances. So, we created a new system. The only people that come over here usually have an appointment. Anyone that tries to enter without stating their identity is thrown out. No questions asked.

Sarah looked up at the woman in front of her, her face contorted into a fierce glare.

"What? Don't give me that look." Maryam spat. "If you hadn't come here none of this mess would have happened in the first place."

Carmen could feel the blood coursing through her veins with every second that passed. She couldn't remember the last time she had been so impatient or when she had let the words of another woman bother her so much.

"Who do you think you is?" Desiree shouted.

"I'm a girl who has taken on about seven before I got here. So, I'd think about addressing me with a bit less tude that you're doing now."

"Bitch, do you think I'm afraid of you?"

"You probably should be. I don't take too kindly to people yelling in my face."

"You don't know me. I'm the most cordial woman here but if you going to be uncooperative then I'm going to have to bring my girls around to straighten your ass out." Desiree's eyes popped until the red veins appeared in them.

"Bring them on over here I don't care," Carmen exclaimed. "As far as I'm concerned, they're just practice."

"You don't know me. You don't know my girls and you certainly don't know Maryam," Desiree warned. "She's a national champion. I guarantee you won't talk so tough after she's done with you. I'd consider changing your tone before its too late."

"And you best change your tone right now," Carmen barked. "I don't care about your posse. I'll slap you right here."

Sarah and Maryam had barged in just in time, each choosing to address the friend and confidant who had accompanied them.

"Carmen stop. Calm down," Sarah ordered. "This isn't helping." She pulled her friend back while Maryam restrained Desiree.

"Did you hear what this girl said?" Desiree exclaimed, turning towards Maryam after she was shoved back. "I asked her a simple question and now she wanna throw hands. Like I don't care. I'll fight her but I didn't want to get in your way."

"Oh please, you were trying to start something, and you know it. So don't get mad when you find yourself up against a real woman who isn't afraid to bite back."

Carmen's words were like thunder quaking. A few more of Maryam's posse appeared and sprung into attack mode but Maryam held them back. Sarah restrained Carmen at the same time.

"Carmen. Carmen, remember why we're here."

"She threatened to slap me," Desiree said, her voice cracking a bit.

Maryam's face contorted in anger. "Who she going to slap?"

"Me."

Maryam shook her head. "Uh uh. Let's go inside. We handling this today." She pulled Desiree and the two girls headed back inside.

"Carmen let's go," Sarah said.

"With these bitches? Please, we don't need them."

"Carmen."

"They probably invited us to jump us, anyway, seeing how they like to travel in packs."

"Carmen enough. Let's go," Sarah ordered, raising her voice.

The four girls entered the apartment and made their way to

Maryam's room. A few of her guards stood outside on watch. The two teams would now be allowed to discuss their differences like civilized women but there was one person in the group who wanted something different out of the situation.

"Okay, let's start at the beginning," Maryam insisted as she sat down on her sofa.

"That would be a good idea," Sarah agreed.

"You come all the way over here to warn me about some girl."

"She's not just some girl nitwit," Carmen barked.

"Carmen," Sarah scolded her. I'll handle this."

"You better check yo girl," Maryam said with a threatening point in Carmen's direction.

"I don't need to be put on a leash. Unlike you and your gang of chimps over there."

Maryam's body flared up in protest. "Whatchu say?"

"You heard me."

"Anastasia's a psychopath," Sarah carried on, ignoring her friend. "The most dangerous sort of person you could ever encounter. Every person in this town is at risk as long as she dwells here. She'll maim and murder every man that has ever entered your life or that you've ever cared for."

Carmen turned towards Sarah. "Which, judging by this girl's looks, isn't very many." Maryam's eyes widened to a dangerous length.

Sarah shut her eyes in embarrassment. "Carmen."

"What?" Carmen protested. "You know it's true."

"Carmen it's time to get serious. I brought you along to help. Or would you rather wait in the car with Amy?"

"Lord help me. I am going to lose it today," Maryam muttered while shifting in her seat in a frantic motion. Desiree placed a comforting hand on her.

"She ain't worth it."

"Maryam," Sarah addressed the girl sitting down in front of her. "I know despite our proximity it's like we come from two different worlds.

There's no magic wand that I can wave that'll make you trust me. But unless you try, unless you let me help you The Pride will butcher all your friends and loved ones. First the men of this town; then the children. And then she'll turn to your squad, possibly turning them into one of her own in the process. Trust me when I tell you, despite all of your training and all of your power." Sarah shook her head. "You ain't ready for that."

"I ain't ready?" Maryam contorted her head as she gazed up at Sarah with wide perplexed eyes. "Who do you think you are? Coming into my place telling me what I can't do or what I'm ready for. Uh uh, this bitch about to make me pop off." She stood up and Desiree went into panic mode. She knew how things would escalate from here.

"No girl. She ain't worth it."

"Oh no, yes she is. From what I heard she's worth a whole lot."

"No. She didn't know no better." Desiree turned from one to the other in a frantic motion. "She didn't know no better."

"She about to know." Maryam moved Desiree's hand out of the way with as gentle of a nudge as she could muster. "Stay in your lane." She walked towards Sarah but was intercepted by Carmen who stepped in between the two.

"Oh no, don't think that you can step up to my girl like that. Not without going through me first."

"Oh, you want some of this too?" Maryam threatened.

"I want all of it," Carmen said with a conniving smile.

"Carmen, this isn't why we're here," Sarah reminded her.

"Speak for yourself girlfriend. This is exactly why I'm here. I came for a good scrap, and it might be a while before Anastasia shows herself, so I think I'll settle for this bitch right here."

Maryam edged closer, standing face to face with Carmen Rivera. "Oh, you're going to get a lot more than a scrap if you challenge me. Best believe that."

Maryam was at least an inch taller than her. Still, despite the high stakes Carmen couldn't help but smile. "Bring it on. I've got nothing to lose."

"Oh, you going to lose a lot." Maryam shrugged. "But it's your funeral. I'm just going to warn you I'm crazy and could easily get carried away. I killed a man recently. Put his head through the ground. And I had to lock up my own granddad when The Pride came."

"You should see my former boyfriend. You don't scare me."

"You should be scared. And if you were smart you scoot back over there with yo friend." Maryam pointed at Sarah, who stood rubbing the tip of her nose with her forefinger and thumb. Carmen ignored the suggestion and leaned in closer to her adversary.

"So, how do you want to do this? Outside, right here?"

"How about we take this in the ring?" Maryam prompted. "There's a gym not too far from here where I do most of my training. My girls will send you the address." Maryam jabbed her finger towards her chest.
"You better show or they'll hunt you down."

"Oh, honey that won't be necessary. Trust me I want to be there."

"Coo," Maryam said. "Now get the hell out of my house."

"Or what?" Carmen challenged.

"Or we'll show you out."

"Come on Carmen. Now's not the time for a fight," Sarah said.

"There isn't a better time. Sarah, are you really going to let this bitch talk to you like that? She doesn't even have half the power that you do."

"Get the hell out of my face. I don't want you breathing all over me." Maryam placed a hand on Carmen's face and shoved her backward. All her senses flared up at once and Sarah instinctively extended her arm as a barrier between her and Maryam.

"Oh honey, if you didn't want to wait until we met in the ring all you had to do was say so."

"No, no Carmen." Sarah shoved her backward, utilizing the full force of her arm. "We are not doing this here. If you really want to fight, then it's going to have to wait."

"Yeah, we'll settle this in the ring," Maryam agreed. "I prefer to fight in front of an audience anyway. You better be there too. Both of you." Sarah turned and met Maryam's gaze. The two girls locked onto each other as the true intentions of their actions were revealed. Sarah now realized who the real object of Maryam's scorn was.

Amy sat in the passenger seat and wore one of Sarah's shades while speaking to Kyle Harper over the radio. This would be the last time that she would have time alone away from her sister and she would make the most of it.

"She has no respect for me, like at all."

"She just doesn't want you to get hurt. None of us do." Her friend said over the radio. He was the voice of reason, the one thing keeping her fractured mind together.

"It's just so frustrating. I mean I know. I'm the baby. But does she have to be so demanding all the time? I mean doesn't my input count for something. Doesn't it?"

"It counts a hell of a lot more than that other woman you're riding around with that's for sure," Kyle added with an annoyed sigh.

"I mean I get it. Carmen grew up on the streets. She was in a gang blah blah blah. But so what? Girl thinks she's so gangsta just because people call her Queen C or whatever. I bet I could take her. She's fast but not that strong. It's just her killer left hook that I have to worry about. But I've been training a lot too. Heck, I could probably take Sarah now if it ever came to it."

There was a slight pause before Kyle replied. "Uh, Amy-"

Amy chuckled. "Yeah, your right. Sarah's too strong. That was just my out-of-whack emotions talking. Crazy people are stronger than regular people anyway. Look don't read too much into what I say okay. This is a rant. Something we girls like to do every now and then. Especially with a guy who's a really good listener. Like you. Just don't take it too seriously. Half of what I say I don't mean."

"Yeah, I get that."

"Just know that at the end of the day she's my sister and-"

But before Amy was able to finish her sentence, she saw a group of women off in the distance marching forward in her direction. She picked up a pair of binoculars that Sarah left and peered in. Her heart sank in her chest. In front of her was the thing that she dreaded more than any other and yet it was the thing that she would pursue with full intent if given the chance.

"Kyle, I'll call you back.

Amy, what is it? Your heart rate just skyrocketed. I don't even need to see what's in your head you to know."

"It's okay Kyle. I got this. Just take care of whatever Sarah asked you to do. Don't worry about me."

Amy jumped out of the driver's seat and looked into the binoculars once again. They were as far into the distance as she could see and luckily for her were taking their time. They were women who believed that they owned this town, and it would be up to Amy and her sister to prove them wrong.

"Amy, just tell me what you see? I'll feel much better if I think it's something you can handle."

"I said I'll be fine Kyle."

"No. No, Amy, wait."

But Amy pressed the button and ended the call before her friend could pry any further. She was tired of relying on other people to solve her problems. Still, she knew that taking on an entire gang by herself wasn't a feasible course of action.

"Okay, Amy you got this. Just remember what she taught you."

Amy muttered to herself as she scanned her surroundings. She had about ten minutes at most until they made it to her and much faster if they charged. She couldn't afford to wait. It would depend on her.

"Just think. She's, my sister. What would she do? What would she do?'

The answer hit her like a bolt of lightning. Amy Stryker fixed her expression into a stern glare. She cracked her neck before summoning all of her will and authority. She placed her forefinger and pinky in her mouth and blew into them utilizing the full force of her lungs.

Saliva sprayed out of her mouth as her windpipe strained and her face turned red. She took a deep breath and blew into them again but nothing resembling a whistle escaped her mouth. There was no other option. She would have to play it straight. She cupped her hand over her mouth and bellowed.

"SARAH!"

Chapter 8: Brawl

Sarah Stryker perked her ears. The voice was faint, but she could decipher its identity from anywhere. She turned her head towards the window.

"What is it?" Carmen asked. Her question caused Sarah's heart rate to spike. She approached the window and peered through it. She could see Amy yelling and pointing ahead of her. Sarah and Carmen surveyed their surroundings until they noticed the group of women marching several yards away. They had arrived at just the wrong time.

Sarah sighed. "Well, here we go again."

"Is that them girls?" Maryam asked from behind them. Carmen shot her head backward.

"Of course it is. What are you? Deficient?"

Maryam contorted her face into a stern and confused glare. "Whatchu say?"

"You heard me."

"Carmen," Sarah called her. "We need to get out there now. Help Amy park the car. I'll be there in a second."

"So, what do we do?"

"It's time to send Anastasia a message."

Carmen squinted her eyes as she grabbed onto the doorknob.

"A message as in?"

Sarah gave Carmen a look. Her glacial-like pupils glistening in the sunlight, shone with confidence.

"That's my girl," Carmen said before departing.

"Maryam. We could use all of the muscle that we can get right now." Sarah approached her with cautious steps.

"I ain't yo muscle. These girls ain't nothing. I'll plow right through em."

"Now's not the time to be stubborn, sister." Sarah extended her arm, placing a gentle hand on Maryam's shoulder. "We have to work together if we want to get through this."

"Getchyo hand off me." Maryam swatted her hand away and Sarah's eyes widened. "And I ain't yo sista. I'll handle this my damn self."

"Is that really how you want to play this?"

I'm not playin. And you best get to stepping. Those girls look like they are ready to fight. Something we both got in common."

Sarah glared at Maryam as she stepped into the shadows. Uncertainty glistened in her eyes, but Sarah couldn't afford to dwell on it. She was needed elsewhere.

All the hairs on Amy's arm stood up at once. She couldn't believe what was happening. In just a few moments she would face the thing that murdered Leland and she wasn't prepared for it: not in the least.

She entered the driver's seat figuring that it was a good idea to get Sarah's vehicle out of the way first.

"Come on. Come on."

Amy started the ignition and kicked the gear shift into reverse. She backed out of the curb and switched the car to drive and steered the car towards the nearest parking lot. The spot was stationed in front of a local diner, and it was largely empty. Amy could have picked any parking space she wanted but her anxiety made her foolish and she hit the curb jamming hard on the breaks before letting out a sudden yelp.

"Amy, what did you do?"

Amy's heart skipped a few beats. She looked out the window to find her older sister gazing at her with a bemused expression.

"I-I thought I was supposed to park the car," Amy spoke with a hoarse breath, still in shock due to the current situation.

"Yeah, you were, but what do you call this?"

"Well, I uh." Amy's thoughts were a scrambled mess.

Sarah waved her hand dismissively. "Nevermind. Come on."

"Come where?" Amy curled her eyebrows.

"Where do you think?" Carmen spat.

"I thought we were going to make a quick getaway," Amy whined.

"We're done running. It's time to take the fight to them," Sarah declared.

"B-but there's so many."

Carmen and Sarah exchanged glances, both of their expressions shone with annoyance and disbelief.

"Come on girlfriend." Carmen yanked Amy by the arm, pulling her out of the car. "You said you have what it takes to hang with the big girls, don't you? Well, it's time to find out."

The three girls marched through the street in unison. Amy could feel her heart thumping in her chest every step of the way. Whereas Sarah and Carmen's heart remained steady and their eyes unflinching. They both knew that this is where they wanted to be.

"About how many?" Sarah asked after the trio stepped in front of the group.

"I count about twenty. What do you think, girlfriend?" Carmen turned towards Amy.

"Yeah," Amy's eyes widened. "Yeah, I think so."

Carmen shrugged. "I say we each take on six apiece. We'll have them on the ground and begging in no time."

"Sarah. Oh, Sarah."

The advancing team called out her name. They were still a few yards away, but their tone of voice shook her. The degrading mocking way in which they spoke her name. It was all too familiar. Sarah led the march forward with her friend and sister beside her.

"Sarah Stryker. We were wondering when you were going to show up."

Before They knew it, the all-female gang stood a few inches in front of the trio. From what Sarah could tell they were identical in appearance and demeanor. They were tall black-haired women with broad shoulders and wore sleeveless shirts that exposed their bulky biceps. There were twenty-four in this group, but Sarah was sure to remain alert. Odds were that there were more scattered around the neighborhood, ready to ambush or lure Sarah into a surprise attack.

"Yes. We heard that you were in Georgetown. We have plans for you. Sarah Stryker."

"Where's Anastasia?" Sarah asked.

"Around," One of the girls said with a conniving smile.

"She'll see you soon."

"Oh yes. Anastasia has wanted to see you again for quite some time. Ever since the last battle. Remember the tower? And the Island?"

"How could I forget," Sarah said, with no change in tone whatsoever.

"She's going to make you pay for sabotaging her plans, Sarah."

"And you too Amy," Another girl added.

"What about you?" A girl turned her facial expression towards Carmen. She raised her eyebrows. "We know all about you too. Why fight against us? You detest and deplore men for what they did to you. Fight with us and you'll have free reign of them all. It's your only chance, sister. To finally have revenge."

Carmen glared at the girl. "The offer is tempting." She shot a side glance towards Sarah and their eyes met. "But I'll have to refuse. Don't get me wrong. I'm not above giving a man a good beating on occasion, and I plan on doing just that. Prevent them from crossing me or my girls over here. But I'll do it at my discretion. I don't need you harpies to make decisions for me."

The Pride each spread their lips into a wide smile. "You're making a serious mistake Carmen Rivera. One that you may not live to regret."

"Neither do I need any of you invading my mind, to make me into your little pawn," Carmen said, ignoring their threat. "Did you think I would just forget about that? I never forget. You crossed the line and for that, I've got a queen-sized ass-kicking with your name on it." She pointed to each of the girls. "And yours. And yours, And yours, yours, yours. And yours."

The squad leader turned towards Sarah. "What about you, sister? You must desire revenge. More so now than ever before. Your heart yearns for it. We can sense it."

"You don't know the first thing about me," Sarah spoke through gritted teeth.

"We know you lie awake every night, weary from the nightmares that haunt you. We know that the thrill of the hunt is all that sustains you. And how do we know? We know because we are the same, Sarah. Feathers of the same bird, forged through torment, and born from a single soul."

Sarah raised her eyebrows. "Feathers of the same bird? One that murders, steals, and betrays their leader and everything that they once stood for?" Sarah shook her head. "I don't think so. I'm not that. I'll never be that."

Carmen cracked her knuckles. "Alright, that's enough talk. Let's get on with the ouchy part, shall we?"

"Let's," Sarah agreed.

Amy's mouth twitched and her insides churned. She couldn't believe what she had agreed to do and yet with her sister and one of her newest friends by her side there appeared to be no other option. All bets were off. This was a battle that none of these women could afford to lose.

The army was of one mind just as they had said. Without a spoken word amongst themselves, they lunged towards the trio in unison. Sarah noticed one with a mace, several with sharpened daggers, and a few with long clubs that would assuredly bash their brains in if caught off guard. In only a few moments the entire street would become a war zone.

Carmen Rivera was the first to withstand the power of The Pride. Three girls pounced on her in unison. She shoved two off, but one charged at her from behind, causing her to stagger backward. She was kneed in the stomach before being knocked backward with several heavy blows to the ribs. The attacks came one after another until before she knew it Carmen found herself thrown into a leasing office behind her.

"Stupid bitch! You never should have defied us."

The women working in the office ran screaming for their lives. So did a few of the families surrounding the group and within the various apartments and buildings. Carmen could hear them as her ears rang and the foggy blur around her returned to her line of sight. She was knocked into the bathroom and one of the gang members placed her into a headlock after she sat up on her knees then lifted her and socked her in the stomach.

"How does that feel? Huh bitch? Not so tough without your girlfriend to protect you huh?"

The feeling of hardened protruding knuckles against her abdomen was like a wake-up call. It had been a few months since Carmen had felt anything like it. It didn't help that a few of the girls there were almost twice Carmen's size and height.

"You think you can scare us? You have no idea what fear is but believe me, when we're finished, you'll understand."

One of the girls lifted Carmen and threw her against one of the mirrors in front of the sink. The glass cracked and Carmen went smack against the ground.

"We're not done yet. Stand her up. I want to see her bleed."

Carmen was lifted and then punched into the wall. She surveyed her attackers, Five girls, each over six feet tall, taller than her and even taller than Sarah.

"You're going to suffer for your betrayal Carmen. If you got any apologies to make or any begging to do you best do it now. Because you may not have a chance in the next few moments," The girl warned.

Carmen felt the inside of her swollen cheeks. She spit out the excess blood before wiping the corner of her mouth.

"Oh, honey." She chuckled. "Princess. You should not have done that." Carmen put her best foot forward, at last deciding to take the fight seriously.

Sarah led the charge as she countered the advances of the warrior women around them. The first girl to attack swung at her with a bat and Sarah raised her forearm, blocking it in an instant. Frost enveloped the bat, and the girl gritted her teeth, the sudden impact causing her to rattle in place. The woman's head snapped back from a swift left hook across the jaw and her leg was swept out from under her by Sarah.

The gang attempted to beat their opponents with every asset they had in their possession. They swung with their bats and pointed weapons in quick succession one after another and even all at once. But Sarah's superhuman speed was something that none of these girls had ever experienced before. She parried their weapon attacks with her hands before hardening them into angry fists and pummeling away. Frost enveloped Sarah's hand and forearm with every strike.

During her time spent with The Pride and training in combat Sarah learned how to combine the power of frost with her knuckles. She punched concrete, sand, and hot coals in a fervent effort to harden her hands. After two years of intense training Sarah's hard work paid off. The frost that protruded from her knuckles made her attacks lethal in their precision and power. It required more effort to hold back to keep from murdering her opponents.

"Amy, you take the girls on the right. I'll take the ones on the left."

Amy stayed one step behind her sister. Her eyes nearly popped out of their sockets after a girl tried to smack her with a mace. She ducked just in time for Sarah to catch the weapon single-handedly before kneeing the girl in the stomach and flooring her with a vicious over-the-head toss.

"Amy," Sarah scolded her.

"I-I'm sorry. It's just. There's so many."

The two sisters did an evasive back dash in unison. "I could do this by myself, but it would go a lot smoother with your help."

"There's too many." Amy's voice shook.

"No there isn't. Focus Amy. Believe in yourself."

"What's the matter, Sarah? Scared?" One of the girls mocked.

"Fight like you mean it, Amy," Sarah ordered. Amy felt her chest tighten up at the sound of her older sister's command. It was like an alarm, one that she couldn't ignore. "Fight with everything that you have."

"I-I'll try," Amy stuttered.

"No Amy. You have to believe it. Believe it and it will happen."

"O-Okay. I believe it," Amy said, her breathing steady once again.

Just as she announced her newfound confidence a girl lunged toward her with a knife. Amy dodged a few swipes before elbowing the girl in between the eyes and sending her flying backward with a punch to the rib. The attack motivated Sarah, who lunged toward three young women at once. Their teeth clenched as they attempted to overwhelm her with an explosion of speedy punches and kicks. Sarah twirled, avoiding a powerful kick attack by less than an inch before connecting with a precise kick of her own to the girl's abdomen. The attacker soared several yards away before crashing into the trunk of a van in the parking lot.

Sarah could feel her heart swelling with every attack. With each bone that she crushed and with every woman immobilized the knowledge that she was closer to her goal dawned on her. Sarah wrapped a firm grip around the wrist of one attacker just as she swung with a knife. With a mere tug of her hand, Sarah spun the girl around, causing her to fall and drop the weapon before pounding the girl's face into the cement with her bare fist.

Sarah perked her ears, sensing four attackers lunged toward her in unison, two in front and two behind her. The two in front attempted to defeat Sarah barehanded and were given a severe punishment for doing so. She punched one in the ribs before stomping on the legs of the other, causing her to shout at the top of her lungs before she collapsed. Sarah then homed in on the attacker in front of her, unleashing a six-hit punch combination and ending it with a penetrating kick to the girl's cheekbone. Blood, saliva, and frost splattered across the girl's face, and she twirled into the air, her mind fluttering away just as her body lost its equilibrium.

One of the attackers had almost stabbed Sarah from behind but at the last possible second, the woman froze in place, her body shivering as frozen icicles dripped down her face and a cold powdery mist oozed out of her mouth. Sarah had elbowed her in the stomach, a sensation that while not as lethal as a knife proved to be just as painful. Another swung at her with a bat and Sarah clutched onto it with her fingertips. She pushed the girl before yanking the weapon and clocking her upside the head with it.

Sarah took a breath in and out. She wasn't fatigued in the slightest. She had been in a fierce battle before arriving back in Seattle over a week ago. Compared to that and compared to the coming battle with Anastasia she knew that this was nothing more than a warmup.

An attacker twirled a ball and chain in their grasp. Sarah raised the bat in defense just as the girl threw it at her. The girl was a bit stronger than she appeared, and the bat was yanked from Sarah's grasp but not before she managed to get a firm grip on the chain. She froze it until the entire chain went from black to blue. She pulled the attacker by the chain and sent her off her feet with a graceful high kick to the chin that shot her head up to the sky. She then yanked her back to the ground and sent her reeling with another kick to the mouth.

Sarah wrapped the ball and chain around the girl's neck before throwing her over her shoulder. She took two mace weapons and twirled them in her hands. The warriors shivered as they gazed at their opponent. If they thought this would be just another street fight, they had another thing coming.

Amy kept her eyes glued to the footing of her opponents. They came at her from all directions and as expected didn't let up for a second. Amy parried the attacks of two women in front of her before sending them crashing into the concrete with her debilitating strikes but was immediately shoved backward and kicked by two women behind her and one in her blind spot. She clutched onto the metal bat that was swung at her before knocking the girl holding it with a sudden head butt.

Amy swung the bat in her hand, getting a solid feel for its maneuverability before she was attacked once again. Several gang members leaped into the air and Amy backflipped just as they came crashing down in front of her. She swung in a wild chaotic maneuver, hitting several women before one plucked her arms and held her in place.

Amy was hit with a barrage of punches that felt more like rock and concrete being smashed against her temple than flesh. She gritted her teeth just as the pain began to sting and jumped, knocking her attacker with a vicious boot kick before breaking out of her other opponent's strong-arm lock and throwing her over her head.

"Amy, relax. You're letting your emotions get the better of you. These girls aren't much stronger than the ones who attacked us downtown."

Amy didn't understand how Sarah was able to do it. Somehow her older sister was able to fight while guiding Amy every step of the way. "Are you kidding? They're way stronger." Her backtalk was rewarded with a hard punch to the face that caused her to collapse; her jaw clenched under the weight of it.

"Amy. You have to focus."

"I am focusing." Amy spat the excess blood from her mouth and sat up.

"Don't argue. Just listen to what I'm telling you." Sarah's voice hadn't changed. "Just follow my lead. I'll guide you through this. Same as I always have."

Amy looked up and her jaw dropped. She watched as her older sister twirled the ball and chain weapons in her hand with ease, her facial expression remained placid as the gang of attackers lunged toward her. Sarah twirled in a circular motion, covering all three hundred and sixty degrees of her surroundings. Sarah used the weapons as grappling hooks to pull her enemies toward her. She wrapped the mace around the wrist of two women before pulling them forward and pummeling them into submission. She pulled a few by the neck and knocked them flat on their back with a staggering kick between the eyes.

Amy carried on with the fight, utilizing her fists as her primary weapon of choice. None of the combatants were able to keep up with her hand-to-hand combat so they decided to improvise with small knives that each warrior appeared to be a surgeon with. Amy's heart stammered in her chest as she ducked, dodged, dashed, and weaved out of the way with all her fervor.

Sarah shifted her eyes towards her sister as she struggled to keep up with the sudden burst of knife attacks. She dropped the mace weapons and pulled out two of her own creations. Two frozen daggers appeared in her hand, and she twirled them with lightning-fast speed and inhuman finesse. "Amy."

The sound of her sister's voice made her shoot her head upward. Her eyes popped out of their sockets as Sarah threw one of her frozen daggers in her direction. Amy reached up and wrapped her grip around the blunt end. She winced as the frost of the blade enveloped the skin of her palm.

"Sarah."

"Use it."

Amy lifted the icy blade in her grasp. For such a tiny weapon it was quite heavy. She gritted her teeth as she attempted to find equilibrium with the object.

"Don't think. Just act."

"B-but I can't. It-it's not me," Amy whined.

"It's in you, Amy."

Sarah decided to step aside for a moment and watch. Amy raised her sister's weapon just in time to block a knife attack from another woman. She parried each swipe of the knife before poking the attacker in the rib with her borrowed weapon and punching her in the chest, causing her to slide backward. Amy spun the dagger in her hand and picked up the pace with every swipe. She stabbed an attacker from behind before plucking a wooden club from a girl on her blind side. She weighed the two weapons in her hands, the bat in one and the frost covered weapon in the other. She put some distance between herself and her attackers. She raised the dagger in front of her face, fixing her gaze into a stern glare, one that gave her older sister a sense of Deja vu.

"That's my girl," Sarah said, her face shone with pride as she watched her sister's movements. She was so enthused by the sight that she almost hadn't noticed one of the women lunge toward her, but it didn't matter regardless. She raised her foot and kicked the woman directly in the nose. The attacker's mind was thrown out of orbit as she crashed into two gang members behind her.

The moment that her enemies made her bleed Carmen Rivera decided that she would have a field day. The feeling of dominating her opponents, the crunch of hardened bone, and the wriggle of flesh and leaking blood. It gave her life. She was now a wild animal without hinges, lock, or lid. She swung with terrifying force, almost inhuman for a girl of her miniature size. It wasn't long before all five girls were overwhelmed with the power of her heavy blows. She pounded a girl after cornering her to the bathroom wall. The walls began to crumble, and the pipes busted. One grabbed her from behind and was punished by a bone-crushing stomp on the foot. Carmen turned and sunk her teeth into the girl's neck. The attackers soon realized that the fight could mean the difference between life and death so two pulled out a pocketknife to help even the odds.

They would regret their decision in an instant. Carmen ducked, evading swipes of the girls' knives with ease before slashing at their stomachs with her purple painted fingernails, which were much sharper than they appeared. She scratched two girls in the abdomen, and they shrieked in horror. She picked them apart with brutal elbows to the face and a breathtaking knee to the abdomen where one woman had been cut.

Carmen lifted one girl and hung her over the handlebar with the shower curtain. She turned around and her head spun backward from a brutal punch to the face of an enraged fighter. Carmen recovered in a split second and pounded her rock-hard fists into the girl's abdomen. She then yanked on the girl's hair, causing her to wince as a result. Tears streamed down the girl's cheeks as her hair was stretched beyond what it ever had been before. Carmen pounded on the girl's face at the same time. She continued for a full thirty seconds, never letting up even for a bit. She wouldn't stop. She couldn't; not until these girls knew who she was.

Sarah and Amy mimicked each other's movements as they fought, every step in sync with the rhythm of a beating drum. They stomped on the ground and spread their legs and arms into a fierce fighting stance. Amy gave a side glance towards her older sister as her knuckles hardened. Sarah stared at the enemies ahead of her as frost enveloped her knuckles. She couldn't let up; not even for a second. The soon-to-be woman beside her was counting on it.

"Alright. It's time to see what you can do. Think you can keep up with me?" Sarah asked.

"Yes. I know I can," Amy said, in a voice that was very much like her sister's.

"Then show me."

The two sisters lifted their frozen daggers just as the enemy spiraled into another chaotic frenzy. Sarah led the charge and Amy remained an inch behind her, attacking another who charged towards the blind spot. She hit one girl in the rib before elbowing one behind her in the stomach. She ducked out of the way of a sudden knife attack, and it cut a strand of her hair before she swept both girls off their feet with a smooth spin kick to the legs. Sarah rammed her icy knuckles into an attacker's abdomen several times before grabbing her by the collar and pulling her into a visceral headbutt. Frost enveloped the warrior's esophagus and her jaw dropped as her body lost all its mobility. She fell in disgrace, cracking like a broken statue after hitting the ground.

Sarah and Amy utilized their weapons for attacking and deflecting as the rival gang grew even more desperate in their desire to subdue them. Sarah parried three weapons simultaneously before stabbing one girl in the leg, launching one into the air with a head-snapping uppercut, and finishing the third with an elegant scorpion kick. Amy pounded the ground at the same time, causing the concrete beneath the rest of the squad to burst, flooring them all instantly. All twenty warriors were subdued, and Amy only had a few cuts and a spot of blood on the corner of her mouth to show for it.

The sisters shot their heads towards the small building in which their friend had been knocked in. They could hear terrible shouting and incessant banging on the walls. Something was attempting to burst out of the building.

"Carmen," Amy exclaimed. She took a step forward towards the building, but Sarah pulled her back by the forearm.

"Ah, ah. She's fine Amy. Relax."

Amy turned towards her sister; her mouth gaped open in disbelief. "Are you sure?"

"Mmm-hmm. Just give her a minute."

Amy watched with protruding eyes as the banging increased in volume, cracking the wall of the building. She involuntarily dashed to her left when a girl was knocked through it and came flying towards her. Sarah didn't react and instead stretched her arm out to catch another girl just as she crashed into her; another skidded across the floor and the last was launched into the air. Sarah threw a frozen dagger in her direction and the girl crashed into a nearby building, the weapon freezing her into it like glue.

Carmen Rivera appeared amidst the debris and shattered rock. She took slow and purposeful steps, proud of the work that she had done. The building collapsed behind her in the wake of her triumph. She cracked her knuckles as she approached the two sisters. Amy raised her eyebrows as she examined the cuts and bruises on Carmen's face.

"Carmen? Are you okay?"

"I'm good. You should see the other girl."

"We were worried about you."

Sarah crossed her arms. "This girl was. I knew you could handle yourself."

Carmen wiped the corner of her mouth as well as the minor cut on her left cheek. "I gotta tell yah; a scrap like this makes me wish I joined you guys sooner."

Sarah shot her head to the right and cocked her head. "Well, it's not over yet."

Amy and Carmen turned in the direction of Sarah's gaze, noticing breaking glass and the Earth quaking all around them. A tall muscular girl burst out of one of the nearby stores. She stomped her feet in an authoritative stance. The Earth beneath her quivered in the wake of her power. She ran her fists along the side of the building, creating two steel armored fists that she would use to beat the women into submission.

"So, which one of us is up?" Amy asked, examining the warrior with a bemused expression.

"Seems a little extra," Carmen added.

"I've got her."

Sarah took a step forward and squeezed herself between her two teammates. The girl lunged toward Sarah. She let out a thunderous war cry that echoed through the city and neighborhood streets. Sarah remained steady as she walked forward. She raised her fist the second that the warrior attacked.

The steel fists shattered, and a chill ran through the girl's arms. She winced as the blood that ran through her veins slowed to an unusual degree. Frost enveloped her knuckles. She let out a gasp that seemed to go on forever, though it was only a split second after Sarah attacked. The moment her icy knuckles connected her muscular opponent was locked in a chamber of torment for which there was no escape.

Sarah allowed a sly half glare, half-smile to escape her lips. Her heart swelled in her chest as the pain of suffocating cold surged through the warrior. She was half this woman's size but twice the warrior.

Sarah parried the warrior's counterstrikes before ramming her fist into her chest, sparks of frost and powdery mist shot out of the girl's back. It covered the street and froze the glass windows and the walls of all the buildings on the block. Making an example of lesser women was what Sarah lived for. It would give her life no matter where she went.

The warrior's jaw dropped, and she let out a hoarse breath. All the oxygen had been sucked out of her lungs in an instant and her sanity along with it. Her mind tunneled into a black abyss that suffocated her stomach as much as her body. Sarah placed a finger on her forehead and with a gentle touch tipped her over on her back.

"Oh my god. Sarah, that was so awesome!"

The sound of her younger sister's praise snapped Sarah out of battle mode, if only for a moment. She turned to find Amy beaming up at her, eyes shining with enthusiasm.

"The way you fight. It's like you're not even trying."

Sarah shrugged. "There's not much to it. You just have to believe it."

"You say it like it's so easy," Amy replied, her voice oozing with skepticism.

"It is," Carmen interjected. "I mean against these low-level fighters?" She scoffed. "We could break them like toothpicks if we wanted. They're just practice."

"I don't know. Some of them seemed pretty strong to me."

Sarah and Carmen exchanged looks. "Tell you what. Why don't you take on the next one?" Carmen suggested. "All by your lonesome."

"Really?"

"Yeah. I was going to take my turn next but I'm a little winded after that last ambush. You fight the next girl and I'll take the one after."

"Okay."

"You sure you can handle it?" Carmen asked.

"Yeah, I got this."

The three teammates marched forward, alert as their eyes scanned the environment around them. The sounds of broken glass and concrete sounded in their ear. It only took a few feet for the trio to arrive at the next wave of opponents.

Amy shot her head forward. Three women had entered the battlefield, backflipping with superb athleticism until they reached the middle of the road where the trio was standing. Amy could tell that they were from The Pride but something about them appeared to be different from the rest.

"Well, time to see what you're made of."

"What?" Amy shot her wide-eyed gaze towards Sarah in protest. "You're not going to help?"

Carmen chuckled. "What part of you take the next one didn't you understand?"

"Yeah, but there's three of them. Sarah only had to beat one."

Carmen shrugged. "So? What, are you not woman enough to take on three?"

"Oh, that's so not fair and you know it."

"What are you, deficient? This is war sweetie. It ain't supposed to be fair."

Amy furrowed her brow, more frustrated with the girl than she had been in a while.

"Don't worry Amy." Sarah patted her sister on the back. "These girls aren't that tough. Just remember what I taught you."

“Okay, but in case they aren't pushovers you think you could I don't know maybe lend a bit of a-"

"Oh, just get in there will yah? Quit your whining."

Carmen shoved Amy forward in the middle of the three attackers before she could even register what had happened. She saw her opponent's fists inching towards her face half a second later and placed her arms in front of her in a defensive maneuver. She blocked a few attacks but was knocked to her knees by a spinning cartwheel from one of the girls and then kicked in the face for good measure.

Amy placed her fingertips on the ground before raising her legs and springing herself back up on her feet. She raised her two fists in the air before putting on her game face, the strongest one that she could muster. If her sister wanted to see her fight, then she would give her a show worth watching.

The attacking felines were much quicker on their feet than Amy had predicted. It only took a second after she stood up for them to go on the immediate offense. They fought in unison; every attack seemed to be coordinated. Each punch was thrown at the same time from each angle. Amy used not only her hands but improvised with her forearm and elbows to block the attackers. Her fist collided right dead in the center of the knuckles of two girls, and she was shoved backward just in time for the third to leap off the ground and attempt to floor her with a flying spin kick to the left cheek. Amy raised her arm just as the kick collided with her. She was able to catch the girl off balance with a swift punch to the stomach that shot her backward, but Amy was kicked in the rib by another surprise attack.

Amy slid backward and placed a hand on the ground to stabilize herself. She charged forward, leaped into the air, and pounded into the ground. The attack created a ripple in the Earth and the squad performed an invasive somersault, catapulting in the air just before the ground erupted from beneath their feet.

"Stay calm," Sarah muttered. "There will be plenty of time to showcase your power later. Right now what you need to remember is technique."

Amy increased her speed as she lunged forward. The next wave of attacks was fierce, with her opponent attempting to connect with a powerful spin kick. With superhuman reflexes that Amy had almost forgotten that she had, she bent her upper torso backward, balancing herself on the balls of her feet as she leaned her body and watched the girl's steel-like legs pass her field of vision. She tried sweeping the girl's legs, but she jumped, somehow predicting Amy's movements. The second warrior ran towards her and sprung into attack mode at the same time, springing into a handstand and twirling in a circle before kicking at Amy with the full force of her legs.

Amy gritted her teeth before harnessing the power within her grasp. She increased the mass and weight of her fist before ramming into the first girl's ribs and sending her reeling with a devastating uppercut. She wrapped her hands around the legs of the girl standing on her hands before lifting her off the ground and kicking her in the stomach, causing her to collide with her comrade.

She had just enough time to react to the third girl who dove towards her and entered the fray with a new weapon. The attacker elongated their nails in an instant. The new development caused Amy to raise her eyebrows in dismay.

The girl slashed at Amy with her new weapons. Amy felt her eyes sink into the back of their sockets.

"Sarah."

"It's okay Amy. I know it's nerve-racking but don't let your emotions get the better of you. You're still in this fight.

Amy dashed backward as she avoided the swipes of the girl's weapons by a narrow margin. The other two members of the squad joined in, elongating their nails to an absurd degree before attacking.

Carmen shot an annoyed gaze toward Sarah. "She's hesitating."

"She's learning," Sarah corrected her. "Give her a chance. She might surprise you."

"Not like this, she won't. She's holding back Sarah. Can't you see that?"

Sarah didn't respond. She kept her arms folded as she examined the fight. A slight purse of her lips was all that gave away her thoughts, but it was all that Queen C needed.

"Uh-huh you can can't you? It's just like I said. She hasn't been pushed over the edge; not like us."

Sarah refused to turn in Carmen's direction. "Maybe she doesn't need to be."

"Uh if she wants to hang with us then she better. Think about it. We're not just up against some bitch. This is Anastasia we're talking about. Do you really expect her to be able to take her on fighting like this?"

The scales had begun to tip once again. Amy had managed to avoid any lethal swipes, but her opponent's nails had cut and grazed her skin multiple times. She was so busy avoiding the weapons that her opponents managed to get a few solid kicks in, even ramming their elbows in her face a few times, leaving a visible bruise that thumped in her mind like a beating drum.

Carmen pointed a finger at Sarah, her voice laced in a warning. "All I'm saying is that you better get her ass in gear or I'm doing it for you."

Sarah gave a fierce side glance to the girl beside her. "Am I supposed to be threatened by that?"

Carmen shrugged. "You can take it however you want. I'm just letting you know."

Amy squeezed her fingers in between the elongated nails and wrapped a firm grip around her hand. She squeezed with all her fervor before kicking the warrior in the midsection, causing her to topple over.

"See," Sarah said. "You're too quick to judge. Amy's got this."

Carmen sighed. "Finally."

The eyes of Amy Stryker lit up as she sprung into a frenzy. Her knuckles cracked as she tightened them, and her spine tingled with anger. She threw right hook after left, increasing her momentum with every strike.

She clutched onto the hand of one girl and bent it back towards the ground. The girl cried out and Amy took advantage of her moment of weakness to deliver a swift spin kick that floored the woman in an instant.

Sarah felt her muscles settle and her breathing return to normal as she watched her sister dominate the fight. She didn't realize how tense she was until then. Carmen Rivera was silent, not as irritated as she was before but stern as she pursed her lips. Both women watched as Amy finished off the final two opponents, one by kicking her several yards away and the second by lifting her off the ground and throwing her into a nearby building with two hands.

Amy wiped the excess dirt and blood from her hands as her breathing settled and her mind stopped racing. She allowed a proud smile to escape her expression, sensing the pain of her swollen cheek and bottom lip at once. She turned as Sarah and Carmen came to greet her.

"Did you see that? Did you see what I did?"

Amy's voice squeaked as she spoke, and a thin line of blood dripped down her nose. She wiped it and examined the placid expression on her teammates. "So? What do you think?"

"Yeah," Sarah said with a slight nod. "You did good."

Carmen said nothing, responding with only a lukewarm shrug of her shoulders.

"Good?" Amy was flustered. "Come on. When I picked up that girl and threw her. That was great and you know it."

"You could use some improvement."

Amy's jaw dropped in disbelief. "Sarah, are you kidding?"

"No, I'm not kidding. You have a ways to go Amy."

"You're trippin. When that girl tried to kick me and I bent over all the way to the ground without moving my legs. Like in that one movie when the guy bent backward and dodged those bullets in slow motion."

"Yeah, but none of that fancy stuff is going to matter if you keep holding back," Carmen interjected.

"What?" Amy couldn't believe what she was hearing.

"It's true. Someone had to say it," Carmen protested, noticing Sarah's silence.

"You do pull punches an awful lot," Sarah admitted.

"Thank you," Carmen said with a sigh of relief.

"But Sarah," Amy whined. "Considering my power is that really such a bad thing?"

"Amy." Sarah lowered her voice, speaking to her sister in as intimate of a tone as she could. "Your heart is your greatest weapon. Your kindness is a strength, not a weakness, despite what some would have you believe."

"But in this case," Carmen prompted, raising her voice to a tone that Sarah found irritating. She gave a stern sideways glance towards her before carrying on.

"But these women don't deserve your kindness, neither your sympathy nor even much of your mercy. They wouldn't hesitate before destroying you in an instant. Always remember that."

Amy shrugged. "So basically I have to be like them? Shut off everything and just go for the jugular?"

"Pretty much."

"But I'm not a killer," Amy protested.

Carmen smiled. "I heard differently."

At that moment all the hairs on Amy's head stood up at once. She turned towards Carmen, glaring at her with the most sinister look that she could muster. Carmen was unaffected by the gesture and merely raised her eyebrows in amusement.

"If you're going to fight The Pride then you better be close to it. Otherwise, none of your training will mean anything. It's a hard road ahead Amy. And if you're to be by my side I need you sharpened and ready at all times. Do you understand?"

Amy stood still as she caught her breath, the reality and precision of her sister's words hit her like a thunderstorm.

"Amy, do you understand?"

"Yes. Yes, I understand. I'll do my best. I promise."

"Good. Let's go," Sarah ordered.

Amy allowed the words to settle in as Sarah walked off. She stood still, noticing Carmen staring at her with that trademark smirk of hers. It was just the sort of face that Amy would consider punching had Sarah not been there.

"What?" Amy wiped the thin line of blood that dripped from her nose. "You want some of this?"

Carmen shook her head, closing her eyes in embarrassment before walking past her. Amy heard her mutter under her breath. "You'll learn, someday."

The trio continued down the trail along the sidewalk. The streets appeared to be desolate. There wasn't a pedestrian insight as far as Sarah could see. The lack of activity on the streets made her perk her ears even further. Sooner or later this battle would escalate.

Sarah stopped in her tracks, noticing a strange disturbance in the ground beneath her. Carmen collided with her, and Amy bumped into Carmen at the same time. Both gave Sarah a bemused look.

"Why are we stopping?" Amy asked.

"I don't know. I'm following this girl," Carmen spat. "She's the brains of this operation. I'm just looking to crack some skulls."

"I wasn't talking to you. I was talking to Sarah."

Carmen twisted her upper torso, raising her eyebrows in a warning. "You giving me lip?"

Amy shifted her gaze up to the sky above, her expression shone with annoyance.

"Don't roll your eyes at me, little girl. I asked you a question."

"Carmen." Amy narrowed her eyes. "We're kinda in the middle of something right now. We really don't have time to get into it."

"Oh honey, I've got all the time in the world for you. Don't worry about that."

"Shut up," Sarah commanded.

"So what? You're taking her side now? I thought I was supposed to be next in the chain of command."

"Of course, she's taking my side. She's my sister," Amy exclaimed.

"Shut up. Both of you," Sarah hissed. "I think I hear something."

It took only a second for Amy and Carmen to pick up on it as well. The ground quaked in its presence. Both of their eyes lit up in dismay while Sarah remained placid, her hair flapping in her face as she waited.

"Sounds like it's time for round three. Mind if I take this one girlfriend?"

Sarah shrugged. "Go for it."

Carmen turned towards Amy. "Time to show you how it's done."

Amy scoffed. "Please, you're not going to show me anything."

"Oh yes, I am. If you're going to throw down with us, then you best be prepared. Class is in session sweetie. So, take lots of notes because I'm going to quiz you afterward."

"There's nothing that you can teach me, Carmen."

"Is that a fact?"

Sarah turned to address her sister. "No, actually I think there's a lot that you could learn from her."

"What?"

A sly smile escaped Carmen's lips. "You heard her."

"Carmen's a natural-born fighter. Despite her lack of finesse. It would do you some good to see her in action."

"Exactly," Carmen said, agreeing with Sarah before she had stopped to consider her words. "Wait what? Lack of Finesse? Who do you think you're talking to?"

Sarah shrugged "Your fighting style is a bit on the messy side. It's just an observation."

"Oh really? An observation? Well, how about this for an observation." Carmen jabbed her finger near Sarah's chest. "You're quickly becoming like the same stuck-up bitches you claim to be against. Your recent successes have gotten to your head. Oh, that just because 'oh look at me I'm a hot blonde that knows karate' that you can pass judgment on how I fight? I don't think so. Unless of course, you're feeling so gong ho about it that you want to step up and prove it."

Amid Carmen's passionate rant, the team hadn't noticed the ground split open, or a pair of deceased hands pop out of them.

"I don't need to prove anything to you, Carmen. My battle record speaks for itself. And you should be mindful of who you're speaking to." Sarah raised her eyebrows in a fierce warning. "I told you before. I'm in charge. I call the shots and I make the judgment calls. It's part of the job. And your job is to fall in line. Same as this girl here."

"Yeah, Sarah's the boss. Not you 'sweetie,'" Amy taunted while mimicking Carmen's tone and hand gesture.

"She may be the boss." Carmen approached Sarah with slow meticulous steps until their toes touched. She locked onto her, sporting a glare every bit as focused and unwavering as hers. "But I'm the queen. Which means if you want to keep this little crusade of yours afloat, you'll let me have a say. I followed these girls for months after they went rogue. I have more intel than just about anyone you're likely to meet. Are we clear?"

Sarah squinted as she studied the girl's expression and fierce brown pupils. There was so much in them, anger, fearlessness, and above all desire.

"You really thrive on conflict don't you sister?"

Carmen smiled "What can I say? It's my curse."

At that moment the face of the next group of enemies appeared in front of the team. Three deceased female corpses all popped out of the ground. Amy recognized them as the ones that attacked her on the day Leland was murdered. They climbed out of little potholes in the ground before cracking their necks and shoulders in unison. Much of the skin on their faces had been melted off, rendering their skeleton bone structure and much of their muscle tissue visible to the human eye.

"Well, it looks like you'll be getting your wish today," Sarah said after the team turned toward the three walking corpses. They turned their necks at a three-hundred-and-sixty-degree angle before limping toward the team. Carmen cocked her head to the side, a gesture of smug fearlessness, before taking an authoritative step forward.

"Good. I get the twisty bendy ones."

Sarah crossed her arms over her chest as she studied Carmen's posture. She couldn't believe it, but Carmen's attitude had humored her. She was now more eager to see this girl fight than ever before.

"Be careful Carmen," Amy called out.

"Being careful was never my forte. But you can bet your ass I'll pound these freaks into the cement before I let them take me out."

The three walking corpses turned their gaze towards Carmen in unison, their desire for destruction and appetite spiking in an instant.

"Yeah, that's right. I'm talking to you," Carmen raised her eyebrows in a threatening glare. "Not sure if you can understand me but if you can, if there's any trace of human feeling still inside, you're going to wish that you were back in the dirt when I'm finished with you. You got that?"

One of the creatures screeched at the top of its lungs, exposing all its rotten molars for the three girls to see. Amy couldn't help but wince at the mere sight of it.

"I thought so," Carmen said. She bawled her hand into a tightened fist, clenching until her protruding veins popped. "Well? Which one of you screeching harpies is first?"

One of the creatures stepped forward, its claws stretched out and ready to pounce on its prey. Carmen smiled, still amazed by how exciting this entire ordeal was for her.

"Hmm. You seem eager."

Without warning, the creature lunged towards her and in an instant, Carmen redirected its attack and threw it over the shoulder by the arm. She planted her knee in its jugular at the same time, before turning to pummel the other two.

"Amy? Do you see this?" Sarah asked, leaning towards her sister.

"Yeah. Yeah, I'm watching," Amy said, conveying no enthusiasm whatsoever. She watched as Carmen made the creatures punch drunk with her enraged strikes to the face. She knocked one creature so hard that its head bent over the back of its neck. She then plucked its legs out from under it before swinging it in a full three-hundred-and-sixty-degree motion and chucking it into the other.

'You, see?" Sarah added. "She's got a limited arsenal but makes the most of it. Puts her heart into every strike. It's what's needed to win."

"So?" Amy shrugged. "I put my heart into it also."

"Amy," Sarah scolded her. Amy sighed, watching the fight ensue with a narrowed expression. She watched as Carmen took on all three of the deceased women simultaneously, flooring them all with a single right hook.

"I could do that," Amy muttered.

Carmen brought her arm in front of her as one of the creatures slashed at her with its claws. She hammered the creature with ten strikes in a row, knocked it on its back, and mounted herself on top of it. It thrashed and its knees buckled as Carmen sunk her nails into its eye sockets, poking them out.

"Can you do that?" Sarah asked.

"Uh, maybe not. But I have my own style." Amy shot her head towards her sister. "And you really think that I can't beat her? Even you said that she lacked finesse. "

"I never said you couldn't Amy." Sarah gave a gesture of warning with her forefinger. "I said that I wasn't sure. There's a difference."

Amy turned her gaze back to the fight. "Whatever. Still not happy."

Sarah said nothing in reply but gave a mere side glance to the girl beside her, just to confirm whether she was as upset as she appeared to be.

Carmen pounded the creature into the cement, effectively burying it underneath. She was yanked off the ground by another and with superhuman reflexes elbowed it in the rib before turning and sending it spiraling to the ground with a brutal haymaker.

Carmen smiled, relishing the high of a solid beatdown. The sudden burst of excitement left her temporarily vulnerable. She gasped when an unsuspecting hand burst out of the ground and wrapped a firm grip around her ankle. Another creature lunged at her from behind at the same time, seizing her shoulders and biting onto her neck with the full force of its teeth.

"Carmen," Amy exclaimed. She took an involuntary step forward but was pulled back in an instant.

"Hang on." Sarah pulled her towards her as she spoke. "Hang on. Carmen didn't interfere with your fight during your momentary struggle. Even when she wanted to. Let's give her the same courtesy."

Carmen cried out as she struggled for control. Three of the creatures jumped on top of her all at once. The one that was buried beneath the concrete emerged and Carmen was tackled to the ground.

"This doesn't look good," Amy said, watching the events unfolding with wide eyes.

"Give her a minute," Sarah said, her voice steady.

Carmen's vision darkened as her enemies attempted to bury her. They bit onto her skin and clawed all at once. But it didn't take long for Carmen to realize that the pain she felt wasn't anything new. In fact, she found it comforting. She had been in the same situation numerous times before.

Before the creature could even register what had happened, it staggered backward in response to a terrible blow from its adversary. Carmen thrust her foot upward, smashing her heel into the chin of one of the feminine creatures, its head snapping as it was launched into the air. Carmen sprung to her feet before smashing her fists into each opponent one by one. She smashed a creature's nose inside of its body. She then hit one with an uppercut to the chest, blowing a hole inside it. She unloaded a series of rapid-fire punches, juggling the airborne opponent before burying it in the ground face first with a two-fisted hammer.

Carmen finished her work just in time to notice the enemy that she had kicked in the chin falling in front of her. She lunged towards it and threw her fist forward at just the right moment, snapping its spine in two and sending it hurtling toward Sarah and Amy.

The sisters performed an evasive sidestep just in time. The creature caught itself and landed on its feet before attempting to pounce on Sarah from behind. Without batting an eye or even turning to face the creature she halted its movement with a swift back fist to the nose. Amy's jaw dropped as the creature's teeth clenched and its body went limp. Slowly it tipped over as frost enveloped its jaw.

Sarah and Carmen exchanged a warm smile. The battle appeared to be going in their favor, but Sarah got a glimpse of something on one of the tall buildings ahead, and her expression darkened in an instant. For a split second in time, everything around her disappeared. The object of her glacier-colored pupils and the impending danger that it posed to her friends were all that was present.

Without another second of delay, Sarah lunged forward, dashing past Carmen, and penetrating the creature behind her with a fatal stab to the jugular. The creature let out a breathless hoarse gasp as its internal organs turned to ice and its vision turned milky white.

"What do you think that you're doing? That one was mine," Carmen barked. Sarah shot a look of warning towards her friend, her eyes bulging out of her sockets.

"Take cover."

"What?"

"Take cover. Now."

The alarmed look on Sarah's face was all that Carmen needed to make her move. She lunged towards Amy, placing a protective arm around her shoulders before heading behind a building next to them. Sarah performed an evasive somersault just as the first round of gunfire began.

She managed to take cover behind a building to the left of Carmen and Amy as the bullets sprayed where she had been standing.

The next minute was a blur of chaos and carnage. The rapid gunfire seemed unending and covered the entire circumference of the battlefield. Amy covered her face in protection against the exploding debris. The bullets collided against the wall in front of them. Carmen brought her in close and shielded her to the best of her ability. Sarah poked her head out from her cover and shifted her eyes upward. She could see a muscular woman standing near the edge of a building, a minigun in hand as she surveyed the streets and fired away.

"Sarah?" Amy whined. "What's happening?"

"Don't worry I got you, girl," Carmen assured her. "I won't let anything happen to you."

The sound of the gunfire had all but deafened the trio as they waited for an opportunity to play their hands. Sarah peered over the cover, examining the soldier firing at them with a watchful eye. The answer hit her like a freight train. She whistled across from her before pointing at her own two eyes and then toward the woman she had addressed. Carmen nodded, catching onto her signal in an instant.

"Alright listen." Carmen shook Amy from where they stood. "When big sis gives us the signal, we're going to storm in that building and take that bitch down."

"What?" Amy opened her eyes and looked up at the girl, her face shone with confusion.

"I said we're going to attack when Sarah gives the signal."

Amy covered her face, as the dust particles surrounding the duo began to build. "Attack who?"

"The one with the minigun. Who else? Wake up, girl." Carmen covered her face as another round of machine-gun fire blasted beside them. She turned towards Sarah, sensing that the opportune moment to strike would come soon.

Sarah created a makeshift knife in her hand, positioning it towards her hip, in preparation for her attack. She raised her free hand and motioned a count to three. Carmen watched her with a careful eye.

After counting to three Sarah threw the knife into the air. It twirled in a swift and smooth motion as it approached its target.

"That's the signal. Come on."

Carmen pulled Amy forward as she made a quick run for the building ahead. The gunwoman raised her weapon to the knife and fired before it had reached her. She was surprised that her opponents believed that she could be bested by such a simple maneuver. The frozen blade shattered in front of her but rather than bursting into what should have resembled shattered glass, a cloud of foggy mist blew out of it. The gunwoman's jaw dropped as the temperature of the surrounding air became dangerously low. She never felt such a suffocating presence before. It not only distracted her long enough for the trio to make a quick escape but also stiffened the grip that she had on her weapon, exactly like Sarah had planned it.

By the time the gunwoman had regained any sense of equilibrium with her surroundings her enemies had already reached the top of the building and burst through a door outside, ready to greet her. Sarah led the charge as she and Carmen lunged forward, taking cover as their opponent opened fire like a rabid animal, still not able to fully see due to the lingering fog. Sarah threw multiple knives in quick succession, distracting her enemy long enough to make her move. Sarah then ran forward, slid onto the ground, and kicked her enemy's weapon upward just before she opened fire again. She then kicked her in the midsection and Carmen brought her to her knees with a two-fisted hammer. The woman spat blood as she lost control of her body. She placed a hand on the ground as her vision blurred. Sarah grabbed her by the tip of her shirt. The next part was crucial.

"Listen to me. I want you to send a message. It's for Anastasia. Tell her that her days are numbered. I'm coming for her. Her and all of her ilk."

The woman's eyes widened as horror enveloped her entire being. For a moment she thought she saw a creature where a person should be. It was covered in the cold mist and had its jaws outstretched, ready to consume her but at the last minute, the woman saw her true adversary. Sarah knocked the gunwoman out cold with a severe headbutt. A gash of blood appeared on her forehead as she lay on the ground, twitching and shivering involuntarily from the power of Sarah's blow.

Amy stood at the other edge of the building beside the door that they had entered. She was gobsmacked, both at what had just occurred but even more so how her teammates had chosen to react to it.

Carmen lifted the minigun that the opponent had been using and examined it.

"Would you look at this? You know in the future we should probably consider going into battle with one of these."

Sarah folded her arms in front of her, allowing herself to relax a bit. "You're more than welcome to but I'm not."

"Why?"

"Too unwieldy. I couldn't rely on something that isn't my own. Besides," Sarah shrugged. "It would hardly make taking down Anastasia's posse as enjoyable now would it?"

Carmen's expression lit up in excitement. She threw the minigun to the side and approached Sarah. "Damn right. And let me tell you something else. None of these bitches are on our level. They're wannabes. Lost girls without direction. We're women. Survivors who have been through hell and back. Anastasia never had to deal with the two of us together before. My guess is she isn't woman enough to handle the both of us either."

Sarah placed a tongue in her cheek. Carmen's words triggered her imagination, the possibilities ahead, and the chance of victory seemed tangible at last.

"You feel me?"

"Can't argue with you there."

The two girls pounded their fists together in unison, the result of which sent a shockwave through the earth. At that moment they were one; the scars of their past and the impending threat that lurked in the shadows were just obstacles to overcome. It was with Carmen by her side that Sarah knew that she wasn't alone.

Chapter 9: A Lesson in Humility

Carmen Rivera kept her stern expression locked onto the punching bag in front of her as she hacked away at it with her lightning-fast strikes. The object crumbled under the weight of her power. Carmen didn't let up, not for a single solitary second. She only had one day to prepare for the boxing match against Maryam and she was determined to make the most of it. She threw jab after jab, right hook after left, and with the occasional haymaker that caused the bag to swing. Her heart thumped in her chest and beads of sweat poured down her face as a result. By the time she had decided to take a rest, she was certain that she had thrown over a thousand punches, relishing the power and magnitude of every single one.

Carmen wrapped a small towelette over her neck and caught her breath. Desiree called Carmen after the street brawl against Anastasia's posse, informing her of the time and location of the boxing match. Meeting Maryam for the first time the previous day had done much to bring all that was inside of her bubbling up to the forefront of her mind. She had become stronger than she thought possible and yet still she could sense that something was missing, something gnawing at the back of her brain.

"Hey."

Carmen shot her head back, noticing Sarah approach her. The two girls dressed identically, sporting a bra, and sweatpants with their hair wrapped in a neat ponytail for the occasion. Both women were in exquisite physical shape. Their abs were toned to perfection and their ripped arm muscles served as a mere glimpse of the immense strength that dwelled within their collective physique.

"Hey, girl. What are you doing here?"

"Thought you could use some company."

Sarah lifted two bottles of water, handing one over to her friend.

"Thanks."

The two girls took a swig of water in unison, allowing their minds to settle as it entered their bloodstream. It was a nice change of pace after the intense battle the team had the day before but Sarah, knowing that she would have to cut to the chase eventually, decided to break the soothing silence with a question.

"So, do you want to talk about it?"

"Talk about what?"

Sarah gave Carmen a stern look. "You know what."

Carmen rolled her eyes in response.

"Are you really going to fight her?" Sarah carried on. "She's a renowned fighter. With multiple titles under her belt."

"Yeah? Well, she won't be so renowned when I'm done with her," Carmen fired back, before taking another swig of water.

"I had Kyle look up her profile last night," Sarah revealed. "She's thwarted hundreds of warriors. Both The Serpents and The Pride. And not just beaten Carmen. Decimated. She's even managed to kill a few of her opponents single-handedly. She's not one to be trifled with."

Carmen let out a silent chuckle. "Who said I was trifling?"

"I think you haven't thought this through. You're just reacting on blind emotion."

"You think you know what I'm feeling?"

Sarah shrugged. "I could tarry a guess. Sure."

Carmen smiled, before leaning against the punching bag. "Alright. Let's hear it then. Go on, read me. Let's see if your perceptive powers rival those boy toys of yours. Go on."

Sarah exhaled through her nose before replying. "You want me to be honest? You're not going to like it," She warned.

"Sweetie you're in Carmen's corner. Down here honesty is mandatory. There are no other options."

"Alright. I think you're stubborn. Set in your old ways because you feel that it's all you have. You're strong but also a little conceited. It's rare for you to ask for help even when you need it the most. And you disregard the sensibilities of those around you out of fear that you'll be seen as weak or vulnerable. So, what do you think? Getting warm?"

Carmen pursed her lips before allowing a subtle smile to escape them. "That's not bad," She admitted.

"Am I wrong?" Sarah said, raising her eyebrows in an authoritative manner.

"You're not wrong but you're missing the point."

"And that would be?"

"That this all boils down to one specific thing. It isn't about not being vulnerable or anything like that. It's all about one thing. Just one. She disrespected me. Disrespected you too by the way. Which I guess you didn't notice or were too slow to pick up on. But me? I don't take too kindly to being disrespected. I tolerate a certain amount of lip from you and the little sis because you're my girls. But from a bunch of second-rate ghetto ass bitches?" Carmen shook her head. "I don't think so."

"So that's it then?" Sarah shrugged her shoulders. "It's all a pride thing then? Are you really prepared to risk it all based on that? This could make the difference between life and death."

Carmen pointed a finger of warning in Sarah's direction. "Yeah, that's right sugar. And don't think you're so high and mighty either. This whole ordeal is about pride. It's all one big game that you're prepared to win no matter what. So don't go thinking that you're any different than me. I'm just a bit more honest about it."

Carmen strutted past Sarah, proud of her ability to put the young woman in her place.

"Alright," Sarah said after she walked past her. "Then you leave me no choice. How long do you plan on training?"

"Four hours at least. Why?" Carmen turned to face her friend; a bemused expression washed over her though it only took a moment for her to guess what her response would be.

"Need a sparring partner?" Sarah placed her hands on her hips, feigning casualness as she spoke.

"I could use one. You got time?"

"I've got nothing but time," Sarah declared.

Carmen nodded. "Alright. Let's get cracking."

The girls ventured towards a ring near the edge of the gym where there was a punching bag stationed right in the middle of the arena.

"Alright now tell me oh wise one, what do you know about boxing?" Carmen prompted.

'It's a combat sport. One where the fighter relies on the power of their fists to win."

"Well duh," Carmen exclaimed, raising her voice to a heightened level. "I meant what do you know about it through experience? Have you ever fought in a boxing match before?"

Sarah paused; a bit flustered by the question. "Well, uh, no. No, I haven't. But I do have a black belt in Karate. Plus, we trained in many forms of combat during my time with The Pride. From Tae Kwon Do to Tai Chi, we even dabbled in some Wing Chun. "

"Blah, blah, blah." Carmen cut her off in an instant. "Why can't you just say no? Look I know you know how to throw down. It's not like I haven't been around. You know how to fight using the assets that you've been blessed with but you're not going to be able to rely on those should you face a boxer in the ring. It's just you. With only your fists to rely on. Can you do that?"

"Sure. I've been trained in several forms of fighting before. How is this any different?"

"It's different because it is. Didn't you say you used to play soccer when you were younger?"

Sarah nodded. "Yeah, Amy and I both. It was a favorite pastime when we were younger. Bonded over it. Even won a state championship once."

"That's lovely," Carmen said, feigning sweetness. "Now can you play football?"

"No."

"But why not?" Both involve kicking a ball, don't they?

"Sure, but I don't know the first thing about football. The rules or how they're implemented in practice."

Carmen raised her eyebrows. "Don't you think the same applies to boxing?"

Sarah shrugged. "I suppose so."

"Honestly if you weren't my girl, I'd smack you in the face for that kind of thoughtlessness."

Sarah's neck stiffened and her eyes widened, serving as a sharp warning to the woman in front of her. Carmen rolled her eyes.

"Girl, I'm just playing."

"If it's a fight that you're looking for Carmen you're well on your way with that kind of attitude," Sarah warned.

"Oh please. I'll happily take you on." Carmen returned Sarah's threat with a half-smile half glare. "Once I'm finished with Miriam, we'll have all the time we need. This gym is open like what? Twelve hours a day? Whenever you're ready just let me know. We'll settle this like women. Find out which one of us is really on top."

Sarah placed her tongue on her cheek, allowing her mind to settle.

"Look. All I'm saying is you gotta respect boxing and its differences. I respect all that kung fu stuff you and your sister learned. Why not return the same courtesy?"

"Do you?" Sarah questioned.

"Of course. In fact, why don't we make a pact? After I decimate that bitch in the ring, I'll train under you a bit. You can teach me all the fanciest moves that you know. I'll even follow your lead just like you want."

"Really?" Sarah's eyes widened. She was surprised to hear Carmen hop off her high horse for once.

"Sure. You're my girl, remember? I'm the nastiest bitch that you're likely to meet when I want to be. But it's like you said earlier. I'm much more than that. I'm also a Queen. And there isn't anything that a queen wouldn't do for a woman under her care. But right now, you're in my corner. For as long as you are in this ring, I make the rules and I give out the orders. I'll be meticulous." Carmen raised her voice, pointing a finger toward Sarah. "And I won't hesitate for a second before calling you out if I deem you less than stellar. And that's putting it mildly. Are we clear?"

Sarah shrugged. "Yeah, we're clear."

"You got a problem with that, Sarah Stryker?"

"Nope. No problem at all."

"Good. And I don't want to hear any whining 'wah Carmen's being mean to me. wah.'," She imitated an exaggerated crying voice and gestured fake tears rolling down her cheeks as she spoke. "Got it?"

"Carmen," Sarah said, glaring in stern defiance. "You couldn't make me whine if you tried."

Carmen raised her eyebrows. "Really? Is that so?"

"Very much so."

"I think I'd like to test that," Carmen replied with a whisper.

Sarah raised her eyebrows back at her in a fearless dare. "Would you?"

Sarah and Carmen locked expressions, each sporting a stern glare that they used just before pouncing on unsuspecting prey. It was only for a moment but that mere instant in time seemed to stretch on for eons.

Without warning, Carmen swung at her opponent. Sarah raised an arm and blocked the attack just seconds before impact. Sarah threw a straight jab to which Carmen raised her glove, parrying the attack as well as the swift combination that was launched afterward. Carmen then pounded Sarah in the ribs unexpectedly before arching her fist forward toward her cheek. Sarah only had half a second to lean backward, avoiding the powerful blow by a narrow margin.

The fight was on. Sarah and Carmen gritted their teeth, increasing their momentum and speed with every strike. The two circled each other after the first combination of fisticuffs. Carmen danced around the ring, keeping her mind on her footing as she prepared for her next onslaught. Sarah shifted the weight on her feet before switching combat stances. She squinted her eyes as Carmen launched her second attack. She saw her monstrous fist inching towards her face in slow motion. Sarah bobbed her head to the left, dodging the punch before throwing a swift counterattack. Sarah threw jab after jab, right hook after left but Carmen's instincts were much sharper than she expected.

Every movement was timed with the rhythm of a beating drum. Carmen shifted her guard, instantaneously, sporting sharp wit as she defended herself from Sarah's onslaught. She blocked every strike before raising her arm and parrying a swift hook that Sarah had thrust her hip into. The maneuver had not only halted her advance but caused her to stumble just the slightest bit. Sarah was sent spinning into the ropes with a mean right hook.

Sarah clutched onto the ropes, composing herself and nearly reeling in dismay from Carmen's strike.

"What do you think?" Carmen whipped the sweat from her brow. "Pretty spry for such a little thing, aren't I?"

Sarah turned to face the fierce woman in front of her. Her eyes widened and her heart tightened in her chest.

"How does it feel? Hurts, don't it?" Carmen placed her hands on her hip, her expression shone with pride. "What was it that you said? That you thought that I was all bark and no bite? Well, this female dog is about to hand your ass to you on a silver platter." Carmen pointed a finger at Sarah in a fierce warning. "You can expect to get smacked around like that quite often if you don't get your act together."

Sarah turned her body towards the woman in front of her and wiped her mouth with slow methodical movements. She felt a tiny cut on her bottom lip and her blood stirred with adrenaline. At that moment it dawned on her, that despite the opposing temperaments She and Carmen Rivera were very much alike. This was the sort of conflict that both women lived for.

"That's it," Carmen instructed. "Let the hurt in. Let the anger in. Let it marinate a bit. And then dish it right back out."

Sarah cocked her head to the side, letting Carmen's punch swell in her pores. As Carmen ordered she let the anger and the pain in but something else entered her bloodstream as well. Bliss. There was nowhere else that she would rather be at that moment. Carmen's attack had brought her to life in a way that nothing else had before. The trash talk, the adrenaline rush, and the flow of attacks one after another. It was a thrill and one that she hadn't relished so much in months. Despite Carmen's unsavory manners Sarah couldn't help but be immensely grateful that she had met the girl.

Sarah Stryker raised her gloves and Carmen returned the same courtesy. The two approached each other before plunging into another bout. Carmen blocked each attack through a slight stagger before striking Sarah in the stomach and the rib. Sarah placed her gloves over her stomach, blocking the next round of attacks before striking Carmen across the cheek with a stunning blow.

Carmen placed her tongue in her cheek, feeling the same embarrassment that Sarah had felt earlier. She cracked her neck before swinging her fists forward, this time thrusting her hip into it just like Sarah had done.

The ring vibrated and shook under the tremendous weight of the two women as they stamped their feet. Sarah swung as her opponent lunged forward. Carmen crouched to the ground, relishing the look of dismay on Sarah's face as she avoided her strikes by a wide margin before hitting her with a three-punch combo to the ribs. She intended on finishing it with a brutal uppercut, but Sarah leaned back and dodged it at the last possible second. Carmen parried Sarah's next string of punches with her gloves before throwing a feint toward the body and striking her across the cheek when she misplaced her guard.

The next minute was a blur in Sarah's mind. She remembered her struggle to recover after Carmen sent her head spinning with a three-hit combo. She placed her forearm in front of her and caught Carmen in the chin with a swift uppercut after she made a predictable attempt at a body blow. The maneuver put some distance between the two girls and Sarah was able to gather her thoughts and formulate a plan.

"Alright stop."

The sudden declaration by Carmen snapped Sarah out of combat mode. She stared at Carmen with a wide-eyed expression, noticing a tiny cut where she had hit her.

"That's enough for now," Carmen said.

"What's the matter? Don't think that you'll be able to go on?" Sarah challenged, still reeling with adrenaline.

Carmen chuckled. "Oh no, trust me there's nothing that I'd love more than for this to go the distance. But if I did then I wouldn't have the strength to fight that other bitch and if what you said about her is true, I'm going to need all that I can spare. But don't you worry." Carmen narrowed her expression. "When this business with Miriam and Anastasia is finished, we're duking it out, right here in the ring," she said, deliberately mispronouncing Maryam's name in a condescending tone. "Because by then there will only be two alpha females left in this city. And that may just be one too many."

Sarah's expression perked with intrigue. She contemplated Carmen's words, perturbed by the fact that they filled her heart with excitement rather than dread.

"Hey guys!"

Sarah and Carmen hopped out of the ring, taking notice of the energetic blonde that came to visit.

"Did y'all start training already?"

Amy Stryker stormed through the gym, dressing in a similar getup as her teammates, and carrying three water bottles in between her delicate hands. Her expression oozed with naivety yet her muscular physique seemed to display a similar level of power as her two older, and more experienced teammates. She handed one bottle to Carmen and another to Sarah before taking a sip of her own.

Sarah took a large gulp of water, choosing to close her eyes and savor the swoosh of it in her mouth. She gulped down and sighed in relief.

Amy eyed her sister with an observant gaze. “Better?"

Sarah nodded. "Yes. Thanks, Amy."

"No problem."

"Girl, you're a lifesaver you know that?" Carmen took a large swig of water. Her eyes widened as she rinsed it in her mouth, the desire to speak reaching her before she swallowed. "You just missed it. This girl and I just had our first sparring match."

Amy's eyes widened in disbelief. "What? You two fought? For real?"

"Yeah, I mean it was only for a few minutes but man what a rush."

Amy gave a stern look towards her sister. "You showed her who's boss right?"

Carmen scoffed. "Bitch, please. I kicked that ass," She said before taking another gulp of water."

Sarah shrugged, crossing her arm to mask her awkwardness. "We hadn't gone on long enough to say for sure."

Carmen let out a forced chuckle. "That's a lie."

"Excuse me?" Sarah shot her glaring eyes toward the woman beside her. She tapped onto the back of her earlobe with her forefinger. "Mind repeating that?"

A sly smile escaped Carmen's lips. "You heard me."

Sarah lowered her voice to a stern whisper. "Are you calling me a liar?"

Carmen leaned her head forward before speaking to her blonde-haired counterpart with intent. "Well, last I checked that's what you are when you tell a fib now, isn't it?"

"Guys." Amy's naive tone of voice snapped both girls out of their standoff. "We're supposed to be working together, remember? Because I'll put both of you in your place if I have to."

Sarah and Carmen shot a fierce gaze toward the girl in front of them, their eyes shone with bemusement as they locked onto her. Amy could feel her feet sink from where she stood. She widened her mouth into a phony smile, wincing a bit before she spoke again.

"Just kidding. Thought I'd you know lighten the mood. Because the tension was really brewing in here."

Carmen took another gulp of water before pointing her finger at Amy in intrigue. "You know what though? You just got me thinking. I'm ready for the next round."

Carmen sat her bottle down on the bench before rolling underneath the ropes and back into the ring. She bounced up and down on the balls of her feet, warming her body as she prepared for the next onslaught.

"Alright, so who's next?" She scanned the two sisters in front of her, squinting as she scanned one from head to toe. "I've already taken on the head, given her plenty of reason to consider me a legitimate threat.
So how about you?"

Amy's eyes widened as Carmen locked onto her. "What?"

"You're up little sis. It's time for a spanking and believe me when I tell you that I'm going to enjoy it quite a bit."

"Me? B-b-but what about you and Sarah? I-I thought that-"

"B-b-b but nothing," Carmen said, imitating Amy's voice. "You want to be a great fighter like your sister or not? Or do you want to be the same scared little mouse that you were when you two were kids?"

Amy's heart sunk in her chest. She furrowed her eyebrows in protest. "What?"

Carmen smiled. "You heard me."

"You don't know anything about what I was like when we were kids. You weren't even there."

"I don't have to be. I can tell."

"You don't know anything," Amy walked towards the edge of the ring, her heart rising in her chest. "You think that you're so tough and you have all the answers to everything, but you don't. You think I'm some scared little mouse? I get scared. Everyone gets scared. That doesn't mean I won't fight if I have to. If someone threatens me or my sister you better believe I will," She spoke through her teeth.

"Oh," Carmen questioned. "Then show me."

Amy gave a concerned look to her sister behind her. Sarah stood still with her arms folded. She hadn't spoken a word during the exchange, instead choosing to give Amy her answer with a subtle nod of approval. The gesture produced a thousand emotions within Amy, she felt her muscles tense as she turned her gaze back toward Carmen.

"Well? Are you just going to stand there all day or what?"

"I'm not a boxer. I don't know the rules."

"There's a first time for everything. Don't you worry about that. I'll walk you through it, show you the ropes. I promise I won't hurt you." Carmen shrugged, realizing that she was lying. "Much."

Amy said nothing in reply. She curled her lips as she weighed the girl up and down. She was no more than a hundred and forty pounds. She had the same muscle mass and stood at the same height. Then what was it about this girl that allowed her to exude so much authority and grace?

"Come on? Weren't you the one that said you could take me back downtown? This is your chance to prove it. This may be your last chance to pay me back for pushing you off the bed back at the hotel."

"Oh, so now you remember?" Amy exclaimed. "Because as I recall when I cornered you about it, you decided to play dumb."

"Bitch, get your ass in this ring before I drag you in myself."

Amy leaped into the ring without a second thought. She edged towards Carmen, sporting the meanest gaze that she could muster. Carmen placed her hands on her hips, examining the girl from head to toe, reading her with even greater precision than she did her older sister.

"Well, here I am," Amy said with a gentle shrug.

Carmen locked onto her prey; her lips fixed into a conniving grin. "You ready?"

"Yeah, I'm ready."

"Alright. Time to see what you got little girl." Carmen raised her fists in front of her. Amy could feel them clench and tighten. She began to consider whether Carmen had lied about holding back. "Come on. Put 'em up."

"Oh." Amy mimicked her friend's gesture, raising her fists and tightening them with equal force, causing her knuckles to crack under the weight of her strength.

"Don't get me wrong. I don't mind staring at your pretty little face all day but personally, I'd rather punch it in."

Amy scoffed, shaking her head in annoyance as she prepared to attack. Her heart swelled up as she circled her opponent around the ring. Carmen wasn't any stronger than she was. She had a chance to win.

"Alright. We'll take it slow for the first minute and then go all out for the last two."

"Okay." Amy furrowed her brow. "Wait what? That leaves us only three minutes."

"Well, you'll most likely be on the ground by then."

"Yeah right. Or maybe you'll be on the ground. Ever consider that?"

"Sweetie," Carmen spoke with condescension oozing out of her voice as she bounced up and down. "I doubt that you'll be able to land a single blow, to be honest. You're too clumsy."

Amy's heart sank into the pit of her stomach. "Oh yeah?" She arched forward, taking a massive swing towards her target. Carmen performed an evasive sidestep, reversing their position in an instant.

"Like that."

"Come on Amy," Sarah called out from where she stood outside the ring. "Keep your balance. Don't let the pressure you're under get to you. This is just another fight and you've been in dozens just like it."

"Not just like it," Carmen corrected her. "She was dealing with grunts then. Now she's dealing with a Queen. And Queens don't play nice when they're instructing students under their care. You should know."

"Oh, just shut up and fight," Amy exclaimed, her voice oozing with irritation.

Carmen's eyes widened in dismay. "Oh really? You want me to shut up and fight don't yah? You want me to shut." She thrust her arm forward and jabbed Amy in the nose. "Up." She jabbed her again, causing her to bop her head back and forth. "And fight?"

Amy gasped, sucking air into her lungs in response to Carmen's attack. She gritted her teeth and threw a wide right hook in her direction, but the experienced Latina was far too sharp to be taken down by such a simple maneuver. She parried her attack before sending Amy spinning with a powerful right hook over her own.

"I told you if you keep giving me lip, we're going to have problems."

Amy turned back towards her opponent, her face reddened as adrenaline pumped through her veins and flowed through her bloodstream.

"You want to talk big like a grown woman? Fine, then I'll beat you like a grown woman. I was going to take it slow but now you'll have to learn the hard way."

Amy bit her swollen lip, her entire being fuming with anger as she lunged forward. She decided to mimic Carmen's movements and threw several jabs at her head. Carmen leaned back, bobbing her head several times instantaneously before ducking low and halting Amy's advance with a few breathtaking body shots.

Amy heaved as Carmen's attacks triggered a current through her body, causing her to lose control of her motor functions just long enough to be hit with a swift four-punch combo, the last of which was a stunning uppercut from Carmen's left hand. Amy staggered backward, nearly tripping on her own feet as a result.

"Focus Amy. Remember your technique."

Amy caught herself and her footing at the last possible second. Sarah's words surged through her ears like wildfire. She positioned herself on the balls of her feet before taking a few protective steps away from her opponent.

"Yeah, come on Amy, focus. I haven't even put any weight behind these punches. You're better than this. You're letting your fear get in the way like I said."

There it was. The sly smile that Carmen had been wearing before plastered over her face. Her opponent was enjoying this. She was enjoying embarrassing her in front of her sister.

Amy decided to mix things up. She ducked a forward jab from Carmen before aiming a fierce body shot that she hoped would throw her off guard. Carmen crouched and brought her arms in front of her stomach before Amy was able to connect with a second blow. Amy gritted her teeth as she swung wildly, hitting her opponent with multiple blows in quick succession. Carmen countered her attack before sending Amy reeling back with a five-punch combo, two blows to the body and three to the chin, ending it in another uppercut that popped her out of her crouched state.

"Keep your guard up. Relax. Your opponent is unpredictable. Be the same," Sarah said.

"Yeah, kinda hard when you're used to being as predictable as the sunrise," Carmen said, responding to Sarah's advice. Amy rolled her eyes in annoyance.

"Ignore her," Sarah addressed her sister. "Focus on your own actions. Don't let her words get to you."

"Wrong," Carmen exclaimed with a fierce point of her forefinger towards Sarah. "Let the words in. Let them do their thing. Those emotions are there for a reason."

Sarah sighed. She knew what Carmen was doing but it didn't make her backtalk get to her any less. She could only hope that Amy hadn't internalized those words, or the match could end for her at any second.

"Come on girl. I haven't even broken a sweat. Are you really going to let a tiny little thing like me do this to you in front of your sister?"

Amy curled her lips, taking a few deep breaths in and out as she summoned her energy.

"That's it. Get mad," Carmen muttered, her expression shone with delight as she prepared for the next round of fisticuffs.

Amy lunged forward once again. Carmen blocked her initial attack as expected only this time when she struck her back, Amy brought her arm in front of her blonde hair, shielding herself and giving her ample opportunity to counter-attack.

The next minute was a whirlwind of fast strikes. Amy blocked Carmen's swift body shots and gritted her teeth once her opponent had risen to her level, throwing a right hook after left with the occasional jab. The two girls unloaded a series of combo attacks at a rapid pace. It seemed that the reminder that her sister would be disappointed if she failed was all that Amy needed to spur her on.

At the last minute of the barrage of punches, Amy managed to sock her opponent in the belly. Carmen hunched over and Amy socked her again and again before rising and sending her staggering back towards the ropes.

"That's it, Amy. You're improving," Sarah said. "Be as relaxed as you can but remember to stay focused. Don't forget your breathing either."

"Damn girl. Gotta admit I wasn't quite expecting that." Carmen wiped the bit of blood that dripped from the corner of her mouth. "That's the hardest I've been hit in months."

"Told you that I can fight," Amy said, her face shone with a sly confidence. "Watch, and I just might be able to beat you too."

Carmen stiffened her neck in shock. "Really? Is that what you think?"

"It's what I know," Amy confirmed.

Carmen placed a tongue in her mouth, sizing her opponent up and down. "Alright then. Time to get serious."

Amy narrowed her eyes as she prepared for the plunge. To her surprise, Carmen didn't strike right away. She dropped her hands at her sides before stretching her arms out in front of and behind her. She stretched them back until they popped, causing Amy to wince a bit before she dropped her jaw. Carmen tilted her head back and forth, cracking it in the process. She then pounded her gloves together and stomped her feet on the ground in a stern combat stance. The gesture sent a ripple effect through the ring, one that rivaled Amy's ability to shift mass and weight in her favor. Her eyes widened with a look of slight confusion as she raised her fists to match her opponent.

"For the next two minutes, we go all out. The last woman standing gets bragging rights," Carmen declared.

"Come on Amy," Sarah whispered.

"You ready?" Carmen challenged.

"Yeah, I'm ready. Are you?" Amy fired back.

Carmen lowered her chin and shifted her right foot from side to side. She stretched her hands out as she prepared for the plunge. The next bout would be the fiercest of the night and she was determined to make the most of it.

The two girls lunged forward at the same time, swinging their fists forward in unison. Amy threw a barrage of strikes toward her opponent and Carmen bobbed and weaved before unleashing a swift combination of her own. Amy raised her guard and shifted between parrying with her left and right arm. She caught Carmen with a two-punch combo that nearly made her stagger, but she caught herself and jabbed her in the nose. Amy's eyes watered with disorientation, but she knew she couldn't let up yet. She rammed her fist into Carmen's abdomen before shooting her head upward with a sudden uppercut.

Amy went for a follow-up attack and the two girl's fists collided with each other, causing the ring to shake with chaotic fervor. Amy blocked a punch with her forearm before ramming her closed fist into Carmen's nose repeatedly. She swung her fist forward and smashed it into Carmen's left cheek, making her spin backward. Amy lunged forward but was thrown off guard by Carmen, who spun back towards her and threw a feint towards her left cheek before hitting her in the right.

The next minute was a series of blows sustained by both fighters. Amy caught Carmen with a few strikes, but her opponent managed to recover before ramming her fist into Amy's breasts and ribs. She felt her breath being knocked out of her and brought her arms in front of her body in defense, allowing Carmen to smash her over the head with a fierce barrage of strikes. In all the confusion and loss of coordination, Amy hadn't even expected or noticed when she tripped over her feet. Amy fell, landing on her rear end with a sudden thud.

"Well, that was a rush."

Carmen flung her gloves across the room, savoring victory and her solidified status as queen. Sarah's eyes widened.

Amy bent her head backward and caught her breath. It was only a few seconds ago that she was elated, the most enthralled she had been in months and all it took was one fall to reduce her back to the woman she was before.

"We'll look at you. Thinking you're all high and mighty one minute and the next you're ready to call the quits?"

Carmen noticed the look in Amy's eyes and gave a gentle nudge on her foot to snap her out of her frozen state. "What's the matter, girlfriend? You wanna go for another round or what?"

Amy shook her head.

"Yeah, me neither. That took the wind out of me." Carmen wiped her sweating forehead, slowly regaining control over her breathing before placing her hands on her hips. "That was something. Still, the outcome was pretty much what I expected."

"Yeah. I guess I'm not a real woman in your book huh?" Amy said, lowering her gaze in embarrassment.

Carmen examined her opponent from head to toe before giving her a reply. "No. Not yet. But hey you're under the tutelage of the two baddest bitches that you're likely to meet. Stick with us. We'll get you there."

Carmen then did something that Amy hadn't predicted and offered her hand. Amy looked up noticing a warm smile on the girl's face. Amy accepted the offer and was given an even more pleasant surprise when Carmen lifted her off the ground and pulled her into a gentle embrace. She released her and cupped her gentle hands into her own.

"I love you. You know that right?"

"I love you too." Amy squinted, questioning her choice of words. "At least I think I do. Most of the time."

"It's okay." Carmen shook her head, her expression shone with more understanding than Amy had seen on her in a while. "You don't have to love me back. I'm a lot to deal with. I know. From time to time I'm going to kick your ass into shape. I know it ticks you off but what you're feeling now? A girl needs that if she's going to survive in this world. Better you learn through me than through the next bitch who decides to stab you in the back when you're not looking. But if you need anything I'm here for you."

Sarah smiled; her expression shone with contentment.

"Tell you what. Because you were a good sport, I'll let you use the bag for the next twenty minutes. I'm going to take a breather and spend a bit of time with your girl over there. Pound away. Imagine it's me in place of it. It's not like you have a chance of beating me anyway," Carmen said with a conniving smile. Amy rolled her eyes as Carmen walked towards the corner of the ring. Amy approached the punching bag as Sarah entered the ring.

"What do you think? Am I teacher material?" Carmen said, addressing the girl beside her.

Sarah shrugged. "You've got the strength. Though teaching requires commitment and quite a lot of patience."

Sarah and Carmen stood side by side as they watched Amy approach the punching bag with her fist raised in the air.

Amy hit the bag with all her might, adrenaline still running through her like boiling water. Carmen's words had elevated Amy beyond what she had expected. Her heart surged with fervor. She had not only one but two women in her corner who were both as determined to make her the strongest that she could be.

Sarah and Carmen's jaws dropped in unison. The punching bag was detached from its support line in an instant, soaring through the air and flying through the door of the gym, leaving its contents flying everywhere after it burst open. Amy stood with her hand stretched out and her fist tightened, bending the mass around her.

Sarah stood with a wide-eyed expression. She had a feeling that she could see the same feat several times and still be fascinated with it. Amy turned around, beaming at her peers, her expression shone with innocence and naivety. Carmen turned towards Sarah.

"Now imagine if she was as pissed off as we are?"

Later that night, Sarah sat on her bed at the hotel with her legs stretched out, leaning against the wall as she spoke on her cell. It had been a minute since she had an update from her teammate downtown and her heart churned as a result. If nothing else, she at least wanted to hear that Kyle Harper had an inkling of the identity of the man that she was searching for.

"Sorry Sarah. I still haven't found a name."

"Sarah's eyes widened in dismay. "Nothing?"

"Well, I mean I found a great deal about The Serpents. But it seems like they cover their tracks pretty well." Kyle scanned his surroundings, standing outside of his welding shop as he spoke. "I know that there are a lot of predators among the bunch and a lot of them participate in some rather perverse methods of torture, manipulation, and control. But none based on the reference that you're looking for. Neither based on the specific rather heinous action that you described. Either this guy has hidden himself well or his action isn't unique and the rest of them do the same."

"No," Sarah chimed in. "The rest of the gang was perverse but there was one that was different. I'm telling you with him it was more intimate. He treats it like an art form. There are bound to be reports on it. Check for survivors."

"I did," Kyle replied. "No such luck. There weren't very many survivors of The Serpents when they were in power and at their peak and now well, let's just say that they are pretty scarce. Very few will risk a confrontation with anyone formidable.

"So? Anything else?" Sarah prompted.

"Not at the moment," Kyle admitted.

Sarah pursed her lips, as she contemplated what her next action would be. Even though Anastasia was a bigger threat than her mystery man could ever be, she wanted this man dead more than anything else in the world. In fact, she wanted him worse than dead. He had humiliated her, and she would return the same courtesy. She wanted to wrap her cold sturdy hands around his throat just to watch him wriggle in agony. Then she could have her way with him. It had been a dream of hers for several months and yet the man she had trusted to help bring it into fruition wasn't living up to her expectations, either because he didn't want to or maybe he wasn't the genius that she believed he was.

"Sarah?" Kyle squinted in thoughtful bemusement. "You seem tense."

"Can't imagine why," She bit back.

"Hey, I spent all day yesterday searching the web for a lead. I'm doing the best that I can here."

"Do better."

Kyle's neck stiffened and he let out a nervous chuckle before giving his reply. "Uh, Sarah. I'm sorry who do you think that you're talking to?"

Sarah raised her eyebrows. "Who do I think I'm talking to?"

"Yeah. I'm not your errand boy."

Sarah shook her head. "I would never demean you like that. And to answer your question I think I'm talking to a man with a two hundred plus IQ whose knowledge and expertise extend to every field of study. I don't think it's unreasonable to expect him to locate a lone predator in Seattle, do you? If so, then perhaps you're not who I thought you were."

"And who do you think I am?" Kyle challenged.

"Someone that I can trust. The one in a sea of a thousand that I can count on."

Kyle's heart skipped a beat. "Well, when you put it that way."

Sarah stroked her hair, lowering her defenses before speaking again. "Plus, once I find him and raid The Serpents warehouse there's bound to be plenty of money stashed inside."

"Money?" Kyle's eyes widened in intrigue.

Sarah nodded. "Hmm hmm."

"Well in that case, yes ma'am I'll get right on it." Kyle changed his tone to that of a soldier going to battle. "I don't care where he's gone or how elusive he thinks he is that fiend is not escaping the knowing ever-watchful eye of Kyle Harper."

Sarah placed her tongue on her cheek. "I thought so."

"So, how have you been holding up? Any luck locating Anastasia?"

"Well, she's certainly located us. But the hunt for Anastasia has to be put on hold. Carmen is challenging Maryam Bahira to a boxing match."

"She's what?" Kyle exclaimed.

Sarah shook her head in annoyance. "Yeah, I don't like it but-"

She stopped in her tracks and averted her gaze towards the door, noticing the voice of a woman shouting from the other side. "There she is now."

"Ah hell," Kyle said, his voice oozing with irritation.

"Let me know when you make any progress in locating our mystery man. I'll call back soon."

"Will do. Be safe Sarah."

"Alright bye."

Carmen came barging into the room only a second after Sarah hung up. She was on the phone as well, having an intense shouting match with Maryam's friend Desiree, presumably over the argument that they had the day before.

"No bitch I say what I mean, and I mean what I say. What don't you understand about that?"

Carmen leaned over her shoulders, speaking with ever-increasing volume as she walked towards her friend's bed. "No, we are not going to negotiate. Your girl wants to throw down and so do I. Birds of a feather we are. So, you're going to be a good little girl and not interfere, okay?"

Sarah wasn't certain but she thought she heard Desiree mention something about her not wanting to instigate or start a fight and Carmen's eyebrows curled with anger. "Bitch I don't care how old you are. Hope you learned a valuable lesson. Don't step up unless you're prepared to take it all the way, cause you better believe that I am."

Desiree said something else in reply. All Sarah could decipher was the name, Anastasia.

"That's what my girl tried to tell you, dumbass. But she tried to make it all about her. Well, that's fine. Two can play at that game. Tell her I'll be at her place in the arena. Tomorrow afternoon. Be there. Bring all of your friends Because my girls will be there too. We can have us a mini brawl after the match is over if you all feel raw about losing."

Sarah heard Desiree say, "Okay but you're asking for it." It was the clearest she had heard her speak during the entire exchange.

"Right back at ya. Bye bitch."

Carmen looked up at Sarah after she hung up, noticing her staring at her with the same thoughtful expression she often wore on her face when she was concerned.

"What? Why are you staring at me like that?"

"This is really important to you, isn't it?" Sarah spoke in a low-level voice. The words triggered Carmen's sensitivities. She shrugged before averting her gaze toward the floor.

"I don't know. I guess I just like to be here for my girls when I can. I didn't appreciate how uncooperative that bitch was. I mean yeah, I like to stir up trouble as much as the next, but I'll be there for you in a pinch if you need me, especially in a fight. I've proven just as much so far, haven't I?"

Sarah nodded. "I just wish you could help in a way that didn't involve fighting Maryam. She could be our best shot at beating Anastasia."

"Yeah, well if wishes were horses. Speaking of which I really wish your girl would stop hogging the bathroom so much."

"Oh no." Sarah's eyes widened. "You're on your own on that one. You may end up getting into another fistfight over it."

Carmen squinted her eyes in annoyance. "How do you put up with her?"

"I mentioned patience, didn't I?"

Amy barged into the room right on time. She had a moist towel wrapped around her body and beamed as her two teammates turned toward her. "Alright, all freshened up and ready to go. Your turn Carmen."

Carmen rolled her eyes before approaching Amy. "Bout time you took a shower. You smell."

"No, I don't," Amy protested.

"Yes, you do. Like really smell. Literally, I thought a man followed us inside the room when we came back. That's unacceptable."

"Bitch," Amy muttered under her breath. Carmen shot her head back after hearing that remark, letting go of the door handle to the other room.

"What did you just call me?"

"You heard me."

Carmen shook her head in disapproval. "We already had this convo sugar. You want me to embarrass you in front of big sis?"

"Yeah, and we're going to keep having it," Amy bit back. She stepped in front of the Latina's face and jabbed a finger towards her chest. Carmen could taste the hot water and moist shampoo soaked in her hair. "I respect you. But don't think that I'm going to let you push me around because you're older than me. From time to time I'm going to give you a little attitude if I want. Let you in on my feels. Sarah knows and gives me leeway. Bout time you wise up and deal with it, sugar. If not and you've got a problem with that then we can go at it in the ring for another round."

"Really? Anxious to go back after how much I beat on you the first time. I mean I'm not tired of it, but I figured you'd want a break," Carmen said with a sly smile.

"Didn't you say you've been boxing since you were a little girl? It's my first time. I do karate like Sarah. I feel handicapped without being allowed to kick or elbow or use my knees. It's a lot to get used to. But give me a few months to get into the swing of things. I'll take you down."

"Really? Care to wager a bet on that?"

"Yup. And you'd lose," Amy declared.

Carmen couldn't help but be amused by her friend's newfound confidence. "Alright. I'll let you slide this one time. But next time I'm taking you up on your offer. And you better not back down. And don't hesitate or whine either. I'm going to put you through the wringer little girl."

"Oh, please do." Amy challenged. She turned towards her sister after Carmen had left the room, beaming with newfound vigor. "What do you think? Stood up to her like a boss, didn't I?'

Sarah nodded, allowing a faint smile to escape her face before turning her attention back to her cell phone. Her attention was so diverted by it that she hadn't noticed Amy bounce on her bed with the full weight of her rear end and peer over her shoulder.

"Who are you talking to?"

"Oh, no one. Just a friend I met online." Sarah noticed that she had received a text message from Stephanie White, asking when the best time for the two to speak again would be. Sarah wished that she had texted her another time. She couldn't deal with this now.

"What friend? Someone from school?"

"Uh Amy, it's kinda private," Sarah said, stumbling over her words.

Amy's neck stiffened. She examined Sarah for a moment, confusion plastered over her face as she tried to ascertain whether she had misheard her.

"I mean it's not that I don't want to tell you. It's just that a lot going on right now. You know with The Pride and everything. I would just rather not burden you with this," Sarah thought of the quickest excuse she could come up with. She didn't think her sister would buy it but to her relief, Amy stood up.

"O-okay. Sure. We don't have to talk about it if you don't want to. It's just, it seems like it's been a while since we just you know talked? I mean I spoke to you about Leland. Why can't you tell me about your friend?" Amy prompted, softening her voice to a degree that she hoped would make her sister vulnerable.

"We can talk. It's just-" Sarah paused, thinking of the best reply. "There are some things that I need for myself. You understand, don't you?"

"Sure," Amy said. She yawned and stretched her arms out before heading for the door.

"Amy, you understand right? I mean I can always tell you about it later. I just-"

"No, no, it's okay. I get you. You want your privacy." Amy shrugged, feigning nonchalance. "That's okay."

"We're cool, right? I just have a lot on my plate right now."

"Yeah, I get you. I just wished you would be more consistent. First, you want my help. Then you don't. One minute you bare your soul, next you feel too shy to tell me who you're texting. I just wish you'd make up your mind."

"Things are really complicated right now," Sarah said.

Amy gestured with her hands. "That's why having someone to confide in can help-"

"Amy," Sarah scolded, her eyes raised in warning. Amy raised her hands in mocking surrender.

"Okay okay. I know when to back off."

"We'll talk later okay."

"You promise?" Amy asked, her expression shone with tenderness and concern. Sarah nodded in affirmation.

"Alright, that's all I need for now." She tightened the towel around her bosom. "I think I'm going to mess with Carmen a bit more. Lord knows that I love putting that bitch in her place. Night Sarah."

"Night." Sarah waited until Amy left to mutter to herself. "Master of the guilt trip, same as always." She put her phone down on the dresser beside the bed and lay backward. She remained in a meditative position, relaxing her muscles until her breathing became faint and the warm affectionate embrace of deep uninterrupted sleep found her at last.

Chapter 10: Raging Fists

Sarah felt her body swimming through the vortex of her subconscious mind. She wanted to reach out with her hands, to grip onto anything that would help anchor her back to reality as the sounds of screeching voices and malicious taunts violated her eardrums. Upon every turn of her head, she saw them, the enemy that she was determined to defeat surrounded her from all sides. That was when it hit her. The dark tunnel was created by the woman she was hunting, the one warrior who unnerved Sarah more than any other.

"Sarah. Oh, Sarah. Where are you?"

Sarah continued to fall, her body weightless as the evil conniving voice of the woman soon to be her greatest adversary, penetrated her heart. She tumbled through several stories before the dream ended, all the while catching glimpses and flashes from her past amidst the suffocating darkness. She saw images of The Serpents, the men who through their actions had been the root cause of her damnation, one sickly pale-skinned, black-haired Serpent drew her attention and boiled her blood. There were also images of her mother and sister scattered throughout, images that she was desperate to reach out and grasp but they faded away from her the quicker she fell.

One image stayed with her throughout the dream. It was hardly visible, the silhouette of the woman that she would soon meet once again filled her heart with dread and uncertainty.

"Who are you?" Sarah asked.

"I'm you. Free of your inhibitions. I'm what you could have been had you not allowed your weakness to consume your fragile heart. I'm everything that you desire and all that you crave. And for as long as you are here, I will be as well."

Sarah Stryker awoke to the sudden sunlight of the early morning and the greeting of an unwelcome obstacle. It only took her a few moments, still reeling from her lifelike dream, to remember what was in store for the team that day.

"How are my girls doing? Get a good night's rest?" Carmen stormed inside the house after Sarah entered the room and Amy sat up, jolted awake by the loud opening, and shutting of the door. Sarah nodded, before crossing her arms uncomfortably.

"Yes," She muttered.

"No," Amy said at the same time, rubbing her eyes with her palms as her vision and awareness returned.

"Well, maybe this will help wake you up." Carmen threw a granola bar toward Amy and she caught it with her two hands.

"Thanks," Amy said, her voice shone with tenderness.

"You bought groceries?" Sarah said, with a bemused look towards Carmen.

"Just a few things from the store that's all. I got fruit and a few granolas. Some bread. Let's see." Carmen ruffled through the bags. "Oh yeah, eggs. After I beat that bitches ass we can make ourselves an omelet in celebration."

"Those apples are ripe right?"

Carmen got the hint and picked one of the apples from the batch and lunged it toward her friend. Sarah caught it and used the tip of her ice blue polished forefinger nail to slice it open before placing it on her tongue. Sarah closed her eyes for a few seconds, savoring the taste of it. The nourishment, however small did much to filter out the toxic thoughts swimming through her head because of her latest dream.

"Better?" Carmen asked. Sarah nodded. "Now what do we say?"

"Thanks."

"Yeah, thanks, Carmen," Amy chimed in, her mouth full of food. "You're a cool chick once you get to know you. You're not like what people say that you are."

Carmen averted her gaze towards the ground, biting her lip in a bashful gesture. "I just have a soft spot for my girls that's all." She walked towards the bed, pulling the covers over her legs and sitting beside Amy.

"So, are we going to work out before we go?" Sarah asked.

"Oh no, I'm ready," Carmen said, her eyes widening with fervor.

"The fight is not until this afternoon, right? We still have a bit of time," Sarah suggested. "Maybe we could have another sparring match."

"Nah I'm good. I tend not to work out too much when I know I'm going to fight that day. I'll warm up a bit about half an hour before the fight but that's it."

Sarah gave a stern look towards the woman soon to be in the ring with one of the great boxers in the country. "You sure you're going to be okay?"

"Yeah, I'm sure. We already talked about this yesterday girlfriend," Carmen said, her voice tinted with such the slightest bit of irritation. Amy gave an eager wide-eyed look towards Sarah's apple and Sarah, without a word, cut it in half, giving her sister the bigger piece. Amy beamed in delight before taking a massive bite out of it.

"We talked and now we're going to talk again," Sarah said, her voice laced in a fierce warning. "You don't have to do this."

"Yeah. I herdbb she wwb reeelly sstorng." Amy struggled to speak after stuffing her face with a bite out of her apple."

"Wwhhta hhs what was that?" Carmen mocked. "Do you want to repeat that girlfriend?"

Amy smiled in embarrassment, taking a moment to catch her breath and swallow before speaking again. "I heard she was really strong."

Carmen glared in response. "So am I. You found that out yourself yesterday."

"Okay? Sure. But what if she's stronger?"

"Remember what I told you? I've been in more fights in my life than I can count. I've fought entire gangs single-handedly."

"Okay?' Amy shrugged. "That's great but maybe she has too. You don't know."

"There's no maybe about it. Maryam Bahira has earned her reputation for a reason," Sarah said, crossing her arms as she addressed Carmen. "Despite her less than graceful personality, she's immensely powerful and shouldn't be taken for granted. You haven't heard the stories of what has happened to the fighters she's beaten."

"Not my problem. Now stop crowding me. I've already made my decision."

"Girl, would you stop being so stubborn and just listen to Sarah? She's smart and she knows what she's talking about," Amy said, her voice rising with irritation oozing out of them.

Carmen's eyes widened in a stern warning. "You take that tone with me again and I'll kick you off this bed."

A sly smirk appeared over Amy's face. "Oh, I wish you would Carmen."

"Oh, you wish I would?" Carmen repeated, leaning forward in a threatening manner.

"I really wish you would. I'm known to be rather cranky in the morning. Even Sarah knows not to mess with me when I'm like this."

"Uh guys," Sarah prompted, snapping the two girls out of their playful banter.

Amy shot her gaze towards her sister. "Oh. Sorry."

"This is serious. Don't let your guard down Carmen. Not for a single solitary second. It'll make all the difference in the world. Remember that."

"I gotcha. Don't worry. I've handled girls like her my whole life. Anastasia is the one we have to worry about, right?"

Sarah's eyes widened, showing the faintest amount of concern. "I'd say there's more than enough worrying to go for the both of them."

"Well, I'll tell you what as a gesture of good faith, I'll let you get the first crack at her, Anastasia I mean. I hate to admit it, but that bitch is crazy. Maybe even more than I am, and should we get her cornered there's no guarantee that she'll fight fair. If she throws us a curveball, I trust you to be the one to get the job done."

"I appreciate that," Sarah said.

"What about me?" Amy asked.

"What about you sweetie?" Carmen replied, her voice shone with condescension.

"Well, who do I get the first crack at?" Amy exchanged glances between her sister and her friend, eager for an immediate response. Instead, all she was given was a sharp glare from the expressions of both girls. Amy sunk into her seat.

"Just thought I'd ask," She mumbled, averting her gaze down towards the bed.

The team arrived at their destination relatively early. The arena was a combination of a gymnasium as well as a well-financed stadium. It had twice the equipment that the previous gym had and over ten times the crowd. Carmen decided to spend the last bit of time that she had to herself to train on one of the punching bags in the locker room. She punched, stretched her muscles, performed jumping jacks, anything that she could do to keep her body warm, her blood pumping, and her mind alert. Sarah and Amy stayed on the sidelines and waited for their friend. After Carmen was finished the trio walked toward the arena in unison.

"Look at that. Dead woman walking."

The girls shot their heads backward, noticing the voice behind them. Carmen knew at once who it belonged to. Maryam Bahira stood with her hands on her hips as she examined her opponents. They stood down the hallway, between the locker room and the door that led to the arena. She had a sinister look on her face, one that Carmen took note of almost immediately.

"Bout time y'all showed up. I was beginning to wonder if you hadn't decided to run. I wouldn't have blamed yah. I wouldn't want to be in front of me if I was you either."

"You must not know me very well. The name is Carmen; Carmen Rivera and I never run from a fight." The Latina stepped closer to her prey.

"You sure? Once I start it's hard to get me to stop." Maryam raised her eyebrows in a sharp warning. "I'll give you one mo chance to walk away."

"Bitch are you deaf or just plain stupid?"

Maryam took two steps forward. "Oh, now I know you asking for an ass-whooping now, calling me a bitch?"

"It's what I call everyone sweetie," Carmen said. "So don't go thinking that you're special, okay?"

Maryam's voice rose as her heart thumped in her chest. "No, what I'm thinking is that I'm going to mess up that pretty little face of yours, you keep this up."

Carmen curled her lips in amusement. "Well, I would say the same thing to you." She circled her forefinger around her face. "But considering the face in question that would be a big fib."

"Girl, you better stop. I'm warning yah. Today is not the day." Maryam took a single step toward Carmen and her heart rose when the tan-skinned girl took two steps toward her. The two were standing less than an inch away and at near eye level.

"Yeah well, it is for me. What? Do you think I'm afraid of you? That you thumping your chest has any effect on me whatsoever? Bitch please, I've known girls like you my entire life."

"I've known girls like you too."

A sly smile escaped Carmen's lips. She shook her head. "No, you haven't. But let me tell you something, by the end of today you're going to. And rest assured I'm going to enjoy every minute of it."

Maryam pointed ahead, addressing Sarah, who stood with her arms crossed and eyes locked in observation. "Come get yo girl."

"She can't help you," Carmen replied.

"Come get yo girl."

"Bitch did you hear what I just said?" Carmen's voice rose to new heights. "This is between you and me."

Maryam shook her head in disbelief. "I'm about to pop off. Aye," She called out to Sarah, her eyes widening in crazed fury. "You better come get yo girl."

Sarah shook her head, her mannerism near expressionless as she addressed her. "No Maryam. I don't have to do anything. You asked for this fight. You made this bed. Now you have to lie in it."

Maryam's neck stiffened. "So that's how it's going to be?"

Sarah shrugged. "That's how it is."

Despite their heated confrontation both Carmen Rivera and Maryam Bahira agreed that it would be best to settle their differences in the ring. They stood in their respective corners as they waited for the referee to call out their names. Sarah and Amy stood directly outside the arena. They would be the closest to the fight and would have plenty of opportunities to cheer their friend on. At least half of the bleachers behind the two girls were filled with both men and women eager to watch. Most were loyal fans of Maryam Bahira and had been watching her fights for years.

One of the male trainees placed a mouthpiece in Carmen's mouth while another wrapped her smooth hands in bandages before placing red boxing gloves over them. She locked onto her opponent across from her and frowned, her blood sizzling with anger.

The two women approached each other in the center of the ring, locking gazes in an instant.

"Alright, now I want a good clean fight," The referee warned. He turned to address Carmen first. "I've read a bit about your past and reputation. It's quite an impressive resume but there will be no hair pulling or scratching in this arena. You hear?" He then turned towards Maryam. "And you. You already know the drill. Just a reminder. If I tell you to stop, you stop. Is that clear?"

Maryam nodded; her gaze locked onto Carmen's brown eyes. "Alright. Now, will you both go to your respective corners so that we can begin?"

"Don't go crying to your girl when I start whooping on you, you hear?" Maryam barked. "I ain't gonna hold back."

Carmen cocked her head to the side. "I won't if you won't."

The two girls pounded gloves before retreating to their respective corners.

Amy leaned towards her sister's ear. "Do you think Carmen can beat her?"

Sarah gave a quick side glance in response. "I think she has a chance. Maryam has the advantage when it comes to experience and strength, but Carmen has sharp instincts and quick wit. Beyond that, it's really up to the two of them, what comes of this."

"Sarah, are you sure this is such a good idea? What if she can't beat her? What if she's too strong? What do we do then? How are we going to stop Anas-"

Sarah placed a finger on Amy's lips before she was able to finish her statement, silencing her immediately.

Carmen stretched out her arm muscles and bounced up, fixing her body into position as she prepared for the plunge. She took a moment to reflect on the fistfights she had been in recently due at least partially to Sarah's influence. They had all been immensely invigorating but few had been in front of as big of an audience or her two newest friends. It was time to summon all her courage and show these girls how far she had come.

The sudden ding of the bell surged through Carmen's eardrums, signaling the start of the match. The two warriors encircled one another as they locked expressions, covering the full circumference of the ring before coming into contact.

Carmen threw the first punch, going for a quick forward left jab that Maryam parried with what seemed to be no effort whatsoever. Carmen threw a second jab. Then a third before throwing a feint and unleashing a swift right hook that would have thrown a lesser boxer out of orbit. Maryam leaned backward, watching Carmen's arm pass over her head.

"That's all you got?" Maryam taunted; her voice muffled by her mouthguard. "Come on Latina. Put yo weight into it. Come on."

Her words pushed Carmen into immediate action. She stomped onto the ground and lunged toward her opponent, thrusting her arm, and twisting her waist with authority. She threw a barrage of punches, a few of which collided with her opponent's elbow and ribs.

"Come on girl. Need me to show you how to throw a punch."

Maryam applied her guard to her lower body before arching her fist into a mean left hook aimed at her opponent's head. Carmen brought her hands in front of her face at the last minute. Maryam's punch collided with her arm. The sudden maneuver was like an explosion and Carmen staggered backward as a result. She caught herself on her tiptoes before balancing herself on the balls of her feet and unleashing a second combination.

Carmen took an unconscious step backward after Maryam blocked every attack with a surprising amount of ease. Her arms shook as the power of the punches that she unleashed reverberated back on her. She couldn't remember the last warrior she had fought who made her feel that way. But her training taught her that dwelling on it would only lead to self-doubt, and she couldn't afford that. Not with Sarah watching.

Carmen gritted her teeth, unleashing a furious wave of attacks that made the crowd erupt with a gasp in enthusiasm. Maryam decided to meet her opponent halfway and raised her fist to counter-attack at just the right moment. Their fists collided, sending ripples throughout the stadium and causing both Maryam and Carmen to clench their teeth.

The force of the fists of the two women sent a current through the arena, causing the referee to stumble and the ground to vibrate from underneath the seats of the audience. Amy gasped from where she stood beside Sarah as Carmen lunged on the offensive. With all the fights that she had been in recently colliding fists was something that she was able to recover from despite the sudden shock to her system. She rammed her fist into Maryam's abdomen before causing her head to bop back and forth with a few precise jabs to the nose. She finished her combo with a vicious left hook that caused her to spin as she staggered backward.

Maryam twisted on her ankle and turned around just in time to parry Carmen's second wave of attacks. Maryam brought her arms in front of her face, a series of ten punches hitting her before her opponent left her room to counter. Maryam decided to give her opponent a taste of her own medicine and threw a series of punches in her direction, beginning with three forward jabs and ending with a massive swing of her arms. The smashing of Maryam's fist against her barebone sent an electrical current and various sound waves swimming through her entire circulatory system.

Carmen knew exactly when Maryam would strike low and timed her guard so that when she did her opponent would be vulnerable to a brutal uppercut that would set her world ablaze, and that was what she did. The attack shot Maryam's head upward, forcing her to balance herself on her heels as her toes were lifted off the ground.

Carmen wasted no time in proceeding with her follow-up attack. She bent her knee and thrust her body upward, smashing her fist into her opponent's chin. The second strike proved to be just as powerful as the first. Maryam's head swam inside of her body. The shimmering light above blended, changing her vision into a strange blurry color that she found disorienting. But her opponent wasn't finished yet, far from it.

Maryam raised her arms to block but by now, Carmen had managed to predict her movements. She threw a feint before striking Maryam in the shoulder and then throwing her off guard with a merciless punch to the chest. She then ducked underneath Maryam's arm, dodging her right hook by a narrow margin before striking right at the center of her abdomen. Maryam heaved because of the sudden attack. In all her life, she couldn't recall being punched so hard in the stomach before. Carmen took advantage of her temporary immobility to deliver a swift beat down, connecting with a series of rapid-fire punches to her lower body before pulling her arm back and hitting her near her back.

Maryam hunched over to massage her body and was left temporarily vulnerable. Carmen struck Maryam with precision, her gloves landed right in between her eyes, causing her to lose her equilibrium. For a mere brief second in time, she couldn't feel her legs and much of the world around her was a foggy haze. When the world returned to her, she felt her body tipping, so she thrust herself forward. The sudden maneuver caused her to trip and land on her knee.

The crowd gasped in unison. Amy's jaw dropped and even Sarah raised her eyebrows in intrigue. The referee lost focus and merely gazed at the sight in front of him in bemusement. For many of her loyal fans in the audience, this was the first time that they had seen Maryam floored by an attack. The sight alone was enough to alert the entire stadium as to the nature of the girl she was fighting.

"Well, would you look at that? The Great Maryam Bahira, put on her knees by an amateur. How will she ever live this down?"

Luckily for Maryam, the ref was too distracted to start the countdown right away, but it didn't matter regardless. Carmen's words were enough to make Maryam pop up off the ground without a second's notice.

"Oh, you going to hell now," Maryam said, her face contorted with rage.

A fearless smile washed over Carmen's face. "You're late to the party sweetie. I've been there and back again. I even have my own cellmate. It's about time you join the club."

Maryam curled her lips, taking a few deep breaths in and out as she contemplated her next action. Within seconds she knew what to do. She thrust her arm into Carmen's forehead, holding her back just long enough for her reactionary swing to miss and to finally be given an opening. She jabbed Carmen in the face, the maneuver causing her head to snap backward on impact. Maryam proceeded with her follow up attack, hitting Carmen with five powerful punches before sending her spiraling towards the ground with a massive right hook.

The crowd 'oohed' and 'awed'. This was how they had expected the fight to go from the beginning, still, the fact that it took a bit of struggle for the undefeated champion to gain the upper hand only made the match more exciting for her fans.

Carmen stood up as the world came back into focus. The first thing that she noticed was the referee and his count from ten to one. By the time Carmen stood up he was at seven. She wiped her nose, the blood dripping from it tickling her skin. She locked onto Maryam, her blood boiling with venom and uncontrollable hatred. She would end this girl no matter what it took.

"Not talking that smack anymore huh? Yeah, that's what I thought."

Carmen cracked her knuckles from the inside of her gloves before raising them in front of her. At first, she had only intended on humiliating Maryam in front of her fans but the desire to hurt pulsed through her veins. She wanted to hear the crunch of her bones as she hammered away at her body. Her mind fluttered, as flashes of her previous fights flowed through her consciousness.

Carmen stomped her feet on the ground and raised her glove in the air. She had only a split second to act. It was only when the bell rang that she realized that Maryam had performed the same maneuver, raised her fist, and froze at the exact time.

The two girls left their fists raised for a few seconds; both knew what the other was thinking. They had half a mind to continue the fight, despite being signaled not to. With slow, hesitant movements the two lowered their fists before marching back towards their respective corners, both of their hearts still pounding with adrenaline.

Carmen sat on the bench in her corner as the men stationed there tended to the minor bruises on her cheek and bottom lip. She kept her gaze locked onto Maryam, intending never to waver but that all changed when two girls approached her.

"Carmen."

She recognized that voice anywhere. "Hey girlfriend. Enjoying the show?"

"Yeah. You're doing great Carmen," Amy said.

"You're holding your own so far. You've got the skill," Sarah replied. "But like I told you before Maryam is another breed of fighter. Pretty soon she'll tap into a well of power that there will seem to be no end.
She's just getting started."

"So am I," Carmen spoke through gritted teeth before one of the men gave her a portion of water through a straw.

"Maryam. Maryam." Desiree called out to her friend as she approached her corner from underneath the ring. "You okay?"

"I'm Coo. But she won't be in a few minutes. Best believe that."

"Girl, you need to be careful. I watched some of her recorded fights. She's strong. Stronger than any fighter that you've faced in a long time."

"She ain't nothing. Got lucky with her first couple of moves. Just like that snake man I beat on the other day. But once I hit my stride I'll be good. She better hope that she down for the count once this match's over with. Because nothing else will stop me."

"Maryam."

Desiree said nothing else after uttering her friend's name. She wanted to say a whole lot more but only when her friend would give her the courtesy of looking her in the eyes. Unfortunately, Maryam knew her friend all too well.

"I got this. I don't need no talking to. When this is over with we'll grab a bite to eat on me. How about dat?"

"Maryam. I'm sorry about what happened earlier but you don't have to do this," Desiree exclaimed. "You don't have to start a big fight every time that I or someone around you gets into trouble. Pretty soon you won't be able to stop. Is this it? Is this where you want your life to be in the next ten years? Don't you want something more for yourself?"

"Girl, you better stay in yo lane." Maryam's voice rose in a stern warning. "This ain't about you. And this ain't about what's going to happen in the next ten years. Don't nobody know that. This is about what I want right now."

"And what do you want?" Desiree prompted.

"To beat this bitch's ass."

Maryam stood up, motivated by the sound of her declaration. She refused to turn towards her friend, who called out to her as she approached the center of the ring, along with her adversary. The bell rang and the two warriors wasted no time in plunging into the next round of fisticuffs, each more determined and unrestrained than before.

Carmen was quicker to the punch than her opponent. She threw a five-punch combination, ending it in a sly gut punch and stunning haymaker to the chin that popped Maryam's eardrums and threw her senses out of orbit for a few seconds. Carmen ducked out of the way of an incoming fist before ramming her glove into her opponent's nose.

A fire was lit inside of Maryam's belly. Her eyes watered and her skull seemed to rattle inside of her body. She countered Carmen's next string and tightened her fist before punching at her opponent's biceps, loosening them up just enough to unleash a series of jabs onto Carmen's stomach. She ended her combo with a direct uppercut to the chin. The attack sent sparks surging through Carmen's body. Blood splattered out of her mouth and nose as she was lifted off the ground, Time seemed to come to a screeching halt in front of her. The sudden thud of her backside crashing against the ground was all that she heard and its vibration as a result was all that she could feel.

Carmen squinted her eyes as the ceiling spun around in a blurry haze. The first thing that she could make out was the ref standing over her, beginning the countdown. For a second it appeared that there were three men in his position. Carmen stood up after a few seconds, taking note of the proud half African, half American warrior that stood over her with her hands on her hips.

"What's the matter, Latina? You said I ain't never met a girl like you before? But you seem to be going down just as easy as any that I've ever fought."

"Don't push me bitch," Carmen hissed through her teeth.

Maryam smiled, noticing the anger infused in her opponent's eyes. At that moment she realized that she had never enjoyed a battle as much as this. She considered prolonging it, just for the sake of seeing that same look on her face. "I ain't going to push yah," she said, lowering her voice and speaking in an intimate declarative tone. "I'm going to beat yah. Do you think that you can come to my town and start this mess? That you can just show up, mess with my girls, and think you and yours over there can decide how to run things? Not going to happen."

Carmen stood up, pushing Maryam's declaration to the back of her mind. To say that she was surprised by the sudden change in the battle was an understatement. But what hurt most of all was that she didn't see this coming. She had been warned about Maryam and yet she had been so stubborn that she couldn't be bothered to heed her friend's warnings. Why was that?

"You ready?" Maryam asked, raising her eyebrows in a fierce gesture. Carmen raised her fists in front of her, taking a deep breath in and out, focusing all her intent and will on one goal; to annihilate this girl, no matter the cost. She had decimated several others before, all she needed was one more. Just one more added to the list and then her heart could rest.

The next minute was a blur. Carmen and Maryam exchanged blows, sustaining noticeable damage as they became more and more desperate to claw their way to the top.

Amy counted fifty hits by the time they stopped to catch their breath. Sarah counted seventy. The crowd began to cheer, a few stood up to bellow at the top of their lungs. For loyal fans of the renowned champion, this was bound to be Maryam Bahira's most exciting show to date.

Carmen slugged Maryam across the cheek, and she spit out blood as her head snapped backward. She retaliated by delivering a vicious uppercut that caused her to stagger a few inches back. Carmen threw a feint before connecting with a right hook on the other side of Maryam's face. She responded by burying her fist into Carmen's abdomen. She hunched over and coughed up blood, allowing Maryam to launch her into the air with a ruthless uppercut. Carmen latched onto the ropes after she landed, nearly toppling over the edge of the ring.

Maryam proceeded into her follow-up attack and Carmen spun in place, pivoting herself on her leg before throwing the fiercest haymaker that she could summon. Maryam parried the advance before smashing her in the rib twice. The attack hit her like a penetrating knife, triggering some of Carmen's worst memories of being stabbed and beat down during gang fights. An animal-like instinct overcame her and without pausing to consider her options, she wrapped her arm around Maryam in a clutch, holding her in place.

The ref stepped in between both girls, utilizing the full strength of his hands to spread them apart but was unable to do so. Maryam decided to take matters into her own hands and spun in a circle, using her momentum to lift Carmen and flung her to the ground. She popped up and charged toward Maryam for another bout.

Carmen grunted as she swung with more fervor than ever before. Maryam curled herself into a ball as her opponent's blows connected with her forearms and elbows, each one reverberated back onto her opponent. Carmen's arms rang out loud, signaling an alarm that she couldn't ignore. She raised her guard just as Maryam saw an opening and attempted to strike. She blocked Maryam's first few strings, though the force of the blow caused her to slide backward and eventually stumble. Maryam raised her hand high into the air, hitting her over the top of the head, smashing her into the ground face first. It was the most humiliating attack that Carmen had endured in ages.

Carmen let out an enraged war cry as she stood up. It was something akin to a screech and a roar. Neither Sarah nor Amy had ever heard Carmen do that before. Though despite her unhinged state Maryam chose to spread her lips into a conniving grin.

"Oh, so you mad now huh?"

Carmen's chest heaved as she fought to keep her composure, despite how much the girl angered her since they met, she had no idea just how far her hatred could go.

"Well, two can play at that game," Maryam said. She gestured with her glove. "Come on bitch. I got something for ya."

Carmen charged toward her opponent with her rage flowing through her chest. She transferred all her rage into her fist, pounding away at Maryam's body with increasing momentum. She struck at her chest, stomach, and her face to hit her anywhere that she could reach. But with every passing second Maryam's body seemed to grow more impenetrable. Carmen utilized the full force of her arms to block Maryam's string before sending her head snapping backward with a sudden punch across the face. Carmen didn't have time to unleash her follow-up attack, as Maryam penetrated her stomach with a precise blow before knocking her back with an uppercut. Carmen propelled herself up off the ropes and back into the fray. She decked Maryam in the face, utilizing the full strength of her fist, she then ducked, dodging out of the way of an incoming attack by a narrow margin. She rammed her fist into Maryam's abdomen, rushing in for a lightning-fast ten-punch combo.

Maryam raised her arm over her face after Carmen attempted to finish her combo with a vicious right hook and knocked her head backward with a swift counter, unleashing much of her hidden strength on her opponent. The next few attacks were the most painful that Carmen had ever experienced before in her life. Her head was sent spinning due to Maryam's rhythmic strikes. She hit her again and again, anger and hatred swelling through her chest as she hacked away at her opponent. Maryam then hit her with a punch to the stomach that caused her to pop off the ground for a brief second in time. Carmen clutched onto her opponent's body once again.

As she held on for dear life, a million thoughts began to swim through Carmen's head all at once. Questions of why she had decided to enter this fight and where it would lead her were the most pertinent in her mind. She was a woman who had always concerned herself with her own pleasure first and foremost. It was why she managed to attain as much power as she had and yet there was something else gnawing at the back of her mind. She thought of the look that the two girls standing outside the ring would give her if she failed. There were very few people left in her life who was willing to trust her with anything important and yet the two sisters had come to her during one of their most trying times. What kind of a woman would she be if she failed now?

Carmen socked Maryam in the rib as she held onto her. The blow threw her opponent off her game just as she intended. She hit her a few more times before Maryam finally found the strength to shove her off. The African warrior gritted her teeth in twisted anger and threw a devastating blow that would have been deadly had Carmen not pulled her into another clutch. She punched her in the rib a few more times and when Maryam shoved her off rammed her face in with a disorienting headbutt that made her brain rattle inside of her skull.

"Foul!"

"That's a foul! Come on ref!"

Several members of the crowd bellowed in protest. They were in complete dismay and floored by the sliminess of the maneuver. The ref pulled Carmen aside as Maryam cupped her hands over her bruised cranium.

"That's a strike. Headbutting is strictly prohibited."

"Yeah, yeah, yeah. I got it," Carmen replied.

"You know better than that," The ref scolded her. "Another stunt like that and I'll see to it that you're disqualified. Do you hear?"

Carmen cocked her head to the side. She had half a mind to punch the man's face in, but she knew that her energy would be better spent elsewhere. "Loud and clear."

Maryam's vision gave out on her for almost a full minute. She regained her composure just in time to see Carmen lunge toward her with a charging fist. She mowed Maryam to the ground with five devastating haymakers in a row, first a right then a left hook, and three uppercuts. The last one lifted Maryam off the ground by less than an inch. She splattered on the ground, her arms outstretched and blood pouring down her nose and the corner of her lip.

"Bitch," Desiree bellowed.

Sarah shook her head in disapproval. This was the second time that Carmen had chosen to embarrass her with her slimy tactics. She made a mental note to herself that once this battle was over, the two of them were going to have a talk.

The ref began the countdown. Maryam felt her vision become blurry and disoriented just as Carmen had been before. In all the matches she had been in, never had she felt such indescribable pain. She would be surprised if Carmen's sneak attack had not given her a concussion. For a second she was worried that she was at death's door but then the slightest prickle restored the feeling in her legs, and she sat up.

Carmen slouched her shoulders. Never could she have imagined that this girl would wear her out so much. It was enough to give her pause and question her decision. But as Maryam stood up and tightened her fist, she knew that that was a line of questioning that she could no longer afford to take.

Carmen and Maryam raised their fists in unison. Both warriors were now prepared to bring all the energy inside of them up to the forefront. Their heart rate rose to dangerously high levels, nearly bursting out of their chest as a result. They each took an authoritative step forward, prepared to take the final plunge that would bring an end to the match. The bell sounded throughout the room, stopping both girls in their tracks before either of their punches connected. Carmen and Maryam dropped their hands at their sides before reluctantly marching towards their respective corners.

Desiree slid into the ring after Maryam sat down. She knelt beside her and gestured towards one of the trainees at her side.

"Can I?" She asked. The trainer nodded, handing over a rag and cotton swab to Desiree. With gentle fingers, she cleaned Maryam's now swollen cheeks to the best of her ability. "You're doing good girl. Just hang in there. Keep an eye out in case that bitch has any more tricks up her sleeve."

"I was going to hold back," Maryam said, her face fixed in a firm dead-eyed frown. "But she done pushed me off the deep end now."

"Let her have it," Desiree said, finally giving her friend a seal of approval. "Just be careful out there, okay? I want you back in one piece."

Carmen Rivera sat at her corner as she allowed her mind to settle and the men in front of her to do their jobs. She detested it. Having so many wounds on her face that required a whole team of men to fix. She took a few deep breaths in and out as she replayed the last round over in her mind. She had nearly hardened her resolve but less than a minute before she was called back Carmen's skin prickled. Someone was staring at her, Carmen gazed back at them from the corner of her eye.

Sarah locked onto her friend, sporting an incessant and observant gaze. Their eyes met and for a while, it seemed that all the warmth had left Carmen's mind. But at the last second, she allowed the faintest smile to escape her lips. Sarah bit her lip, giving her friend a subtle look of sympathy before she was called back into the center of the ring once again.

Maryam and Carmen both stood up. They walked with slow and purposeful steps until they stood face to face in the center of the ring.

Only the ref stood in between them, with widened fear full eyes.

"No more games. We fight to the finish, you understand?"

Carmen cocked her head to the side, strangely amused yet also invigorated by Maryam's words. "It's why I'm here."

Maryam attempted a gloved fist dap in solidarity, but Carmen removed her hands out from underneath her at the last moment. "Oops."

A sly smile escaped Carmen's lips as she took a few steps backward. Maryam's eyebrows furrowed. At last, she knew where she stood with this girl.

Sarah bit her lips as she prepared to take it all in. She had a gut feeling that the fight would only get more disastrous from here on.

Carmen and Maryam proceeded to unleash a plethora of blows to the face and body, both sustaining heavy damage as a result. Jabs, hooks, uppercuts, and haymakers were thrown like wildfire in desperation. The cuts that were previously tended to were opened, causing both girls to bleed more profusely than before.

"Oh my god."

"Unbelievable!"

The crowd exclaimed in dismay as the girls exchanged lightning-fast blows. At a certain point, the immense pain that the two were in was ignorable and all that was at the forefront of either of their minds was the desire to win.

Carmen hit her opponent with a fierce right hook that threw Maryam off guard. She staggered and blocked Carmen's follow-up attack with her glove before sending her reeling with a fierce left hook of her own. When she turned back towards her opponent, Maryam numbed her senses with a brutal backhand and penetrating belly punch for good measure.

Carmen blocked two of Maryam's attacks before clamping her gloves down on her ears, returning the same feeling of numbness on her opponent. It was at that moment that both warriors reached their breaking point.

They lunged forward with both of their arms stretched out in unison, thrusting their full body weight into the maneuver. What happened next had the audience awestruck. Amy's jaw dropped at the sight of it and so did many others. The crowd let out an almost never-ending gasp, surrendering to the might of these women as the spectacular sight in front of them stretched on into what could very well be infinity.

Carmen and Maryam unleashed an endless barrage of punches, unloading them onto each other and deflecting in perfect synchronicity. They punched and punched with insane speed, authority, and willpower. After fifty strikes were thrown in the first fifteen seconds Sarah lost count but still, the warriors continued to punch away, even as their environment grew increasingly more chaotic and unstable. The ring shook and the walls around the stadium began to crack because of the power radiating from their fists. For these two warriors, this contest was no longer a game; it was war.

Sweat poured down the girl's cheeks as they pounded away. Their feet stomped the ground as the barrage increased in speed and power with every second. They continued the chain of attacks without ceasing for a full two minutes. The speakers blasted in the ears of those closest to it. Desiree and Amy gritted their teeth and cringed from where they stood. Only Sarah remained still, the thundering waves that emitted from their attacks blowing her hair into her face.

Carmen gritted her teeth, leaning closer as she increased her speed. Maryam roared, her arms growing sore through so much speedy movement. This was the first time she was forced to exert herself to such an insane degree, yet she couldn't falter now; not with so much at stake. The crowd 'oohed' and 'awed' dropping their jaws and widening their gazes the longer the rush went. Sarah examined them noticing that one man seemed to be particularly affected most of all. He had taken a massive swig of his drink before the barrage of attacks began. The vibration from underneath his feet, as well as the insane barrage in the ring, caused him to shoot the beverage out of his mouth like a fountain for the duration of the exchange. Sarah had never seen something so strange in all her life.

The rapid-fire attacks went on and on. For a while it appeared the two warriors, Carmen Rivera, and Maryam Bahira, were at a stalemate. Neither of them would let up, not for a single solitary second. The ground beneath their feet didn't matter, and neither did the crowd watching in disbelief and elevation. Between the two of them, Carmen was the faster fighter. She knew it in her gut. There was a reason she had wanted to fight this girl ever since she had first laid eyes on her. This would mark a turning point in her life. No one else would look at her the same after that day.

What Carmen had counted for in speed she failed to do so when it came to strength. Her arms gave out on her for just the briefest second in time and that was the only opening that Maryam needed. She connected with a few debilitating strikes to the chest. Carmen heaved under the weight of her blows, the pressure of it, causing her lungs to constrict. She threw a right hook in an involuntary reaction. Maryam crouched, dodging the blow with ease before shoving her fist into her opponent's abdomen, and watched as her world was ripped asunder.

Sarah and Amy both widened their expressions in an instant. The crowd suddenly became silent, all gazing at the sight before them in awe and reverence. None of them had ever seen anything like it. They each could have seen it ten times over and it still would have floored them as much as it did at that moment.

Carmen let out a shrilled scream. She had been stabbed nearly to death at one point in her life and yet despite this attack not being fatal, the pain that she felt was far greater than any stabbing wound could ever be.

Carmen's jaw hung open and a thin line of blood elongated from the corner of her mouth. Maryam stood triumphant, her heart swelled with pride as she took a deep breath in and out. She had persevered and won the exchange with little cost. The situation couldn't have been more in her favor and less in her opponents.

Carmen felt her entire body cave in on itself. She couldn't believe what had happened. She was sure there was some scientific explanation for this sudden turn of events that she wasn't educated enough to know. She couldn't move, neither her lower body nor her arms. For the first time in years, Carmen Rivera was reminded of what it was like to be helpless.

To add insult to injury and to solidify her dominance over her opponent, Maryam used the fist welded in Carmen's gut to lift her off the ground like a limp noodle. This next part was something that she wanted Sarah to see. With this simple act, she would prove once and for all that she was far stronger than any of her detractors could comprehend.

Once Carmen's feet were off the ground Maryam brought her up over her head, turning to the right before slamming her to the ground. Carmen felt as if she had been run over by a car or worse. Amy cupped her hands over her mouth and nose, flabbergasted by what she had just witnessed. Sarah remained still but inside a blizzard stormed through her heart. Her eyes widened and her mouth hung open by just the faintest bit. She feared that her friend had bitten more than she could chew when she challenged Maryam. But until that moment she had no idea just how formidable the renowned boxer was.

The ref began the countdown and Carmen gritted her teeth, attempting to use all her mental faculties to block out the pain but to no avail. It surged through her entire system, turning her thoughts into a foggy haze in which she was unable to see her destination.

"The winner is Maryam Bahira!"

The bell sounded and the crowd erupted in triumphant applause. The referee raised Maryam's hand up high. She smiled, relishing her victory despite her aching wounds.

Carmen's heart sunk into her chest. The realization of what just happened allowed a minuscule of her strength to return to her. She noticed the soreness of her muscles the moment she sat up and her arms wobbled as a result.

"Hey, bitch. I'm not done with you yet. So stick around."

Maryam turned around, floored by the sound of Carmen's voice.

"You're just like how they all say."

Maryam curled her eyebrows in confusion. "What? You get yo ass whooped and you still running yo mouth?"

"Shut up," Carmen hissed. "You haven't won anything."

"Look around you. It's over. I put you flat on yo back. Face it. You picked the wrong battle. I'm stronger. I'm better. More of a woman than you are."

"No. You're not. You're no woman. You're a thing."

Maryam chuckled. "Whatever you say."

"You're just like they say. At first, I thought they were just bigots. Those Serpents but it's just like they say. Most of you are good for nothing trash."

"Whatchu say?" Maryam's voice flared with anger.

"She tried to help you. But your kind never listens. Good for nothing black trash!"

Carmen bellowed at the top of her lungs, her voice fuming with hatred as she spoke. All logic and reason flew out of the window, her only desire was to bring down the behemoth of the woman in front of her. The match didn't matter anymore, her humiliation was the only thing that did.

Sarah's eyes sunk into the back of her head and Amy cupped her hand over her mouth in response.

At that moment Maryam felt a chill surge through her body. Her eyes locked onto her opponent. Her heart rate increased along with her breathing. She flashed to her battle with the serpents several days ago. Maryam hardened her fist, gritted her teeth, and lunged toward her opponent with all her fervor.

Carmen brought her hands up in a half attempt to defend herself. Her head rattled as she was knocked against the ropes from the sheer force of her blow. Her arms ached as much as her body. She threw a half-hearted punch and was punished for it in an instant. Blood burst out of her mouth as she was knocked into the corner by a brutal haymaker.

"Maryam!" The ref lunged towards the revered fighter, only to regret it a second later. She punched him in the chest, causing him to fly backward. He landed on the ground in disgrace, his body limp.

Carmen raised her fist in defense, but Maryam was able to break her guard with ease. Blind rage had risen her strength to new heights. She pounded away at her opponent's flesh. Punching her again and again, the sound of it blasting Carmen's eardrums.

Sarah couldn't believe it. She had feared for her friend since the match began but never could she have predicted this turn of events. Amy's eyes watered in disbelief as she watched the beating unfold. Maryam blacked out. She didn't know how many times she had hit Carmen. It could have been fifteen or twenty times. But all that she knew was that despite her reducing her face to a bloodied mess, it wasn't enough. She could never do enough to repay her enemy for just how far she had crossed the line.

By the time Maryam was finished Carmen's body and face went numb. Her cheeks were enlarged, and blood streamed down from her reddened puffed-out eyes. Maryam hit her with one final punch to finish the job, sending her collapsing unconscious on her back.

"Maryam!" Desiree approached her friend, sensing the dire circumstances of the situation. Maryam felt herself reeling from the surge of adrenaline. The deep fatigue and battle wounds had all come rushing to the surface.

"Girl. You need to calm down. You're hurt." Desiree stepped into the ring and placed an affectionate hand on Maryam's face. "Medic!"

"The match was over."

Maryam was snapped out of her momentary fatigue. Somehow despite the pain, she recognized that voice immediately.

"That was unacceptable."

A group of medics approached the two warriors as well as the referee who had been injured by Maryam as well.

"What? You want some of this?" Maryam challenged, locking expressions with the girl outside the ring, the one person who the revered prizefighter had had her eyes on from the beginning.

"You should show more restraint."

"Hey," Maryam shrugged, struggling to catch her breath. "This is the house of pain little mamma. If you don't want to get hurt, best not to enter."

"You're completely out of line," Sarah said, her stern expression glaring at the woman above her.

"Am I?"

"You are. You're also out of your depth. Clashing with forces that you have absolutely no comprehension of."

Maryam curled her lips. "Oh, I got plenty of comprehensions. And you should watch yo mouth. Unless you want to end up like yo friend over there."

Sarah narrowed her expression. "That's going to cost you."

Maryam raised her eyebrows. "What? Girl, you better speak up. What's that going to cost me?"

"Your title. And once I've taken it you're going to regret what you've done," Sarah declared.

"Bitch who do you think that you're talking to?" Maryam puffed up her chest and took an authoritative step forward.

"No." Desiree attempted to block Maryam's path but was shoved aside with minimal effort.

"You should've listened to me," Sarah said.

"Bitch, don't talk at me from behind the ropes. You want my title, right?" Maryam challenged. "Idn't that what you just said? Well, my title don't just go to anybody. You want it? Then you better come get it."

Sarah said nothing in reply. There was a much bigger battle on the horizon. Still, she couldn't let Maryam go unchecked. Something needed to be done about her now.

"Girl, today is not the day." Maryam shook her head. "I know you heard me. After all the mess you done said you better get yo ass in this ring. Right now!"

Sarah unfolded her arms and latched onto the ropes in an instant.

"Sarah!" Amy called out to her, but Sarah ignored her sister's words, concerning herself only with the powerful fighter who had knocked out her friend. She walked towards Maryam, standing as close to her as possible before the two exchanged another word.

"So, when do you want to do this little mamma?"

Sarah locked her eyes with her opponent as she spoke to her. They stood at the same height, both primed and ready for the next showdown. "I'll give you two days. After that, we meet here the same as before."

"That's coo with me. Just be ready. You don't want me to embarrass you like I did to your Latina friend over there. If we do this we go all out. You better bring yo A-game."

"Count on it."

Chapter 11: Through the Valley

The first thing that Sarah did after the match was over and Maryam exited the ring was to speak with the paramedics concerning her friend. Amy stood behind her, leaning against the wall in a fit of agitation as a few able-bodied men loaded a battered, bruised, and still unconscious Carmen Rivera on a stretcher.

"I assure you that she will receive the best of care," One of the men said.

"How bad is it?" Sarah asked.

"It's difficult to say for sure. She's received heavy damage. She's quite strong. It's practically a miracle that she's managed to survive such injuries but I'm afraid it'll be a while before she's made any sort of recovery."

"You'll keep me posted? Let me know if she wakes up?"

"Of course." The doctor nodded in agreement and Sarah returned the gesture. She turned around, noticing Amy rubbing her arms like she often did when things went wrong.

"So?" Amy asked after Sarah edged towards her. "How is she?"

Sarah hesitated before giving her a reply. "She'll be fine. She just needs time. That's all."

Amy responded with a gentle nod, lowering her gaze towards the floor.

"I'll drive you back to the hotel. But I'll be out for a while. I have a few things to take care of." Sarah proceeded towards the door but stopped when she noticed her sister still standing in the same place.

"Amy."

She spoke in a gentle tone, doing everything that she could to mask the storm thundering inside. Amy met her gaze. Without another word, Sarah gestured towards the door.

The two sisters remained silent during the ride back. There was so much that both wanted to say but neither believed it was the right time.

"I should be back by tonight. Call me if you need anything. Okay?"

Amy nodded. "Okay." She opened the car door before turning to face her sister once more. "Sarah. Is there anything that I can do? To help I mean?"

"Amy, right now the best thing that you can do is-"

"What you tell me to do. I know. I know." Amy rolled her eyes and took a single step outside the car with her left foot.

"Amy," Sarah called out to her. The sisters met each other's gaze. "We'll get through this. You just have to trust me."

Amy examined her sister, there was a stillness to her expression that was quite soothing, though that didn't do much to stop her anxiety. It clogged her throat and squirmed through her gut. Finally, after what seemed like ages, Amy returned her sister's declaration with an understanding nod before exiting the vehicle.

"Be safe."

Sarah could only hope that her words could help her sister in a way that her presence couldn't. She needed time and space. She also needed to do something productive to detach herself from the scene in the ring before. She kept her mind on the road ahead as she drove off into the distant fading sun.

For Sarah Stryker, there was only one thing on her mind, retribution. She wanted it. She needed it more than just about anything else in the world. She had only a short window to train before she would have to face her newest opponent in the ring. And after that, it was only a matter of time before The Pride would reveal themselves. She took a cruise around Georgetown, hoping to find a distraction that would take her mind off the current situation. She needed something to punch; something to stave off the cravings of the demoness within. She had just hardened her resolve when she received a sudden call from downtown.

"Kyle?"

Kyle Harper sighed in relief. "Sarah. Oh, Sarah. Boy, am I glad to hear from you."

Sarah tensed up her body, knowing that she would have to go to great lengths to mask herself when speaking to this man. "What's up?"

"What?"

"Is there something wrong?"

"Hmm? Why does there have to be something wrong?" Sarah

glared, seeing right through his cool facade.

"What? I know you're giving me a look. You always call me when you need something, so you assume I'm the same?"

"Kyle," Sarah said, speaking in as patient of a tone as she could. "If you don't stop giving me the run-around-"

"It's probably nothing."

"If it was nothing, then why did you call?" Sarah challenged.

"Well." Two towns over, Kyle approached his window and peeled down the blindfolds. "There are these women standing outside of my home you see. And they give me this vibe-"

"How many?" Sarah interrupted.

"Sarah. There's nothing to worry about. Like I said it's probably nothing."

"How....many?" Sarah gave up trying to hide the irritation in her voice.

"About five. Or so." Kyle hesitated. "There are several cars parked in the driveway. They're just standing there. Not sure what for but whatever it is it can't be good."

"Stay inside. I'll be there."

Kyle's voice grew bashful. "I mean Sarah look. I understand you're busy. I can handle this if-"

"Don't argue. I'll be there."

"Sarah."

But she hung up the phone before he could say anything else. She pressed onto the ignition and stormed through the streets as she headed back downtown. She would send Anastasia a message that she wouldn't soon forget.

A team of women stood in front of the man who they knew was a friend of their former colleague. They would give him one chance to surrender, after that, all bets were off as to what they would end up doing to him.

"Face it. You're still the same man that you always were. No matter what you do or how hard you try. You're still the same, impotent in more ways than you can imagine."

"No. This time I'll use it. I swear I will."

Kyle Harper stood in front of a group of three, one of them with elongated nails to which he had no doubt would be her first method of attack should she have the opportunity. They had managed to break into his home due to their violent nature. Now all he could do was buy enough time for his friend to show up. She was his only hope. He held his shotgun and pointed in the direction of the squad leader, who stood closest to him. He would shoot her first, should she or any of her posse make any sudden movements.

"For a supposed genius you're remarkably stupid," She hissed.

"What do you want with me?" Kyle asked, through a shaking jawline and rattled teeth.

The squad leader laughed, her expression shone with excitement and almost uncontrollable anticipation. "How many times do we have to explain it to you? You're nothing to us. It's not what we want with you." Her voice oozed condescension as she spoke. "It's how we can get what we want through you."

"For god's sake would you stop with the word games," Kyle's voice shook. "For once would one of you actually talk to me like a person?"

The squad leader glared in reply. "That would require just a bit more suspension of disbelief than I'm willing to grant at the moment."

"Get out of my house," Kyle hissed, his heart rate skyrocketing to a dangerous level.

"No," she said in reply. "It's not your house anymore. Everything you see belongs to us now."

Kyle squinted in disbelief. "I would say over my... well, you know? But that would be a bit predictable don't you think? Considering that's what you want."

The squad leader smiled in reply. "You're cute. "I think I'll play with you for a little while. Girls, what do you think?"

"Yes, definitely," One of the girls agreed. "Hate to snuff him out before we get to have any fun."

"Oh no. I'm not letting you degenerate harpies play with anything."

"What did you just call us?" The squad leader exclaimed.

"Back away," Kyle ordered. "Take your desire to maim and murder somewhere else."

"No." The girl said, her voice oozing with desire. "I think I like it right here. It's unfortunate for you but not everyone can be a winner, right?"

"Get out. Now. I'm not joking."

"Let's make him hurt!" One of the girls exclaimed.

"You take one step forward and I'll shoot. I swear I will."

"Then do it."

"Don't test me."

"Do it. You worthless feeble shrimp of a man," The squad leader spat, her eyes lit with contempt.

"I will." Kyle cocked his gun. "In about five seconds. I'll blow you through the wall."

The squad leader's eyes widened. "Oh, you better. You better put everything you got into that shot. Because if you don't the next few minutes will be the most painful you've ever experienced in your life. I guarantee it."

Kyle began the count to five. "One. Two."

"We'll beat you until your skin turns purple. We'll cut you, leaving shallow marks that'll drag out for what will feel like hours."

"Three. Four."

"We'll start with what's between your legs."

"Goddammit! Would you stop with the threats of castration? For men, that's crossing the line in more ways than you can imagine."

"I can imagine just fine. In fact, I'm imagining what I'm going to do to you right now. We'll cut you. And cut you. And cut you. We won't stop cutting until-"

Before the squad leader was able to finish her remark, she was knocked into the wall beside her with a brutal kick to the midsection. Sarah stormed into the room and pounded her face into the wall with a series of quick precise strikes, utilizing a large portion of the strength in her knuckles. She turned around as the two remaining squad members lunged toward her with an angry fist. She raised her palms, catching the opponent's hands in a firm unyielding grip before freezing them stiff. With a mere flick of her hand, she bent their wrist and a vile sensation flowed through the girl's bloodstream.

A cracking sound surged through Kyle's eardrums as the girls cried out. He could sense the shivering confusion in their hearts as Sarah pounded on them with little restraint. She punched one in the chest, knocking her into the wall. Sarah proceeded to pound the pinned opponent into submission. When the second warrior attempted to ambush her from behind Sarah stomped on her foot and rammed the back of her cranium into the girl's forehead.

Kyle watched with widened eyes as Sarah decimated the women that had caused him so much distress with ease. She hit one with a precise strike to the rib that made her muscles clench. She spiraled through the air a second later after Sarah's fist grazed against her cheekbone.

All the opponents of The Pride were left in various states of frostbite and agony as Sarah turned to face the freaky-haired, green-eyed man staring, her facial expression placid as if nothing had happened.

Kyle nodded in a half-attempted greeting as he struggled to catch his breath. "Hey, Sarah."

"Hey Kyle," She replied in a whisper.

"Nice of you to drop by so suddenly. Though I'd imagine there are other things you'd rather be doing right now."

Just then the girl that had been pinned against the wall had regained a bit of her strength and screamed as she lunged forward in rage. Without turning around Sarah pinned her against the wall again, this time with a foot against her throat. The air turned frosty as she held the girl still, freezing her body through her jugular vein, then released her foot and rammed her head into the cemented wall with a swift kick. A loud *thud* sounded throughout the house and the girl fell unconscious, sliding down to the floor in disgrace.

"It's like I told you before," Sarah said as she walked past her friend. "Whenever you need me. I'm there."

Kyle turned to face her, allowing a sigh of relief to escape his lips. "Good to know." He sat down at the bottom of the staircase near his dining table. Sarah chose to stand but turned an observant eye in his direction.

"I don't suppose you've made any progress in locating a certain nameless man," Sarah prompted.

"I have actually," Kyle revealed. "I managed to find a few stories of women that were violated in the specific manner that well- that you were. Based on all the links it's a single man with a single fetish. The evidence is conclusive. Now all I have to do is tie it to a name. I have several listed but well-" Kyle hesitated. "You seem to be having a lot going on right now."

"It can wait," Sarah confirmed. "Just don't think for a second about holding out on me. You may be the mind reader." Sarah placed two fingers underneath her eyelids. "But I assure you that no deception will make it past these eyes. We clear?"

"Yeah, we're clear."

The two exchanged a warm smile. Kyle felt a slight relaxation in his muscles upon doing so. "I heard about what happened with Maryam. It seems you two weren't able to reach common ground huh?"

Sarah lowered her gaze, but it was too late. Kyle had already read what was at the forefront of her mind.

"She'll be okay you know? It wasn't your fault. There was little that you could have done. Carmen knows that."

"What about you? I got here before any of them managed to do any damage, didn't I? Because if not then I can take a look, patch up any wounds."

"No. No." Kyle waved his hand dismissively. "I'm fine. Besides a bit of an adrenaline rush, I'm all good."

Sarah raised her eyebrows. "You're not just saying that are you?"

"What? You calling me a liar?" Kyle said, with a sly smile, echoing her words. Sarah smiled. "Anyway, you better get back. Amy and a boatload of people need you in Georgetown right about now."

"Kyle." Sarah lowered her voice to a soft intimate tone. "Don't be stupid. I'm here because I want to be here. I'm asking you with all sincerity. Anything you need. Just ask."

Kyle could read the openness in her words, something that he hadn't heard from Sarah in months. With them, he saw a golden opportunity; one that he wouldn't dare pass up.

"Well," Kyle said, his voice dubious.

"What?"

"There isn't anything that I need. I told you I'm fine. But if you are really that adamant about paying it forward there is one thing that you can do for me."

"What's that?" Sarah asked, her voice oozing with skepticism.

"Tell me about your mother."

Sarah turned away in an instant, her body flaring in protest. "Kyle."

"Sarah, come on. Don't be like that. Sarah, please? Work with me here."

"Kyle." She turned to face him once again, irritation ringing in her voice as she spoke. "I understand that you desire intimacy. But this-" Sarah broke off. "Prying into people's personal affairs and demons like this. It's not the way."

"No, I know," Kyle protested, raising his hands in surrender. "I know. In general, your right. Despite how much I want to. I can't force myself on the world and expect to fix its problems overnight. I know that. I'm not the tactless busy body that you think I am."

Sarah glared in reply, still visibly perturbed by the man.

Kyle rolled his eyes. "Okay. Okay. Maybe I am. But that's not the point. The point is we're not normal people. You and me. Both in our abilities but also in our suffering. We're going to need to take drastic measures in order to heal. We met when we were at our lowest. Or have you forgotten?"

Sarah shook her head, confirming the truth of Kyle's words.

"We got to know each other pretty well these past two years. More than most people do in ten. So, considering what I already know about you and how much you've entrusted in me I think asking you to share just a little smidgen of your personal life isn't too much to ask, don't you think?"

"But she's my mother. All I have are memories."

"I understand and I'm sorry." Kyle raised his palms. "But getting to know her will help me understand you that much more. In fact, I think she's the missing link. To help me understand, well you, everything that there is to know about you both good and bad. The ugly and the magnificent. And it may just help you too. There's a lot of pent-up aggression in you and I'm sure some of it will alleviate once you've spoken up about it."

Sarah didn't say anything at first. She continued to glare at the man, though despite how much she wanted to, she felt no genuine anger towards him.

"Come on Sarah. I was just attacked by a merciless pack of assassins hell-bent on my destruction, who I might add threatened to cut my balls off before you showed up here. You gotta give me something."

"Alright." That single word of approval spread a warm smile across Kyle's lips. But Sarah raised a forefinger in warning before she would allow him to get too excited. "One look. One. That's all you get."

"Baby, one is all I need."

Sarah Stryker sat still on the dining table, her entire being tensed up in anticipation and dread for what was to come. It was just two years ago that she wouldn't have trusted this man, nor any other within a thousand yards of her. And yet here she was, waiting as the strangest man that she had ever met prepared to hack into her mind, exposing everything that she worked day and night to hide from the world.

"Alright. Sarah, I want you to relax. Empty your mind of all unwanted thoughts."

Sarah curled her lips. "Alright."

"I know you have a lot on your plate right now. We all do. But try not to think about it. Just focus on right now. The present."

"M'kay."

"Sarah?" Kyle squinted as the two locked eyes. "I said to empty your mind."

Sarah shrugged. "I am."

"No, you're not. I can still read you. I wouldn't be able to read you if your mind were empty."

"Kyle," Sarah said, narrowing her eyes. "Would you just get on with it? I practice meditation nearly every day. I know how to keep my mind focused. Just go."

Kyle shook his head. "Not unless you cooperate. If I enter a cluttered mind, it could break my concentration."

Sarah's eyes widened. "Oh, I'm definitely going to break something if you keep stalling."

"Hey," Kyle protested. "Attitude problem. Keep in mind who your source of intel is during this little crusade of yours. You have a vested interest in keeping me happy at all times. Whether you like it or not."

Sarah averted her gaze towards the ceiling and sighed. She didn't like it one bit, being placed in someone else's care. But if there was one thing that Kyle Harper knew better than anyone, man or woman it was the world of the mind. Sarah allowed her breathing to settle as this simple fact dawned on her.

"That's it. That's it. Relax. Forget about your problems. At least for now. Focus on me. Sarah, look at me."

Sarah locked eyes with the man sitting across from her, her expression placid, giving away little. She stared at Kyle for a solid minute, the air growing thick and the sound of car noises outside drowning in the distance. The weight of the chair underneath Sarah began to shift and at a certain point, she could no longer feel it. For a brief second all that Sarah could see was the misty green eyes of the man in front of her, then blackness.

The first thing that Sarah saw after her consciousness drifted was an image of a five-year-old with pale blonde hair and misty blue eyes. The girl edged towards an older woman who lifted her into the air with a warm embrace. The woman beamed as she raised the small girl into the air, both of their teeth shone with glee. The girl melted as the woman's lips grazed against her cheek. The middle-aged woman kept her hair in a ponytail. It was similar though a bit of a dark shade of blonde than the girl. The image began to fade after a few seconds.

"That was one of my first memories of her," Sarah said.

"I see," Kyle replied. "What about this one?"

Sarah saw another image of her mother, this one in a much worse state than before. Her mother sat down on her couch in a bloodied state. There were cuts all over her face and swollen cheeks. A seven year-old Sarah Stryker sat in front of her and applied cotton swabs, water, and alcohol to her cheeks. The young and frightened Sarah's eyes grew moist as she applied the cotton swabs with as delicate and as gentle hands as possible.

"Also, one of my first memories of her," Sarah said, though she hesitated to say the words.

"I've seen these images before," Kyle said. "But we need to look beyond them. There is a truth that you're trying to hide. That will put all of the pieces of your life back together again. What is it about your mother that you miss? The vivid memory that you're desperate to hold onto."

"So many things," Sarah revealed. "The way she smelled. It was the sweetest fragrance even when she smelled like smoke, which was her primary vice when I wasn't around. She devoted so much time to her living and domestic responsibility. But when I was there, when she was in front of me it was like nothing else in the world mattered; not like I did."

Sarah's mind tunneled through the images of her past, each one made her heart swell with even greater longing than the last. Images of her and Amy being held by her mother soared through her consciousness, as well as images of a teenage Sarah having to tend to the wounds of her mother as she did as a child.

Just when Sarah thought her mind had settled, she sensed something vile. A wraith-like creature appeared in front of her, blocking the image of her mother in an instant. Sarah was sent tunneling through the pit of her subconscious, descending into darkness, and losing grip of reality in the process.

Chapter 12: Down for the Count

The Pride had a base of operations within Georgetown. The facility was guarded by two female soldiers who were vigilant in reporting any suspicious activity. It was a building that concerned many people though most made it out unharmed. It wasn't the primary entrance but the back end that concerned most of the women who dwelled near it. They all knew the rumors of not only the Queen who dwelled there but the unspeakable acts that she would exhibit on her subjects.

The screams could be heard from yards away, sometimes even from outside the building. Most of the women who worked there were used to it. They all knew that during this time their boss was busy and was not to be disturbed for any reason, though it didn't matter regardless. The room on the basement floor was blocked by a magnetic lock and keypad. Only a few of the higher-ups from The Pride knew the passcode and even then, they were more likely to witness an eclipse than to enter the forbidden chamber, lest they should spend the rest of the week wide awake consumed by nightmares.

If a member of the squad was brave enough to enter the room, the first thing they would notice is the stench of rotten flesh. It was a smell that could burn their nostrils and dull out their senses entirely. Nothing would make them forget except of course the second thing a person would notice upon entering the room and that would be the bodies lined up in both rows and columns scattered throughout the entire chamber.

The victims inside the chamber were hung from chains attached to the ceiling, some by their wrists and even a few of them by their necks. Most of these victims were male though the caretaker of the chamber made it a point to bring as many rebellious women to the prison as she could spare. It was diabolical, a wealth of torment, pain and suffering reserved exclusively for these people, many of whom for the mere crime of existing.

"Please. Please. Let me go. I promise. I won't tell anyone. I won't," a man begged. His hands had been strung up by a rope that hung from the ceiling.

But the woman in charge of the facility took no heed of the innocent man's pleas. Instead, she rammed a canned carbonated drink into his cranium, causing it to burst open and spill some of its contents on the floor. The man fell slack jawed. He saw a pair of red eyes out of the corner of his own; eyes that stared him down like a hawk. This combined with the long vibrant red hair of the girl in question mystified him. He was certain he had never seen a creature, man, or woman that resembled anything like her, yet her basic features appeared unremarkable.

The dwellers of the chamber would come to know this girl as torturer but the soldiers on the top floor knew her as not only the commander and chief but the soon-to-be crowned Queen of The Pride.

The blurry image in front of her slowly became clear as the feeling in Sarah's limbs returned to her. The first thing that she noticed was that she was in a darkened room, illuminated by a single lightbulb attached to the ceiling. The next thing that she noticed was that she was restrained, metal straps on each hand. Ordinarily, this would be only a minor inconvenience for her. The third thing that she noticed was the sense of numbness and fatigue that had all but violated her body.

"Hello, Sarah."

She looked up; the silhouette of the woman who had addressed her stood still just outside the center light. Sarah was certain that she had never heard her voice before, but the tone was familiar. The woman who had addressed her stepped forward, revealing facial features and much of her upper torso. She was of average build with large, red rimmed spectacles perched on the edge of her nose. She wore a placid expression, examining Sarah up and down with a look of suspicion.

"How are you feeling?" The woman asked. Sarah saw right through her words, which were dripping with feigned concern that she found downright insulting.

"Who are you?"

"My name is unimportant. What is important is my purpose," The woman said. "As is yours. So much of what you are and will be remains to be discovered."

Sarah leaned back against her seat; her eyes narrowed in fatigue. She had a feeling that this woman was here to play mind games with her, and she couldn't be less in the mood.

"What do you want with me?"

The woman shrugged, feigning bashfulness before she replied. "Well by me I assume you refer to Queen Anastasia. She has plans for you, numerous and ever reaching in scope, starting with this. But if you're referring to me specifically, well it's odd actually."

The woman lowered her voice, speaking to Sarah in an intimate tone as the air grew thick and suffocating. "You asked for my identity and more important than my name in relation to you is my curiosity. I have a question to ask you. It's something I've wondered about for a long time. Ever since I found out about you. Why? Why would you turn your back on your sisters? Why would you risk your standing, your assets to save the lives of such retched low-life scum? You were a young woman with your whole life ahead of you; one that represented the pinnacle of what The Pride had to offer. Why throw it away? Why choose exile?"

Sarah felt her breath growing hoarse, the fatigue eating away at her insides. What had this woman done to her while she was unconscious? "Because it was the right thing to do."

The woman nodded, a half-smile escaping her otherwise blank expression. "I see, and that's all that concerns you? Right and Wrong? Altruism? Is that what you tell yourself? Is that how you justify your nightly escapades?"

"So, is this Anastasia's game plan?" Sarah challenged. "Pick my brain until I succumb to my base instincts. Seems rather prosaic don't you think?"

"No, As I've already said her plans are far greater than what either you or I could imagine. Like you, she is a rather unusual specimen. But unlike you, she doesn't let her feelings, or her comfort get in the way of becoming the woman that she is meant to be."

"You don't know the first thing about me. My life is anything but comfort."

"Maybe," The woman admitted. "You suffered. Anyone with half a brain can see that. But you no longer have to. You can have an entire army by your side. You no longer have to fight on your own."

"And ignore Anastasia's activities on the basement floor?"

The woman contorted her expression. "Basement floor? What do you-"

"You know what I'm talking about," Sarah said, not buying her feigned confusion in the slightest.

"Anastasia was right about you. You're a rare find indeed. It'll make me enjoy your fight even more."

It was Sarah's turn to feign confusion. "How do you know?"

"Like I said. We know all about you. That was quite a brave declaration. Challenging a prizefighter in front of an entire audience. It would be rather remarkable if you managed to beat her at her own game. But we're going to need to adjust the stakes a bit."

It was at that moment that Sarah noticed a small desk stationed in front of her seat, a syringe, and a bottle of a strange yellow liquid substance. Sarah's heart slowed down as it hit her. She recognized it from her time studying medicine in high school. She exchanged looks from the syringe to the woman who held it in her grasp.

"So, this is your plan? Weaken me so that I'll be an easy kill."

"We don't want to kill you, Sarah. The Prizefighter is on her last legs after her previous fight. She would hardly be a match for you in her current state. So, I say we make things just a little more interesting. You've come a long way, Sarah. I speak for not only myself but Anastasia and the rest of The Pride when I say I can't wait to see what happens next."

Sarah's mind tunneled down memory lane the moment she was injected with the needle. She saw flashes of her mother, Amy, Kyle, and a few of her training sessions with The Pride. She had indeed come far in such a short period. Mountain climbing, Martial arts, and knife throwing were among the activities that she engaged in most frequently during her time spent with these women.

Sarah felt as though her mind was catapulted out of her body. The injection seemed to take immediate effect. How could she have let this happen? She had anticipated a conflict with Anastasia for months and yet in all that time, Sarah had never considered that her adversary could be so cunning.

Sarah opened her eyes as the world came back into focus. The flashes had ceased half an hour after she had been injected. She scanned the room. Her guest was nowhere to be found. Fortunately, the light had been turned on, exposing the way out.

Sarah attempted to lift her free hand, only for it to be halted in an instant. Her limbs were still confined to the chair by metal straps. Sarah gritted her teeth as she rammed her wrists against them. She felt something vile surge through her as she did so. She saw an image, a single image of a snake with glowing red eyes. Its scaly skin almost made her jump.

It was a sensation that Sarah Stryker hadn't experienced in over two years. It was despair; a carnivorous predator that welcomed Sarah into its clutches with its hands outstretched and its jaws wide open. It was damn near impossible to quantify yet was sharper than any blade she had been attacked with before. She needed an escape, right that very second, or the darkness would consume her whole.

It took ten hits for the metal straps around her wrists to bend. The slight opening gave her enough room to slip her hands through the straps. She applied an even greater amount of force to her legs, using the tip of her shoes to push the metal strap off. The physical strength was still there but much of the equilibrium associated with it was gone. Sarah stood up after removing the metal straps. Her legs wobbled and it took only a few seconds after she was on her feet to collapse to the floor.

"Sarah. Oh, Sarah."

Her heart skipped a beat. She knew that she was alone yet the voice inside of her head was clear. Sarah knew that she could never rid herself of the nightmares but for once she thought that the daytime hallucinations had ceased. It was the drugs speaking to her. It had to be.

"Sarah."

"You are no one."

Sarah crawled towards the door in front of her. She dug her piercing blue polished nails into the ground and drudged herself forward. She moved for a solid minute and gripped the side of the doorknob. She gritted her teeth and lifted herself by her arm.

The first thing that Sarah did after mustering the strength to enter her vehicle was head towards the invaded home of Kyle Harper. She had gotten a text from him revealing that he had been somehow miraculously returned home after a brutal interrogation by The Pride. On one hand, Sarah was relieved that just like her Kyle's abduction had not been fatal. On the other hand, it seemed rather peculiar that the enemy would capture such an important player and then dump him back in her lap as though he were nothing. She needed to see him again to confirm the truth of the matter.

"I'm sorry Sarah. I'm so sorry. I had no idea."

Kyle Harper sat at his dining room table, still reeling and in the worst state that Sarah had seen him in. There were cuts and bruises all over his face. He sat still, taking deep breaths in and out and wincing in a futile attempt to fight the pain.

“It’s alright,” Sarah said, leaning against the wall beside the table. “The two of us were in another world. One of Anastasia’s posse must have burst in when you were inside of my head. We must have been so focused on what was inside that we hadn’t noticed.”

Kyle shook his head, perturbed by Sarah’s excuses for him. “No, no it’s not just that. I mean I was pretty deep in there but usually, I’m able to jack out relatively easily. But today, well,” Kyle sighed. “I’ve thought about it from every angle. It’s clear. There’s only one possibility. Anastasia has another telepath within her close circle. It’s the only thing that makes sense. Someone was able to sabotage our minds when I was down there. It’s the only way that she could have rendered us comatose for so long.”

Sarah squinted her eyes. “Are you sure?”

Kyle nodded. “As sure as I am about anything. Not only does it make logical sense, but I can feel it in my gut. There’s something that we’re missing here.”

“Yeah, like why they let you go? They know about our connection, and this is the second time that they’ve managed to get you in their clutches.”

“Yeah, and this time they didn’t interrogate me. Gave me a good beating but that was about it. “Kyle turned towards Sarah. “They wanted you. It’s always been about you, Sarah. You’re the one Anastasia wants. I guess in the grand scheme of things I’m just not that important.”

Kyle averted his gaze to the table after uttering that last statement. Admitting that took more strength than he knew that he had.

“No, you’re not,” she said.

Sarah examined the man up and down, then with gentle movements approached him, placing a hand on his shoulder. “You’re essential.”

The two exchanged a smile, in that moment, the gravity around the room seemed to have lessened. But Sarah knew that she couldn’t dwell on it. She was needed elsewhere.

“I should get going. I need to train.”

"Your match with Maryam is tomorrow, right?"

"Yes," Sarah said as she walked off towards the front door.

"Well, how on earth are you going to be able to compete in your condition? If I'm reading you right, you seem eerie similar to the Sarah I met two years ago. How on earth are you going to be able to fight the match and deal with Anastasia and her posse when they attack? What are you going to do?"

"What I can." Sarah turned to face him one more time. "You feeling alright, need some patching up?" She gestured towards her face.

Kyle shrugged, feigning nonchalance. "I'll be alright. It's not as bad as it looks."

Sarah tilted her head. "Kyle."

"Go Sarah," he said, his voice stern. "I'll be fine. I even got a new security system installed; in case those bitches try anything again. But something tells me that they're finished with me. It's all up to you now Sarah."

"Hang tight. And stay safe. I'll be back later," she said stepping outside and shutting the door behind her.

Sarah texted Amy that she would be late in returning to the hotel. She couldn't afford to waste any more time. She had already lost way too much by falling into The Pride's trap. Now more than ever was the time for her to be vigilant and unyielding. She would formulate a plan and stick to it. She couldn't depend on Amy or Carmen. This was her fight. Anastasia had placed a hit on her. Involving anyone else would most likely get them hurt.

Sarah drove to the gym that she and Carmen had trained in to find it empty and abandoned, which she appreciated. She spent ten minutes in the locker room, getting a feel for her body. She was as lean and muscular as before, though her body was sore and seemed to weigh considerably less after the injection. Sarah wrapped her hair in front of a mirror as she hardened her resolve. She removed her top, dressing in bra and sweatpants just like she did when she practiced boxing previously. This time she wouldn't stop, not for the rest of the night, not until the art of boxing was as natural to her as that of Karate, Tae Kwon doe, or any other martial art. She would give Maryam Bahira a fight that she wouldn't forget.

Sarah stood in the ring for three hours straight. She pounded away at the bag as her inner turmoil drowned her surroundings in the distance. Something was off. Not only had her abilities of frost manipulation disappeared but in addition, her physical strength wasn't quite what it was supposed to be. She couldn't believe that she had allowed Anastasia to do this to her. She saw her adversary in the place of the punching bag she was wailing on. She saw Anastasia, Maryam, as well as the Serpent men that she was hunting. She would beat them all to a pulp, no matter the consequences.

"Sarah."

She closed her eyes and sighed. Why? Why did she have to be here? Why now? She hadn't even finished her recovery. Sarah dropped her hands and let them slouch at her sides. She couldn't falter. So much was depending on this fight. And yet the desire to submit was more pronounced than it had been in ages.

"What are you doing here?" Sarah said, her voice low as she made every effort to be as steady as possible. "You were supposed to be back at the hotel."

"I figured that you would be here." Amy approached the edge of the ring, choosing not to enter and keeping her distance to judge her older sibling's temperament. Sarah could tell, even without turning around, that Amy was fidgeting. "After everything that's happened, I just- I was worried."

"How did you get here?"

"Taxi," Amy replied. "Is everything okay?"

"I'm fine," Sarah said. She cringed the moment that she had uttered the word. Amy would see right through it. She always did. The answer would spur her on further in her desire to ascend to her older sibling's level.

"Is there anything that I can do?" Amy's tone was needier than she had intended. Sarah cracked her knuckles and stretched her neck.

"Honestly. The best thing that you can do is just hang tight. I'm going to need to do quite a bit of training if I'm going to be ready."

Sarah raised her gloves in front of her and proceeded to pound the bag once more. She alternated between straight jabs, hooks, and uppercuts right at the center of the bag. She tried to avert her attention, but she felt a slight prickle on the back of her neck. It took her a full minute to realize that the feeling was caused by the fact that Amy hadn't left the room.

"I'm here. Might as well make the most of it, right?" Amy jumped into the ring and stationed herself behind the bag. "Come on. Show me what you got."

Sarah glared in response. "Amy."

"What? Two hands are better than one, right?"

"Not now Amy. This is something that I need to do on my own."

"Why?" Amy exclaimed.

"I just do. Boxing is an entirely different discipline for me. I need to master it on my own before I share the experience with someone else. Especially with someone that is as unfamiliar with it as I am. We'll train together later, after the fight with Maryam. There will be plenty of time then."

"There's time now, Sarah. You don't need to do it all on your own. Let me in."

Sarah glared in annoyance. "Amy, why are you here?"

"I told you. To help you."

"Are you?" Amy's eyes widened at the sound of her older sibling's questioning. "Because from what I can tell, the only person that you seem to be here for is yourself."

Amy's heart sunk inside of her chest. Of all the cuts and scrapes she had endured in her various fistfights, those words hurt most of all. "Sarah."

"No seriously." Sarah raised her expression, determined not to let Amy's emotional protests get to her. "Are you here for your own ego? To prove something? Because I already told you what I need. And that is for you to fall in line. Same as what I told you before we came here. And if you can't do that then it's best that you get a ride back home."

Amy's jaw loosened. It seemed to require strenuous exertion to even form a syllable in response. "You don't mean that." Sarah shrugged. "I said it, didn't I?"

Amy looked as if a bug had entered the back of her throat.

"This isn't a game, Amy. What? Did you think this was a road trip? That we're here to have fun as we used to playing soccer when we were little? We aren't little girls anymore. We're women. It's time to start acting like it."

Sarah had nearly hardened her resolve but then she took notice of the flustered look on Amy's face. Just as she feared her younger sibling hadn't foreseen this turn of events, which meant that she was oblivious to just how dire the situation had become.

Amy stood with her mouth hung open as she waited for a followup comment, but none came. Sarah merely gazed in her direction, her expression cold and unwavering. It didn't matter how long Amy would stand there staring at her with those gaping hurt eyes. Sarah would stare her down all night if she had to, hoping that somehow her eyes, as scornful as they were, would serve as a warning that would keep Amy out of harm's way.

After almost a full minute Amy exited the ring, realizing that to her great dismay, she was no longer wanted. She placed a tongue in her cheek to keep her twitching bottom lip in place as she stormed out of the room. Her disposition had reversed in an instant. She'd rather be anywhere else in the world at that moment.

Sarah sighed, releasing the tension from her body. It took only seconds after Amy left for her expression to imprint itself on the back of her mind. Sarah cocked her head to the side, realizing that her frustration would only give her that much more power.

Sarah stood in the locker room outside of Maryam's boxing arena, wrapping bandages around her hands as she waited to be called. She examined her left hand and balled it into an angry fist. She pursed her lips as she attempted to lower her body temperature. She squinted her eyes, noticing just a tiny bit of frost around her hand before it evaporated. The injection she had received was still strong in her mind. She felt as though a meteor had been dropped on top of her; its radiation still coursing through her veins. How long would it take to flush it out of her system?

"Sarah Stryker," One of the trainers called out.

Sarah followed her trainers out into the main hallway after her name was called. She found Amy waiting by the doorway with her arms wrapped around her chest. Sarah stopped once she stepped in front of her, examining her from head to toe before deciding to speak.

"You okay?"

Amy looked up, still sour from their previous conversation. She cocked her head to the side. "Do you care?"

Sarah glared in reply. She knew that Amy's words were a challenge as much as they were a cry for attention. She figured that she would cut her a break.

"Okay then," Sarah muttered to herself before averting her eyes away in acceptance. She walked out into the arena. It took her only a minute to spot her opponent in the corner of the other side of the ring.

Maryam Bahira stood with her head held up high, stiffened by the fatigue coursing through her veins like boiling acid. Her match with her previous opponent echoed like wildfire, her chest, jaw, abdomen, and knuckles still ached from it. She couldn't believe what she had allowed the miniature Latina to reduce her to.

Sarah stepped into the ring, making sure to take a deep breath in and out as she summoned her might. The two girls were then called to step forward. Sarah walked with slow hesitant steps, and she noticed her opponent mirror her movements. They stood only a mere inch away after stopping. Sarah and Maryam both furrowed their brows as they prepared for the plunge.

"You good? You're looking a little sluggish there."

"I could say the same to you," Sarah bit back.

"Been getting in a few fights recently? As practice?"

"Something like that," Sarah replied, making sure to be careful with her words. She couldn't give her opponent any weakness to prey on. The referee approached the two women, exchanging wide-eyed glances between them before speaking.

"Alright. Just like before I want a good clean fight. We had a few slips up last time. I understand this is a sport of passion. But you must obey the rules at all times if you want to remain in the ring. Are we clear?"

Maryam turned to face the referee. "I'm coo. As long as she is." She pointed to Sarah, who glared with a fierce dead-eyed expression.

"I'm fine," she said, with a focused eye that hadn't turned to face the referee even once.

"Alright, well will you please head to your respective corners so that we can begin?"

Sarah and Maryam took a moment to size each other up. For both women, this battle was so much more than just a contest of strength and dominance. They locked expressions as the blood within turned to steel, sharpening them both for a fight that was sure to go the distance.

"You sure about this?" Maryam warned. "Like I told yo girl I don't hold back."

"I'm sure."

Maryam's eyes widened. "You better bring it."

"I intend to."

"Aight din."

The two warriors pounded gloves before heading to their respective corners. Sarah bounced up and down, as the adrenaline welded up inside of her. She took notice of the crowd as well as a fidgeting Amy standing just outside of the ring. With a swift reminder of her sister's presence, Sarah's destination was solidified. This was a battle to which there was no return. Sarah cracked her knuckles as she turned to face her opponent.

"Tonight, we have our champion, Maryam Bahira. Against the respected veteran of The Pride, Sarah Stryker."

The bell rang, signifying the start of the match. Amy gripped her fingers around her elbows in agitation. Sarah and Maryam circled each other, each getting a solid position of their footing before taking the plunge. Maryam bounced on the balls of her feet, noticing a slight tingling in her body that alerted her to her reduced strength. She would have to play this one smart. She couldn't afford to waste any more energy.

Sarah threw the first punch. A forward jab that Maryam was able to deflect in an instant. Sarah threw another jab, gauging her opponents' reflexes. Maryam responded with a swift combination of jabs that ended with a body shot to the abdomen. Sarah deflected the body shot leaving Maryam open for no longer than a brief second in time. Sarah took full advantage and decked the African boxer in the face, causing her to stagger backward.

Maryam shot a livid expression toward Sarah. She roared and exploded into a full-on frenzy. If her bout with Carmen taught her anything it was not to hold back. She didn't know how she had let Sarah get a hit in so early during the match, but it didn't matter. She would make Sarah regret it.

Sarah raised her fists and blocked Maryam's fierce combo. Every attack felt like an avalanche. The muscle relaxants had done a number on Sarah. She staggered and her body was sent rocking back from the pressure of Maryam's heavy blows.

Through a moment of clumsiness uncharacteristic of Sarah, she dropped her guard, her forearms stinging from the collision of Maryam's fists against them. Maryam struck her opponent, timing it so that her gloves slid in between Sarah's arms just as she dropped her guard, connecting with a fierce uppercut to the chin.

Sarah felt as though her head had been knocked off her shoulders. She had been punched numerous times by various people, but never in her life had she been hit with a haymaker so earth-shattering.

Maryam pounded away without hesitation. She struck Sarah twice in the chest, once in the stomach, before winding her hand back as far as she could and flooring her with a vicious right hook. Sarah spiraled to the ground and a look of triumph washed over Maryam. Never in her life had she experienced such catharsis when beating an opponent.

Sarah sat up on her hands, watching as a thin line of blood dripped out of the corner of her mouth. She took a moment to catch her breath, realizing that her stamina was also hampered by the drugs.

"Stay down. You know ya can't hang with me."

Sarah lifted her leg, leaning against it before springing herself back on her feet.

"Girl, you better stop. Think about this. You keep going there ain't no going back. I'm the champ for a reason. I fight to win, which means my opponents tend to end up a bloody mess by the time it's over. That is if they lucky to still keep walking afterward."

Sarah took a moment to catch her breath then placed her hands forward and balled them into fists. She chose not to say a single word in reply. She wouldn't give this girl the time of day.

Maryam's expression remained placid. Fighting was her passion. The crunch of a woman's bones under the power of her titanium-sized blows. It was what she lived for. But for some reason, this girl's stubbornness filled her heart with dread rather than excitement. "Aight din."

The two warriors lunged toward each other in unison. This time

Maryam was hesitant to strike, and Sarah took full advantage of that. She broke Maryam's guard, arcing her fist around to her earlobe, and gritted her teeth as she pounded her temple, knocking her into the side of the ring.

Sarah pinned her opponent to the ropes and unloaded a series of rapid-fire punches that left Maryam stunned. She could feel the coldness of her forearms return to her by the end of it, finishing her combo with an uppercut that shot Maryam's head into the air, causing her to spit out her mouthguard. A mixture of saliva, sweat, and blood splattered on Maryam's face, freezing in mid-air as well as clouding her vision.

The audience gasped in utter dismay. Some of the women in the audience cupped their hands over their mouths. A booming noise enveloped the room the moment Maryam hit the ground. It was like she had made a crater in it. Her jaw clenched and swelled with the coldness of Sarah's attack. The pain increased once the Ref began the countdown.

After seven seconds of disbelief and denial surging through her, Maryam found the courage to stand up again. She popped off the ground after a wave of self-awareness hit her.

The bell rang signifying the end of the round. The two girls stood with their hands outstretched, their fists raised towards each other. They both had half a mind to resume their fisticuffs immediately but with slow hesitant movements, they each lowered their arms, accepting the momentary pause in battle.

Sarah and Maryam retreated to their respective corners. They slouched on their seats as their trainers approached them. Both kept their eyes glued onto each other as the men applied cotton swabs and cue tips to cuts and swelling on their faces.

"Maryam"

Desiree approached her friend's corner with her eyes protruding in fear. She gripped the edge of the ring as if she was hanging onto her last breath. The longer that she stared at her friend, the higher her heartbeat rose.

"You okay?"

Maryam took deep breaths in and out as her expression locked with the blonde-haired warrior that sat only a few feet away from her. For the first time in her life, her feelings about her opponent were difficult to decipher. The rage that she felt for all her enemies was there but there was something else as well; something that she couldn't quite place her finger on.

"Girl, answer me. Are you okay?"

"I'm fine," Maryam said through gritted teeth.

"She really did a number on your left cheek."

"Mmm-hmm. She going to hell now."

Maryam's declaration was frightening. It was what she often said about any person who pushed her over the edge. With those words, Desiree knew that the match was headed towards disaster.

Maryam took a swig of water before standing up. She couldn't stand sitting down any longer, not when her opponent had gained so much momentum. She stomped her feet on the ground before approaching Sarah, her eyebrows curled in deep unyielding focus. If Sarah would dial her fervor up to a ten, then Maryam would dial up to a fifteen. It was her sole desire and one that she trained her entire life for.

Sarah's head snapped backward. A mixture of saliva and blood splattered across the arena. She lost her footing and stumbled for a brief second. Maryam had hit her with a vicious hook to the left cheek right out of the gate. Sarah raised her hand in defense and made an evasive back dash to regain her equilibrium. She couldn't believe that she had left herself wide open like that. She danced around the ring as her blurry vision returned to normal.

Maryam lunged forward into another offensive maneuver once again, wasting no time in taking her opponent into account. Sarah aimed a punch straight for her head and to her surprise, Maryam ducked low to the ground, avoiding the attack by a narrow margin before causing her to heave with a well-timed body shot. Maryam then sent her off the ground and into the ropes with a brutal uppercut to the nose. She lunged forward and attempted a follow-up attack, but Sarah performed an evasive sidestep at the last second and struck Maryam straight in the cheekbone. The sound of her knuckle crunching against her made the audience cringe. The unexpected maneuver caused Maryam to bleed out of the corner of her mouth. If she thought her bout against Sarah Stryker would be an easy one, she was in for quite the awakening.

Maryam and Sarah struck in a rhythmic sequence, without thought or much technique. The sheer chaos and desperate dire circumstance of the fight tore into each of their hearts, leaving little left other than blood and sweat. Their gloves pounded into each other over and over. They exchanged a few blows along the way. Maryam punched her opponent in the chest, nose, abdomen, in between the eyes and Sarah returned the favor. Both seemed to be on equal footing despite the difference in style and experience.

Sarah winded her arm back, preparing for the ultimate punch. She would subdue her opponent. She was tired of playing games. She was tired of saving face for the sake of her sister. The lioness within would not be satisfied until all her adversaries were subdued, starting with this woman. She thrust her arm forward, utilizing the bulk of her strength. For less than a split second, the effects of the drugs were gone. There was only her body; her fist; and her own decision.

Sarah had successfully landed her attack, though not before Maryam struck her with a swift shot at the same time. The two girls reeled in response, their heads rocking back in unison under the weight of their immense strength and desperation. Amy's jaw dropped in disbelief as both Maryam and Sarah crashed to the ground. The entire audience fell silent. This was an unexpected turn of events that none of them had seen before.

"Come on, Sarah. Come on."

Amy spoke in a low whisper, her heart thumping in her chest. It required all her willpower to keep her composure. She knew that she would need it to weather the storm ahead, but she could already feel her insides churning.

"Maryam. Maryam, come on. Get up."

Desiree screamed, though to her dismay much of her voice was drowned out by the incessant noise surrounding her.

Sarah squirmed from where she lay on the ground. Her mind had been thrown out of orbit by that last punch. She rolled on her back and dug her gloved fist into the mat. She felt as though her brain had been disconnected from her body. The sensation was enough to make her consider throwing in the towel, if only for a brief second.

Maryam raised her head, getting a good look at the floored woman in front of her. Who were these women? How could she have let them weaken her like this? She curled her lips as blood dripped down her nostrils. In all her life, she couldn't remember the last time that she wanted to beat an opponent so badly before. By the time she managed to push her self-deprecating thoughts to the back of her mind, she was on one knee, mimicking her opponents' actions.

The two women lunged toward each other the moment that they made it to their feet. Neither of them had a game plan. Neither of them knew what their method of attack would be. All they knew was how badly they wanted to subdue the other. Their fists were only an inch away from each other's faces when the bell rang once again, signaling a momentary pause in the great contest between two of the strongest warriors that The Pride had to offer.

Sarah stumbled on her way to the corner. Two of the male trainers assigned rushed to catch her in an instant. On a normal day, she would appreciate it. But this time Sarah felt herself resisting their help.

"No. No, I'm fine. I said I'm fine"

The men acted with their hearts and ignored Sarah's defensive protests. As did her sister who rushed to her corner immediately.

"Sarah. Sarah are you okay?"

There was a delay in response, which only increased Amy's hysteria. She raised her voice in an instant.

"Sarah!"

"I'm fine Amy."

Sarah raised her voice in reply, hoping that her rudeness would shut Amy down and dissuade her from any further questioning.

"Sarah, you're not okay. I can see it. Come on. You're worn out. Even before she hit you. Whatever it is you can tell me."

Sarah's vision turned blurry. She looked to Maryam's corner, slouching as her arms hung down her sides. For a second, the dark-skinned warrior in front of her faded out, and a pale-skinned Redhead sat in her place, but Sarah knew it was an illusion. There was still a bit of time remaining before she faced her true adversary. Maryam still sat in the same spot across from her as she did before.

"Sarah, why won't you talk to me?"

Sarah could tell even without looking that Amy's eyes were beginning to water. This was the last thing that she needed. In a moment of thoughtlessness, in which her heart had gotten the better of her, Sarah uttered a single sentence that could've very well been her damnation.

"It's not the fight. It's the injection."

"What injection?"

"It was The Pride they-"

Sarah stopped in her tracks, realizing what she admitted at the last possible second and what it would mean to the girl across from her.

"You were injected? By what?" Amy couldn't believe her ears. Her eyes and jaw both widened in unison. Her heart sank into the back of her chest, further than it ever had in months. "Oh my god. Sarah, why didn't you tell me?"

Sarah lowered her gaze and took a deep breath in and out. She could feel not only her insides churning but her heart clenching. Everything was disorienting and it seemed as if the feeling wasn't going away any time soon. "I-it just happened."

"Sarah, stuff like this doesn't just happen," Amy scolded. Her voice was startling. It was striking in its familiarity with her own. "It was planned. They planned it." Amy's eyes widened. "It's Anastasia! It has to be."

"We'll deal with her later," Sarah said.

"Sarah, call off the match. Tell them what's going on."

"No."

"Sarah, please. If you keep going you're going to get hurt."

"Amy, not now."

"Yes now!" Amy barked. She had enough. She was done taking orders. "Sarah, you need to let me help you. Let me step in. I'll fight her."

"No. No, Amy, you can't. It's too dangerous. She's experienced. You're not ready."

"Yes, I am. I've trained with you, With Carmen. I can do this. Please, Sarah. I need you to believe in me."

"This isn't about that Amy. Right now, I need you to listen to me. I know what I'm doing."

"No, you don't," Amy reprimanded. "Please, Sarah. Just let me go for one round. We'll see how I fair then. Just give me a chance."

"You'll have a chance. Soon enough. There's no need to rush this," Sarah said in a hoarse breath.

"Sarah, this isn't about me. It's about you. If you keep going like this, I might lose you." Amy's eyes began to turn red as the tears welled up inside of them.

"Amy, stop. I've already told you."

"Sarah-"

"Amy." Sarah spun her head in her sister's direction. Amy's whines and pleas helped to restore some of her strength. "I said no."

Amy felt a knot tighten around the back of her throat. The tone in her sister's voice shook her like thunder. She knew that there was a weakness for her behind them somewhere but trying to reach that before this match ended would be futile. It was for this reason that Amy chose to keep her silence as Sarah stood up for the next round.

Sarah and Maryam raised their arms as the bell rang again, signifying the start of round three. Both warriors had become sluggish from the brutal double knockdown in the previous round. They could see the weakness in each other's eyes; a mirror of what was happening within their bodies.

Blood splattered across Maryam's teeth as her head rocked backward from the force of Sarah's heavy blow. She had seen the fatigue in her opponent's eyes and the attack that landed still ranked in the top percentile of punches that had ever been thrown her way. She performed an evasive back dash and swung back with a swift punch to the side of her opponent's head.

Sarah felt her neck stiffen as Maryam buried her fist into her cheekbone. The punch was so great in its magnitude; so precise in its destructive capabilities that Sarah lost all motor control for at least five seconds. Maryam was able to connect with a soul-stealing punch to the gut. Sarah gasped, her breath giving way as her opponent used the fist buried in her abdomen to lift her off the ground.

Sarah's mind tumbled into chaos. Her mind raced as she struggled in panic. She couldn't let this happen. Not now. Not after all the effort that she put into coming here. Sarah swung with all her fervor, knocking Maryam's arm off her. She threw a series of rapid-fire jabs toward her opponent; before hitting her in the mouth.

Sarah didn't let up for a second, placing her entire body weight into her next series of attacks. For the second time in this brutal and increasingly unstable match, Maryam found herself overwhelmed by her speedy and formally trained attacker. She was struck in the chest and the nose several times before her head twisted to the left in response to a vicious right hook by Sarah.

Maryam roared and threw a massive right hook in Sarah's direction and when she blocked it; Maryam held onto her, ramming her fist into her opponent's abdomen several times. Sarah shoved her off in agitation but not before her head was smacked in with another swift right hook.

Blood poured down Sarah's nose as she positioned herself on the balls of her feet and prepared for the next barrage of attacks. She took a few hesitant, mindful side steps; mimicking Maryam's footing as she struggled to find an opening. Sarah and Maryam lunged forward at the same time. The two women decided to let loose and pull out every ounce of fervor that they had in their arsenal. The next minute was sheer chaos. Sarah and Maryam exchanged blow after blow, their minds lost in the abyss of rage and torment. They struck each other repeatedly in the face, the chest; the stomach; between the eyes, and a few in the ribs. They struck at any and everything that they could reach.

Sarah ended the barrage by connecting with a ten-punch combo to the chest. She whined her arm backward and finished the combination by ramming her hardened glove into Maryam's temple. Her opponent was knocked into the ropes and Sarah proceeded into her follow-up attack. Time was at a standstill for the African boxer. The Earth fluttered beneath her feet as she was knocked into the corner of the ring. She was now in the danger zone. Just a few more moments of agony and her title would be lost, possibly forever.

With that thought in mind, Maryam spurred into action, utilizing her most advanced defensive maneuvers. She swayed, avoiding Sarah's strikes by a narrow margin before smashing her in the ribs, escaping from the corner and asserting herself back in the fight. Both women threw their arms in an aggressive frenzy, ignoring the prickling pain that had infiltrated their hearts to claw their way to the top.

Sarah connected with a three-punch jab to the nose before twisting her body for a right hook that would floor her opponent. She had seen it in her mind before attempting it herself. However just before her right hook landed Maryam raised her arm, halting the attack in an instant.

Sarah's jaw dropped. In her moment of triumph, she had gotten careless, and her opponent was sure to take advantage of that fact unless she stepped it up. She threw several left and right hooks to make up for her previous blunder, but Maryam had picked up on her pattern, blocking and parrying with a rhythm akin to a beating drum. Maryam rammed her fist into Sarah's chest and abdomen with a swift five-punch combination that set her world in flames.

Sarah heaved as the sounds of the audience, announcer, the referee as well as even that of the woman in front of her drowned in the distance. Her breasts and stomach ached with debilitating agonizing pain that she was certain she had experienced before, though it wasn't quite as pronounced. Still, Sarah chose to lunge forward. Her opponent was bound to be just as tired as she was. Sarah arched her fist forward in a swift maneuver that she was certain would turn the tide of battle for good. In less than a split second, all the pain endured during this fight would pay off. She was certain.

The next thing that Sarah felt was a sensation indescribable to man. A fountain of blood sprayed out of her nose after it had happened. She had been launched off her feet and into the air by an uppercut of the heavens. Sarah's soul turned to shattered glass. She couldn't believe she had allowed this to happen. Time slowed down as the reality of her situation settled into her consciousness. She crashed to the ground in disgrace, sending a rippling effect that vibrated throughout the arena.

Amy cupped her hand over her mouth as her eyes moistened. Her heart sunk into her chest. She had seen this turn of events coming though to her dismay it did nothing to make the sight any easier to witness.

Maryam held her arm high into the air even after the attack had landed and Sarah lay flat on her back. She caught her breath and gazed at the woman beneath her, a look of relief escaping her fatigued expression. She had never felt more elated in her entire life. To see the woman who looked down on her subdued and bloody under the weight of her blows was a thing of beauty. She had put everything that she had into that last punch. More than what she used against The Serpent gang who attempted to ambush her and nearly as much as what she used to knock Carmen Rivera out cold.

Sarah lay sprawled out on the floor. She had a runny nose full of blood and her body was wobbly under the weight of Maryam's attacks. She noticed the Ref standing above her, beginning his count. she was now in the danger zone. It was only a matter of time before she would have to face her true adversary. Perhaps she was better off accepting where this situation had left her? She could still come out of the mission in one piece if she played this smart.

But then Sarah remembered the girl that was watching; the girl who had been by her side since the beginning. The girl who depended on her since she was a small child. How could she do anything other than fight with that girl watching from the sidelines?

With that single thought in mind, Sarah found the strength return to her limbs once again. Like the missing pieces of a puzzle, all it required was a bit of brainpower. She rolled on her back and dug her fists into the mat. This next action would change everything. She was certain of it.

Maryam's eyes widened at that moment. A petrifying sensation entered her bloodstream. It wasn't fear. It couldn't be. She was certain that fear was something that she was incapable of. And yet watching as the woman who she had nearly knocked into the next century, attempt to stand up, produced emotions within that Maryam never knew that she had. Desiree's eyes widened at the same time. To both women this appeared to be a dream; how could someone from this girl's background be able to withstand such a beating?

Sarah looked up, her eyes glaring at Maryam with animosity as she stood on one knee. Her opponent was weakened by her momentary victory. She had to be. Sarah would take advantage of Maryam's moment of rest and beat her into submission. It was as good of a plan as any other she had come up with during this journey. She had to go the distance. It was the only option left.

Sarah's legs wobbled the moment she stood up. She buckled and crashed to the floor. Sweat dripped and beaded down her forehead, her cheeks, and her nose as the reality of just how wounded she was had hit her. The vile toxin was still there; laying dormant and waiting for the right opportunity to strike. All that Sarah could do was crumble under the weight of its pressure.

"The winner is MARYAM BAHIRA!"

The sound of the audience was like thunder. Many of them had been fans of Maryam for a long time. They were certain that Maryam would win this fight before they arrived. The fact that the fight and everything it entailed produced so much uncertainty only made the champion's sweeping victory more rewarding.

"Told you, you couldn't hang with me," Maryam said, approaching Sarah with slow hesitant steps. Sarah refused to look up when she addressed the woman. She'd rather not say anything to her at all.

"You haven't won. You know nothing," Sarah said, as she sat on her knees with her eyes averted towards the ground. Maryam was thrown. During the short time she had known this woman she hadn't heard her address her in such a manner. Something was off.

"Look. It wasn't a bad fight. You and your Latina have potential. Maybe we could train sometime. Pass on a few notes."

Maryam extended her glove, hoping for a bit of leeway. Sarah stood up and knocked her hand out of the way, stumbling as she approached her frantic tearful sister and male trainers who attended to her wounds.

Maryam was left on her own. She had won and yet the sense of triumph left her in an instant. She stood with her eyes widened as the voices and celebration of her fans drowned in the distance. By the end all that was left was silence.

Chapter 13: Anastasia

Ten women stood at the center of a dojo huddled in a circle, their hands dripping with trepidation as they prepared for battle. They gritted their teeth and their petrified expressions locked onto the behemoth of a warrior standing in the middle of the group. For that person what would transpire in the next moment was nothing but a training exercise but to the rest of the group, this was a confrontation that they had been regretting all week.

The team of female warriors lunged forward in unison, screaming at the top of their hysterical lungs as they summoned up the atom's weight of courage that they had inside of them. They raised their hardened fists, each taking turns striking their opponent. The first three women to attack were knocked back before they had even blinked.

Two of the black belts were hurled through the wall and into the next room while one was sent soaring through the ceiling. The sight made a few of the women pause before attempting to strike themselves. They had all heard stories of this woman, but it was another experience to witness her inhuman strength themselves.

The warrior in the center of the mat hadn't moved her feet from where she stood. Any of these women would be lucky if they could get her to even break a sweat during this session. She stood at over eight feet tall and sported a thick muscular body though at a closer glance one could spot the unique curvature of a feminine physique. She wore long jet-black hair that extended past her shoulder blades. Her name was Olga, and she was one of the few women within the organization who had served The Pride her entire life.

Olga tightened her fists as she prepared her mind and spirit for battle. For years she was a warrior who was considered by many to be a one-woman army. Her reputation had granted her worldwide acclaim and praise. The mere mention of her name inspired fear and reverence in the hearts of many of The Pride, but all that changed when she met Sarah Stryker.

The mere clench of her fists made the ground beneath her quiver and the walls crack. The last thing that any of these women wanted was to face Olga. They all knew that it would take only one mighty punch to send them to an early grave.

The remaining seven took a few hesitant half steps as Olga's merciless eyes surveyed each one. These women were just appetizers before the main course. They did little to satisfy her thirst for battle but that didn't mean she would take it easy on them either.

Olga remained still as the team charged toward her. She floored one with a backhand, using minimal effort and causing her to crash into the ground face first. She then proceeded to knock the others back with her elbows and fists.

One woman pulled out a chain, twirled it in the air, and threw it; attempting to subdue her by the neck. The Muscular brute spun around; utilizing more speed than most believed that she was capable of, wrapping a firm grip around the chain and immediately pulling the girl into a suffocating chokehold. Olga lifted the girl off the ground as she gagged in frantic desperation. Olga tried to imagine that this girl was her sworn enemy, maybe then the emptiness prickling away at her mind would dissipate because of it.

Greta, the girl with the ability to control reanimated corpses, leaned against her crutches for support after arriving in the dojo from the stairs above the team. A proud grin spread across her face. She had made it just in time to witness Olga lift two women into the air: holding them up with a single hand below the stomach. After a few seconds, she hurled them off the mat in a moment of triumph.

"How is it that I knew I would find you here?"

Olga looked up, noticing the tattooed girl in front of her. She cracked her knuckles and pursed her lips.

"Because you're a busybody who always pokes their nose where they don't belong."

Greta chuckled. "You're cute when you're angry."

The rest of the squad stood up, rubbing the back of their necks, and headed towards the door beside Greta. Only about six out of the ten women were able to do so, the others who had been knocked through the wall were still unconscious and would be for at least a day. This had been a daily routine for the past month. Olga would break as many warriors as possible even if it would only bring her an inch closer to her goal.

"Where is she?" Olga asked, her expression placid and uncaring.

"Upstairs, dealing with a few guests," Greta replied.

"I need to see her." Olga barged towards the door, hoping that that would be the end of the conversation, but Greta couldn't resist opening her mouth once again.

"You know you're still not ready to face her right?"

Olga stopped in her tracks. The blonde was a blip on her radar, but the words of her colleague hit her like a fist. She contorted her body towards the girl beneath her. She leaned in closer; dangerously close. Greta stood at average height and with a slim build akin to the warriors Olga had just taken down. She appeared to be at a clear disadvantage and yet despite that the sly grin had never left Greta's expression. It remained plastered on her face as Olga spoke to her.

"I'm sorry. Mind running that by me again?"

Greta shrugged. "I think I spoke very clearly, don't you?"

Olga shook her head. "Oh, you better hope that you weren't. I'm not in the mood."

"You faced her in battle. You know what she is capable of and how sharp her instincts are. Do you think that little display is going to cut it?"

Olga gave a glance towards the dojo; taken in all the damage that had been done. She had created a massive dent in the ground and there were several holes in the wall in which she had plowed her enemies.

"I'm on the path. You'll see once I get my hands on her.

Greta shook her head. "You rush into this half-baked and things will end up just like last time."

"You're one to talk," Olga fired back. "You think you're so crafty, yet she was able to not only subdue you but break your leg as well."

Greta's smile dissipated. She chewed on her bottom lip. "I wasn't at one hundred percent."

"You don't say?" Without warning, Olga shoved Greta into the wall behind her. "Well contrary to what you might believe I am at one hundred percent. And believe me, when I face that bitch in battle, she'll discover it first-hand."

Greta didn't fight back. She knew that such an act would be futile for the time being. But that didn't matter. What did was the effect her words had on Olga.

"I'm Anastasia's number one girl. And you best remember that."

"Things change," Greta replied, smiling once again though her voice was laced in a fierce warning. It was Olga's turn to respond with a grin.

"Yes. They do. One day it might be you who is called to serve me. Be a good lap dog and go back to raising that undead army of yours. Leave the actual fighting to the big girls. Now if you excuse me, I have a Queen to attend to."

Olga condescendingly slapped Greta's cheeks before heading up the stairs outside of the dojo. Greta turned around, staring in her direction long after she left, the wheels in her head spinning like a clock as she plotted her next move.

Inside one of the rooms on the top floor, near the main office, dwelled a woman of seemingly unparalleled power and influence. She was a warrior whose very soul was at peace only when torment and pain engulfed all her surroundings.

It was this person who had placed the hit on Sarah Stryker, who had targeted her from the very beginning. She had long elegant illuminating red straightened hair that extended past her neck with a small green beanie on top of her head. Her Carmine red eyes made her two Prisoners shudder from where they stood. She was of average height and build and her demeanor was like an ocean without waves. Few knew her identity and even fewer knew what her real name was but those who served her or were unfortunate enough to be sentenced as one of her subjects would come to know her by the name of Anastasia, the current Queen of The Pride.

Anastasia stepped into the limelight. She stood unapologetic, her eyes shone with confidence as she scanned the bodies of her male and female subjects. The prisoners stood naked, their hands tied by two individual ropes, spreading their arms out across the ceiling. Both were bloody and bruised from the various beatings that had been inflicted on them.

"Please. Please. Let us go. I beg you."

The man was the first to beg. He couldn’t believe what this beautiful and seemingly ordinary woman had reduced him to.

"Let you go?" Anastasia mimicked a whiny voice. "But we just got started."

"I-I’ll give you anything." The man pleaded.

"Oh, begging already? I love this part." Anastasia approached the man and leaned in close. She leaned against a pillar for balance as her gaze penetrated his heart like a laser.

"P-please."

"Now, what could you possibly give me? What could a wretched pathetic shell of a man possibly offer that I don’t have in spades? Go on. I’m waiting."

"B-bbb," The man stuttered as he attempted to speak.

"What’s the matter huh? I thought you were desperate. Come on. Show me what you know. It’s your life on the line after all. Or do you want me to break out the scissors, and remove your essential assets down there permanently?

"No. No, please. I’ll tell you anything."

Anastasia smiled. "There's nothing that I want to know sweetheart. I already have the full package. Which is more than what could be said for you."

"STOP." The woman tied beside him complained.

"Mind your tongue bitch." Anastasia spat. "Before I cut it off."

"Leave him out of this," The woman insisted. "If you want to punish someone, punish me."

"I SAID MIND YOUR TONGUE. I do what I please and with whom I please." Anastasia stood up, leaving the man's side, and approached the female captive. She grabbed her chin and pulled her in close. "And you get no say in the matter. Unless you wish to be placed under a great deal of pain yourself."

"If you want to kill me then get it over with."

"Oh, no. I'm not finished with you, not by a damn sight. Your punishment is just getting started. And it'll only get longer with that attitude." "I did nothing wrong."

"Oh, really? You did nothing wrong? And who exactly are you to judge that?" Anastasia squinted as she examined every inch of the girl's face. "This isn't a girl's camp. This is an army. My army. And as long as you are in my presence you will serve me."

"I don't serve you. I serve The Pride."

"I am The Pride. For as long as you claim to be one of us you will do as I say. I decide your every action. And I decide when you've earned a break. Is that clear?" Anastasia squeezed the girl's cheekbone with authority. She had half a mind to squeeze her head in with the force of her palm. The female captive waited too long to respond, triggering Anastasia's impatience. She pulled out a knife and grazed the girl's right cheek, producing a shallow cut down to her chin. "I've got a wealth of pain in store for you, unbearable sensations that you never even dreamed of if you don't answer me. Now, are we clear?"

"Yes. Yes." The girl exclaimed. "We're clear. God, we're clear." The girl sobbed in defeat. Anastasia turned away, realizing that her work was now finished.

"What's the problem? Plenty of the other girls have boyfriends too."

Anastasia turned back towards the girl, baffled by the absurdity of what she was suggesting. "Yes, but they are not all caught making out on the job when they're supposed to serve me are they?"

"So that's what this is about?" The man said. "Purging the male end of the population. How do you expect to continue our species afterward?"

Anastasia lifted a glass of water off her desk. "The plan is more accurately described as subduing rather than purging." She placed the glass against her lips and took a modest sip of her drink before continuing. "I mean, in order to effectively subdue a population, one has to initiate a bit of purging. But one takes precedence over the other."

"Why?" The man asked, his voice oozing with desperation. "Why do you have so much hatred for us?"

Anastasia chuckled, shocked by the absurdity of what the man was asking. "Hate? Is that what you think this is? This is an act of passion, of artistry most assuredly but hate?"

"But there must be some reason that your-"

"Look into my eyes," Anastasia commanded, silencing the man in an instant. She placed her two forefingers underneath her eyelids. "I want you to look deeper. Allow your entire field of vision to be consumed by them. Now, tell me, do you see any hatred in these eyes?"

The male prisoner's eyes widened to an alarming degree. "No," he said suddenly. "There's nothing. Nothing at all."

Anastasia allowed a morsel of delight to wash over her expression. "Bingo."

"Please, let us go," The woman asked.

"Nope. I think I'll keep you up here for a few more hours."

"Please, you don't have to do this."

"My word is final," Anastasia said.

"You can't. We could bleed out-"

"DO NOT SPEAK OVER ME." The self-appointed Queen of The Pride bellowed to the height of her lungs. The two prisoners silenced their pleas in an instant. "Now as I was saying, I'll give you a few hours to reflect on your decision. Maybe next time you'll avoid displays of public affection if you know that your boy toy will suffer for it."

"He's not my boyfriend," The female prisoner murmured.

Anastasia lowered her chin and squinted her eyes. "What?"

"He's not my boyfriend. The man I was with is already dead."

Anastasia placed a finger under her chin, contemplating what she was being told. "Then why did they bring you to me? Are you a spy or-"

"No," The man pleaded. "I've never even met this girl."

"Huh," The Queen muttered in nonchalance. "Well, that's unfortunate, isn't it?" She threw her hand up in the air. "Oh well. What's one more fuel to the fire?"

Anastasia left the room, leaving her two prisoners to contemplate their next agonizing hours of torture and bask in the depravity and sadism of their captor. Whether they lived through the next few hours or not one thing was for sure, the look in Anastasia's eyes would remain within the recesses of their subconscious minds forever."

Olga made it upstairs to find a lounge full of women from various backgrounds, barging from one office to the other. She stormed through the halls of the lounge, nearly bumping into a few of the women working there in the process. There was only one woman on the floor who concerned her, and it was the one stationed in the main office. In the furthest corner of the top floor, she found who she was looking for.

"Anastasia? Queen? Are you there?" There was no response right away. Olga pounded on the door. "It's me? You wanted to see me?"

"Yes, of course. Come in."

The voice was warm and oozed with a gentleness that seemed foreign every time Olga heard it. She opened the door with hesitation, ducking to keep her head from pumping into the ceiling, and greeted the one woman in the world who unnerved her to the point of submissive obedience.

"Hello, Olga."

Olga replied to her leader's greeting with a gentle nod, signaling her acknowledgment of it. "You wanted to see me?" She prompted.

Just then a black boy approached Anastasia. He bowed his head as he extended a cup of tea in the woman's direction.

Anastasia lifted and placed it against her pink glossed lips. "Thank you, Ahmed." She took her time and sipped a morsel of it as Olga waited to be addressed.

"Madame?"

"Patience." Anastasia's voice was light as a feather yet there was something behind it that compelled her to remain silent. "You know I don't like to be rushed."

"You're right." Olga bit her lip. "My mistake. I'm here whenever you need me."

Anastasia responded to her Olga's apology with an understanding nod. "I'm only teasing. This is an urgent matter. I can understand why you would be eager to get things rolling, especially given what is at stake."

Olga shrugged, displaying the utmost confidence despite the storm raging within her. "Everything is in order as far as I'm concerned. The girls are well trained though between you and me only so many will be able to go the distance.

Anastasia kept her eyes locked on the massive brute in front of her; sizing her up to see if she believed what she was being told. "It's all part of the plan. As is the role that you will play in the coming conflict."

Olga perked her ears. Her entire being lit up upon hearing Anastasia's words elevating her.

"You're my muscle. The enforcer that will come to subdue all of our enemies." Anastasia lowered her voice, choosing to address Olga in an intimate tone. "You may not believe this, but I understand your pain. The missing hole in your chest. I feel it too. Ever since she defied us and managed to survive. It's not something that has ever happened before, not in the entire history of The Pride. And if we don't do something now it will happen again."

Olga's heart sunk into the pit of her chest. She knew what she was going to be called upon to do but the anticipation hurt all the same. "It can't happen. Not again."

"Not if we act," Anastasia replied, anticipating her subordinate's needs. "What's the latest on Sarah Stryker; her whereabouts? Is everything in motion?"

"Yes. The ploy worked. We managed to subdue both Sarah Stryker and the Telepath for a time."

"And what of the Telepath?"

"We let him go. Once we had Sarah he was no longer needed."

Anastasia nodded in approval. "And what about Maryam Bahira? How did the fight go between the two of them?"

"Pretty much exactly how you predicted."

A sly smile spread across Anastasia's lips. "Good. We are in the final stage. Sarah Stryker must be brought to justice for her crimes."

"And the Latina?"

"And The Latina," Anastasia answered in the affirmative. "They are our primary concern though that doesn't mean that I will tolerate carelessness."

Olga remained attentive and alert as her commander and Chief gave out her final orders. They would be imprinted in her skull and would remain there long after the conversation came to an end.

"We can't afford to leave our tracks uncovered this time. That means any and all bystanders must be eliminated. Anyone out after curfew must be killed. No exceptions."

"What about the men?" Olga asked, despite her instincts telling her not to question the Queen curiosity got the better of her.

Anastasia glared in response, clearly irritated by Olga's questioning. "Did you not hear what I just told you?"

"It's just that some of the girls- they enjoy the company of-"

"Do I look like I care what they enjoy?" Anastasia corrected her. "Last I checked the Queen's pleasure was prioritized before everyone else. Or am I mistaken?"

"No ma'am. You know I could care less. This isn't my request." Olga made sure to distance herself from anyone who could incur Anastasia's wrath. "It's just that some of the girls would be more eager to cooperate if-"

But Olga froze in her tracks before she could finish her last thought. Anastasia balled her hands into a ruthless fist, changing the atmosphere of the room in a mere instant in time. "Do you see this? Do you see it? If you want cooperation, loyalty, and respect then this is all that you need."

The sound of Anastasia clenching her fist echoed throughout the room. Her arm shook with fervor as the power of it extended down to her elbow, leaving a dent on top of her desk where it had been resting. "Are we clear?"

"Yes. Of course, Madame. We're perfectly clear."

"Good." Anastasia's mouth spread into a subtle smile. "I expect nothing less from you, Olga. Things didn't fare well for you the first time that you faced Sarah Stryker. No one blames you of course. She's unorthodox and completely different from any opponent that you ever faced. But I know you. I know what you're capable of. You're one of the finest specimens that The Pride has to offer. As a matter of fact, you have the potential to be one of the most powerful warriors in the world. But you won't as long as you have her dangling over your neck."

"I won't fail you," Olga said with authority.

"You have my full confidence. Just remember that my patience and mercy only extends so far. Nothing can go wrong this time. Nothing.
All The Pride's enemies must be taken into account. Sarah Stryker, The Latina, and The Prizefighter."

"Yes ma'am," Olga repeated.

"And remember every man that you see-" Anastasia prompted.

"Kill him."

"Every man. NO exceptions."

"I will see to it."

"Good."

Olga took a few steps back towards the door. "I'll hasten preparations."

"And Olga" Anastasia called out to her just as she grabbed onto the doorknob. She had one more thing to add before it slipped her mind. Olga turned towards her; her eyes lit up in bewilderment.

"Make sure to take care of the little sister too."

Maryam Bahira was given a lead by an unknown informant who had called her after the fight against Sarah Stryker. She drove to a small, abandoned building and roamed the halls in silence. Her primary thought was the nagging feeling that had entered her ever since she had exited the ring. She hoped that this meeting with one of the higherups would do something to put those feelings to rest.

"Hello, sister."

A woman walked by, casually greeting Maryam as if she were one of her own. Her eyes squinted in dismay as she locked expressions with her.

"Maryam Bahira."

Maryam's eyes darted forward, recognizing the voice of the woman who had addressed her. She was a scrawny woman who wore large spectacles and whose demeanor was placid, giving away nothing. It was this woman who had injected Sarah with the special serum needed to subdue her powers.

"It's nice to see you again, sister," The doctor greeted. Maryam surveyed the woman from head to toe, taking in the full image. There was something about her that made Maryam's skin crawl despite her not being physically imposing.

"I'm here," Maryam said with a shrug. "You called. Now whatcha won't?"

"Oh, just a moment of your time nothing more," The doctor said in a sly tone. "The Queen would like to congratulate you on a sweeping victory. It was quite the match."

"Ain't nothing but a thang," Maryam said.

"Your opponent has beaten quite a few of our most powerful warriors in the past. What you've accomplished today isn't to be taken lightly. It seems that your reputation as the woman with the fastest and most powerful hands in The Pride is true."

Maryam cocked her head to the side. The doctor's smug face made her blood boil. "Well, you can't always believe what you hear. The power of my fists can only be attested to by my opponents. But if you're eager to find out for yourself, feel free."

The doctor chuckled, amused by the bravado. Maryam wondered if her opponent could see through it and right into her fragile center, but she couldn't afford to worry about it.

"I'm a scientist, Maryam. Not a fighter. I don't compete on that level."

"Because you don't want to or because you can't?" Maryam leaned closer towards the woman, the tips of their noses nearly touching as she examined her. She wouldn't allow herself to be intimidated, no matter how much power these women had at their fingertips.

The doctor didn't flinch. "I have my own talents. Every woman does. Anastasia ensures that we all use our abilities to help each other reach a common goal. You could be a part of that."

"I told you. I'm not interested in being a part of anything. I've allowed your girls to go unchecked for this long only because of what you promised me. But you attack any of my people and we're going to have problems."

"We'll do nothing of the sort. We only seek to support our fellow sisters. Your power is great and would be of great use within The Pride. But I'll let her explain it all." The doctor gestured towards the path ahead of her. "This way."

The doctor led Maryam down a long corridor towards the front office. She knocked on the door and waited to be called in.

"Come in."

Maryam felt her spine tingle with anticipation a mere second before she walked inside the office. She froze, the minute that she entered. She had seen this woman before though it was the first time, she had been in such proximity to her. The green beanie-wearing redhead rested her arm on her chair and leaned back as her eyes widened.

"Well, well, well. Look who it is. The mighty Maryam herself. Aren't you quite the specimen? Even more butch and muscle-bound than what you appear on TV."

Maryam contorted her gaze in confusion. The sound of Anastasia's voice was like a siren. In all her life she had never heard a voice like it, nor would she ever desire to again.

"I was told that you wanted to see me." Maryam tensed her body and raised her chin in skepticism.

"I've been watching you. For a long time. Many of your fights and much of your progress." Anastasia spoke in a softened tone, making sure to make every word count. "The least you can do is give me the time of day."

Maryam contorted her gaze in confusion. "You've been watching me?"

"Yes. I have. I consider myself a more sophisticated breed of warrior, but I enjoy a good scrap as much as the next gal. I root for you too by the way. Why do you think that is?" Maryam shrugged.

"Because more than any other that I've seen in the ring you want to be there. You've proven that with every fight. Watching your battles is like entering a time capsule. You take your audiences by storm, taking us all back to a time when things were different. When your kind ruled in a primitive fashion, bashing the heads of everyone and anyone who stood in their way. When you enter that ring life is simple. The reality of your environment, your decrepit existence dissolves around you. It's the closest thing to freedom that you could ever experience in your life."

Maryam swallowed hard. The words of the woman who sat in front of her were like acid. She didn't know how much more of it she could take. "What do you want with me?"

Anastasia shrugged, feigning casualness and nonchalance. "Nothing much. I just want to make sure that we're on the same page. That's all."

Maryam weighed the woman's words in her mind, just to confirm whether she believed what she was being told. Anastasia shifted her eyes toward her subordinate, the doctor.

"My apologies. I will take my leave, Anastasia."

The doctor exited the room and a Tall muscular woman entered from the other side. Maryam's eyes fixated on her, shifting as they followed her until the woman stopped by Anastasia's side.

"I don't think you've met. This is Olga. I'm sure you know her at least by reputation. I'd say she's at least as savage as you. Maybe you can compare notes?"

Maryam's gaze shifted from Anastasia to Olga. She was contemplating her next course of action as much as she was her words. Everything would have to be carefully laid out and planned. She couldn't afford to take any unnecessary risks.

"Something on your mind?" Anastasia prompted.

"Yeah, I got a whole lot. Whatchu do to that girl? Whatcha got me involved with? What the hell is goin on?"

"Isn't it obvious?" Olga spoke up first. Maryam raised her eyebrows as her gaze shot upward towards the woman. She couldn't believe her ears.

"You were a means to an end," Anastasia said. "Don't fret too much about it. Okay, homegirl?"

"Homegirl? Who you think you talking to?"

"Relax. We want the same thing."

Maryam shook her head. "You don't know what I want. You don't know the first thing about me," She spat.

Anastasia glared in response, baffled at what she was being told. "Point in fact I do know you. It's why my girls approached you in the first place. You're a woman who lives for battle. It's all you have left after the death of your parents. You spent your entire life building your strength only to have that stuck-up bitch steal all the cred. Something like that is bound to drive a girl crazy."

Maryam felt her blood rising. She couldn't believe it. She couldn't believe what she had agreed to. "You don't know what you're talking-"

Anastasia raised a finger, silencing Maryam in an instant. "Remember this was all part of the plan. You wanted to face Sarah Stryker on an even playing field. Woman to woman. With only the strength of your knuckles to rely on. You got your wish. You've proven that your fists are superior to hers."

Maryam squinted her eyes. "What did you do to her? To Sarah?"

Anastasia mimicked a flustered face. "Uh, Thank you, Anastasia?"

"What did you do?" Maryam repeated, raising her voice to a heightened degree.

"Watch your tone," Olga reprimanded her. Maryam's neck stiffened as her eyes locked onto the woman in front of her.

"We took her down a notch," Anastasia said. "Just like you wanted."

Maryam felt her throat sink into the pit of her stomach. She was frantic, barely able to remain standing in place as she shook her head.

"I never wanted this."

"Didn't you? Why was it when my girl called you, you answered? You wanted the chance to face her in battle. You goaded Sarah and her friend into a fight. My girl only played her part."

Maryam couldn't believe it. How could this have happened? How could she have played right into the enemy's hands?

"This is a momentous occasion. You should feel honored. You are responsible for the takedown of the most infamous warrior in the countryside. Our opponent is down and ripe for the killing."

Maryam felt her eyes sink to the back of her sockets.

"And you're invited to join us," Olga added.

"Yes. This is as much your victory as it is mine." Anastasia shifted her eyes and shrugged. "Well, almost as much. anyway. Tell you what, come with us now and I'll let you have the killing blow."

Maryam furrowed her brow. "Killing blow?"

"Enticing, isn't it? Imagine, another woman's life in the palm of your hands. There's nothing in the world like it."

"Bitch, who the hell do you think you're talking to?" Maryam barked, her entire being flaring up in protest. She stomped her feet as she took an authoritative advancement toward her adversary. "I ain't yo lab dog."

A strong-arm halted Maryam's steps in an instant. Olga had stepped in between her and Anastasia who sat still.

"Settle down now. You don't want to start a fight that you can't win."

"Whatchu say?"

"You may be the baddest bitch in the ring," Olga leaned forward, speaking in an intimate hushed whisper. She rested her hand on Maryam's chest, the sheer force of her palm holding her back. "But she's the Queen. And I- well I'm someone not to be trifled with. There's a wealth of power out there, most of which you haven't the slightest clue about. So, know your place."

"You best get yo hands off me. Today is not the day."

Olga allowed a conniving smile to spread across her lips. She towered over Maryam and yet despite that, her opponent seemed unafraid.
That would mean that when it came to a fight between the two of them Maryam wouldn't hold back.

"Today is very much the day. Or haven't you heard what our Queen just said? Before the day is finished and the night reclaims its place there's going to be a slaughter. Care to join?"

"There's going to be a slaughter in a few seconds, you don't get out of my face."

Olga allowed a second smile to escape her once stern expression.

"Oh, I'm going to have fun with you."

"Ladies." Anastasia peered over her desk at the two women as they squared off, clearly enjoying the conflict. "We're on a tight schedule here."

Olga turned around, noticing Anastasia's voice and plea. She exchanged looks between her and the woman in front of her. Maryam remained still; her eyes locked upward. Every bone in Olga's body screamed at once. She wanted nothing more than to make Maryam bleed, to feel her hands wrapped around her throat but she knew her time was better spent elsewhere.

"We go to war. This afternoon." Anastasia declared. "You're more than invited to join us. But by tonight this town will belong to The Pride. Tread carefully."

Chapter 14: Connection

Sarah Stryker was alone. On most days this was nothing more than a mere statement of fact. But on the day of her loss against Maryam Bahira, it was so much more.

Sarah couldn't believe it. She couldn't believe where she had ended up and where this scenario had led her. In many ways, she had entered Georgetown with intentions that were the exact opposite of the decisions that she had made for herself. Her initial quarrel was with Anastasia. Why then had she allowed Maryam to provoke her into a fight? Nothing was certain, especially concerning the younger sister who stood watching her from the doorway.

Sarah sat still for several minutes before leaning up off the couch and examining her wounds. Her abdomen had turned red from all the poundings that Maryam had inflicted on them. There were also several cuts on both cheeks as well as one on her left brow. Her opponent had indeed earned her reputation though Sarah was certain that she was only at a third of her strength after the forced injection, possibly less. This gave scope to her suspicion that this was all a ruse by The Pride to demoralize her before the final conflict. And yet here she was, an open target falling into their clutches despite her awareness.

"What is it?"

Amy stood by the door, rubbing her arms like she always did when she was afraid. Sarah had half a mind to ignore her. She had avoided her gaze for several minutes but even out of the corner of her eye, it was as clear as day. Amy would never stop. She would never leave, no matter what.

"What?" Sarah wiped her face with a wet cloth and averted her gaze to the ground. She raised her eyebrows. "Why are you staring at me like that?"

"You look terrible," Amy said, not caring to be polite.

"I wonder why."

"Want me to clean you up?" Amy heightened her voice in sarcasm. "I mean I don't want to encroach on your territory but you're bleeding all over the couch."

Sarah threw her arms up in defeat. "Might as well. If you're going to stay, might as well make yourself useful."

Amy grabbed the wet cloth from her sister's grasp and applied the faintest touch to her cheek.

"How's Carmen?" Amy asked, speaking in as casual a tone as she could.

Sarah shrugged. "Last I heard she was making a steady recovery. That was yesterday. Not sure if she's regained consciousness though. Only time will tell if she's sustained any permanent damage."

"And Kyle?"

"He's safe," Sarah replied.

Amy nodded before averting her gaze toward the ground. What she wanted to say next would require a bit of strength.

"You piss me off sometimes."

"Excuse me?" Sarah snapped her head forward. The sound of her sister's voice was barely over a mumble, but it still bothered her more than anything else in the world. "What was that?"

"You heard me."

Sarah glared, noticing that her sister still refused to look at her. She shook her head in reply. "You are unbelievable. You know that?"

"Takes one to know one."

Sarah raised her eyebrows. "Amy, you're treading on thin ice."

"What's your problem?" Amy spat, finally raising her gaze to meet her.

"My problem? I don't know Amy. What do you think my problem is? I only just found out a few days ago that Anastasia put a price on my head. And the one woman who I hoped would help ended up challenging me to a fight."

"I know that. I was targeted first. The Pride murdered Leland right in front of me," Amy yelled. She could feel her heart rising in anger with every second.

"Which is why we need to exercise caution. You of all people should know that."

"I do," Amy exclaimed. "What do you think I am? Stupid?"

"Well, your previous reluctance hasn't exactly inspired confidence."

Amy's jaw dropped.

"I need you to fall in line. You follow my lead. I told you that from the beginning."

"I know that, Sarah. I've always followed you; ever since we were little. But if I'm going to fight and risk my life, I need to know that you have a plan. That you're not just running off to another suicide mission."

"That's my problem; not yours."

"How can you say that?" Amy exclaimed.

"Very easily, as it so happens."

"Look, maybe you're okay dying in the heat of battle. Maybe that's how you dream this will all end but I'm not. Be as upset as you like but I'm not going to stand by and watch."

"You will if you expect to accompany me the next time I go on a mission."

"Sarah."

"I mean it, Amy. Yesterday was the last straw. I can't have you jeopardizing this mission. It's too important."

Amy had enough. She decided to spite Sarah, though it could very well mean the end of their time together. "More important than me?"

Sarah felt her heart sink into the back of her chest. "I never said that. And it would be ill-advised for you to put words in my mouth."

"But you just said that that's what's important. If so then-"

"Amy, don't yell at me." Sarah pointed a finger toward Amy in a fierce warning.

"Sarah, I need you to trust me. To let me in. You've always been like this." Amy's eyes moistened as she confessed her inner thoughts.

"Yes, because this is the way I get things done. You know this."

"Sarah, please. I don't want to lose you."

"I'll be fine," Sarah assured her. "You just play your part. I'll handle mine."

Amy froze in place, realizing that there was no getting through to her older sibling. After a few minutes of treating Sarah's wounds, Amy stood up and headed for the door.

Sarah had nearly hardened her resolve, but she couldn't end it there. She had to give Amy something to hold onto, to weather the storm that lay ahead.

"Amy."

Sarah leaned forward and called out to her sister just as she made it to the front door. Amy turned around. Her facial expression was placid, finally akin to the girl whose wounds she had tended to.

"There will be time later. We'll talk." Sarah softened her tone, her voice more akin to the older sibling that Amy knew.

"Sure," Amy muttered. It was better than nothing but not enough for her to shake the feeling that Sarah was holding out on her. She turned around and headed for the door, uttering her last words to Sarah as she did so.

"Whenever you need me. I'm here."

Sarah Stryker was cut off from all that she knew and all that she cared about. She would have to summon and rely on her strength more than ever. She couldn't afford to falter now, not with a price on her head and Anastasia still in hot pursuit.

Sarah took a much-needed bath after cleaning the rest of her wounds. She had to get her powers back. The doctor had injected her with muscle relaxants that were bound to only last a few more hours or another day at the very most. She could wait till then to meet Anastasia on the battlefield. But how many innocent lives would The Pride take in pursuit of her?

"Hello, Stephanie? Stephanie White are you there?"

Sarah sat on the ground against the edge of her bed as she waited for a reply. She couldn't believe that it had been a few days since she had spoken to this woman and yet for some odd reason, in this trying hour this one phone call to a seemingly total stranger seemed to take precedent in her mind before anyone else.

"Sarah?"

The voice was a comfort unlike any that Sarah had experienced in days, weeks even. She had only recently met this woman and not even in person. What was it about her that kept drawing her back?

"Hey," Sarah said, attempting to sound as casual as possible. "I've been meaning to call but I've been really busy the past few days. I hope you can understand."

"Of course. I was wondering when we would speak again. What's up."

"Well," Sarah hesitated. "Things haven't been going very well."

"Were you not able to work things out with Maryam?" Stephanie's voice rose in curiosity.

Sarah shrugged. "It's not like you didn't warn me. As far as I can see the only way that she's able to work out her differences with a person is through a fistfight. Guess we both have that in common," She admitted.

"Did you win?"

"No."

Stephanie spread her lips in a sympathetic expression. "I'm sorry. If you were able to put up a fight at all you should be proud. Maryam is the best boxer in the country, some say in the entire world. There's no shame in losing to her."

Sarah averted her gaze towards the floor. "I know."

"Then why do I get the sense that there is still something bothering you; something beyond just a mere fight," Stephanie prompted. Sarah looked up, seeing an opportunity that she couldn't have predicted staring at her in the face. She couldn't believe what had just entered her mind, but odds were based on the woman's previous calls she already knew her secret anyway. It would take strength to say it out loud but perhaps that morsel of power was all that she would need to weather the storm that this conflict had placed her in. She was on her last legs. It would be the only chance that she would have left.

"Stephanie," She began. She took a deep breath in and out, sensing the fragility of her body and tethered humanity. "There's so much. . . .so much about me. . . . so much that you don't know."

"Well, that's why I'm here."

It was as open of an invitation that this girl was likely to give her. Sarah scanned the room, making sure that she was alone before returning her attention to the phone in her hand.

"Sarah, you can tell me anything. Whatever it is that you want to say. I'm here for you. I mean it."

Why did she believe this woman? What was it about her that oozed such trustworthiness and admiration? Whatever it was Sarah couldn't afford to dwell on it. The likelihood that she would meet someone else like this seemed minuscule.

Sarah exhaled, sensing her heart rate and the thickness of the air around her. At that moment it was as if time no longer existed, nothing did except the presence of the girl with whom she would share the source of her greatest turmoil. She blinked as her eyes moistened, for the first time in months.

"I was raped."

At that moment it was as if someone had pulled out her umbilical cord. These were words that she had once uttered to another person, one who was a stranger at the time, very much like the woman on the other end of the receiver. Part of her was ashamed that she had put herself in this situation again, but she had already opened the gate and sent the demons flooding out. It would now be up to her to face them. "I was raped just two years ago."

There was no immediate response. Sarah felt a tear roll down the corner of her eye and she blinked, freezing it in place just as it reached her cheek. There would be time for her to break down later. "I was abducted. By The Serpents; The most infamous group of men on the planet. It took me an entire two weeks to escape. They took pleasure in what they did. Tortured and violated my body in unspeakable ways. Ways in which I only choose to revisit at night."

There was still no response. "I can't escape it, no matter how hard I try. They did something to me, on the night that I was locked in that dungeon. A snake bit me; put something in my blood. Now they are everywhere. I can see them. I can feel them."

Sarah felt her chest rising as she spoke. Each word brought back some of the human feeling and awareness that she desperately tried to ignore in the ring. "So, to answer the question that you asked me when we first spoke. That's why I fight. Because there's nothing else that I can do. I pummel, stab, and strangle as I hunt day and night. The rage inside of me, flowing like a river and as acidic as bile."

After what seemed like ages Stephanie found the strength to respond. "Sarah, I'm sorry."

"My mother is gone, and I am all that is left of her, forced to tackle all of the great evils of the world on my own. It was bad enough having The Serpents on my tail, but it wasn't long after that The Pride was taken by authoritarian rule and I was one of the first to be abandoned, offered up as a sacrificial lamb to the most heinous of criminals."

Sarah took a deep breath in and out. "And I have a sister. Who, thanks to my influence, is every bit as stubborn and unyielding as I am. Having to survive on my own is one thing but she's all that I have left. How can I march off into battle; into what may be certain death knowing that she's as likely to do the same? I made a promise a long time ago; a promise to look after her. But how can I keep it when my enemies target her as much as they do me?"

Sarah took a moment of silence after that outpour. Amid her confession and revealing her hidden secrets and insecurities, Sarah had a moment of self-awareness. This was still a new person in her life after all.

"I'm sorry. I know this is a lot. But right now," Sarah took a moment of pause. She sighed before carrying on. "Right now, there's no one else that I can tell; no one else that I can talk to about this."

"It's okay, Sarah. It's okay."

The voice of Stephanie White did much to slow the beating of Sarah's chilled heart. "No, it's not. It's really not. You have no idea what it's like. To live like this. To have so much pain and anger stored inside of you. To have to deal with it on a daily basis."

Stephanie's heart stopped. Everything stopped. She lowered her breathing at the same time as her voice. "Actually, you might find that I do understand."

Sarah perked her ears in an instant. Her eyes widened as she zoned in on Stephanie's words. What came next would shake her to the core of her being.

"Sarah, I have a confession to make. I knew who you were. Like so many others, though I sought you out for my own personal reasons."

Sarah squinted her eyes. The oxygen grew cold in the room around her, probing her for the sudden revelation that would change everything.

"The same men who abducted you two years ago attacked me over three years prior. And like you, nothing has been the same since then. When I saw your name on my desk, I saw it as an opportunity to finally confront what had happened to me."

Sarah curled her lips, suddenly it hit her. It all came so suddenly but now she understood why she had begun this journey in the first place; the true purpose of it. It all made sense. "I knew about you as well. That's why I accepted your calls. I didn't want to pry so I waited. Until a sense of comfort was built into the conversation."

Stephanie replied with a gentle nod. "Same here."

"Does it ever get easier?" Sarah asked. She couldn't believe the words that had come out of her mouth, but it was a question that she needed an answer to more than any other. "You've lived with The Serpent's poison in you for over five years now. Does it get any easier?"

Stephanie squirmed and sat up in her chair. "That's a hard question, Sarah. If you want the short answer, then I'll say yes. But also no. As for the long answer, well over time, you learn to cope with it, the trauma, the fear, anxiety, and depression. Those unresolved feelings will resolve themselves over time. It just takes faith."

Sarah raised her eyebrows. "And the anger?"

"Well, that's where things are a bit complicated. I can't pretend there's an easy solution for everyone. It really depends on you. You see, I had to make a lot of sacrifices to get to where I am today. After the Serpents, I was broken. Like you, I needed to do something drastic in order to cope, though my own journey was decidedly different from yours."

"But it doesn't go away completely?" Sarah prompted.

"It did in my case."

Sarah's eyes widened to an alarming degree. She remained silent as Stephanie clarified her simple yet Earth-shattering statement; one that would remain in Sarah's psyche long after the conversation was finished.

"It took a while, a lot of self-reflection. But at this moment I feel no anger; no animosity or hatred towards my attackers."

"None?" Sarah felt as though she had entered another realm entirely. Such a thing couldn't be possible.

"Part of me thinks that I should. What those men did was a vile deed that no one should have to endure. But if you let it the memories of what happened will consume you."

"I know," Sarah muttered with a sigh. "I know all too well."

"But you seem like the self-aware type. In fact, if I could tarry a guess, I would say that you might end up like me. One day the pain, the hate, and the anger," Stephanie shook her head. "It'll wash over you completely. It'll just be another part of your past."

"I doubt it," Sarah said. Stephanie's suggestion brought out some of the strength back into her body as well as her anger.

"What makes you say that?"

"I need it. For me it's important. The hatred and Anger swelling through my veins; it allowed me to survive, took me across continents. Without it, I doubt I would be sitting here speaking to you now."

Stephanie replied with a gentle understanding nod. "Perhaps. But perhaps you don't give yourself enough credit."

Sarah raised her eyebrows in intrigue. This woman seemed too good to be true.

"In any case. I agree that it's important to fight. People like the ones who attacked us exist on a global scale. Men and Women around the world are suffering, even more than you and I. And I don't blame you for how you feel. Though I bear no animosity there are still a few nights when I'm jolted awake by a sharp and unsuspecting memory. A side effect of my choice to suppress the pain of that fateful day."

"Is there a chance? Is there any hope for me? For us?"

Stephanie spoke in a voice clearer than any Sarah had heard before. "Yes, absolutely. More than hope as a matter of fact."

Sarah gave a side glance towards the phone on her ear. "Are you just saying that? How could you know?"

"Think about where you began. Think about how far you've come. What did people say then? What are they saying now?"

The beating of Sarah's heart rose and was more pronounced than it had been during the conversation so far. For the first time since the fight, Sarah sensed her humanity as well as the energy of everything around her. It was stunning, that one phone call could alter her entire biology.

Sarah's moment of ease was halted by a loud thundering noise outside of the room. Sarah snapped her head towards the window, immediately distracted by the sound. Something was going on outside.

"Stephanie," She muttered, unsure of how she would end the conversation. "I-"

"Go, Sarah. You're needed out there. Fight with all of your desire and all of your will. And above all else remember what you're fighting for and that there are those of us cheering for you on the sidelines."

"Thanks, Stephanie," Sarah said, as her heart swelled with renewed strength. "Thanks for listening."

Stephanie smiled. Sarah could sense it through the phone. She could almost see it. "It's my pleasure. Good luck, Sarah."

Sarah hung up the phone. She stood up and stammered towards the window. She pulled down the blindfolds and looked outside.

A car burst into flames through a controlled explosion. A second was taken out just a few seconds later. For several minutes a series of disruptive explosions spread throughout the city's streets. Out of the rubble a silhouette of a woman appeared; then another and another.

There were few people left outside. Every single male within a thousand-mile radius of The Pride was snuffed out. They were stabbed, pulled into dark corners, and inside abandoned buildings before being taken out. The conniving, knife-wielding warriors spread themselves out into a vertical line. They had one target in mind though they would make sure to have as much fun as possible in the meantime.

Sarah took a few steps backward, removing herself from the window and the vicious warrior women who echoed her power in almost every way. The hour that she had been waiting on had finally arrived. She bawled her hand into a fist. The frost was there. She could feel it. All the muscle relaxants had done was suppress the strength inside.

Thankfully The hotel had managed to clear itself out in little time at all. Sarah was shoulder bumped by several people as she ventured through the hallway. Everyone was in panic mode.

Sarah Stryker barged into the janitor's closet and made preparations. She cleared out everything that could be used or seen as a distraction. It would require all of her will to accomplish what she was about to attempt.

Everything had to go just right. It would make the difference between life and death.

Sarah sat crossed legged in the center of the room. She relaxed all her muscles as well as her spirit. She made every intention to block out all unwanted and anxiety-ridden thoughts. What was happening outside would only be relevant once it faced her directly.

Sarah inhaled and waited five seconds before exhaling. She closed her eyes, blotting out the images of The Serpents and The Pride that desired to consume her. Sarah was almost as still as an inanimate object. Her sole desire was to make herself ready and battle sharp as the final conflict converged in on her from all sides.

Sarah took another deep breath in and out. She felt something cool and tranquil washed over her; a cold and powdery white mist that signaled her rebirth.

After fifteen minutes of meditation, Sarah Stryker opened her eyes. Her will was precise, and her gaze was placid, giving nothing away. She was a woman who had been through hell and back during the past two years. Anastasia would regret what she did to her. Sarah would guarantee it.

Georgetown was being ambushed from all sides. The roar of fire blazing and the crackling of exploding gasoline could be heard for miles across town. Most civilians remained inside and safe for the time being. The few who were foolish enough to remain outside would be dealt with severity. Only one target mattered to these women, but they wouldn't allow a single person to escape and risk jeopardizing their plans.

A man with a broken leg and bleeding profusely from his knee to his ankle stormed through the streets in a frantic attempt to escape the chaotic destruction. He ran with a limp. The explosions sounded all around him; his heartbeat rising like the banging of a drum. The man quickly slid underneath a nearby car after spotting it.

The man's heart sunk into his chest as the sun beamed down on him. One of The Pride had lifted the car with only one hand. The pedestrian could sense the power radiating from her as she smiled. She was one of the tallest and most imposing women that he had ever seen. If he had time to consider her identity the pedestrian would have assumed that she was a lieutenant or even the leader of the gang. Though in actuality she was nothing more than a grunt.

The warrior woman lifted the pedestrian by the collar of his shirt. She brought him to eye level with her and sized him up. The man grunted and wriggled with his legs dangling in the air. Not only had she lifted him with ease but with a strength that seemed impossible to break away from.

"Well, look at what we have here. A man; out and about past curfew."

The woman spoke with a much lighter tone of voice than the pedestrian imagined. She feigned sweetness and naivety as she spoke. Her voice oozed with contempt. Just the feeling of her breath washing over his face caused his spine to tingle in alarm.

"Question is now that I have you in my grasp. What should I do with you?"

"You know what to do," Said one of the girls behind her. Much of the group had joined the tall muscular woman. The man saw up to five warriors huddled all around him.

"Anastasia said to kill any man we see but I don't know. Seems like such a waste if you ask me."

"Be careful sister," One of the others warned. "She doesn't take kindly to insubordination. Remember what happened to the last woman who stepped out of line."

"Relax. I can fall in line. This man is as good as dead. I can guarantee that. Still, doesn't mean I can't have a bit of fun with him first?"

Each member of the female gang spread their lips into a conniving grin. At that moment they were of one unified desire coursing through their entire being to provoke their enemy and cause as much pain as possible. Nothing else mattered.

"Ah, what's the matter? Scared?"

There were six women present and they all bellowed at the top of their lungs; glee and insatiable hunger glistening in their eyes as they prepared to strike.

A blue-colored knife soared through the air and struck the tall woman in the center of her back. She collapsed and her male victim fell from her grasp. The rest of the squad shot their gazes toward the direction that the weapon had come from. Their eyes sunk into their sockets after discovering the identity of the one who had abused them.

One of The Pride had entered the fray just in time. She was the one woman who they had been seeking out yet one of the few who inspired dread and apprehension upon her entrance into the battlefield. She was a girl who had traveled the world and back for this opportunity and she wouldn't risk missing out on it now.

The gang lunged toward Sarah Stryker in unison. They were of one mind and spirit. Sarah ruffled her hair, tucking a few strands behind her ears before preparing her mind and spirit for battle. She couldn't afford to hold back. Not with the fate of so many men and women at stake. She would make sure that The Pride experienced the full brunt of her fury.

Sarah's fists were like Iron and her speed was that of an Olympian. The warriors summoned all their energy as they sprang into attack, only to be shut down by Sarah's superior technique. Each attack seemed like being hit by coal after a winter's chill. Sarah was able to keep her opponents overwhelmed with her bare hands for most of the fight but then the gang decided to play dirty and elongate their nails, pulling a maneuver straight out of Carmen Rivera's playbook.

Four throwing knives appeared in Sarah's hand. She anticipated her opponents' method of attack and within milliseconds she responded with a series of pokes to the neck and abdomen. Five warriors attempted to slash at her with their nails in unison. Sarah twirled her makeshift weapons in her smooth and delicate grasp, parrying her enemies with keen instincts. She clipped the nails of a few opponents and applied her freezing ability to others, rendering each woman powerless to her attacks.

The last woman to challenge Sarah was the tall opponent who had attacked the innocent bystander just a moment ago. She lunged toward Sarah and wrapped an intrusive hand around her throat and lifted her off the ground. Her grip was strong, much more than almost any fighter that she had faced during her stay in Georgetown, but it only took Sarah a moment to figure out what to do. She placed a hand on the warrior's wrist, freezing her skin and then twisting it until her arm bent backward. Sarah then twisted her arm again, bending it with ruthless fury. The woman cried out and was temporarily immobilized, allowing Sarah to knee her in the stomach. The tall woman's eyes widened as she was lifted off the ground within seconds. Sarah held her high in the air, keeping her weight balanced with both hands before slamming the girl onto the concrete with tremendous fervor.

The six opponents lay on the ground, pain surging through them, unlike anything that they had ever experienced in their lives. Most of the girls were partially frozen, their limbs crunched together like pretzels, and a faint breath of powdery mist was the only thing that sustained them. The tall woman lay groggy on the cracked earth, her body motionless and numb from the sudden jolt to her system. Sarah was done playing games. She would make these women pay.

"Oh, Sarah."

The voice made her shudder from where she stood. She would recognize it anywhere. Sarah turned her head as her eyes locked onto the person who had traveled across the country to face her in combat; her sworn enemy.

Amy Stryker was alone. She couldn't believe how rude Sarah had been during their last conversation but deep down she knew it was only because her older sister was hurting. Somehow despite Sarah's insistence on handling things alone, Amy knew that she would need her help soon. Though she figured that she had time to kill before the big finale, so she decided on a short walk, hoping to clear her head. Amy was just on her way to the hospital to visit Carmen on the other side of town when a gargantuan fist unexpectedly ran into her cheekbone.

Amy stood back up as the world came back into focus. She felt her muscles tense as the eight feet tall muscle-bound behemoth of a woman loomed over her, edging closer with slow methodical steps. Her eyes widened and her jaw dropped to the floor. In all her life she had never seen such a woman.

“So, you must be the little sis.”

Amy’s mind spun out of orbit within seconds. She was decked in the face, with a blow so severe that for a moment the world grew dark, even though it was mid-day, with the sun beaming on the faces of the two women. She rolled on the ground as blood poured down her cheek. She couldn’t think of a worse spot that she could have been in and to make matters worse, she was far from the protection of her sister, who had recklessly chosen to isolate herself.

Olga beamed as she stared down at her prey. "I had hoped to run into Sarah but you’re the next best thing. With your death, she’ll have nothing to hold onto."

Just as Olga reached down to lift Amy, she was knocked off her feet with a sudden punch to the cheek. She stood up, enraged but also flabbergasted. She knew that Sarah was in another part of town. She couldn’t have predicted that Amy would receive help from a most unlikely guest.

"Uh uh, You ain’t coming anywhere near her."

Maryam Bahira stood, with her arms balled into fists. Amy’s jaw dropped in dismay as the two veterans from The Pride squared off.

Chapter 15: Mirrored Lines

Amy's jaw hung open in bewilderment. It was only yesterday that the woman in front of her had faced her older sister in the ring. What happened to change that?

"Well, well, well. Look who it is. The mighty prizefighter herself. I was wondering when you would show up."

Olga took a few threatening steps towards Maryam Bahira as the two locked eyes, positioning their feet at the same time as they prepared to pounce.

"I warned Anastasia about you," Olga said as Maryam's eyes shifted, surveying her every movement. "Told her that you were too much of a loose cannon. That you were a liability. But she always had a soft spot for you. Enjoyed your matches every so often. I enjoyed them too, but I always knew that no matter how many opponents you beat it never changed what you are. Just like the men seized by The Serpents you're nothing more than an animal. An abomination. And if you ask me, it's about time you learned your place."

Olga's words triggered Maryam into immediate action. She charged toward her with the full force of her legs and aimed a brutal punch straight for her nose. Olga wrapped her gargantuan grip around Maryam's knuckles. The sly smirk remained plastered over her face as her opponent gritted her teeth and struggled for control. She attempted to pull back and Olga squeezed her hand, forcing her to use the full brunt of her strength to escape the painful death grip. Olga struck Maryam in the chest and abdomen before lifting her by the trousers and the strap of her bra and chunking her a few feet backward.

Maryam spat blood from her mouth and with slow hesitant steps stood back up. All her life, she had never been hit with such a devastating attack. What Olga lacked in technique she more than made up for through sheer willpower. Maryam stood up and placed her two fists in front of her. For a moment her vision became blurry and at that moment she felt something that she was certain that she could never feel and that was fear; real genuine fear that inspired a wave of panic in her pores.

"Hey girl, you gonna just sit there all day, or are you going to help me take this bitch down?"

"What?" Amy's eyes widened. She couldn't believe the callous way in which Maryam addressed her.

"Ain't you ever been in a fight before? Girl, you better wake up."

Amy popped up off the ground at the sound of Maryam's demand. She stammered her feet and approached Maryam. The two girls were now standing shoulder to shoulder.

"Alright. Sarah's your sister ain't she?"

"Yes," Amy said, her eyes remaining stern, locked onto the tall beaming woman ahead of them.

"I take it that you're a fighter like her huh?" Maryam asked though it was a rhetorical question more than anything.

"Of course, I am." Amy didn't appreciate the question and decided to add in a snide remark to throw Maryam off. "If you want, I can give you a demonstration after we beat this girl."

Maryam responded with a sideways glance and Amy met her gaze with a look of equal authority.

"She's strong. The only way that we'll be able to beat her is to fight together."

"Alright," Amy agreed.

"Try to keep up. I ain't like yo sista. I'm not going to hold ya hand if you fall behind."

"Please don't."

Amy and Maryam stomped their feet, cracking and shooting debris into the earth as they lunged toward Olga with their hands outstretched and their fists tightening to an insane degree. They rammed their arms together and aimed a punch straight for Olga's nose. The two girls were of one mind at that moment; nothing penetrating their hearts but the sole desire to bring down the warrior in front of them.

Sarah Stryker remained silent as she glared up at the woman in front of her. Much of the chaotic destruction and carnage had ended. Sarah perked her ears in preparation for the final bout. She knew that it would require all her faculties simply to remain standing throughout the fight. It would take even more to win.

Anastasia locked eyes with her opponent. Her red eyes glistened in the sunlight and a fixed smirk rested on her pale-skinned face. Her straightened red hair flapped in the wind in perfect synchronicity with Sarah's blonde hair. She stood with an equal amount of stillness and determination. The girl in front of her may have been trained by the best warriors of The Pride but her desire and moral compass made her weak. She'd never be able to achieve what she did; no matter how determined she was, and it was for one simple reason. There was a point that she wouldn't go beyond.

"How long has it been?"

Sarah shrugged. "A few months, give or take."

Anastasia nodded in understanding. "Feels like a year, to be honest."

"You ain't kidding."

Anastasia raised her eyebrows in intrigue. "Have you improved?"

"I do my part."

"Good. I'd hate for this to be boring. With any luck, you'll surprise me even more than last time."

"Stick around and see what happens," Sarah challenged.

"That's what I like about you, Sarah. Valiant until the end. Even on your last legs. Always a fighter. Of course, I still hate your guts but oh well."

Sarah glared as she studied the woman in front of her. Her heart rose in her throat in response to Anastasia's jab at her. Normally insults were as frivolous as the wind but there was something else behind Anastasia's words that struck her.

"What is it about you? What is it about your very nature that's inspired so much change? I've spent weeks trying to figure it out. When I ordered the hit on the little sis, I knew it would lure you. Though what I hadn't counted on was the Latina and The African boxer getting in the way."

"Yes. And I hadn't counted on your goons either."

"It seems that both of us have been rather busy as of late."

"It appears so," Sarah agreed.

"When I think about how far you've come, I can't help but be impressed," Anastasia confessed. She lowered her voice, almost as if she was imparting a secret to her. "You are, without a doubt one of the finest specimens that The Pride has ever produced. It's unfair actually, how powerful you are."

Sarah raised her eyebrows in confusion.

"In all actuality, I had considered the possibility of offering you a job; a permanent place among us. Despite my feelings towards you, snuffing you out right now would seem like such a waste. With you working by my side we could get quite a lot of things done."

"But you know that I won't accept that," Sarah said. She found it quite humorous that even after all the vile actions that Anastasia commanded and after all of the trouble Sarah caused her, she would still make at least a half-hearted attempt to recruit her.

"Yes, because you're a stubborn and conceited bitch too shortsighted to see a good deal. Or have I misspoken?"

"No," Sarah admitted with an uncaring shrug. "That's pretty much the long and the short of it.

"So that's it then? We fight till the finish?"

"Guess so."

Sarah Stryker and Anastasia squared off and fixated their expressions. Their eyes locked onto each other; contempt shone in their glazing eyes.

The two girls stared at each other for a long time; neither of them moved out of fear of missing their opportunity. Neither of them could sense anything except the wind, which blew strands of their vibrant yellow and red hair in their faces.

The two women stared at each other until their own eyes were the only thing that either of them could see. After a solid two minutes, a tiny share of ice protruded from between Sarah's thumb and forefinger. A tiny throwing knife appeared in Anastasia's hand at the same time. This was a reunion that both women had spent weeks preparing for; that both yearned for yet had greeted with delicacy and apprehension. They couldn't afford to be careless; not for a single solitary second or they would be ripped apart from the inside out.

The two warriors threw their knives in unison: initiating the first attack of this decisive battle. The pointy ends of both weapons rammed into each other causing one to engulf the other in frost; freezing them both in an instant. The maneuver triggered both Sarah and her redhaired foe into sudden action. Both stormed forward, moving at full speed and twirling the knife in their grasp.

Anastasia and Sarah met in the middle of their street, clashing weapons at the same time. Their teeth clenched the moment that their knives met. The two of them tugged with their wrists, utilizing much of the strength that they had in their arms to do so. At the last second, Anastasia pulled her arm away, and another small throwing knife appeared underneath her sleeve.

Sarah brought her icy dagger up in front of her just in time to deflect the first wave of attacks initiated by her foe. She attempted to poke her opponent, first in the neck and cheekbones, then in the chest and abdomen but to no avail. To her surprise, Anastasia knew just how to respond and pulled out an extra dagger on each hand to swipe out her icy weapons from Sarah's once firm grasp.

It wasn't long before the fight broke into a fierce round of fisticuffs. The next few minutes were a blur of lightning-fast blows of the girl's fist and feet. It had been ages since Sarah had fought a woman with a style like hers. Both women fought with all their fervor and all their will. They parried several jabs before unleashing a massive spin kick in unison. Their heels smashed against each other, and their legs hung in the air for a few seconds. Sarah and Anastasia then placed all their weight on their legs, shoving each other backward with authority.

Anastasia snuck a forward jab within a split second of her discovering an opening. She smashed Sarah's nose in and proceeded on the offensive. She hit Sarah with a few more jabs before unleashing a second and more devastating spin kick in her direction. Sarah crouched and managed to avoid the attack but was hit with a follow-up sweep attack by Anastasia.

Sarah fell and rolled out of the way just as Anastasia rose her heel high into the air and attempted to smash her into the concrete. Sarah pivoted herself on her right elbow before delivering a well-timed kick to Anastasia's midsection. Sarah then leaped off the ground and sent her opponent reeling and soaring backward with a bone-chilling uppercut.

Anastasia sprung herself back on her feet utilizing the power of her legs and fingertips. She threw a barrage of attacks toward her opponent. Sarah raised her palm and caught Anastasia's elbow in her grip. Sarah dug her feet into the ground and gritted her teeth in agitation. Sarah shoved her elbow away but hadn't reacted fast enough and was sent reeling backward from a brutal punch across the cheek.

Sarah sensed her ears ringing in response to her opponent's attack. She brought her hands in front of her as Anastasia continued her combo in quick succession. Sarah brought up her hands in defense, parrying her advances with smooth technique. Her instincts were sharp, but Anastasia knew just when to strike. She hit her in the stomach. Sarah was then sent into another realm. The moment that the tip of Anastasia's shoe rammed into her chin thunder overcame Sarah's senses. She was lifted off the ground before crashing back into the concrete; leaving a crater after she landed.

Sarah sprung herself back up to her feet, ready to unleash her fury but then she noticed something out of the corner of her eye. More soldiers. There was at least one woman stationed on each rooftop within twelve yards of Sarah and her opponent. Anastasia wasn't known for fighting fair.

Sarah curled her lips in anger before lunging towards her opponent with her cracking frost-covered fists. She would make Anastasia pay, for turning The Pride against her, for Maryam's distrust, and even for Carmen's hospitalization. She would make her pay for everything that had happened during the past few days, whether she was directly responsible or not.

Sarah parried Anastasia's punches before slugging her across the cheek with a vicious right hook that cracked the frost and ice shards around her knuckles. Blood splattered across Anastasia's face as time seemed to lose its equilibrium and her body grew numb from the surrounding cold.

Sarah took advantage of her opponent's temporary immobility and decked her in the face again. She pummeled Anastasia with her fists and feet unaware of what was happening around her. All that mattered in Sarah's mind was that the girl in front of her was demolished, no matter the consequences.

The Pride caught onto the turning tide and the battle and grew desperate as they struggled to execute their plan. Two women twirled their knives in their fingertips as they watched the fierce battle between the two youngest and most prodigious warriors of The Pride.

Sarah snapped her head back just in time to catch a dagger that spun like a bullet from a rail gun straight towards her. She held the weapon by the tips of her fingers and her eyes widened in fervor.

Unfortunately, the split second that Sarah had utilized to catch the dagger was all that Anastasia needed to regain her footing. She dodged a sloppy haphazard spin kick from Sarah and proceeded on the offensive. The two were once again locked in a deadly and unpredictable bout of fisticuffs. At the last second Anastasia was able to gain the upper hand and sent Sarah sliding backward with a kick straight to the abdomen. A second knife was lunged by one of The Pride and Sarah bent backward, dodging it by a narrow margin.

Anastasia looked up, noticing something that she was sure would distract her from her battle with her sworn enemy. There was a group of civilians stationed on the rooftops behind Sarah. The Red-haired warrior squinted her eyes, taking in the sight that could turn the tide of battle against her. The soldiers that stood on the opposite side of the battlefield were African American males. Three of them pointed their rifles in her direction. This entire conflict would be over in just a few moments if she didn't do something.

One of the men fired a single shot toward his target. Anastasia turned around, noticing that the man had been aiming at one of her guards. If these men thought they had a prayer against her power they had another thing coming. Anastasia placed her forefinger and ring finger in her mouth and whistled at the top of her lungs.

The Pride responded to their leader's call without hesitation. A grappling hook was fired from one of the buildings, the pointy end penetrating the concrete where the group of men stood. Several members of The Pride zip-lined from one building to the other in a single file line.

Sarah glared at the woman in front of her with all the animosity and rage that she could muster in a single look. Anastasia stood still for a moment, her vibrant hair swishing back and forth as her lips slowly spread into a conniving grin. Despite Sarah and the locals' preparations, she had seen this chain of events coming.

The Pride sprung into formation the moment that they landed. They twirled their signature daggers in unison before raising them over their shoulder. The male soldiers opened fire the moment that the scorned women lunged forward. They had managed to take down a few but not before the fastest from among the group plowed through them, cutting a few with their knives and pummeling them into the cement barehanded.

Anastasia and Sarah locked expressions, examining one another for the second time in this fight. They could both sense it, the venom and rage oozing from the other, and at that moment; despite their stern opposition and conflicting philosophies they were one.

"So, this is it then?" Sarah said.

"This is it," Anastasia confirmed. "We fight to the finish. No interruptions. No holds barred. No mercy. Well? How does that grab you?"

"I wouldn't have it any other way."

"Hmm, I'm glad," Anastasia replied, with such a tinge of animosity in her voice. "Let's get this bout over with, shall we?"

"Let's," Sarah agreed.

The two women lunged forward in unison, digging their feet into the earth and causing it to quiver in the wake of their tremendous power. The concrete below them cracked and sent a wave of panic throughout the city streets. Both Sarah and Anastasia spun in a circle before delivering a triumphant kick toward their opponent. A massive chunk of the earth burst out of the ground in between both warriors and their heels smashed the concrete into debris before they made contact.

Olga latched onto the fists of the two women in front of her, wrapping the full circumference of her palm around their hands. Amy and Maryam gritted their teeth as Olga squeezed down hard. Both women decided to unleash everything that they had in them. Amy and Maryam threw a barrage of their best attacks, utilizing the full force of their forearm and knuckles.

Olga placed her arms in front of her, defending herself against the sudden onslaught. Her blood boiled and her heart rate increased like the rhythm of a beating drum. This was more of a challenge than what she had expected and upon that realization, adrenaline swarmed through her like wildfire. She swatted both of their attacks away before raising her arms and bopping each on top of the head with her elbow. Maryam and Amy were smashed into the ground, creating a fierce dent in the earth upon doing so. The two girls winced, stunned by the imposing nature of their opponent and Olga took advantage of that. She kicked Amy into a parked car just a few feet away, creating a massive dent and shattering the glass windows at the same time. Olga then grabbed Maryam by the ankle and tossed her forward, causing her to tumble and roll in the cement before landing on her face.

"Come on. Don't tell me that this is it. This is what I spent all this time waiting for? Pathetic."

Olga's taunting rang in Amy's ear as she stood up. She felt a cut on her left cheek and the bottom corner of her lip. She leaned her palms on the ground as she struggled to stand. She felt her back stiffen the moment that she did so. She had heard her sister mention this woman before and how fierce she was, but it wasn't until now, with her presence looming over her that Amy considered what she was facing.

Maryam hunched over and spat blood as the pain of the embarrassing attack oozed into her pores. Never in her life had she experienced anything like it. And worse of all she had enough battle experience to know that her opponent was just getting warmed up.

"Aw, what's the matter? Scared?" Olga teased. "Face it, you had no idea what you bargained for when you challenged me. Neither of you did."

Maryam stood up and cracked her neck, making sure to keep her rage in check. This woman was an opponent, like so many others that she faced in the ring Olga had a weak spot. Maryam just had to keep clawing away at her until she found it.

Amy staggered as she stood up. She took deep breaths in and out, heaving with great intensity. A thin line of blood dripped down her nose. She couldn't believe that she had agreed to this fight. Was her desire to prove herself to Sarah worth dying over?

"Aye!" Maryam called out to Amy. "You aight?"

Amy didn't respond right away, her mind was still tumbling towards chaos; anxiety, frustration, and fatigue shone like the sun in her eyes.

"Aye, you deaf or what?" Maryam exclaimed for a second time.

"What?"

"You all there? You hurt?"

"Yes. No. I'm fine," Amy answered unconvincingly.

"We need to work together if we're going to put this bitch in the ground."

"Yeah. I hear ya," Amy said, amid her hoarse breath.

Maryam examined her opponent. Olga stood proud, sporting an eager grin. She was still unfazed by the girl's desperation. "Okay. So, here's what we're going to do. We attack on opposite sides. Me from the front and you from the back. You good with that?"

"Yeah," Amy said, raising her fists in front of her. "I'm good with that."

"Good. Then let's toast this bitch."

Amy and Maryam lunged forward in unison. They bolted at full speed towards their opponent. Olga spread her legs and prepared her defense but was taken off guard the second that Amy leaped into the air and vaulted over her. She turned her gaze just as Maryam struck with her fists.

The blows sent a tremor through Olga's body. It had been months since she was struck with an attack even remotely like it. Amy whined her arm backward and struck Olga in the back with a punch of equal strength. Olga roared. The pain rang in her ear like a bell, triggering her animal instincts.

The next few minutes of the fight happened too quickly for the warriors to recall. Maryam hit her opponent with a four-hit combination to the stomach and across the cheek. Olga recoiled before going on the offensive. She slugged Maryam and elbowed Amy behind her at the same time.

Maryam's eyes turned watery and her vision blurry as Olga punched her nose in, causing blood to gush from it like a fountain. She hit Maryam until she smashed against the concrete. She was then left to grab Amy by the ankle and lunged her forward. Amy clutched onto a metal pole beside her and swung across, utilizing a skill that she learned from gymnastics during her time at high school. Amy spun around the pole, catapulting herself off it and aiming a fierce kick straight towards Olga.

Olga was floored by her opponents' athleticism but at the last second managed to extend her arm and floor Amy with a triumphant close line that caused her to crash across the street.

Amy popped off the ground and utilizing the full strength of her legs, aimed a vicious rising boot kick towards her opponent's temple. She performed several somersaults as Olga staggered backward. She had only a half-second to back dash as Amy's fist came crashing down on the concrete below. The staggering amount of force from Amy's fist caused the debris to shoot out of the Earth.

Amy leapt into the air and aimed a second punch at her opponent. Olga remained still, studying Amy's position in the air. At the last second, she plucked Amy out of the air with her two hands, one wrapped around the throat and the other balancing her with a hand on her stomach. With the full force of her legs, she slammed Amy to the ground, sending a sudden shock through her system. Amy let out a hoarse breath. In all her life, she had never felt anything like it. Who was this woman? Was she even human?

"Aw, I'm sorry. Did that hurt? You'll have to forgive me. Sometimes I let the adrenaline get to me. I forgot my manners. The name is Olga. The fiercest and strongest woman that you're likely to meet."

Amy felt blood building up in her throat. She felt as though she hardly had any strength to stand let alone keep fighting. But what kind of woman would she be if she stopped now?"

"And you're the brave little sister of Sarah Stryker, the most infamous and wanted traitor of The Pride. You see, Sarah hurt me tremendously the last time that we met. And now I intend to pay her back. But with Anastasia having her fun at the moment I'm fresh out of luck. Guess you'll do. Hope you don't take it personally."

Olga twirled her hair in her fingertips as she gazed down at Amy. She was preoccupied with reveling in her apparent victory that she hadn't noticed when Maryam jumped off the ground and lunged toward her. She hit Olga in the chest and the wind behind her trembled in response. Amy popped off the ground and hit her again. Olga regained her footing and threw a punch, but Amy swayed out of the way, kicking her in the ribs and causing her to stagger and trip off her feet.

The momentary advantage did much to swell the hearts of Maryam and Amy, whose attacks grew more ferocious and coordinated with every second. Together the two of them overwhelmed their opponent, hitting her with a barrage of attacks before ramming her face in with a unified punch that sent her flying off her feet for the first time in the fight. Olga plowed right into a building behind her. Maryam and Amy stood still for a few seconds afterward, their arms glued together, and their faces shone with relief.

The ground beneath the two girls trembled. Amy's eyes widened as she averted her attention to what was happening beneath her. Small bits of debris shot out of the ground and the shaking engulfed the entire area, creating an earthquake, unlike anything Amy had felt in months. The situation was dire; more than either woman could imagine.

A shrill scream caused both Maryam and Amy's eyes to pop. The scream had come from inside the hole in the wall of the building and it was vile; almost inhuman. Loud thunderous footsteps sounded in the ears of both girls; until Olga, eyes bloodshot red with anger, came rushing out of the building.

The three warriors burst into an all-out frenzy. Olga's fighting style was wild, chaotic, and even more unhinged than before. She was done holding back and now her enemies would be forced to experience the full brunt of her power. Her fist collided in between the knuckles of Amy and Maryam, taking huge chunks of concrete and debris off the ground. Amy and Maryam balled the fists in their opposite hand and aimed a strike at Olga's head. She raised her palms in response, clutching her fists and holding them still with stiff movements. Amy roared and hit Olga's rib with her extended leg. She bent over and Maryam took advantage of her temporary immobility to catch her off guard with a brutal right hook.

Olga roared and popped up, punching with authority. She lifted Amy with a brutal uppercut to the chin. She then punched Maryam, sending her sliding into the wall of the building behind her. The blow left Maryam stiff and stunned, unable to move as Olga advanced toward her. Maryam raised her fist in protest, but she was rendered helpless by Olga as she smashed her face into the concrete over and over. If things went her way, she could kill her here and now. Olga was done playing games.

Amy bounced up off the ground and approached Olga in haste. She was floored by a sudden backhand that brought her to her knees. Olga stood triumphant, with her right fist planted on Maryam's cheekbone. Amy sat with her back facing Olga. The stiff and bitterness of fatigue had reached her at last. She clutched onto her cheek, feeling the reddened scrap that Olga had left with her attack.

"Anastasia tried to warn you. You had a chance to help us bring that girl to her knees. Now you ally yourself with that bitch, with this bitch. Is this really how you want to end up?"

Maryam took deep breaths in and out after Olga lowered her fist. Blood trickled down her nose as she found the courage to respond. "You going to try to talk me to death or what?"

Olga raised her eyebrows in intrigue. "So that's how you want to play it? I'll bite." Olga wrapped a firm grip around Maryam's throat and squeezed with little more than a slight clench of her hand. Maryam felt her vision darken the moment she did so. Olga spread her lips into an evil grin, which burned its way into Maryam's consciousness.

Maryam felt the weight of her body sinking into the wall to the point of her smashing against it. She felt her tongue loosen and her body lose its equilibrium and feeling the more her opponent tightened the grip around her neck. Slowly Olga lifted Maryam off her feet, tightening her grip with every second. By the time Olga had lifted Maryam to her level, she was squeezing with all her strength. Maryam winced, gritted her teeth, and grimaced. The pain that she felt was like a siren, a signal that the end was near.

"You know something?" Olga spoke in an intimate tone, lowering her voice to little more than a whisper. "I've dreamed of this from the moment that I saw you. I watched your matches, in person and on TV. I always knew that despite all your bravado you were all hype. And now I have the chance to prove it."

Olga stood still, intrusive. Standing so close that Maryam could feel the hotness of her breath. "Do you feel it? The sense of defeat sinking into your pores. It's the end. All your victories and all your strength. In just a few moments it'll be gone. And I'm going to revel in every second of it."

Olga's full attention was on the woman in front of her. But with superhuman reflexes, she grabbed Amy by her ponytail. "I was going to have you watch but better yet, why don't you join her?" She slammed Amy against the wall with a stunning amount of strength. She clutched onto Amy's throat with her free hand and lifted her off the ground with ease. Olga then planted Amy against the wall, shoulder to shoulder with Maryam, measuring their pained expressions with hungry eyes. "This is what I live for. And to think they told me that you were two of the strongest warriors in Georgetown." Olga let out a shrilled laugh, relishing the moment. "The fact is that you're nothing. Both of you. You got lucky. None of the people that you've fought had any real power. But now you're facing a woman that has. Consider yourself blessed that in your last moments you can rest assured that your death will come at the hands of a true warrior."

Maryam was certain that Olga was using her full strength but surprisingly, she felt the grip around her throat tightening even more. The world began to blacken around her as the defeat that Olga spoke of loomed over her like a hungry animal. The oxygen was gone, her breath became a lifeless gag, and the numbness consumed her entire being. There was nothing left to do but to accept where her actions had led her and despite her frustration, she couldn't imagine herself anywhere else.

It hit Amy like a sixth sense. With the greatest amount of strength that she could muster, Amy raised her fingernails and dug them deep into Olga's hand. The gesture made Olga twitch, but her grip remained around the girl's throats. Amy expected just as much but all she needed was the slightest edge to keep her in the game. She kicked Olga in the rib, causing her to hunch over. Amy twisted her arm, causing Olga to release her grip. She then pulled her arm backward and decked Olga in the face as hard as she possibly could. Olga flew backward and made a crater when she hit the ground. Amy was given a moment of reprieve and used the opportunity to rush to Maryam's aid, who stood coughing and massaging her sore strangled throat.

"Are you okay?" Amy said, placing a hand on her and massaging her back.

"Yeah," Maryam said in between coughs. "Yeah, I'm fine."

Amy darted her head forward, noticing that Olga had slowly returned to her feet. Maryam looked up, apprehension building inside of her like bricks. Her neck was still throbbing, and her body was thrashed. She was certain that the girl beside her was in pain as well but somehow, she was still able to keep fighting. If she could then how could a professional like her give in now?

Maryam stood up, stretching her muscles, and cracking her neck in defiance. Amy raised her fists as well, mimicking her posture. The next exchange was bound to be the fiercest contest yet.

"Maryam, I have an idea."

Amy spoke in a slow whisper, making sure not to give anything away to the titan in front of them.

"Do you? What, yo big sister actually teach you how to fight?"

Amy felt her heart tighten in response. "Yeah, she did. And I could do without the attitude if you don't mind. I'm trying to get us out of this."

Maryam sighed. "Alright, so what's the plan?"

Olga cracked her neck and stretched out her arms as she waited for the two women to attack her first. She placed her hands on her hips and bent over, her back cracking at the same time. She was still cool, despite her minor injuries; one on her hand, and a bottom cut below her lip. Despite the uncertainty of this battle, Olga was having the time of her life. Never had the chance of killing two women excited her so much; at least not since she had met Sarah Stryker.

Amy and Maryam roared as they lunged toward Olga in unison. She lifted her fists in front of her, predicting where they would strike. Amy leaped into the air just when she expected. Olga winded her fist back in preparation. Amy twirled in the air and before Olga could even successfully throw an attack, she was hit with a devastating kick that knocked her entire world out of orbit. Blood splattered out of her mouth and Olga felt her brain rattle inside of her skull. She hadn't taken the time to let the pain soak in because her head was shot upward with a well-timed uppercut by Maryam.

The two girls knew that they couldn't let up for a second. They hit her with a barrage of punches that they were sure would do the necessary damage, but Olga swept Amy's leg out from under her, before grabbing her by the ankle and tossing her away. Maryam jumped up and hit her with a rising fist and several more in a fierce combination. Olga parried a few of her attacks before punching her directly in the chest, causing Maryam to fly into a nearby car. She slid to the ground, her body becoming groggy. Olga grabbed her by the back of her neck with one hand and placed the other on her back and lifted her high into the air before slamming her on top of a car.

Just as Olga attempted to smash her face with her fist Maryam did something that she never thought that she would and stuck a fingernail in her eye at the last possible second. Olga recoiled instantly, her face reddening and her eyes watering with uncontrollable tears.

"YOU BITCH!"

Amy saw the perfect opportunity right before her eyes. She jumped onto Olga's back and wrapped a firm grip around her arms holding her in place. Olga swung left and right but Amy had expected a fight. Her feet swayed only for a few moments before she planted them on the ground and grunted as she applied the necessary pressure on her opponent. The next move would be vital, she only had managed to practice it a few times in her life.

The concrete beneath the two women cracked as Amy wrapped her opponent in a full nelson. The Mass of her body and the surrounding environment Skyrocketed. Amy focused her mind on a single goal. She wouldn't let go. No matter what.

"NOW."

Maryam lunged forward at Amy's signal, punching away at every inch of her opponent that she could reach. Olga's taunts and advances had produced more rage within her than she could quantify. She punched her until her fists became numb and she was certain that they would shatter under the weight of Olga's rock-hard body. But it didn't matter. It wasn't enough. It would never be enough to make up for how much Olga had humiliated her.

Olga managed to summon up the last of her strength just in time. She spun in a circle, sending Amy spiraling towards the ground. Maryam decked Olga in the face, the sight of her ally being hurt sending a sudden wave of strength surging through her. Blood burst out of Olga's face as she reeled in response to Maryam's attack. At that moment she was certain that her sense of taste and hearing had vanished.

Olga deflected Maryam's next wave of attacks before snapping her head backward with a vicious attack of her own. Amy popped up and proceeded to join in on the barrage of attacks before she was floored by an earth-shattering head butt. Amy wrapped her hands around her face as the pain burned into her subconscious. Maryam was sent spiraling from a vicious right hook from her opponent.

Amy rushed towards Olga once again. Maryam thrust her arm forward, combining her powers with Amy in perfect synchronicity. They struck Olga in the chest then crouched and hit her in the stomach causing a vile sensation to surge through her body. Maryam hit her multiple times in the stomach, parrying a few of her jabs as Amy jumped off her back. Olga had less than half a second to react. She gazed up in wonder as Amy's fist came crashing down. She felt the thundering power engulfing her entire being before she was even touched. It crushed the concrete and the car below and at that moment Olga knew that she underestimated Amy more than anyone else she had ever fought before.

Olga crashed to the floor after Amy's fist smashed against her. She lay spiraled out on the floor with her eyes closed. Amy took a step backward, clutching her arms and letting out a hoarse breath. Maryam approached the unconscious woman, relief sinking into her pores after realizing what the two of them had accomplished.

"Bitch." Maryam kicked Olga's unconscious body. Amy grabbed onto the top of her bra.

"What are you doing?"

"What do you think? This girl almost cost us. Now that she's down I'm making sure she'll stay that way."

"We fight to survive." Amy reprimanded. "Because we have to. We don't do it to hurt people."

"Really? Because last I checked that's what they had in mind for yo sista."

Amy's eyes widened in disbelief.

"Sarah."

It was only a mere second after Amy uttered her sibling's name that she bolted in the opposite direction. She couldn't let Anastasia gain any more momentum. She still had some fight in her and with any luck, her sister did too.

An Icy Fist engulfed Anastasia's entire field of vision. The air slowed down all around her, and her senses dulled out. Her entire body and her cheek collapsed in on themselves. She reeled backward as her nose was smashed into her face. The frost oozed into her pores and blood gushed out of her and she was blinded for a few seconds. She couldn't recall the last time she had been hit with a punch so overwhelming, but she knew that she couldn't afford to dwell on it at such a late stage in the battle.

Sarah's heart swelled in her as she increased her strides and momentum with every second. She threw punch after punch until she had connected with over twenty attacks, penetrating her opponent in the chest, abdomen, and cheekbone with her cold knuckles.

Anastasia clutched her chest after being knocked backward by a stunning ice fist. She couldn't believe that she had let the fight come this far. How could she have let this girl gain so much momentum?

Sarah stood with her arm outstretched and her shaking fist cracking the ice around her knuckles. There were cuts and bruises around Anastasia's face and she knew that they mirrored the same injuries on her as well.

Anastasia pulled out a pair of twin daggers and twirled them in her grasp at a lightning-fast rapid pace. To Sarah, it seemed endless, though it only took her opponent less than a minute to perform the feat. Sarah's jaw dropped as the reality of what she was facing infused itself into her skin. She stood breathless as Anastasia crossed her daggers over her arms. Sarah braced herself as her red-haired counterpart lunged toward her.

Frost covered Sarah's forearm, giving her a morsel of protection against Anastasia's vicious swipes. Sarah gritted her teeth as the knives scraped the frost from her skin. She hated being on the defense and decided to do something drastic. She pulled out two daggers and clashed with her opponent's weapons.

Both girls shoved each other backward, as the opposing teams came to play. Various weapons came soaring through the air, including shuriken, knives, twin, and triple daggers in quick succession. Sarah swayed left and right, dodging a few knives. Anastasia responded to the rebel men who took it upon themselves to defy her and The Pride. She pulled out a flute-like object and blew several darts into the distance. She penetrated several men in the neck and the jugular. She noticed several men peer from on top of nearby buildings.

Anastasia turned around just as Sarah lunged toward her. She raised her weapon and the two knives met with a clank. The next bout would be a contest of strength as well as endurance. Their hands and weapons trembled in the weight of their power. In less than a minute both women would discover what they were made of and who between them was superior.

Sarah's heart sank into the pit of her chest. The ice dagger shattered in front of her, and she knew it would take a considerable amount of time to find the energy to create another. Anastasia twisted Sarah's arm and stuck her knife deep inside of her.

Sarah gasped as all the oxygen left her body. She was certain she had experienced the harshest temperatures known to man but being stabbed in the gut was an entirely different type of cold. Her jaw dropped and for a moment, she held onto her adversary for support.

"You don't know how long I've waited for this moment."

Anastasia's voice oozed with contempt. She stuck the knife deep into her gut and gritted her teeth in excitement as she witnessed the pain in her opponent's eyes up close.

"Sarah!"

The sight made all the hairs on Amy's skin stand up at once. She and Maryam arrived just in time to witness the attack.

Anastasia removed the knife and kicked her opponent in the chest, causing Sarah to roll on the ground, her body limp and wobbly. She raised her knife just in time to defend herself against Amy. The next minute was a blur. She parried a few of her opponent's strikes before sweeping her opponent's feet out from under her. Amy caught herself on one hand and spun her body, performing a spin kick, the likes of which only an Olympic medalist could perform. Anastasia staggered backward, blood splattered out of her mouth because of the unexpected counter, giving Maryam an opening to unleash the brunt of her fury.

Anastasia felt her body collapse on itself as the titanium gargantuan sized fists collided with her upper body. Her bones rattled inside as Maryam struck her over and over. She was lifted off the ground with an uppercut that left her in a daze.

Anastasia sat up. She placed her fingers in her mouth and whistled at the top of her lungs. Several throwing knives were lunged toward the battle arena. Maryam and Amy's wide eyes spun in a circle, getting a complete look at her enemies. It was a moment of uncertainty that overwhelmed them, and that Anastasia was able to prey on.

In an instant, the self-appointed Queen of The Pride pulled three daggers out of each hand. But instead of throwing them directly at Amy and Maryam like they expected the knives encircled them, clashing with the weapons of Anastasia's posse and creating a whirlwind of mayhem. There were now over a dozen knives soaring around the duo, which meant that every step was a tremendous burden.

Amy made the first move. She lunged forward towards her opponent; her brow furrowed in anger and disgust. Anastasia smiled. She could predict her opponent's actions like the sunrise, and she was certain that would ensure her victory. Their fists clashed and the ground beneath cracked in reverence. There would be no quarter and there would be no restraint. For both warriors this fight meant everything.

Amy swung with all her fervor. The sight of Sarah being stabbed was still imprinted in her mind. She saw it even as she fought her opponent. It had engulfed her entire field of vision and there was no escaping it. She slugged her opponent across the jaw before smashing her stomach in. Maryam rushed to her aid and Anastasia was forced to contend with two powerful warriors. She plucked two daggers that were swarming in the air and utilized them as a suitable means of defense. With that act, the playing field had been leveled.

Anastasia deflected Amy's attacks with her knives before jabbing her in the chest and punching her in the throat. Amy clutched onto her neck as she performed a desperate back dash in retreat. Maryam took her spot and lunged at Anastasia.

The boxer proved to be far more durable than the queen expected. Anastasia jabbed at her with her knives and Maryam wrapped a firm grip around her hand, holding her in place. Anastasia pulled her right arm back and raised her left one just as Maryam struck her, sliding backward in an instant in response to her tremendous power.

Anastasia decided to pull out the big guns. She spun her daggers in a lightning-fast motion, creating a deadly windmill as she advanced toward her target. Maryam tightened her fists and lunged forward, believing that she would plow through her.

Maryam lost control of her body before she could land an attack. Anastasia deflected her first hit before using the power of her weapons to knock her hands in the air. She then sent Maryam flying backward with a graceful spin kick to the midsection. With that act, all her enemies were now floored. She would have free reign to do what she liked.

Anastasia gasped in shock. Something vile had entered her bloodstream and she was paralyzed in an instant. She gazed towards the ground noticing that her leg had been frozen by a dagger made of frost.

Sarah Stryker stood with a hand covering her stomach. She took deep breaths in and out as blood oozed out of her eardrums and nose. She hadn't planned that method of attack, her will simply sprang free. A maneuver left over from years of endless preparation and combat.

Anastasia's legs wobbled as the numbness sunk into her nervous system. She sank back before crashing to the floor. Her mouth remained open as a cold white mist shot out of her breath.

Sarah crashed to the ground a few seconds afterward. That last attack had taken everything that she had. She was certain of it. Whatever happened next, her teammates would have to be the ones to pick up the slack.

Maryam and Amy stood up, taking in the petrified and defeated expression on their enemy's face. This was the opportunity that both had yearned for, and it was only after witnessing her floored that the two girls realized it.

A squad from among The Pride stepped in just in time. They leaped from the buildings and landed in front of Amy and Maryam, shielding them from Anastasia.

"Get me out of here," she hissed. Though her breath was hoarse there was no mistaking what she had said.

Several vehicles entered the fray. One of the girls lifted Anastasia off her feet and placed her in the passenger seat of one of the cars before entering and driving off. The rest entered the other vehicles and took off after them. Amy and Maryam stood still for a few seconds after they had gone, both felt as though they should have chased after the vehicles but neither had the strength.

Amy turned around, noticing that a group of men had descended on them. Her eyes widened, realizing what was happening all too late. The men laid Sarah on a stretcher before placing her on the back of a truck.

"Sarah!"

Amy lunged towards the truck, waving her hands in protest. Maryam stepped in front of her just in time.

"Hang on girl. Calm down. It's alright. My boys will handle it."

"Where are they taking her?" Amy asked.

"To the hospital. They'll patch her up. I've called in the best."

"Really?"

Maryam clutched onto Amy's injured arm and grabbed her by her chin. "What about you? You seem like you could use a bit of patching up yourself. You sure you okay?"

"Yeah," Amy muttered with a shrug. "I'm fine."

"You got heart. I could tell when we were fighting. It's not every day that I run into a girl that can keep up with me. The move you used to take down that big girl, well I ain't never seen anything like it. How did you do it?"

"It just sort of came to me," Amy answered.

"Sharp instincts. With moves like that you're sure to survive out here. Just don't let it get to your head, okay?"

Maryam smiled after uttering her remark. Amy returned the gesture without thinking. After a few seconds, the awkwardness of the situation hit her. She contorted her expression into a fierce frown, her eyes unwavering and fixated on the woman in front of her.

"What?" Maryam's eyes widened in dismay. "What is it?"

Amy spoke with a low voice. "You beat up my sister."

"Oh, girl." Maryam shook her head in consolation.

"She came here to help you. And you threw it in her face."

"Look. I ain't got nothing against yo sista." Maryam twirled her braided locks between her fingers as she spoke, her voice casual and oozed with an unusual amount of decorum. "People look up to and fear her. I just had to establish my territory. That's all."

Amy squinted her eyes in confusion. "Your territory?"

Maryam allowed a faint sound to escape her lips in response. "Mmm hmm."

"What are we? A bunch of wild animals? Last I checked we were women."

Maryam shrugged. "There ain't much difference between the two. This group we fought is proof of that." She pointed in a stern warning. "Live long enough and you'll see."

Amy sighed. If this girl was going to make things difficult, she would respond in kind. "Fine, let me establish my territory." She took two steps close towards her peer, to the point that their toes were practically touching. These next words were important. "My territory is by my sister's side. She's all that I have left. You know people keep treating me as if I'm naive but I'm not. I watched a man, someone that I cared about die right in front of me. My mother died just a few years ago. I know how cruel the world can be. Which is why we need to rise above it. Otherwise, we're just repeating the cycle."

Maryam raised her chin in intrigue. "I feel you."

"So, the next time you feel all gung-ho about challenging my sister to a fight, you come through me first. Understood?"

"Coo," Maryam replied, still twirling her pigtail. "I'll happily whip on both of y'all. It's a two-for-one special as far as I'm concerned."

Amy glared in response. Her stern gaze penetrated the heart of the woman who stood opposite her. Despite her cold exterior, Maryam felt her blood boiling, the same as it did when she first met Sarah.

"But for now we're good. I'll give you two time to recuperate first. And I mean what I said, you did great back there. You should be proud.
And I bet she is too."

Maryam took off, approaching one of the cars a few feet away. Amy allowed a subtle smile to escape her lips and stood staring at her even as she drove off. Her mind fluttered, still unsure of what to make of this entire series of events. Since she had agreed to enter this conflict with her sister none of this had gone as planned and that made the possibilities for the future even more uncertain.

Chapter 16: The Cycle

The telephone rang for a solid minute. The house was empty. There were few decorations and no visible tv or electronics to speak of apart from a computer in one of the rooms. This was a house of Isolation; the sort that would drive people mad but was more than accommodating for a disjointed Sarah Stryker. "Hello?"

Sarah edged towards the living room before answering the phone. Her injuries were still visible, from the battles against both Maryam and Anastasia. There were several stitches along her abdomen. There were bruise marks on her cheeks and a small cut on her bottom lip which stung every time she bit it. Sarah had made a miraculous recovery after just a week of medical attention and rest.

"Sarah. I trust that all is well. The last call ended so abruptly I couldn't leave it there."

Sarah sighed, relief and relaxation entered her body at last. "Stephanie, hey. Yeah, Sorry to leave on such short notice. I had to. Anastasia made good on her promise and attempted to subdue the town."

"Well, judging from the fact that you're speaking to me now I'll guess that things turned out rather well."

Sarah shrugged. "All things considered."

"How did you do it? How did you stop her?"

"I had some help. A whole lot of it," Sarah replied, her voice oozing with gratitude.

"So? What's next?" Stephanie asked.

"You know something? I'm not entirely sure," Sarah admitted. "Just a week ago I would've considered myself a woman prepared for pretty much anything. But this fight took a lot out of me. Best to conserve as much as I can. In case The Pride strikes again."

"I see. Probably all for the best," Stephanie agreed.

"Hmm hmm."

"So, all in all everything turned out okay though. I mean despite your injuries everyone is safe?"

"Yes. We all had our fair share of injuries though, some of us more than others. But it's the children that suffered most of all. Having to serve The Pride, answer to Anastasia's every beck and call. I can't imagine a greater nightmare. But we managed to find a few of them."

"I'm proud of you," Stephanie said. It was a statement that gave Sarah pause. Who was this girl? How could someone who she had never even met in person inspire such strength and belonging in her? Sarah was uncertain as to the answer but whatever the reason she wanted this woman in her life. She would serve as an anchor when all else failed.

"Stephanie." Sarah paused as she attempted to gather her thoughts. She thought of a way that she could say what she wanted without feeling exposed, but she knew such a thing was impossible. "Thanks. For listening. For seeking me out when you didn't have to. You have no idea what it means to me."

Sarah could tell that her words had made Stephanie smile, she could practically feel it engulfing her surroundings, giving the room a cool and tranquil atmosphere. She twirled the telephone cord nervously as she waited for the answer.

"You're welcome. I'm sure our time together has benefitted me as much as it has you."

"Probably," Sarah agreed.

"I'll be in touch. Hopefully, we'll have the chance to meet in person soon."

"I'd like that."

"Remember, you're not alone. No matter how suffocating your surroundings are. No matter who tells you otherwise you're not alone. None of us are."

The storm that had entered Georgetown had ended. The men who had helped in the battle against The Pride were now busy with repairs. The damage was visible in the faces of all the men who had been attacked and nearly destroyed by the ambush. Time would be the only thing that would heal the wounds that had soaked into the city streets; nothing else would.

Sarah stood at the back of a large moving trunk as the men inside organized the cargo. Despite her fatigue, she spent a few hours helping the movers transport and deliver boxes. A small boy that she rescued helped as well. Though the locals were unsuccessful in locating most of the missing children. It would be up to someone else to pick up the slack at a later time.

"Figured you'd want to stay inside, given all the hell you've been through lately."

Sarah turned around, noticing a proud and nonchalant Maryam Bahira approach the group. Despite everything that had happened between them Sarah's mind was at ease.

"I probably should," Sarah replied. "But honestly I can't. Too much has happened. Too much to think about."

Maryam nodded in understanding. "I've been there. The least that we can do is make ourselves useful right?" "Right," Sarah agreed.

"Much as I hate to admit it, turns out you were right. Them girls really were as bad as you said. Maybe even worse. You okay, by the way? That stab wound was nasty. If my boys hadn't got there in time-"

"I'm okay," Sarah answered. "It hurts but I've been through a lot worse."

"Yeah, like that beatdown I gave you in the ring," Maryam said, with a sly grin. She couldn't resist teasing her former opponent. "Your face is still covered in bruises." She shined her fingernails on her bra in mocking bravado. "I'm good. I know."

"I wouldn't be talking. Or have you not seen?" Sarah used her finger to gesture toward her face. "You're quite the mess yourself, sister."

Maryam chuckled, realizing that she had run into that one. "You sho right."

Sarah couldn't help but allow a subtle smile to escape her lips in response. "Amy told me that you helped ditch her out of a rather difficult fight. I appreciate that."

"Well, I did my part. Though your girl did most of the fighting. I can tell that she takes after you. She has a strong head on her shoulders. I like her."

Sarah smiled, proud of Maryam's approval.

"I have to confess. When you first came to me I acted a fool to provoke you into a fight. It was something that I wanted most, ever since I heard about you."

"I understand," Sarah said. "Though there would have been plenty of time for that later. By your own admission, you were in way over your head. The Pride has become much stronger over the years, stronger than you can imagine. The best chance that we have is to- "

"Girl, I don't need no talking to." Maryam jabbed a finger at Sarah. "See, that right there. That attitude is what got us in this mess in the first place. You think you can just show up and expect me to run things your way?" She shook her head fervently. "Mmm-hmm, you don't know me or what I've been through."

Sarah lowered her head in a bashful expression. Something about Maryam's words echoed her thoughts and it took her a moment to pinpoint it. "Yeah, well maybe I'd like to," Sarah said, looking at her peer in the eye. The gesture gave Maryam pause. She raised her chin as she examined Sarah, her eyes squinted in skepticism. After a moment she responded with a subtle nod.

"When they approached me, I had no idea why. Like I said I wanted to face you in the ring. And I wanted it to be on an even playing field. I didn't know what they would do or that it was Anastasia who decided to have you injected. I never wanted things to turn out that way."

"Not your fault," Sarah said, her voice stern and reassuring. She shrugged. "Neither one of us was playing with a full deck."

"And still you showed up anyway," Maryam said, her voice shone with pride. "I've been hit a lot but every time I see you I can still feel those punches. You sho know how to throw down." She couldn't believe that she was complimenting her former opponent. She decided to get one last dig in. "Well, For a white girl at least."

Sarah glared in response, though the smile hadn't left her expression. For the first time since they had met, she felt at ease.

"I don't really consider this a win after what happened," Maryam prompted. "But I'm a fighter first and foremost. It's what I do. The way I deal with you is the way I respond to the world. As far as I'm concerned, everybody can get it. No hard feelings, right? I hope not but if so it's no sweat off my back either way. We can gladly settle this in the ring if you still got a problem."

Sarah shook her head. "No. No hard feelings." She raised her finger in a sharp warning. "But I will be taking you up on that offer when my strength returns. And I don't intend on holding back. So, if I were you, I would spend the next few days training to your heart's content, because next time you will receive no mercy from me. Is that clear?"

Despite Sarah's tone Maryam couldn't help but smile. Just a few days ago the idea that she would meet a woman like Sarah Stryker was foreign to her. Sarah was a person who challenged Maryam to her core, she questioned everything that she had worked for yet that had allowed her to excel beyond her limits.

Maryam did something that she hadn't predicted. She extended her hand. It wasn't her intention or why she had come to speak with Sarah, or perhaps it was unconsciously.

"What do you say we start fresh? From one woman to another, acknowledging our shortcomings and put this whole situation behind us?"

Sarah examined her for a moment. What she saw was someone who was very much different from the animalistic warrior she faced in the ring.

She was a proud woman and leader; one who mirrored her desire for survival and achievement just as she did. It was because of that revelation that she took her hand.

"Of course," Sarah agreed, speaking in a gentle tone. "The next few months are going to be tough. In fact, there's a good chance that our lives are going to change forever. Anastasia will recover soon and when she does, we'll be the first on her list. The Pride will hunt us down; no matter what we do and no matter where we go. It's important that we fight as one. That we unite with any person who's willing to help, without prejudice or Pride. Only with gratitude."

"Speak the truth sista," Maryam agreed. "Though I still prefer to work alone. It's how I run things." Sarah raised her eyebrows.

"But," Maryam carried on, rolling her eyes. "If I need to, I know where to find you."

"Good," Sarah nodded. "Well, I better get going. I'll keep in touch." Sarah turned around and walked towards her car but was stopped by Maryam.

"Sarah!" She called out. Sarah turned around; her eyebrows raised.

"Your friend, That Latina girl, the one I knocked out." Maryam paused. Did she really want to say it? Yea she did. It would cement where she stood with these women. "Tell her to watch her mouth next time."

Carmen Rivera lay on the hospital bed. The fight with the renowned boxer had backfired on her in a worse way than she thought possible. Since then, Carmen felt as though she had been cut off from the outside world, so much so in fact that it was almost as if she had died and wherever she was now was her punishment for her various blunders. The weight of her failure lingered in her mind; until she was reduced to a near-catatonic state, but that all changed when the door opened and Sarah Stryker entered her room.

Carmen turned around, her eyes lingering at the sight in front of her with intrigue and perplexity. For a moment she thought it was a mirage but there she was. Sarah stood still by the door, a handful of flowers in her hand and a somewhat placid expression. Carmen noticed a reddened area around her friend's pale-skinned face, alerting her that this couldn't have been a hallucination. Her friend had finished her mission and had finally come to visit.

"Hey, girlfriend."

Carmen spread her lips into a wide smile, stretching the liquid tubes around her. The numbness of her body as well as the unexpected arrival of her friend gave the sight a sense of euphoria. She felt as though she had floated off the ground at that moment; a feeling that only increased when Sarah spoke.

"Hello, Carmen."

Sarah approached her friend with slow hesitant steps. This was how she always felt when someone close to her had been hurt; like they were contagious and by being in proximity to her she would catch whatever they were inflicted with. She walked towards the edge of Carmen's bed and set the flowers in a vase and sat down in front of her.

"How are you?" Sarah asked, deciding that it was best to cut straight to the point.

"Well let's see," Carmen said. "I can't feel my face. My head is throbbing, my body is aching and the food here sucks. So, all in all, I'd say that I've been better."

"I know," Sarah muttered. "I'm sorry I didn't come right away. I wanted to. I just-"

"Don't be," Carmen interrupted. "You had a lot on your plate. I get it. I wouldn't be my priority either if I were you."

Sarah glared in confusion. "You are my priority," She declared.

Carmen felt her lips curl a bit. Why did she have to go and say that? It would only make the situation even more awkward. She decided to divert the subject. "Well judging from how pretty you look I'm guessing you and homegirl had a bit of a tussle after I was knocked out, possibly over what happened to me. Am I right?"

Sarah averted her gaze towards the ground. Her friend was in the hospital and yet her degree of power over her remained. "Yeah. It's from Anastasia as well."

Carmen's eyes widened in intrigue. "So, Team Sarah won after all huh?"

"Yes, and with Maryam's help," Sarah confirmed.

Carmen's eyes widened.

"We managed to stop her from seizing the town. But she'll be back."

"Figures. Nothing is ever over and done with like you plan it to," Carmen muttered to herself. She turned towards Sarah, her eyes pleading before she spoke again. "I screwed up, didn't I? "

Sarah curled her lips. "Probably best for us not dwell on the past."

"Sarah," Carmen said, glaring in mocking irritation. "Remember what we talked about. You're in Carmen's corner. There's no sugar coating and no lying to spare hurt feelings." Carmen asked the question again, this time in a stern tone of voice. "I screwed up, didn't I?"

Sarah placed her thumb and forefinger together, gesturing in the affirmative. Carmen replied with a silent chuckle. She didn't realize how much she missed Sarah till that very moment. Nothing in her life had been the same since she met this girl.

"I honestly don't know why you put up with me." Carmen shook her head in disbelief. "I mean if I saw someone get their ass kicked after running their mouth off like I did-"

"I'm not you," Sarah said, putting Carmen in her place.

"Yeah, you're not. It's why I like you so much," Carmen admitted. The two girls locked expressions, a wave of understanding and belonging entering their pores. Carmen sat up, stretching her muscles, feeling more relaxed because of her friend's attention.

"It was such a rush, discovering my skill for fighting. I wanted to make my enemies cry and wail in pain. Most of the girls I fought had no real staying power. But I knew that she was different. It was why I provoked her initially; to test myself. That maybe if I could beat her, I would prove that I had staying power also."

"I know," Sarah confirmed.

"Guess I have a lot to learn huh?"

"We all do. That's just the deal. Your journey is just beginning; the same as mine."

Carmen slouched in her bed and scoffed. "Yeah, what journey? Learning the ins and outs of a hospital ward?"

"We're going to get you out of here. As soon as possible."

Carmen placed a finger on her bottom lip, pondering Sarah's words.

"You're going to receive the best of care. I'll train you personally so that the next time Anastasia attacks you'll be there as the first line of defense."

"Why?" Carmen asked, her voice oozing with skepticism. "Why would you want me?"

"Why?" Sarah paused. "Because you're one of mine, and that look of defeat is one that I can't bear to see on another woman. Once upon a time, I was there, sitting where you are now after a grueling battle. But I had friends, teammates who stood in my corner and helped me to my feet. Now that you're under my care I extend the same courtesy."

"You shouldn't trust me. When people leave their guard down my first instinct is to stab them in the back. It's my nature."

Sarah glared in reply. "Carmen, are you going to make things difficult? When I offer you take. As I was told it's a normal healthy part of being a woman. You're going to accept my help even if I have to drag you out of this hospital myself. Might as well save yourself the effort and accept it."

"I accept it," Carmen replied graciously. "I just thought I should warn you. Just in case things turn sour between us in the future. And just so we're clear, I don't owe you anything. Okay?"

Sarah shrugged, allowing Carmen's harsh words to roll off her with stunning nonchalance. "Never said you did. I'm doing this because I want to. And if it may lead to you stabbing me in the back well that's just a risk I'm willing to take. Besides, I doubt you could take me, even on your best day. So, I'm not too worried about that."

Carmen locked onto Sarah's expression, taking note of the challenge in her tone. For a moment the two girls glared at each other, then without warning, Sarah spread her lips into a warm smile. Carmen scoffed in disbelief but couldn't help but return the grin, realizing the massive break that she had been given when she decided to befriend this girl.

Sarah and Amy left Georgetown the next day. Both girls felt as though they had just finished fighting a war though they knew that the last battle was only a warm-up for what was to come. Sarah had spent a considerable amount of time sharpening her relationships with the new women in her life but now was the time to remind herself of the one that mattered most of all.

Sarah and Amy sat on the swings of an all but abandoned playground near their old home in Bellingham. The place did much to solidify the wedge that had been carved between them in recent years. It would be up to the two of them alone to rectify that, a task that filled both girls with dread and a sense of urgency all at once.

"Remember when we used to play? When we were little?" Amy asked.

"Mmm-hmm," Sarah said.

"You were always much faster. So much better. I could never catch you. No matter what I did. No matter how hard I tried. I could never beat you."

"You caught me once," Sarah reminded her.

"I did?" Amy said, turning her head towards her sister as her eyes widened.

"Yep. It was only once. But it was something."

"I think that's why we sometimes fight. You accept me for who I am but most of the time I'd rather be like you."

"There's also the fact that you second guess my every order."

"I know, I know," Amy admitted with a nervous smile, sinking into the pit of the swing seat. "That might have something to do with it."

Sarah pointed a finger in a stern warning. "Which is something that I can handle most of the time as I know that's just how you are but with what you said before the match?" Sarah shook her head.

"What?" Amy protested.

"When I asked you how you were doing and you responded, 'Do you care?'," Sarah mimicked her voice. "I had half a mind to consider Carmen's advice and backhand you for comments like that."

"I know, I know," Amy pleaded. She bit her lip and chuckled in embarrassment. "I'm sorry. I was hurt. I didn't mean it."

Sarah averted her gaze to the floor, bashful about what she would say next. Truth be told she hated that she had pushed Amy to speak that way. Her stern gaze was only her way of saving face. "I admit. I was kinda hard on you back there."

"You have to be. I get that," Amy reassured her. "You may think that I don't, but I do. Honest. I'm not the same person that I was a few years ago. I'm not as meek and I'm a hell of a lot more capable. I can do this. If you'll let me. I'm in it for the long haul. I'll be there for you. Always."

"I know," Sarah said looking up at her. "And you're wrong. You are the same person that you were back then, just as you are the same person that you were when we used to come here as children." Amy's heart sunk into her chest.

"And that person is one who I would trade the world for. A person with a heart so tender that it affects everyone around her. Someone who fights every day for the people that she cares about. Who works so hard to improve herself that she's oblivious to the fact that the one who she has improved the most is right in front of her."

"Do you really mean that?" Amy questioned, her skin melting.

Sarah shrugged. "I said it didn't I? You've always been there Amy. Even when you thought you weren't needed. And I'll return the same courtesy.

The truth is that you're essential. I'll tell you as I told you before. I wouldn't be where I am today if it weren't for you."

Amy stared deep into her sister's eyes, searching for any deception or sign that her sister wasn't being genuine. She saw none. All she saw was certainty in Sarah's eyes. The same unwavering look that she always gave her. "So that means we're good? You trust me, right?"

"There's no one that I trust more," Sarah confirmed. Amy beamed, elated beyond measure. She decided to do something daring and raised her fist in front of her. Sarah smiled, catching on in an instant. The sister's fist pumped, sounding a current through the earth as they did so. It was a symbolic gesture of the unbreakable bond of sisterhood, one that would serve as a formidable challenge to all enemies that they might encounter, past and future. The gesture solidified Sarah and Amy as one in accord; two women born from the same womb determined to improve themselves and each other regardless of cost.

Sarah would spend the rest of her day alone with a man; one of the few that she trusted. He was a man that despite his unsavory manners had come to look out for her with as much care as any of the other friends in her life. It was because of this that Sarah felt guilty about postponing her meeting with him until then but she figured that she would make up for it by treating his wounds.

"Sarah, Sarah wait, stop; it's okay."

Kyle Harper sat on the dining table in Sarah's home as she applied a moist towel to his swollen face and eye. He had been given a solid beating by The Pride before he had been freed. She cleaned his wounds with finesse and great speed; to the point of it being uncomfortable. But she didn't care. This man had done so much for her and asked for little in terms of material wealth in return. This was the least that she could do.

"Sarah come on. it's okay. really I mean it."

Sarah ignored Kyle's words and received a second towel soaked in a bucket of water. She squeezed it with harsh hands before approaching her friend.

"Sarah, come on. I'm okay really. I mean look at you."

"Kyle, be smart. Now are you going to fight me on this or are you going to let me do my job?"

Kyle froze, realizing how important this was to her. Her stare was placid, but he could feel the trembling deep within. He sighed and sank in the chair in defeat.

"Good boy," Sarah said as she bent over and applied the wet towel to his face.

"Owe, Ow, Sarah geez."

"Shh, hold still. This won't take but a minute," Sarah said, yanking him upward by the chin. "Keep whining and it'll take a lot longer."

"I thought that a woman's touch was supposed to be delicate," Kyle complained.

"It is. Or would you rather have me treat you like I did Anastasia?"

"Ha Ha," Kyle mocked. "I see that you got back into cracking jokes at my expense. That must mean that you're in a good mood as of late."

Sarah shrugged, continuing to treat his wounds as she spoke. "I'm good. A little on the tired side. But nothing a bit of rest and meditation won't fix."

"Well, then I'm guessing that this wouldn't be a good time to tell you that I found your man."

Sarah recoiled, taking a step backward away from her friend. She had half a mind to ask Kyle to repeat his statement but there was no doubt what he had said.

"Yeah, that's right. I found him. Wasn't hard once I found the right connections. Had to do a bit of digging but I found a name and from what you told me, it's him all right. It's got Serpent written all over it."

Sarah took another step backward. "What's his name?"

"Marcus Hamilton."

Sarah's heart sank. It was almost as if Kyle's revelation had spoken the man into existence. There was a part of her that didn't want Kyle to continue but it was too late. She needed to know everything.

"He's a Serpent and is one of the sickest and most perverse in nature. He's violated hundreds of women; yourself included and he has a particular trademark; one that involves the fondling of breasts for amusement and humiliation. For hours on end. Just like he did with you. He's still out there Sarah and in all likelihood, he's still hurting people. I'll do what I can to help but, in the end, it'll be up to you to stop it, same as before."

Kyle stood up, noticing Sarah's unease. She hadn't finished cleaning his wounds, but the sudden revelation had distracted her. "I'll be in touch should I find anything pertaining to his whereabouts. But you should know this guy is a slimeball and a crafty one. He knows how to hide. We have to play this one smart."

Kyle took a step away from Sarah and the dining table but was stopped in his tracks in an instant. A strong hand clutched onto his elbow and held him in place. His eyes darted behind him in shock, noticing Sarah's frightened expression. She squeezed him so hard that the freezing temperature of her touch caused him to panic.

"I told you not to linger; only to peak," She muttered, her voice shaking and cracking at the same time."

"I know. I wouldn't betray your trust like that Sarah. You have to believe me."

"What did you see?"

"Everything," Kyle revealed. Sarah's eyes sunk into the dark recesses of her sockets and with it, much of what she had buried in her subconscious had re-emerged. "I saw what they did to you. I saw what he did to you. I saw everything."

Sarah's mouth hung open. She couldn't believe it. The horrors of the dungeon were something that she was certain that she would keep with her forever. But now there was someone else who not only knew what happened but had seen it with their own two eyes. It was almost too much to believe.

"I wanted to escape but you wouldn't let me. Or rather your subconscious wouldn't," Kyle said, noticing that Sarah wanted to protest. "I was locked in that dungeon like you were. For hours on end."

"When?" Sarah asked, still reeling and breathless. "When did it happen?"

"When you came over and I asked about your mother," He revealed. "The world of the mind is complex. A web of experiences, ideas, and knowledge. Opening that gate sent just about everything else flooding out. And like an avalanche, there was little I could do to stop it."

"Then you know?" Sarah muttered. "You know what Marcus did to me.

Kyle bowed his head. "I'm sorry Sarah. Yes, I know. Not only do I know but I felt it. His scaly dirty fingers on your naked flesh. I saw the whole show, Sarah. And believe you me there's isn't A sight that I've found to be more sickening or depraved in all of my life."

Sarah couldn't believe it. She couldn't believe where her actions and her trust had led her. When did she unconsciously decide to let this man in? Why? She was certain that all she ever wanted was solitude but maybe there was something that yearned for more. If she was uncertain before this interaction confirmed her suspicions about her past. She would never escape it. No matter what she did it would remain with her forever.

"Now what?"

"Now I help you find him. And all the other men that had anything to do with what happened to you back in that lair.

"Why?"

"Because like I said I felt everything, but I also felt you. The loneliness, the confusion, the unceasing pain, and paranoia. Normally an eye for an eye is not my philosophy. I believe in making amends. In overcoming trauma. In communication with those we don't understand but I see that that may not be entirely possible in your case."

Sarah curled her lips as her heart hardened into solid Ice. She had a feeling she knew what Kyle would say next and her heart yearned for it, more than just about anything else. She would remember it even after Kyle left her alone. Sarah would meditate, sharpen her knives, and barge out into the day for some early hunting. It was all that she could do to quench her bloodlust and fury.

"I'm sorry Sarah. Truly I am. No one should have to endure what you did. It's an injustice and an even greater one would be to allow this man to walk free for another day with the possibility that he would inflict another. Allow him to experience the full weight of what he has done to you and so many like you. Make him pay even if it is with his life.

I will help you in the knowledge that when you find him you have free reign. Show no mercy. Make him beg. Make him scream. Make sure that when you're done with him, whether you choose to take his life or not, he will be utterly incapable of violating another human being again. Give him hell Sarah."

"I will," Sarah declared.

Acknowledgment

For as long as I can remember the world of fiction has moved me beyond words. I've watched dozens of critically acclaimed movies, my fair share of Television shows, and read a decent number of beautifully written Novels. They all served to inspire me and light a fire under my behind whenever I was feeling lazy or unmotivated but that wasn't where the source of my imagination came from. I've always dreamed of creating my own original work. I still have a handful of memories to this day of plays that I've watched that filled my head and heart with such wonder. Now that I have written a few Novels, two full length ones and a novella I now have a solid idea of what it takes. A lot of hard work and unyielding passion. With those two things there's anything that a man or woman can't do but I would also like to thank a handful of people who helped me along the way.

ISMAIL MAINOR- my good long-time friend. Who followed my story for years, even back when it had a completely different name. He has given me so much in the way of insight. His intelligence on numerous subjects is unmatched. I can always count on him when I need to verify a thought that I have in my head.

SALIM GIOTUS- A man with an extraordinary imagination and with quite a lot of intelligence as well. He's definitely one of the kindest friends that I've had and one who offered a wealth of creative ideas.

RUBEN ROBLEDO- Longtime friend and coworker who allowed me to use one of his characters in my story. The gesture was very much appreciated.

ASHLEIGH REVERIE- One of my first Beta readers who gave me genuine feedback and remains a contact till this day. Her recent success in self-publishing her Novels has inspired me immensely. Because if she can make do it while being a loving wife and mother of two, what possible excuse do I have?

IF VEEN- A beta reader who went out of her way to write a full-length Analysis and glowing review of my Novel and even created a custom cover for it. Honestly girl, you are awesome and if you are still out there, I can't thank you enough.

HAREEM MASABAT SALEEM- An Immensely intelligent Beta reader whom I'm honored to have read my story. Gave me insight and commented on nearly every chapter if not every page.

LAUREN MINKOFF- One of the kindest people within the writing community that I've ever met! This woman spend several months going over my writing and giving me so much insight and feedback. I could never repay her and hope that I have the privilege to work with her again someday.

JENNA BYGALL: My developmental editor. Gave me a lot of in-depth notes and in return I gave her some insight into the world that my story takes place in and what to expect from the future of the series.

SKYE ALLEY: Provided her professional voice over to produce a kickass audiobook for this Novel. Well worth the price of admission and a true work of art.

There are more people that I would like to thank, others that I've influenced me or provided me with feedback or words of wisdom that have helped me on my journey. But these are the most pertinent on my mind, including my loving parents and two wonderful little sisters, who have always had my back and have supported me through difficult times, in the past and even recently. Without their help I wouldn't be even half of what I am today. So, thank you all and lastly thank you. Yes you. You the reader. For taking the time to read the story of dreams. The story that I've decided to devote much of my life to and will continue for as long as possible. It's been a wild ride so far and I suspect things can only get more exciting from here on out.

See how her story began in the epic prequel Novel and origin story

Sarah Stryker And The Scorching Fire

Coming soon to Amazon Kindle and a Bookstore near you.

www.ingramcontent.com/pod-product-compliance
Lightning Source LLC
Chambersburg PA
CBHW020249030826
48979CB00030B/2673/J

* 9 7 9 8 9 8 7 4 9 3 6 1 8 *